SILVER DECEPTIONS

by

Deborah Martin

D1488015

A TOPAZ BOOK

TOPAZ
Published by the Penguin Group
Penguin Books USA Inc., 375 Hudson Street,
New York, New York 10014, U.S.A.
Penguin Books Ltd, 27 Wrights Lane,
London W8 5TZ, England
Penguin Books Australia Ltd, Ringwood,
Victoria, Australia
Penguin Books Canada Ltd, 10 Alcorn Avenue,
Toronto, Ontario, Canada M4V 3B2
Penguin Books (N.Z.) Ltd, 182–190 Wairau Road,
Auckland 10, New Zealand

Penguin Books Ltd, Registered Offices:
Harmondsworth, Middlesex, England

First published by Topaz, an imprint of Dutton Signet,
a division of Penguin Books USA Inc.

First Printing, January, 1994
10 9 8 7 6 5 4 3 2 1

Copyright © Deborah Martin Gonzales, 1994
All rights reserved
Topaz Man photo © Charles William Bush

 TOPAZ IS A TRADEMARK OF NEW AMERICAN LIBRARY,
A DIVISION OF PENGUIN BOOKS USA INC.

Printed in the United States of America

Without limiting the rights under copyright reserved above, no part of this
publication may be reproduced, stored in or introduced into a retrieval system,
or transmitted, in any form, or by any means (electronic, mechanical,
photocopying, recording, or otherwise), without the prior written permission
of both the copyright owner and the above publisher of this book.

BOOKS ARE AVAILABLE AT QUANTITY DISCOUNTS WHEN USED TO PROMOTE
PRODUCTS OR SERVICES. FOR INFORMATION PLEASE WRITE TO PREMIUM
MARKETING DIVISION, PENGUIN BOOKS USA INC., 375 HUDSON STREET, NEW
YORK, NEW YORK 10014.

If you purchased this book without a cover you should be aware that this book
is stolen property. It was reported as "unsold and destroyed" to the publisher
and neither the author nor the publisher has received any payment for this
"stripped book."

"PERHAPS I SHOULD IMPRESS UPON YOU THE DEPTHS OF MY INTENTIONS . . ."

"Truly, my lord, I don't think that will be necessary," she protested, but it was too late. His arm had already snaked around her waist and his mouth was on hers. Then he slid the tip of his tongue between her lips and ran it along her tightly clenched teeth. From the other kisses she'd received from men, she knew what he wanted and feared giving it to him. Somehow she knew such intimacy with him would affect her as those other kisses hadn't. Yet if she didn't respond, he would wonder how experienced she really was. . . .

So she made the mistake of opening her mouth, thus baring herself to a kiss of such fathomless intensity, it made her body ache. All she knew was the plunge of his tongue, mimicking the act he meant them to share. Her pulse quickened and her eyelids slid shut as one of his hands moved to cup her neck, holding her head still closer while he stole her breath from her.

So this was seduction, she thought.

SILVER DECEPTIONS

300,000 NEW & USED
BOOKS · RECORDS
COMICS · TAPES & CD'S
BUY SELL & TRADE
A BOOK NOOK
CLAIRMONT AT BUFORD
404-633-1328

Buy Two Topaz Books and Get One Free Romance Novel!

With just two purchases of Topaz books, you'll be able to receive one romance novel free from the list below. Just send us two proofs of purchase* along with the coupon below, and the romance of your choice will be on its way to you! (subject to availability/**offer good only in the United States, its territories and Canada**)

Check title you wish to receive:

☐ *WILD WINDS CALLING*
June Lund Shiplett
0-451-12953-9/$4.99($5.99 in Can.)

☐ *A HEART POSSESSED*
Katherine Sutcliffe
0-451-15310-3/$4.50($5.99 in Can.)

☐ *THE DIABOLICAL BARON*
Mary Jo Putney
0-451-15042-2/$3.99($4.99 in Can.)

☐ *THE WOULD-BE WIDOW*
Mary Jo Putney
0-451-15581-5/$3.99($4.99 in Can.)

☐ *TO LOVE A ROGUE*
Valerie Sherwood
0-451-40177-8/$4.95($5.95 in Can.)

☐ *THE TURQUOISE TRAIL*
Susannah Leigh
0-451-40252-9/$4.99($5.99 in Can.)

☐ *SO BRIGHT A FLAME*
Robin Leanne Wiete
0-451-40281-2/$4.99($5.99 in Can.)

☐ *REBEL DREAMS*
Patricia Rice
0-451-40272-3/$4.99($5.99 in Can.)

☐ *THE RECKLESS WAGER*
April Kihlstrom
0-451-17090-3/$3.99($4.99 in Can.)

☐ *LADY OF FIRE*
Anita Mills
0-451-40044-5/$4.99($5.99 in Can.)

☐ *THE CONTENTIOUS COUNTESS*
Irene Saunders
0-451-17276-0/$3.99($4.99 in Can.)

*Send in coupons, proof of purchase (register receipt & photocopy of UPC code from books) plus $1.50 postage and handling to:

TOPAZ 🔷 GIVEAWAY
Penguin USA, 375 Hudson Street, New York, NY 10014

NAME_____

ADDRESS_____ APT. #_____

CITY_____STATE_____ZIP_____

To Carolyn Nicholson, who read and believed in my books long before they were ever published.

To my sisters-in-law, Tena Martin and Erica Martin, who keep me posted on sales in Texas and, more important, give me love and encouragement.

To Sappho, who has always been there for me throughout my career changes and myriad stints at BPS.

And to my wonderful editor, Jennifer Enderlin, who understands the very essence of what makes romance work—thanks for taking a chance on me.

Chapter One

"Death, in itself, is nothing; but we fear,
To be we know not what, we know not where."
—John Dryden, *Aureng-Zebe*, Act 4, Scene 1

NORWOOD, ENGLAND
MAY 1667

Dark clouds, their bellies full of rain, hovered over Norwood's square as if waiting until the most crucial moment to dump their burden. Whipping the air into eddying currents, the chill wind sucked away warmth. Dirty piles of winter slush lined the edges of the hard, bleak patch of ground. It was a perfect day for a hanging.

Wrapping her woolen cloak more tightly around her slender body, Annabelle Taylor drew her hood forward to cover her thick raven hair. Her stomach churned from the emotional turmoil of the last three weeks. She inched forward through the crowd, making herself as inconspicuous as possible, given her height.

Slowly now, that's it, she told herself, her cobalt eyes surveying her surroundings to make sure no one had noticed her. If she moved forward a bit at a time, she'd be near the front when the hanging began, without her presence being commented on. She needn't have worried, she realized a few moments later, after she'd gained her spot close to the gallows. The crowd that watched with sickening jubilation for the first sign of the cart scarcely paid her any heed.

Not that it matters. They'll notice me well enough when I claim Mother's body after the hanging.

No one would expect Annabelle to watch her mother's hanging. Indeed, she'd told the sheriff that she'd send a man for the body because she couldn't bear to witness the hanging. She'd also sworn to her mother in a weak moment to stay locked up tight in the manor on execution day.

But she'd told such half-truths for a reason—to confuse the sheriff and his men so they'd be taken off guard when she claimed the body and alarmed them with the sight of her weeping. She sucked in her breath with an effort. That part she wouldn't need to counterfeit.

With any luck, her servant, Charity Woodfield, would create enough turmoil in the crowd that no one would notice when Annabelle and Charity's father, Richard, cut her mother down once the grim deed was done. Annabelle patted the bulge under her cloak. Good. The knife still lay strapped securely to her waist. They'd have to work quickly if they wanted to carry the body to the surgeon's house without being challenged. The surgeon's house. She must cling to the hope of his success. Otherwise, she'd go mad.

A pity she couldn't rely on her usual method of coping with life's pains—a combination of playacting and imagining. Under other circumstances, she'd be recreating herself in her mind as another person in another age. Starting from the toes up, she'd clothe herself in pretend garb, give herself a different name, and act as if she were far away from her surroundings. The trick had gotten her through many beatings.

Today, however, she couldn't escape. The pain burned too close, too fresh, too new. Besides, she had a task to perform.

"I have terrible news," a voice whispered at Annabelle's elbow.

She glanced over at the buxom, fair-haired woman who'd elbowed her way through the grumbling crowd to stand at her side, and a sigh passed her lips. At last Charity had arrived, the even-tempered widow who'd been more like an older sister than a servant to her, since there were only five years between them. At the moment, however, Charity looked not the least bit even-tempered.

"What terrible news?" Annabelle asked. "What's happened?"

"The surgeon can't take yer mother."

Annabelle paled. For a moment she panicked, but she steadied herself with a deep breath. "What do you mean, can't take her? I gave him all the gold I could find. He swore he'd do what he could. He swore it!"

The expression on Charity's pretty face was grim. "It isn't his fault. Some runagate told the sheriff about yer plans, and the sheriff put a stop to it. He's got three burly soldiers at the surgeon's house waitin' to seize you and the body if you near the place. He'll let you take the body to the graveyard and naught else."

Annabelle's heart plummeted. "It was my only chance to save her, and a very small one, too."

She'd read tales of men revived after a hanging. If the neck remained unbroken at the end of the ordeal, sometimes a person lived through it, simply losing consciousness for a time. Only last year, Tom Watkins's friends had taken his hanged body in secret straight to a surgeon's, where the surgeon had warmed and bled it until the man had revived enough to escape the soldiers. To her knowledge, Tom Watkins still lived healthy as a horse somewhere in London.

That memory had sustained her throughout her mother's short imprisonment and her trial. She'd known the trial would come to this, to a hanging. After all, her mother had murdered Annabelle's father—no, she corrected, *stepfather*—before three servants.

Annabelle choked back a sob. No one cared that Ogden Taylor had been beating Annabelle or that his poor wife, Phoebe, could no longer endure Ogden's cruelties. They only cared that a heinous crime had been committed. In their eyes, Squire Ogden Taylor had merely been administering a proper punishment to his recalcitrant daughter when his wife had lost her wits and plunged a kitchen blade into his brawny chest.

The only sentence the magistrate could have pronounced was death by hanging, and he'd done so to the cheers of those who'd jammed the tiny courtroom.

The memory of those cheers still turned Annabelle's stomach. A tear slipped from between her lashes. She rubbed it away. "She can't die, Charity. I can't let her die. If it weren't for me—"

"Don't start blamin' yerself for it. It would have ended like this sooner or later. He pushed her to it, he did. At least yer mother had the satisfaction of seein' him die for all his torments."

Annabelle silently agreed. She couldn't pretend to have loved her stepfather, nor even to wish Mother hadn't killed him. She only wished Mother had done it less publicly.

The moment those wicked thoughts appeared in her head, she banished them. A superstitious fear made the sweat bead up on her forehead despite the brisk spring air.

Please, God, I didn't mean it, she prayed. *Only let her live. I fear I'll think more wicked thoughts if you take her from me. If you save her, I'll . . . I'll . . .*

How could she tempt God into overlooking Mother's terrible crime? Perhaps if she offered to serve Him all her life, to banish rebellious thoughts forever from her mind. Would that cover her past sins and save Mother? Or would God consider Annabelle hopeless?

The squire had called her the "spawn of the devil" because one moment she could suffer his beating with wailing cries and the next present a face of perfect composure to the world. He'd said it was unnatural for a girl to be so changeable.

Often she'd feared he was right. Mother had never been changeable. She'd been saintly always, urging Annabelle to be more apologetic and womanly to escape his wrathful words. It was true that in a moment of unexpected rage Mother had killed him. But anyone else would have done the same, Annabelle told herself. Mother didn't deserve to hang.

"What do I do now?" Annabelle whispered raggedly to Charity.

Charity placed a soft hand on her mistress's arm and sighed. For a moment, her doe-brown eyes met her mistress's and Annabelle glimpsed the lack of hope in them. Then Charity glanced up at the gallows and winced. "Not a thing you can do now, dear heart. At least you made her last days tolerable—bringin' her food in the gaol, sittin' and talkin' with her, readin' to her." Charity's eyes darkened. "I dare say she got more pleasure out of those weeks in gaol than in all the years with yer father."

"My stepfather," Annabelle corrected.

"Aye, yer stepfather. It takes some gettin' used to, thinkin' of him that way, though I never could quite believe he was yer father. Such a cruel man could never whelp a sweet-faced angel like you."

Annabelle groaned. "An angel could save her, Charity. I can't." A spark of hope softened her tone. "Perhaps if we carried the body back to your father's cottage, we could revive it ourselves. You know a bit about medicinal preparations, and we could—"

An old crone standing nearby jerked her head around at the sound of Annabelle's raised voice. Instinctively, Annabelle drew the hood of her cloak farther forward to hide her face. The woman stared for a moment, two beady eyes searching the cloak. Then, with a shrug, she settled her bones back into a waiting position.

Charity edged closer to Annabelle. "You must keep quiet. If the sheriff finds you here, there'll be a commotion, and we don't want that." She sniffed. "And don't be thinkin' about raisin' bodies up from the dead by yerself. I never had much faith in the surgeon's ability to bring her back. I know I can't do it meself. There's nothin' left but to flee this wicked place, turn yer eyes from the evil here, and set yer feet toward London."

"I'm not leaving until the end." With a shudder, Annabelle stared at the gallows cross-piece, the rough wood worn smooth in the middle where the rope was tied. "A miracle could happen. God may look down on her and see the injustice. He'll spare her. He must.

I know she killed a man, but God surely understands how far a mother will go when her child is threatened.'' She swallowed. ''I mean, He is Himself a father.''

''God helps those who help themselves, and yer mother's put herself beyond helpin','' Charity said without rancor. ''Come on with you. We'll travel to London. Like I told you t'other night—my cousin works there in the theater. She'll help us find a position. She says the theater's full of women like us. With yer genteel manners, you could get a position easy.''

''Don't worry, I'll go to London soon enough.'' Annabelle strained to see if anyone yet came down the road. ''But I don't know if you should accompany me. You could easily find a position here, what with your reputation for having the finest cooking in the shire.''

''Fie on that! I want to seek my fortune on the stage in London. You should hear my cousin's tales. The nobles fight over the actresses. She says any woman who's half bonny can find a duke with coin in his pockets who's willin' to set her up—''

Annabelle stiffened and faced Charity, her eyes sparking through their pain. ''Don't even think such things! Indecency of that kind is what landed Mother in this position. If she hadn't taken up with a dissolute nobleman, she wouldn't have been abandoned when she was with child. Then her parents wouldn't have forced her to marry the squire and live the hellish life that drove her to murder!''

She barely contained the loud cry of rage mingled with pain that nearly escaped her lips.

''My poor mistress,'' Charity replied, stroking Annabelle's back with soothing movements. ''Come away. This be no place for a woman with yer hurting heart.''

Before Annabelle could answer, the noise of the crowd suddenly increased. Annabelle's blood thundered in her ears. Unable to look elsewhere, she shifted her gaze to the curve where the cart track split from the road.

First strutted the sheriff in his sable robes, appearing very dignified and aloof for a man who coveted the Taylor lands. Her fists tightened. How she'd love to close her fingers around his fleshy throat, to watch his eyes bulge with fear instead of his usual pompous conceit. Had he no pity for a woman whose husband had treated her with utter contempt? No, he was like the squire, eager to punish any sign of weakness to make himself feel more powerful.

He marched ahead of the procession, clutching the rod of power in his meaty hands. The curled gray locks of his new periwig bobbed as he tried to walk with sober dignity. Instead he swayed like a swollen boar, wide nostrils flaring at the anticipation of death in the air. Oh, how she wanted to see him hang in Mother's place!

Unfortunately, that would never happen. Instead, he would soon bid on her stepfather's lands that would be up for auction. How like her stepfather to have disinherited her and her mother in his will. Had he guessed he'd come to such an end? Or had he simply seen it as one final triumph?

In either case, he'd made it impossible for Annabelle to remain in Norwood. After all, she was already twenty-one and husbandless, thanks to her stepfather's refusal to spend a penny on a dowry for her. An unmarried woman with no money would be an easy mark for the likes of Norwood's sheriff.

She gritted her teeth. The sheriff completed the wheel of torment fashioned for Mother by two other pompous, unfeeling men—the nobleman who apparently was Annabelle's real father and Ogden Taylor. A plague on them all! How she hated them!

Behind the sheriff tramped two brawny soldiers. Annabelle groaned. The sheriff was certainly doing his best to keep her from spiriting Mother's body away.

Suddenly the cart carrying her mother rumbled into view. Chains held her, with thick iron shackles that dwarfed her delicate wrists and ankles. Her beautiful, silver-streaked jet hair had been shorn, accentuating her expression of helpless confusion. As she knelt in the wobbling cart, wearing the snow-white gown Annabelle had brought her in prison, she clasped her hands before her in supplication, closing her eyes as her lips moved in silent prayers.

"Mother!" Annabelle cried out, and involuntarily started forward.

Charity held her back, clamping her hand around Annabelle's arm. "No, no, dear heart." She glanced around, relaxing when she realized that the noisy crowd was too caught up in catcalls to note Annabelle's outburst. "If ever we needed that self-control of yours, 'tis today. You must keep still and quiet as a mouse. They'll be watchin' and waitin' for you to make a fuss. You know the wretched rumors. There's some in this town, wicked meddlers, already say you prompted yer mother to murder him. They're waitin' to throw you in the gaol too. Don't give the bastards the chance."

This last was said with such venom it gave Annabelle courage. Annabelle let that venom seep into her soul. She'd need the strength of such hatred if she were to find her revenge. And avenge Mother she would. Oh, not against the townspeople. Some of them might be wretches, but most had been relatively kind to her and her mother. All, however, were as powerless as she to stop the events unfolding before them.

As for Ogden Taylor, Annabelle hoped he rotted in hell at this very moment for his brutality. Unfortunately, she had no choice but to leave him to God's revenge.

One man could be punished, however. One man had acted with complete irresponsibility, eventually bringing about Mother's downfall. That man was her real father, the nobleman Mother had called Maynard, whose gifts—a signet ring and a poem with the signature "The Silver Swan"—Mother had sent her to retrieve from their hiding place in the harpsichord. Mother had told her of him only two days ago, urging her to seek him out and ask his protection.

Annabelle shuddered. His protection. She'd sooner cut out her tongue than ask him for help. She'd find him, all right, but not to seek his help.

She shifted the rough cloak about her shoulders and thought of the father she'd never known . . . and the one she had known. All those years she should have guessed the source of Ogden's virulent hatred of her. She supposed she shouldn't blame Ogden entirely for his reprehensible behavior. Mother and her family had deceived him into believing he was marrying a virgin, when really his fiancée was with child.

As Annabelle's mother had told it while she'd lain in a dank cell preparing for death, Ogden had chosen to keep the secret between them so that he always had something to torment her with, to keep her at his mercy.

Annabelle rubbed her chilled hands together, a sob catching in her throat. If only she'd known, she could have done something perhaps . . . taken Mother away, set out to create a new life for them both.

No, she thought with a trace of bitterness as she watched her mother's trembling form shake with every jolt of the tiny cart. In these harsh times, a woman without a husband could scarcely eke out a living even if she could find a position as a servant in some great house. Mother had never been strong enough for such a struggle.

Annabelle had always been the strong one. Annabelle had been the one to tell whatever blatant lie it took to save Mother from a beating, to pretend to be terrified of her stepfather because he only tormented the one who cowered most. She *had* secretly been frightened of him . . . but not like Mother.

Charity's father, Norwood's cobbler, pushed through the crowd behind them. Mr. Woodfield took a position on Annabelle's left side, clasping his short-crowned hat. "Sorry it took me so long," he murmured. He nodded his balding head toward the back of the crowd. "But I'm all ready with the cart and—"

"Hush, Father," Charity told him. In a few short whispers she explained what had happened.

He shook his head, a mournful expression on his face, then patted Annabelle's arm with a leathery hand. "Ah, then, we must give 'er up to God. 'Tis a sign from Him, it is, sayin' that we got to let her go."

Annabelle started to chastise him for giving up so easily, but Charity's fingers tightening on her arm kept her from voicing her thoughts. They watched in silence as the procession neared, raising up a trail of dust in the dry earth.

A drunken voice in the crowd called out, "What a collar day! Perfect day for a murderess to swing!"

A woman's voice close by took up the cry. "Aye, she deserves to be twisted, she does!"

Though some in the crowd hushed those who spoke cruelly, the few murmurs of sympathy for her mother couldn't enable Annabelle to block out the morbid images brought forth by the word *twisted*.

Bile rose in her throat and she gagged, prompting Charity to slide an arm around her waist. A hawker nearby cried out, "Buy a fresh orange 'ere," and other hawkers added their cries.

Devil take them all for treating it as another merrymaking fair, Annabelle thought with sickening clarity. Her mother's few acquaintances had stayed away in sorrow, so for the most part, those villagers in attendance cared not a whit what happened to the squire's wife. The squire had practically kept Annabelle and her mother prisoners in their own home, so they'd had little chance to build close ties to the villagers. The villagers thus held them suspect, even more so now that her mother had killed a man.

She didn't care what they thought, Annabelle told herself. Still, Annabelle saw her mother struggle valiantly to ignore the hurtful cries of the worst of them.

Annabelle swayed against Mr. Woodfield, who held her up, placing his arm in comfort around her shoulders. "Poor lass," he whispered. Then he turned to his daughter. "The lass shouldn't be here, you know."

"Aye, I know, but she won't listen to reason."

"I must stay," Annabelle said, though her voice shook.

"Don't torment yerself so," Charity muttered. "Yer mother is as good as dead now. You promised her you'd not witness the hangin'. Keep that promise. 'Tis dangerous to stay in Norwood another day. Most won't welcome the daughter of a murderess with open arms, y'know. And then there are the rumors . . . so come on, then. You mustn't watch any longer."

Annabelle fixed her eyes once more on the slow progress of the cart. The taste of sour bile burned the back of her throat. "I can't leave her. Not yet. I have to stay."

Charity shook her head wordlessly, but remained at Annabelle's side. Mr. Woodfield continued to support her with his wiry arm, but his strength and kindness, which she usually relied on to give her hope, she scarcely noticed now.

The rough-hewn cart stopped a few yards in front of them, beneath the gallows with its dreadful rope hanging down like a hideous outstretched claw. Annabelle ached to run to Mother's side, but she resisted the urge. Mother had made her promise not to watch the hanging, because she'd said it would haunt Annabelle forever and she didn't want to pass on such a legacy to her only daughter. If she saw Annabelle there, it wouldn't give her comfort . . . it would make her last hours intolerable.

Annabelle knew all of this in her mind, but her heart wanted to touch Mother's soft hands once more, to kiss her tearful eyes until they closed, to help ease her into the next world with a woman's feeling touch, not the harsh rope of a man's world.

The crowd's coarse cries no longer entered Annabelle's consciousness. Her attention was instead consumed by the sight of her mother being jerked to her feet by a man whose somber clothing and executioner's mask marked him as the hangman. A hatred filled

Annabelle so intense, so hot, she thought she'd burst into flames if she didn't leave the square at once.

Yet she couldn't leave. Not when a miracle might happen. Not when a reprieve could come from anywhere. Her mind told her no reprieve would come, but her heart insisted it must.

The hangman caught in his hands the thick, knotted rope that hung over the cart. The wind whipped her mother's white gown around her like a shroud, forcing Annabelle to choke back a sob at the sight. Then the hangman motioned to her mother to move nearer until the noose loomed close enough that he could widen the knot and slip it over her bowed head. He tightened it around her neck, and Annabelle's own throat went numb.

Please, God, she prayed again. *Save her. You must save her!*

The hangman stepped off the cart. The Sheriff of Norwood repeated the sentence in a booming voice, then asked if the condemned had any final words.

Her mother's soft "Nay" incensed the crowd, who would much rather have heard a long confession of her past sins. After all, the hanging served as an entertainment for them, and they didn't like being deprived of their amusement. It took every ounce of Annabelle's strength to refrain from giving them a few choice words of her own.

The hangman's black hood hid whatever emotion he might be feeling as he took up the reins of the horse teethered to the cart. Then slowly he led the horse forward while Phoebe Taylor's feet dragged along the bottom of the cart until they no longer found purchase.

Annabelle immediately shut her eyes to the sight. The silence of the crowd maddened her, because it allowed her to hear the gallows creak with her mother's weight. But Annabelle didn't scream; she didn't even cry. Instead, she began to pray more fervently than she'd ever prayed in her life.

Let the rope break, God, she chanted in her head over and over. *Let it break. Let her live. They'll not*

*hang her again if the rope breaks. They'll take it as a
sign from You. Let her live, and I'll be pure and holy
all my days, I swear it. Save her and I'll be your
servant forever. Please, God, I swear it!*

She didn't realize she was babbling the words aloud,
her voice rising higher and higher above the hush of
the crowd, until Charity and Mr. Woodfield on either
side of her began dragging her backward, mumbling
excuses to everyone near them.

Her eyes still shut, she clasped her hands together
and dropped to her knees. "Please, God!" she cried
out over the hostile murmurs of those around her. "She
can't die! You can't let her die!"

Charity and Mr. Woodfield now struggled to force
her to her feet. "Come, we're leavin' now," Charity
hissed. "Stand up and walk, for pity's sake! Stand up
and walk! Don't bow before those wretches. God has
taken her into his bosom, He has, where she belongs.
He ain't goin' to release her now. Come on!"

A clap of thunder sounded nearby, and Annabelle's
eyes shot open. It was an answer of sorts, wasn't it?
God would spare Mother?

Then she saw the gallows. A scream left her lips,
though the part of her growing numb didn't notice.
She stumbled to her feet and wrenched her gaze from
the horrifying sight before her, one last supplication
tumbling from her lips.

The rope held.

In that moment, Annabelle shoved her soul, along
with all her childhood dreams, into the tiniest cupboard in her heart. Then she closed up her heart,
walled up her feelings against the pain that threatened
to overwhelm her reason.

And as she hardened her heart against the world,
and most particularly against men and all their cruelties, she vowed that one man at least would pay for
taking her mother from her. Her father.

Chapter Two

"Robes loosely flowing, hair as free:
Such sweet neglect more taketh me,
Than all the adulteries of art;
They strike mine eyes, but not my heart."
—Ben Jonson, *Epicene*, Act 1, Scene 1

LONDON
NEW YEAR'S DAY, 1668

"A mischief upon all Fools!"

Act III of Dryden's *Sir Martin Mar-All* had begun, and the din temporarily lessened in Lisle's Tennis Courts. The old indoor courts in Lincoln's Inn Fields, though cramped and small, had served as theater for the Duke of York's acting company since the theaters had reopened in 1660. Rumor had it that Sir William D'Avenant, who owned the company's royal patent, planned to build a new one, but as yet no one had seen any evidence of it.

So the duke's players had to make do with the present narrow space. Rows of backless benches covered with emerald cloth were crammed into the pit, filled by young gallants, critics, the boldest women of quality, and a goodly number of vizard-masks—ladies of the evening. In the first tier of boxes on either side of the pit sat more women of quality, with only a few men, for the others were too busy making noise in the pit. The royal boxes faced the stage, and there Charles II and his court gathered on the nights when they chose to attend. The second tier contained the more conservative gentry, the few who attended the scandal-ridden theater. And the upper gallery held the cheapest seats, filled with whatever common folk could afford them.

For the most part, only nobility and the court attended the two London theaters. As a result, both the king's company and the duke's company, who held the only patents for theaters, had to struggle to fill seats. They survived by changing the bill as often as once or twice a week to satisfy the jaded tastes of those who attended the theater daily. And where that failed, they sought out the most beautiful women to draw the gallants who watched every night for fresh female faces.

This particular afternoon all eyes were on the actress who'd spoken the first line with contemptuous pride. Colin Jeffreys, Marquis of Hampden, watched her from a first-tier box with particular interest. He glanced at the playbill to make certain she was the actress he sought. It read "Rose, played by Annabelle Maynard."

She's the one, he told himself.

His gaze followed the tall beauty as she crossed the proscenium stage. In the light of the theater's countless candles, Annabelle Maynard's bearing and gestures seemed too patrician for the part of the servant Rose. She wore elegance like a badge of pride, her face a study in striking simplicity. Although the requisite short curls framed her face in front, the rest of her hair tumbled to the middle of her back like a shimmering robe of ebony.

Did she even wear rouge? he wondered as Moll Davies entered the scene, a heavy shade of red on the cheeks of her white powdered face. In contrast, Annabelle Maynard looked fresh and unspoiled as wild rosemary. No doubt she was just as prickly.

In short, the perfect antidote to the jaded sensibilities of an oversophisticated court . . . and not at all what he'd expected. Perhaps he indeed had the wrong actress. He hadn't been to a play at the Duke's Theater since he'd returned two weeks ago from spending three years in Antwerp in the king's service, so he wasn't familiar with all the actresses.

"Riverton," he called to his friend sitting two seats over. Colin had to raise his voice to catch Sir John Riverton's attention, the hum of voices in the theater was so loud. How on earth did anyone listen to a play in this din? he asked himself as he called to Riverton again.

"Not now, Hampden," Riverton replied, drawing closer the giggling vizard-mask who sat between them. "Can't you see this poor girl's lonely?"

The "poor girl" was sliding her bejeweled hand up Colin's thigh even while her other hand worked at tantalizing Riverton on her other side.

"*Lonely* wasn't the word I would have chosen," Colin shot back, his voice heavy with irony as he brushed her hand from his thigh. The woman smirked. "But she'll undoubtedly wait another minute or two. Tell me about the tall actress in white."

Riverton briefly drew his attention from his companion to search the stage. He nodded in Annabelle's direction. "The Silver Swan, you mean?"

Colin's gaze followed Riverton's nod to the same actress he'd been watching. Now he noted the slender alabaster neck, the graceful gestures . . . the silver ribbons she wore not only in her hair but threaded through her lace cuffs and in bows on the tips of her white satin slippers. On her bodice, a silver brooch winked in the lights, though he couldn't discern what it depicted.

"The Silver Swan," he murmured under his breath. An apt nickname for this stately creature.

"Yes," he told Riverton, "the one with the dark hair. I believe her name is Annabelle Maynard."

Riverton chuckled. "That's her. Even though she plays mostly minor roles, she's hard to miss. She's only been with the duke's players for . . . oh, six or seven months."

I've got the right one, then, Colin thought. She was definitely the woman Walcester had described.

Riverton's gaze now also swung to the stage, although his hand idly toyed with the trailing curls of the woman sitting beside him. "She's quite popular. You know how it is. After seeing the same faces week after week, the gallants want new blood occasionally. She's pretty, don't you think?"

"Pretty" was an understatement, Colin thought. "Lovely" was more accurate.

"You know, if you're interested in meeting her," Riverton continued, "I can introduce you to her maid."

"Can you, now?" Colin leaned forward in his seat and fixed Riverton with a speculative glance. "You know Madam Maynard well?"

Riverton's chuckle carried to him over the chatter of those in the boxes surrounding them. "Well enough." When Colin's eyes narrowed, he hastened to add, "But not in *that* way, you understand, although there are some who *have* known her more . . . shall we say . . . intimately."

An inexplicable twinge of disappointment brought a frown to Colin's face. "Typical actress, is she?"

With a nod, Riverton leaned across the scowling vizard-mask between them. "That's what I've heard. Serene and aloof onstage, but in bed, passionate as fire." He laughed. "I imagine pearls and baubles will open the thighs of any pretty actress. And she's no exception. So they say."

Colin's gaze flicked in disbelief over the actress, searching for some sign of this wanton side. "Who exactly are 'they'?"

"Somerset, for one. Claims he's practically put himself into debt buying her jewels, and you know the man can't afford it, since he's only a second son. He says she's repaid him . . . as only a woman could. He's undoubtedly backstage this very moment, waiting in the wings for her."

Only Colin's eyes registered his dismay at the thought of Annabelle Maynard in Lord Somerset's arms. " 'Sdeath, he's a fop if ever there was one."

Riverton shrugged. "Indeed. But that's the sort of man she seems to find attractive. Or at least 'tis the only type I've ever seen her with."

Colin shook his head. She looked intelligent. Her acting was refined, calculated to gain audience approval at every turn. She even had the old matrons in the upper gallery eating out of her hand, so she obviously knew her trade well. She didn't seem like one of those women newly come from a whorehouse who sought the stage only because it provided better opportunities to find protectors. So why did she dally with a lot of silly, prancing coxcombs? It made no sense at all.

Not that anything in this fool's errand for Walcester made sense. "I want to meet her," Colin announced.

Apparently the request didn't surprise Riverton. He shifted in his seat, adjusting his bad leg. Then he stared at the stage. "When?"

"As soon as possible—tomorrow, if I can."

"All you have to do is slip into the tiring-room and wait for her—"

"With the other fops and gallants who are jostling about? No. I want to meet with her alone, where we can speak."

" 'Speak,' eh? Is that what you're calling it these days?" Riverton laughed. "Well, then, suppose I fetch her maid? Maybe she can set up an assignation, if her mistress is willing."

"*If* you know her as well as you say—"

"Don't worry." Riverton stood, ignoring the woman who pouted in the chair next to his. "I never lie about women. I'll catch the pretty bird's servant for you and be back before you can even miss me."

Colin watched Riverton leave the box, then returned his attention to the stage. Annabelle Maynard was exiting with Moll Davies and an actor he didn't recognize. The moment the three vacated the stage, the raucous gallants in the pit called out their disappointment. Judging from the cries of "Swan, Swan," Colin didn't think it was only Moll Davies they wanted.

Undoubtedly, Annabelle Maynard had a score of men, both young and old, seeking her favors. It was always like that when a new actress appeared. Had the attention being bestowed on her prompted Walcester to ask Colin to begin surveillance on the woman? If

so, why was the earl concerning himself with an actress? Simply because of her surname?

Colin shook his head. With any luck, the answer to
that question would come after his dinner with Walcester tonight. He found himself hoping Walcester's motives were above reproach. Because although Colin was
indebted to Walcester, he couldn't stomach involving
himself in something that might harm such a lovely
and talented young woman.

Deep in thought, Annabelle entered the tiring-room
after the third act.

"An orange to whet your whistle for the next one?"
asked one of the orange girls resting her weary feet on
a chair.

A half smile played over Annabelle's face. "That
bad today, is it?" she asked as she hitched up her skirt
and drew a few pence from the pocket in her smock.

The orange girl, who couldn't have been a day over
thirteen, sighed. "Aye. 'Tis crowded enough, but no
one wants oranges." She flashed Annabelle a grateful
smile and handed her the orange, Annabelle's fourth
that day. "Maggie'll 'ave my 'ead if I don't give 'er
somethin' at the end of the day. Thanks."

So young, Annabelle thought as the girl left the
tiring-room. *Too young for hawking oranges in the theater.*

She turned the orange over in her hand and decided
to eat it. The other three she would pass on to the
urchins outside the theater as she always did, but today
she was in the mood to actually eat one.

Charity walked in and caught her peeling the fruit
before she could hide it.

"I swear," Charity muttered crossly, "are you
throwing your pence away on the orange girls again?
'Tis no wonder you can't afford that gown you want.
How many is it today? Two? Three?"

Annabelle sighed as Charity came to her side and
searched her dress for any signs of disrepair. "Only
four."

"All the girls know you're a soft touch," Charity said, shaking her head. "That's why they follow you around all the time. You shouldn't encourage them."

"I can't help it. They are so like me at that age. Maggie beats them when they don't bring in enough money . . . I know she does. And what are a few pence to me?"

Charity only sniffed in response.

"Besides," Annabelle continued with a grin, taking a big bite of the orange. "I wanted to eat one. Who could be part of the theater and not eat oranges?"

Softening, Charity patted her arm. "True, true." She hesitated, surveying her mistress with a critical eye and then kneeling to study Annabelle's loose hem.

"You know, the theater suits you, dear heart," Charity murmured as she drew out the needle and thread she always held ready and began to sew up the hem.

Annabelle had to agree. She liked the smell of hot wax from a thousand candles, the hush of the men in the pit when a scene was particularly good, the sound of lutes wafting down from the musicians' box. She even liked flirting with the gallants, even though most of them were foolish young pups. She enjoyed theater life, every part of it. The theater had been a good home to her these past months.

What's more, she was actually quite good at this acting business. In a perverse way, she supposed her stepfather was responsible for teaching her to control her reactions and trot them out whenever she needed them in order to survive. He'd been the most exacting teacher an actress could have, she thought grimly.

Thinking of her stepfather and his cruelties sobered her. There was only one dark thread through her bright tapestry. Her real father. Seven months in London and she still hadn't found him, hadn't even had one nibble at her trap.

She'd set the trap well enough. She'd taken her real father's surname. After judicious work, she and Charity had also gotten the entire theatergoing court calling her the "Silver Swan," thanks to the brooch she'd bought and her constant reinforcement of the image.

Nonetheless, there'd been no sign of her real father. She'd hoped to draw him out with her names. After all, the poem he'd given her mother had been signed "The Silver Swan" and sealed with his ring, so "the silver swan" must have meant something to both of them. Yet no one of the name Maynard had contacted her. No one had contacted her at all.

Until someone did, Annabelle could do little. There was so much she wished to do once she found Maynard. First she wanted to confront him with her bastardy, and then rub her stage experience and scandalous adventuring in his face. Her unveiling was to be quite public, a supper, perhaps, to which she'd invite all the gallants and nobles who flocked around her. And her father, too, of course. There she'd announce her real identity, her real parentage.

Oh, yes, once she'd done so, her father would become the laughingstock of London for the bastard daughter he couldn't control, who mocked his family name before everyone. She knew gentlewomen whose families, after disinheriting them for some scandal, had still tried to keep them from the stage so they wouldn't truly embarrass the family. Why should her father be any different, even if she were only his bastard?

Her vengeance wouldn't end there, however. She'd continue to humiliate him so thoroughly he could never raise his head among his peers. Then it wouldn't simply be her presence on the stage or even her past wanton behavior that would shame him. No, she'd find his sore spots and press them. If he proved puritanical, she'd spout shocking words from the stage until the skies rang with them. If he hated gambling, she'd gamble, then send her creditors to him with the bills. No doubt he'd refuse to pay them, but he'd still be embarrassed, wouldn't he, to have such an indiscreet daughter?

All the while, she'd throw in his face her reputation for having a string of supposed lovers. His name would ever be on her lips. London would know that he and he alone was her father.

She frowned, taking another bite of orange. What if he were an aging rake, flaunting his excesses as the king and his court did? She dismissed that possibility. She'd not found him among the rakes who populated the theater, so he was undoubtedly a more pompous sort. Perhaps he even had a family who knew nothing of his wild younger days. Her reputation would shame them all and him the most.

That would be a fitting punishment for the man who'd abandoned his lover and daughter to Squire Taylor's punishments, she told herself, trying to dismiss the fact that her plan would also wound her father's innocent wife and children, if he had any. She forced herself not to sympathize with those nebulous relations. At least her father's children hadn't been subject to the squire's beatings. At least they hadn't watched their mother die a grisly death.

Well, she'd make certain he suffered for that death. And when he'd had enough and had come to her with remorse in his eyes and a new awareness in his heart, perhaps she might find it in her soul to forgive him. Perhaps.

Charity had finished the hem, so she rose and began plumping one of Annabelle's satin ribbons. " 'Tis such a shame. All that heat and damp air is takin' the curl out of yer pretty hair and dainty ribbons.''

Annabelle tore herself from her obsessive thoughts and managed to say lightly, ''You're not going to improve them without a hot iron, so why don't you forget about my ribbons? Act Four is going to start any moment. Tell me . . . do you remember my opening line?''

Charity screwed up her face as she thought. Annabelle bit back a smile. Memorizing lines wasn't Charity's strong suit, which was probably why she'd left the acting to her mistress, except for a wordless part once in a while.

Charity had managed to keep busy, however, be-

tween caring for Annabelle, making and selling pork-
pies in the marketplace, and even singing the occasional
song on stage. She couldn't learn lines, but she had no
trouble learning songs. Annabelle regarded Charity
fondly. Charity liked songs. And she did, after all, have
a fetching voice.

"I swear I've already forgotten half the scene," Annabelle muttered half to herself as she finished off the
orange.

Charity's face cleared. "Wait, I remember. Mr.
Young says, 'Good luck, and five hundred pound attend thee,' and then you and Mrs. Davies come in.
Then she says, 'I am resolv'd I'll never marry him,'
and you say—"

"Oh, yes. 'So far you are right, Madam.' This fol-
lows that absurd scene where Warner and Lord Dart-
mouth plot to find a husband for his pregnant
mistress."

"Aye, that's the one."

Annabelle's face darkened. "Dryden has obviously
never known what it's like to be a bastard or to suffer
like Mother with a bastard in her womb. That's why
he can write so blithely about illegitimacy and men
who won't do their duty by the women they seduce."

"Don't start puttin' yer mind on such things now
when the act's about to start. Besides, it hurts you to
think of all that."

"That's why I do," Annabelle said with a burst of
passion. "The more it hurts, the more it resolves me
to set things right, so Mother can rest easy in her
grave."

Charity's brow knitted in a frown. "I know what
yer feelin'. And 'tis right you should torment the man
who harmed you and yer mother. But he's already done
his sufferin', and you can't hurt him more."

A pity, Annabelle thought. " 'Tis not the squire I
wish to harm, and well you know it."

"I know no such thing." Charity sniffed as she
worked on one silver ribbon, curling it around her finger in a useless attempt to revive it. "You think you

hate yer father, but you don't even know the man, nor why he left yer mother. 'Tis no matter how much you cry yer hatred of him. It's yer stepfather as takes up all yer dreadful thoughts, it is.''

Charity smoothed back the curls from her mistress's temple, and Annabelle caught her hand and moved it to trace the delicate crescent-shaped scar there. The squire had once lost his temper and cuffed Annabelle so hard, his ring had gashed her temple. Annabelle had been six at the time.

''My stepfather may have done this to me,'' Annabelle said in a whisper, still remembering the horror of seeing her own blood dripping down her face, ''but it wouldn't have happened if my real father hadn't abandoned Mother. 'Tis only fair that I hate the man who was the true source of my pain.''

Charity shook her head sadly. ''Nay. It's the squire who draws yer hatred, no matter where you want to place the feeling.'' Charity caressed the spot. '' 'Tis a righteous hatred, but don't let it sour yer heart.''

Annabelle's face went all stony, like the masks of the women in the pit. Charity was right. This wasn't the time to brood. She tried to box her emotions carefully away, like the actress she'd learned to be long ago, yet she couldn't swallow past the lump in her throat. ''Sometimes I wish I'd killed the squire myself. If only I'd had the courage.''

''You had the courage to stand up to him. 'Tis yer mother who lacked courage, which was why she did such a cowardly thing, killin' him and leavin' you to fend for yerself.''

Annabelle detected the edge of bitterness in Charity's voice and stiffened, then jerked away from Charity to pace the floor. ''You can't blame Mother. No matter what you say, I know she wouldn't have done it if it hadn't been for my real father . . . Maynard, whoever he is.''

Her thoughts ran along their earlier course. ''I wish he'd simply take the bait. I thought certain when he saw me using the names 'Maynard' and 'Silver Swan' together, he'd have some reaction. Dear heaven, I paid a pretty penny to have this brooch specially fashioned, and it has brought me nothing so far.''

Charity shrugged. ''Perhaps he don't live in London no more. Who knows? The poor man might be dead.''

Annabelle stopped in her tracks, a frustrated expression crossing her face. ''Devil take the man, he'd best not be dead! I want to see that barbarous bastard squirm.''

''Madam! I swear yer letting those gallants turn all yer proper words into obscenity!''

Annabelle opened her mouth to retort, then closed it upon seeing Charity's look of censure. A wan smile crossed her face. Charity would never understand. Annabelle's current role of wanton actress had been a godsend. She could mock the world and be praised as witty for it. She could shake her fist at fate and as long as she couched her words in dry humor, no one guessed at the pain beneath them.

Least of all the gallants who courted her. ''Gallants,'' she remarked thoughtfully to Charity. She shook her head. ''All of these so-called wits are nothing but conceited popinjays. Take Lord Somerset, for example. Is he a wit? I think not. More like a lackwit than a wit, if you ask me.''

Charity giggled. ''That's true, I'll readily admit. That one's so enamored of his face, he don't have the time to sharpen his brain.''

One of Annabelle's finely plucked eyebrows rose. ''Nor the inclination. He seems entirely concentrated on preening and bragging about his supposed bedding of me to his lackwit friends.''

''Ah, but he was a sight, wasn't he, the mornin' after?'' Charity remarked, her eyes sparkling. ''Wakin' up all groggy after swiggin' my tea, and not even knowin' he'd merely been sleepin' beside you the whole night. You should have seen his face when I entered in a flurry and announced you were wanted straightaway at the theater. The simpering fool didn't

know whether to admit he didn't remember his evenin'
with you or boast about his success."

Annabelle remembered well Somerset's inane smile.
"Of course he chose to boast."

"Aye, but 'tis a good thing for you the man's vain
as a peacock. If y'd had a real man in that bed, he
wouldn't have let you go till he'd had another tumble
in his wakin' hours, no matter what I told him about
where you was to be."

Annabelle smiled wryly. "That's why I chose Somerset. He'll believe whatever I tell him about his prow-
ess, and he'll leave when I tell him to." Her smile
faded. "It wouldn't do to find myself in Mother's position . . . my belly full and no man near to claim the
babe."

She bit her lip. It was necessary to her vengeance
that the world think her a woman of no morals, but
like everything else, she refused to do more than play
the role. If her stepfather hadn't cowed her, she certainly wouldn't let some foppish gallant do it.

"I swear, if y'd gone one more month without lettin'
them think *someone* had bedded you, one of those so-
called wits would have had his way with you, willin'
or no."

Annabelle's lips tightened. No, she wouldn't have
wanted to be raped, nor even seduced. Her father's
abandonment made her more testy about men than
most virgins were, although part of her realized all
men weren't like her father and stepfather. Unfortunately, most of those she'd met in London were either
fops or brutes.

A knock at the door interrupted Annabelle's
thoughts, and a muffled voice warned there was only
a minute left until her entrance.

Charity gave Annabelle's gown a few last-minute
smoothings and bent to straighten a ribbon on one of
her slippers. Annabelle watched Charity and wondered when her pretty maid had become more of a
friend than a servant. When had the differences in their
stations so blurred that she felt completely at ease con-

fiding in Charity and depending on her for so many things?

She knew the answer to that. It had happened when Charity and her kindly father had begun treating Annabelle as family, giving her refuge when the squire's temper had raged. They'd taught her to believe that good people did exist, that profession or station didn't define goodness. What was more, Charity's father had taught her not to hate all men. Annabelle had often wished fate had given her Richard Woodfield for a father instead of the squire. And Charity for a sister. Yes, Charity and her father had constantly given Annabelle hope that somewhere men and women could live together in pleasant company, without one needing to beat the other into submission.

"Have I ever thanked you for keeping me sane these past few months?" Annabelle suddenly asked, a catch in her throat.

Charity glanced up at her mistress in surprise. Then she patted Annabelle's hand where it now clutched her arm. "You thank me, dear heart, every time you smile."

Affection for Charity welled up in her. Charity could have left her long ago. A number of the gallants were attracted to the still youthful maid, to her lush figure and quick wit. She could have had her pick, but she'd stayed at Annabelle's side, determined to remain close until Annabelle's plan for vengeance reached fruition. What would Annabelle have done without her?

The call came again from outside the tiring-room. Annabelle planted a quick kiss on Charity's cheek. "Have an orange, love," she said in her best orange girl voice, then swept from the room.

Charity watched her mistress go with a smile on her lips. Annabelle had grown into a fine woman, despite everything that had been done to her. She wore her dignity like a protective cape, this girl who'd suffered wretchedly and still thrust her stubborn chin into the air and stood up to those who threatened to beat her down.

Underneath it all, however, Charity knew a heart lay bleeding from her many disappointments. Her eyes misted. She'd give anything to find the balm to ease that heart's pain.

Ah, well, she did what she could by being with Annabelle. It was no suffering to share London with her. They'd had a fine time since they'd arrived, even if things hadn't yet turned out the way Annabelle wished.

A few moments passed before Charity could dash the mist from her eyes and return her attention to her surroundings. She'd just begun straightening the room, however, when a knock startled her. She opened the door to find Sir John Riverton on the other side.

"Oh, it's you, is it?" Stepping aside, she let him in with a sniff and then continued her work, struggling not to show any interest.

Sir John was a hard man to ignore, however, with his masses of chestnut hair and rakish smile. Aye, his features were a tad coarse and his hair threaded with the beginnings of gray. Everyone knew he'd been in trade before he'd been knighted for service to the king. There was also the small matter of his limp, product of a battlefield injury. Yet none of the ladies minded that much, thanks to his witty tongue and smiling brown eyes. Flirting brown eyes, she amended wryly, for the man was an incurable rake.

"You've missed the actresses," she said. "They're either on stage or waitin' in the wings or—"

"Actually, I've come to see you."

Charity whirled on him in surprise, a becoming flush staining her cheeks. Sir John gave her one of his most ingratiating smiles, instantly dousing the blush and raising her suspicions. Sir John had always treated her with the good-natured tolerance of an older brother. Much as she wished things were different, she wasn't such a fool as to misinterpret his current behavior. He was manipulating her with that tempting smile. No doubt about it.

"What d'ye mean, y've come to see me?" she asked, her tone cautious.

"I have a friend who wishes to meet your mistress."

Ah, so that was it. She rolled her eyes and turned away with a sigh. "Don't they all. I suppose this friend is some old merchant with a droolin' leer, or another of yer bold gallants who wants only a quick tumble."

Sir John moved to block her in her activities, propping his bad foot on the chair she'd been dusting. She found herself watching his thigh muscles shift under breeches that were drawn tight. Her mouth went dry.

"A bold gallant, yes," he said, "but I don't know about the quick tumble. Hampden doesn't seem as eager for quick tumbles these days as he once was."

She opened her mouth, but he forestalled her question.

"That's not to say he's a fop. He likes women, all right. Before he went to Antwerp for His Majesty, he was known to have a way with women, and I doubt he's lost that ability. Of greater importance, however, he has something your mistress's friend Somerset doesn't."

She crossed her arms over her chest and gazed up at him in suspicion. "And what might that be?"

"A title. And a fortune to go with it. Now, wouldn't your mistress like that?"

Charity fought the urge to laugh. No, her mistress wouldn't like that at all. The last thing Annabelle wanted or thought she needed was a protector.

Charity, however, had a different view of things. She would have liked to see her mistress make her way as an independent woman, but Charity, being practical-minded, knew independence didn't exist for women, and certainly not for a woman who had set out to destroy a noble. Only if a woman used her charms to snag a husband could she survive in the world.

What Annabelle needed was a man of her own, with a rake's wit and a cleric's good heart. Charity smiled. A man with a merchant's money wouldn't hurt none either. Of course, the likelihood of Annabelle's ever finding a husband was slim, now that she'd ruined her reputation by becoming an actress. But a protector . . . a good one who'd treat Annabelle with kindness . . . that was an option Charity couldn't get out of her mind.

She thought for a moment, then looked at Sir John, whose amused expression told her he felt sure of her answer. "A gallant, you say?"

"A marquis, with comfortable estates to his name. He's been in the king's service until recently, but now he's returned to England to reap his rewards. Come, now, Charity. Your mistress toys with the fops, but what she needs, both you and I know, is a real man in her bed. You were married once. You know what a difference the right man can make in a woman's life. Lord Hampden will treat your mistress well and give her more than enough money to suit her needs, if it comes to that."

Charity stood there staring at him, a thought suddenly entering her head. "Why is it, Sir John, that you haven't sought her favors yerself? You toy with all the other actresses . . . why not my mistress?"

John stroked his chin with his thumb and forefinger. "Now, why should you ask that, I wonder?"

"And why shouldn't you answer, I wonder?" she mocked him.

He chuckled. "Oh, it's a simple enough answer. Your mistress is far too sober-minded for me, too intense. I like a woman with a sense of humor."

"But she's wittier than any woman I know," Charity protested, wondering why she was arguing for something she didn't really want.

John's eyes warmed to a soft, sweet brown. "Ah, my inquisitive magpie, but wit often masks a wounded heart. I steer clear of wounded hearts."

Then thank heavens her own heart was quite nicely intact, she told herself. "And yer friend?" she asked with one brow lifted. "How d'ye know he would take a wounded heart into his bosom?"

"I don't." Sir John smiled. "But we'll find out how he feels about the subject, shan't we? I tell you what. . . . Why don't you meet him, then let me know your opinion? If you like him, then you and I can get him and your mistress in the same room. What do you think?''

She stared at him, then pursed her lips. A man with a title, eh? One who might treat her mistress with consideration? It was a possibility worth exploring. ''Oh, all right, then. I suppose I won't be missed. This act goes on forever. Lead me to this gallant. But mark me well, if I don't like his looks, I'll fight yer plans every step of the way.''

''Of course,'' he responded, but his light chuckle told her he didn't think for a minute she would dislike his choice.

It took them a few minutes to make their way from behind the stage to the boxes. At three-thirty when the play had started, the house had been packed with nobility, and Dryden's play had always drawn a good crowd. But now that it was half over, some had left to attend New Year's suppers while others were pursuing the consummation of assignations they'd made at the theater. So she wasn't surprised a few moments later when they entered a box to find it empty but for Sir John's friend, Lord Hampden.

Lord Hampden sat with his eyes fixed on the stage. She paused at the entrance to survey him unobserved. Sir John stood quietly beside her, the smile never leaving his face.

No wonder Sir John thinks I'll like his friend, Charity thought as she scanned Lord Hampden with a critical eye. *A splendid specimen of a man he is, and no doubt about it.*

He looked about thirty, the perfect age as far as Charity was concerned, old enough to have a mind of his own and young enough to give a woman enjoyment. A thick mane of golden curls streamed down to gild his richly clad shoulders. And what shoulders! Broad, proud, masculine in every way. He leaned casually back in his chair, his legs splayed in front of him, two thick legs with muscles cording them from hip to ankle. That much she could tell, even under the folds of his rich royal blue breeches.

Legs were important in Charity's estimation. She always noticed a man's legs. In Sir John's case, his bad leg had told her he was capable of great loyalty, for he'd wounded it in service to the king.

In the case of this Lord Hampden, his strong and muscular thighs boded well, for it said he rode a horse with dignity and wasn't a stranger to hard work. In these days, even nobility ought to be able to put their legs to good use, she thought. This man had sturdy legs—already one stroke in his favor.

At the moment he looked bored, however. With the box being empty, she thought, perhaps his friends had forsaken him for other companions. On the other hand, her mistress had left the stage, which might also account for the tedium in his face. Then, as if he felt her gaze on him, he shifted his eyes from the stage and caught sight of her and Sir John.

What eyes, she thought with a tingle. Deep-set and green as oceans, they were, and not a whit of cruelty in them. They narrowed as he watched her and Sir John approach.

"Lord Hampden, meet Charity," Sir John said, pressing her forward.

She bobbed a curtsy, pleased when Sir John cupped her elbow to urge her to rise. Then his hand rested in the small of her back with familiarity. A shiver shook her skin before she returned her attention to Lord Hampden.

The marquis was smiling now, and the flash of even white teeth charmed her to her toes.

"You're Madam Maynard's servant?" he asked.

"Aye, milord." The man had a voice like dark honey, Charity thought. This one could be dangerous to a woman's dignity.

"I wish to meet her."

No mincing of words here, she thought. "So do a great many men, milord, if you don't mind my sayin' so. She's a fine actress, she is, and the gallants all find her fetching.''

The smile broadened. "As do I. So what must I do to ensure I get a fair chance at meeting her?''

She saw the twinkle in his eyes and grew bolder. ''Oh, but yer lordship wants a wee bit more than a fair chance, don't he? If you wanted merely a fair chance, y'd be down there now with the lot of them, tryin' to get her attention.''

"You're a saucy wench," Lord Hampden retorted, though he seemed pleased by the fact. "Is your mistress as bold with her tongue as you?''

Charity ignored the double meaning that no doubt lay behind his words. "Bold enough to fend off yer sallies if she wants, whether or not you enter the fray behind the stage with the others.''

He leaned forward. "I've no need to enter that fray, Mistress Upstart." For the first time, she noticed he held his fist clenched around something. He opened it to reveal several gold sovereigns. "There's a great deal more where this comes from. You see, I'm willing to buy my way into your mistress's good graces. I'll wager that's more than those fools flitting around behind the scenes are willing to do.''

A keen shaft of disappointment brought a frown to Charity's face. Even though she'd wanted a man who could care for her mistress's purse as well as her heart, she hadn't stooped so low as this. She curtsied stiffly. "I'm afraid you've mistaken my mistress for a whore, milord. I don't think the two of you would suit, after all.''

Without another word, she swallowed her dismay and turned to go, brushing off Sir John's hand when he tried to halt her.

"Wait!" Lord Hampden said softly. Something in the urgency in his voice made her pause. When she remained with her back to him, he added, "I didn't mean to offend. I've heard tales and, well . . . sometimes rumors don't distinguish between women who take lovers and women who are whores. But I do know the difference, so there's no excuse for me, is there? Please accept my apologies.''

She glanced at Sir John, whose red face clearly showed who'd been at fault for spreading the rumors. She thought a moment, her eyes burning into Sir John's. He shrugged, his quick uncharacteristic embarrassment now apparently gone. She'd get no help from that quarter.

She pivoted to face Lord Hampden. His smile had faded, replaced by tense interest. Perhaps she'd been too hasty, she thought as she watched him meet her gaze with clear eyes. Any man who could apologize so nicely surely deserved another chance. Most of the men who came to the theater took the actresses for strumpets in costume. This one seemed at least to question that assumption.

"What exactly is it you wish me to do, milord?" she asked in a tone meant to remind him he wasn't out of hot water yet.

He seemed to relax. "I'd like you to arrange a meeting between your mistress and me. One where we'll have complete privacy."

"Of course," she said, her voice icy.

His voice chilled a fraction in response. "I simply want to talk to her."

"Of course," she repeated, but when he refused to take the bait and offer more assurances, she added, "So it won't bother you if the meetin' takes place in the tiring-room, here at the theater?"

"As long as I can speak with her alone, I don't care if it takes place in the middle of London Bridge."

His ready answer calmed her fears somewhat. After all, this Lord Hampden was a fine-looking gentleman. He seemed willing to treat her mistress with some small respect. It was more than she'd seen in any of the others. "I'll see what I can do. But I won't make no promises."

"When can I meet her?"

She crossed her arms over her chest. "I said, I'll see what I can do."

"When?" The green eyes suddenly glittered hard as emeralds in the dim glow of the candlelight.

She sighed, then thought a moment. "Tomorrow afternoon. I'll make certain she arrives an hour before the others."

He dazzled her with a beautiful smile. "Good. I see that your name is fitting. You're the very soul of charity, and I won't forget it."

For the first time since she'd entered the box, she returned his smile. "Oh, don't you worry, milord. I don't intend to let you forget it."

Then she whisked out of the box to the sound of the two men chuckling behind her.

Chapter Three

"Use every man after his desert, and who
should 'scape whipping?"
—William Shakespeare, *Hamlet*, Act 2, Scene 2

Edward Maynard, Earl of Walcester, surveyed the
book-lined walls of his comfortable study, a glass of
claret in one hand, a quill in the other. Thin gray wisps
of hair hung like a fringe from around his shiny bald
pate as he stood there silently in his sober, jet clothing. He shifted his gaze to the portrait of his wife
hanging over the fireplace. Poor fragile Delia. She'd
died during the plague, leaving him without an heir or
even a daughter to comfort him in his old age. Now
he almost regretted his often harsh manner toward her,
his refusal to countenance her lack of sense. At least
she'd endured his coldness when other women would
have thrown tantrums.

He pondered the noblewomen of his acquaintance.
Rumor had it that Lady Wickham, angry at her husband, had flounced off to the country and barred him
from her bedroom. The Duke of Lauderdale's wife had
cuckolded him a number of times. Not that the duke
had cared, of course, since he acquired a new mistress
every year, some actress or dancer or such.

A taut sneer twisted Edward's lips. Actresses. They
were the worst female creatures of all, with their seductive manners and shocking behavior. The actresses
were bringing London to ruin. They encouraged His
Majesty in his profligate ways as his devoted queen
stood sadly by.

At the moment, Edward was most concerned by one particular actress, a dubious woman named Annabelle Maynard. No matter how much he told himself that the woman's appearance probably had nothing to do with him, he still worried she might know something about his past that could destroy him. The Norwood business, for example. If she knew of that, he was in deep jeopardy.

It had taken him years to reach the height of political power he now approached. The king admired his work with the Royal Society and had even appointed him to high office. Yes, with Clarendon fled in disgrace, Edward had a chance to be as powerful as the Duke of Buckingham.

So much could yet go wrong, however. For one thing, the younger nobles like the Earl of Rochester and Sir Charles Sedley disliked him for his sober mien and harsh rebukes. Worse yet, now that he was gaining in power, Buckingham, once his close ally, had become his worst enemy. Oh, yes, Buckingham would delight in drumming him out of the court as he had Clarendon.

It would be easy enough to do, for Buckingham knew about the debacle at Norwood all those years ago, as did His Majesty. If Buckingham ever stopped believing Edward's story that he'd been powerless to prevent the treachery, the duke would pounce. Edward had successfully hidden the truth all these years. He'd trod the thin board of power without a fall. Was he now to be tumbled off and his foolish cowardice exposed just because some actress had come to haunt him?

A knock interrupted his reverie. "Yes?" he called out.

A footman opened the door and announced Lord Hampden's arrival.

"Excellent. Show him in here at once," Edward said, setting his quill carefully down on his writing desk. Hampden could unravel this muddle if anyone could.

In moments, the footman had returned with the marquis. As usual, Hampden was dressed with exquisite taste, his embroidered vest of the finest workmanship and his breeches burgundy velvet of the first quality. If any other man had come before Edward in such clothes, Edward would have termed him a profligate. But he knew Hampden dressed well because he had a zest for life, a zest not dampened by his equally sharp intelligence. Edward might not share that zest, but he certainly couldn't condemn it.

Edward watched Hampden observe everything in the room though without appearing to do so: the papers piled on Edward's desk, the half-empty glass of claret at Edward's elbow, the rumpled quality of Edward's garb. Edward fought the urge to squirm under such scrutiny. Spies like Hampden were inclined to be observant. The marquis undoubtedly did it out of habit.

After their greetings, a long silence fell between them, only broken when Walcester snapped, "Well? What do you think?"

Hampden looked noncommittal. "About what?"

"You know what. That . . . that woman."

Hampden walked to the fireplace and stood staring into the fire. Edward watched him, a tight knot forming in his chest as he waited for Hampden to speak.

At last Hampden pivoted to level his perceptive stare on Edward. "Tell me, Walcester, before I give my opinion of 'that woman' . . . why did you wish me to see her on the stage?"

Edward's lips thinned. How much should he say? He could trust Hampden with his life and his reputation. Still, Hampden had lost much during the civil war. He might not agree to carry out Edward's wishes if he knew Edward's secret. So Edward must reveal only enough to coax the marquis into helping him.

A shame Hampden had no interest in political power, for Walcester could easily offer him that. But Hampden had never seemed inclined to grovel and scrape before His Majesty in order to gain more lands, more titles, more honors, as so many other noblemen did. Since Hampden's return, he'd seemed content to spend his days caring for his investments and his estates and performing experiments with the Royal Society. Edward had seen him at court only once.

No, much as it grieved him to do so, Edward would have to rely on the indebtedness Hampden felt toward him in order to solicit the marquis's help. "You surely have guessed part of my reasons," Edward ventured.

Hampden nodded. "The actress's last name is the same as your own. I assume that's the source of your concern?"

"Part of it."

" 'Sdeath, Edward, dozens of Maynards reside in London. Why should a similar surname concern you? Unless you believe she's a . . . er . . . relative of yours." Hampden didn't say the word *bastard*, but Edward knew he thought it.

"You know me better than that, don't you? If I'd had illegitimate children, I'd have provided for them." Faint irony tinged his tone as he added, "I'm sure that with my station, any woman carrying my child would have hastened to inform me."

"So why the concern?"

He sucked in a deep breath. Now came the difficult part. "Do you remember years ago when I first met you in France?"

Warily Hampden met his gaze. "How could I forget it? You came upon me as I was about to be skewered by a burly soldier who'd caught me sneaking about his wife's rooms and had chased me into a blind alley."

A certain softness entered Walcester's tone. "You were not quite a man then, a skinny, cocky little ruffian. There you stood, without a weapon and so undernourished you could barely stand up, but still facing that man with insolent bravado."

"He would have killed me if it hadn't been for you," Hampden put in quietly.

"Aye."

Hampden sighed. "Yes, I well remember it. You rescued me, and then saw that both me and my friend,

the Earl of Falkham, were given employment. You
found him a place in the Duke of York's army and
introduced me to the Duke of Buckingham in Rotter-
dam.''

"Did you ever wonder how I'd had such connections? Why the brother of a king and another highly
influential duke promptly took the two of you into their
service upon my recommendation?''

Hampden shrugged. "No. Men of your stamp know
everyone.''

"Yes, but you were a bastard son—''

"My father claimed me,'' Hampden broke in with
a frown.

Edward reminded himself to be careful. It wouldn't
do to insult Hampden. "Aye, he did, because he had
no other heirs. But your legitimacy didn't profit you
much in France with him dead and you in exile. I had
to do some fancy talking to persuade Buckingham to
entrust an untried lad known for his gossiping tongue
with England's state secrets.''

The cold glitter in Hampden's eyes told Edward he'd
made his point. "If you're saying all this to ensure
that I'll help you, then you may desist. I've already
acknowledged the debt I owe you. I certainly intend
to repay it in every way I can.''

Edward shook his head. "No, no, that's not the
point.'' He sipped his claret, choosing his words carefully. "I helped you because I knew you'd be an asset
to England. What I'm trying to show is that they accepted my recommendation for a reason.'' Edward
paused. "You see, I'd worked with them myself, in
the same capacity in which you and Falkham later
did.''

Hampden's eyes widened. He surveyed the desk, the
piles of scholarly papers and books, then jerked his
gaze back to Edward. "What do you mean?''

"Before the battle at Worcester, before you ever
knew me, I'd been a Royalist spy. By the time I met
you and Lord Falkham, I had left the king's service,

but before that, I'd spent time in the Parliamentary army, feeding intelligence to the king's army.''

A faint smile crossed Hampden's face. "You. A spy. 'Tis hard to countenance." He assessed Edward with a new light in his eyes. "I suppose you were a spy for His Majesty?"

"Yes. While pretending to support Cromwell, I traveled with the Parliamentary army gathering information for the Royalists. I continued in that capacity until Charles II fled to France."

"I should have guessed," Hampden remarked as he stared at Edward. "You did have an amazing knowledge about who was important and who wasn't." He paused a moment. Then his eyes narrowed. "How does all this concern Annabelle Maynard?"

Edward drew in a deep breath. "My code name during the civil war was chosen from a madrigal. You may have heard of it." He couldn't keep the bitterness from his voice. "My code name was the 'Silver Swan.' "

Hampden stood completely motionless for a second, not even attempting to hide his surprise. Then he dropped abruptly into the nearest chair.

"I see you've heard Annabelle Maynard's nickname," Edward continued. "I haven't been able to convince myself it's merely coincidental that she goes by both names."

With a frown, Hampden stroked his chin. "She's too young to have known you then. She can't be more than twenty-two."

It was Edward's turn to be surprised. "Truly? From what I'd heard others say, I thought surely she'd be older."

"You haven't seen her yourself?"

"I haven't ventured near that theater since I've heard of her. Don't you see? If her purpose is to lure me there, I must resist at all costs."

Hampden remained silent a moment, his brow furrowed in thought. "What do you think she intends?"

"I truly don't know. Only the Royalists received communications from the Silver Swan, but few knew my real name, and certainly Cromwell's army never knew of my existence.''

"In any case," Hampden said, "the war is over and no one should care one way or the other. So why are you worried that anyone might have found you out now?''

Edward stood abruptly and paced the room. He could hardly tell Hampden the real reason. ''That's just it. If this Annabelle Maynard knew both my names and my title, there'd be no reason for her not to seek me out. But she hasn't, which tells me she doesn't know everything.''

"I see your point, but—"

"She or the person she represents may know only my surname and code name. As you say, a number of Maynards reside in London. Without knowing the rest, anyone seeking to find me would be hard-pressed to determine my identity, wouldn't he? This is a way of drawing me out.''

"That still doesn't answer my question. Why should anyone care to draw you out at all?''

Edward rubbed his eyes wearily. "I don't know. Perhaps someone has a grudge against me for my activities.''

Edward could tell from the way Hampden avoided his eyes that the marquis thought him unnecessarily concerned.

"Look, Hampden," Edward bit out, "I wouldn't ask you to check on it if I didn't think I had cause for alarm. I've already done enough questioning to learn that Annabelle Maynard appeared in London out of nowhere. No one knows where she's from. She doesn't talk of her past or her reasons for coming to London. Her secretiveness bothers me.''

"Perhaps her background is too mundane to claim.''

"For God's sake, man, she flaunts her silver swan brooch as if it were a medal and shows off her silver ribbons every chance she gets. Obviously she, or someone working with her, wants to lure the Silver

Swan into the open. I must know why before I walk into a trap.''

Hampden regarded him steadily for a moment. "Is there more to this than you're saying?"

Yes! Edward wanted to cry. But he couldn't, in case he was wrong about her. If Hampden found evidence that this woman knew of Edward's past spying activities, then Edward would assess on his own how much she understood and why she'd sought him out. Then if it had anything to do with the debacle at Norwood . . .

He didn't like to think of it, but it might become necessary to get rid of her . . . pay her off . . . or even have her forcibly taken from England to the colonies.

"Is there more you wish to tell me?" Hampden repeated.

Edward forced himself to meet Hampden's suspicious gaze. "No, of course not. So tell me . . . will you do me this favor? Will you see what you can discover about this woman? Who sent her to London? Why she's here? Who her family and friends are?"

Hampden shifted his sturdy frame in the chair as he considered Edward's request. "You've already gathered some of your own information. What do you need me for?"

Edward fixed him with a fierce gaze. "Because you're the best. And because you're the only man I trust for this."

Their eyes locked for a moment, Hampden's dark with suspicion . . . and something else. Finally he sighed. "All right. I'll look into it." When Edward started to thank him, he held up his hand and added, "But only because the woman intrigues me and only because of what I owe you. I think you're being overly concerned. Or you're hiding something from me."

Edward's breath withered to nothing in his throat, but somehow he managed a smile. "Hiding something? What could I hide from you?"

Hampden shook his head. "You might try to hide a number of things, but rest assured I'll ferret out your secrets if I so desire. At the moment, I don't think I want to know what has you so worried." Hampden rose to his feet. "As long as this remains uncomplicated, I don't mind doing 'research' into Madam Maynard's past and acquaintances. After all, I'm no longer working for the king, so I have the time. But if matters become the least messy, I'll be back, Walcester, and I'll expect answers from you."

"Thank you," Edward said, fighting back the anxiety threatening to engulf him. " 'Tis probably nothing, as you say, but all the same, I would like to know who she is."

Hampden smiled and quirked one brow. Then with an odd expression on his face, he rubbed the edge of his chin. "In truth, so would I, my friend. So would I."

Edward spent the rest of the evening wondering what exactly Hampden had meant by that enigmatic statement.

Chapter Four

"Queen and huntress, chaste and fair,
Now the sun is laid to sleep,
Seated in thy silver chair,
State in wonted manner keep."
—Ben Jonson, *Cynthia's Revels*, Act 5, Scene 3

The day after New Year's, Annabelle Taylor entered the tiring-room at one o'clock, an hour and a half before she normally arrived. No one was there and the emptiness filled her with a vague disquiet.

Already the theater was filling for the afternoon's performance, although most of the people in the auditorium were servants holding seats for their masters. Backstage, however, not a soul trod the boards, for most of the players didn't arrive until around two.

Nonetheless, Henry Harris should be here, Annabelle told herself as she pocketed the orange she'd just bought. Charity had said Henry wanted to meet her at the tiring-room early to rehearse. If that was the case, where the devil was he?

She shook off her uneasiness and searched for the flint box. Though it was midday, the winter skies outside were dreary and dark, and little light filtered through the grimy window at one end of the room. She lit the candles in the sconces, then found a comfortable chair to sit in while she waited.

Clearly, Henry had been detained. There was no other explanation. She swept a wayward curl from her face and wondered if she dared light a fire. Sir William D'Avenant, for all his generous and pleasant air, tended to be a bit of a pinchpenny. Of course, with the theater only half filled some nights, Annabelle could easily understand his need to count every shilling. Nonetheless, last night the house had been full. Surely Sir William wouldn't mind if she indulged herself this once and built a fire. In an hour's time, the servants would be coming to light the fire anyway.

With that reassurance, she went to the hearth and knelt to lay a fire. A sharp pain made her suck in her breath. Devil take her tight laces! On days like this, when the winter damp seeped into a person's bones, she had trouble with her ribs. She wondered if they would always pain her or if there simply hadn't been enough time for them to heal. After all, it had only been a year since the squire had thrown her down, then kicked her hard enough to break three ribs.

A grim smile crossed her face. At least she no longer had to fear being tormented by her stepfather. She fought for control over the ache and in moments had a comfortable blaze roaring in the fireplace.

Rising to her feet, she stared into the fire, thinking how different her life was here in London. Had it only been last winter that she'd been forced to get up hours before dawn to stoke the dying fire in the squire's chambers, working in complete stealth lest she stir him from his sleep? Even then she hadn't minded the work, though she'd known he'd given her the task to shame her. After a night spent shivering in her own small chamber, she'd welcomed the fresh blaze.

She looked down at her clothing, at her simple wool gown that gave her more pleasure than all the finery the squire had made her wear when company came to call. He hadn't wanted the world to know how he treated his daughter or his wife in private. Her mother had become a master at hiding bruises. And Annabelle . . . she'd managed to smile her way through many a formal dinner despite her sore behind, raw from the stiff brush he liked to beat her with.

Her mother had known nothing of those private punishments . . . not until that horrible day when she'd come across the squire in the kitchen, his temper flaring at Annabelle's defiant words and his crop coming down on her back in a fury. Her gown had been low enough in back to allow his crop to bite into the bare skin, drawing blood. Her mother had lost all control at the sight of her daughter's back scored with his marks.

Annabelle fought back tears. She'd been right to maintain the conspiracy of silence between her and her stepfather, to hide the truth from her mother all those years. She'd begun the charade early in life, when she'd realized her mother could do nothing about the squire. Annabelle only wished she could have continued it. Then her mother would be alive. . . .

She pressed her knuckles to her mouth to hold back the sobs that would otherwise escape. Her head ached just thinking about the past and her mother. Forcing her thoughts away from the dangerous subject, she rubbed her temples with frenzied movements. Henry would arrive any moment. It wouldn't do to have him see her upset.

She pulled a chair up to the fire and sat down, gazing deep into the flames as she touched her hand to her intricately worked silver brooch. The Silver Swan. Every time she heard the gallants call her that, it reminded her of the poem her mother had said was written by her real father.

The lines were engraved on her memory after all the hours she'd studied it, looking for some clue to his identity:

> The bard cannot reveal himself,
> Except in song, one last refrain,
> To beg sweet Portia tread with Beatrice
> Far away from the martyr's plain.
>
> Her heart she must keep close and mute,
> Her tongue must whisper not a cry
> Else she be forced by crown-less hands
> To sing the hangman's lullaby.

Scrawled beneath it in what had looked like a man's hand had been the words, "With fond hopes, The Sil-

ver Swan.'' Obviously the poem had been intended as
a message to someone. ''The Bard'' could be a reference to William Shakespeare, particularly since Portia and Beatrice had been characters in Shakespeare's
plays. Was the message to Portia to ''tread with Beatrice'' intended to be the establishment of an assignation?

Perhaps it was, she told herself, but then how had
her mother fit into all of it? All her mother had said
was that during the civil war, when she was still
Phoebe Harlow, Annabelle's father had come to stay
at the Harlow house. The soldiers had called him Captain Maynard. Phoebe had called him Captain, too,
and had never known his first name, nor had he seen
fit to tell it to her even after the two of them had become intimate. Then one day Captain Maynard had
asked her to carry a sealed poem to his friend at a
tavern in Norwood. Maynard had told her mother little
about the poem she'd carried and only enough about
the man she was to meet to enable her to recognize
him. To ensure that her mother could verify that the
message came from him, Maynard had given her his
signet ring.

Annabelle thought of the ring that lay in a locked
box at her lodgings. She'd not yet determined to whom
the crest belonged, largely because she'd not wanted
to ask anyone and give away her purpose yet. Eventually, however . . .

She remembered what her mother had told her about
her visit to the tavern. Her mother had met Maynard's
friend as planned. He'd read the poem and then, when
some people had entered the room, had thrust the let-
ter back at her and told her to leave. Not certain if she
should try to leave the message with him when he was
alone, she'd waited in town. When she'd seen soldiers
rushing toward the tavern, she'd panicked. Too frightened to wait, she'd returned home only to find that
Maynard had fled.

At that point in the story, her mother had refused to

say more. Her mother had clearly known more than she was saying, but Annabelle hadn't been able to coax her into revealing it all. She'd seemed ashamed of something. Now the desire to know the truth burned at Annabelle. Why had the soldiers come to the tavern? What had happened to make her mother feel such shame? Why had her father fled, leaving her mother to bear an illegitimate child alone?

Was there some way she could use her knowledge of the Silver Swan to strike back at her father? It was an intriguing thought.

Aloud she recited the poem's lines to herself, searching yet again for any hidden meaning. Her head ached, but she forced herself to concentrate on the words. She'd repeated aloud the line "To sing the hangman's lullaby" when a noise behind her disrupted her concentration.

"Rather a morbid poem for a beauty such as you, don't you think?" said a resonant man's voice.

She whirled in her seat, expecting to find Henry Harris. Instead, a man she'd never seen stood in the doorway, his large frame filling it. For a second, fear coursed through her. Alone in the tiring-room, she was easy prey for any stranger who chose to confront her.

Then she noted the stranger's rich clothing and rakish plumed hat. No doubt he was a nobleman with amorous intentions rather than some scruffy miscreant from the streets. She mustered her courage and reminded herself she was the Silver Swan, the woman whose sharp tongue all the wits and rakes respected. She could handle any forward gallant.

Chin up, she rose with regal nonchalance. "You aren't supposed to be in the tiring-room, sir. I suggest you return to the pit to await the play."

"Would you banish me to the pit, then, for daring to admire you?" Eyes green as a forest in spring stared back at her with insolent amusement.

Something about the way his bold gaze raked her put her on her guard. The best way to deal with such impertinence was to put him in his place with banter, yet thanks to the way he surveyed her, a faint smile on his lips, she couldn't think of a quip sufficient to cow him.

When his smile broadened at her silence, however, she found her voice. "Better the pit than to be turned to stone, like those who dared to gaze on Medusa. Don't you know that an actress before her performance is as poison-tongued as a snake?"

His low chuckle contained enough charm to seduce a stone. "I hardly believe a swan could be so easily transformed into a serpent. I think Aphrodite stands before me and not Medusa."

He merely played on the fact that Aphrodite's bird was the swan, but she blushed at the pretty compliment nonetheless.

Faith, I must stop this! she told herself. *The man's a smooth-tongued devil. Any woman with half a brain could see that!*

Then why were her palms sweating? And why had her dreadful headache completely fled? "Beware, lest Aphrodite pierce you with her arrows," she said more sharply than she'd intended, determined to have the last word and evict this unsettling stranger.

"I'll risk it." He stepped farther into the room. She tried not to notice his solid build, nor the cleft in his squarish chin, nor even the golden hair that streamed down over his shoulders from beneath his wide-brimmed hat and glinted in the firelight. She tried not to notice . . . and failed. She knew from mythology that one man had been spared Aphrodite's shafts—Adonis. If ever Adonis stood before Annabelle in the flesh, it was now.

To her consternation, the stranger rested his hip against a scarred oak table a scarce two feet from her.

"I'm waiting for someone," she told him coldly. "You can't stay."

"You're waiting for me."

She thought at first he was merely being arrogant, but at the knowing expression on his face, a small suspicion gave her pause. "I'm waiting for Henry Harris."

The smile grew calculating. "But your maid Charity said—"

Her suspicion became a certainty. She groaned. "Devil take that woman! 'Tis so like her to do something like this."

"I take it you weren't informed of our appointment?"

"Nay." Deep in thought, she said the word with casual unconcern. But when he lifted himself to sit squarely on the table, she reacted more fiercely. "Of course not. If she'd told me, I wouldn't be here. You can be certain of that."

"Then I must thank Charity for her discretion."

She leveled a scathing gaze on him. "No, you mustn't, for her discretion will get neither of you anywhere. My maid does not decide whom I will see, so I'm afraid you must leave."

"We haven't even been introduced." With the smooth, frightening grace of a tiger, he slid from the table and stood before her. Then he whisked his plumed hat from his head and bowed. "Colin Jeffreys, Marquis of Hampden, at your service."

A marquis, no less! No wonder Charity had agreed to arrange a meeting between them. Still, Annabelle didn't intend to let something like a title tempt her. How well she knew what farces titles were. Men with titles were as treacherous as men without them, if not more so.

"A pleasure to meet you, my lord. Now, would you please leave?" Her voice trembled. She knew it, but hoped he hadn't heard it, especially since he stood very close to her now, close enough to touch her if he wished.

"You can't throw me out yet. We're just beginning to get acquainted." He tossed his hat onto the table, and she winced. The man clearly intended to stay awhile.

Forcing a flippant tone into her voice, she remarked,

"Then we shall have to continue this interesting acquaintance later, shan't we?" She flashed him a simpering smile. If she'd had a fan, she would have fluttered it coyly as was the fashion. "Why don't you return after the performance? Many others do."

"Precisely, which is why I'm here now."

From the frown etching his forehead, she could tell that unlike the other gallants, he didn't like her flirtatious posturing. His suddenly sober gaze never left her face. So why could she imagine it roaming her body, searching for the chinks in her armor?

Time for another tack, she told herself. She pivoted gracefully away from him to cross the room toward the door. In the best bored monotone she could muster, she remarked, "You are becoming incredibly tiresome, Lord Hampden. If you don't leave this room now, I shall seek out Sir William to remind you of the rules."

His low chuckle gave her pause. "Sir William and I are good friends, so you'll find no quarter there. No, I'm afraid you're stuck with me for the moment."

Why did his words send an anticipatory tingle through her every vein? With a jolt, she realized she truly was alone with this man, and he clearly didn't want to leave.

"What do you want from me, my lord?" Her hand on the doorknob, she twisted her head to look at him. "What must I do to have peace?"

He crossed his arms over his chest as he leaned back once more against the table. "Surely you could guess that yourself." Pointedly he allowed his gaze to travel the length of her.

Color suffused her face, though she fought to maintain her aloof, bantering persona. "Ah, but that would take the enjoyment out of hearing you make the proposition."

He pushed away from the table and approached her with slow, deliberate steps. She stared him down, all trace of amusement gone from her expression.

When he stood only a foot from her, he reached out

and smoothed back one curl from her face, much as
Charity might have done. Only his gesture wasn't
soothing or helpful. His was calculated to seduce, and
she knew it. His fingers brushed the skin of her cheek,
the merest tickle, but enough to make her heart's pace
quicken.

Nicely done, she complimented him silently, and
hated herself for responding to a gesture he'd undoubtedly used with many an actress in the past.

For a moment, his eyes locked with hers, their glittering depths holding promises she feared he might
attempt to keep. She'd scarcely realized she'd stopped
breathing until he dropped his hand and she released
a long drawn-out breath.

His gaze swept down to fasten on her brooch. "Such
a lovely piece of work," he said, with only a hint that
he might be talking about things other than the brooch.
"Where did you find it?"

His question put her on her guard. She backed away
while she still could. Then she lifted her hand to finger
the brooch's cold metal. It wouldn't do to admit she'd
bought such an expensive piece of jewelry herself on
an actress's pittance. "Oh, I scarcely even remember.
Some admirer or other gave it to me, I suppose."

"Have you so many admirers that you can easily
forget who gave you such a gift?" His mocking smile
returned.

"I have more admirers than you can possibly imagine," she replied acidly, hoping to discourage him.

"And not a one that you favor with your returned
affection."

Her eyes widened before she caught herself and
forced a saucy smile to her lips. "Of course I've fa-
vored some with my affections." She tossed her curls
and fluttered her lashes. "What poor actress could resist the sweet blandishments of London's gallants?"

"What actress indeed?" His gaze probed her secrets. "Then you wouldn't resist my blandishments, I
trust."

This began to feel distinctly like a trap, she thought.

"At any other time, with your being a marquis . . . a very handsome marquis—" here she paused to flash a seductive smile his way, "I'd be tempted." Sweet Mary, it was difficult to play the part of a jaded, vapid actress with this man. "But I'm afraid I have quite a *tendre* for Lord Somerset. I couldn't possibly fit in another gallant, since I spend most of my waking hours with him." A blatant lie, she thought, but at the moment, she needed to rid herself of this importunate man as quickly as possible.

"Such a pity. The Silver Swan deserves something better than a fop like Somerset. Particularly when she bears the name Maynard."

She'd been about to give him a frosty retort on the subject of Somerset, when his second line stopped her. "What does my surname have to do with anything?" With studied nonchalance, she moved to put a chair between them, trying to ease the sudden tightness in her chest.

Lord Hampden remained silent a moment, watching her with eyes that gleamed in the flickering firelight. "The Maynards I know, and there are several, are men of repute and title. If perchance you're related to one of them, you should at least have enough pride to uphold the family reputation and not associate with a mere second son like Somerset, no matter how glib his tongue and fashionable his clothing. He buys that clothing at a dear price, as you must know. He certainly can't care for a woman the way another man might."

"Another man . . . like you, I suppose."

He flashed that brilliant smile at her again, momentarily driving all rational thought from her mind. No man should be allowed to walk around with a smile like that, she thought. The men in town must have to conspire to keep him constantly away from their women.

"I would be the perfect choice." Not a hint of vanity marred his tone.

She wanted to cut him with a biting retort, to put

him in his place, but she dared not, for he hadn't yet told her what she wanted to know, and now they'd steered into other waters far more disturbing. She had to bring him back to the subject that most interested her—the Maynards he knew.

She gave him a glittering smile of her own. "You? The perfect choice? How do I know that associating with you wouldn't also put a smear on the pristine family reputation of these Maynards?"

Raising one brow, he rubbed his chin. "You don't. That's why I'll give you time to ask about me before I continue my pursuit. I think you'll be pleased by what you find. I assure you, if any of the Maynards I know were to have a say in your choice of companion, they'd choose me."

Why did she get the feeling he was offering his knowledge of the Maynards as bait? Had her real father noted her presence on the stage and recruited this Lord Hampden to help him discover her game?

She surveyed Lord Hampden in silence, noting the bold, broad forehead, the powerful neck, the wide span of muscled chest. His eyes watched her with an intensity that bespoke more than a cursory interest.

She could hardly believe this well-spoken gallant sought her out merely at some older lord's direction. He seemed too independent for such manipulation, and too intent on having her for himself. The thought sent warm blood to the surface of her skin.

"So tell me, my sweet swan," he remarked, the subtle hint of intimacy in the endearment making her fight a blush all the more furiously, "shall you allow me to call on you in your lodgings, say two days from now?"

His request threw her into a quandary. He knew about the Maynards. He might even know who her father was. What's more, if she could trick Lord Hampden as she had Lord Somerset into believing she'd bedded him, she'd have another weapon against her father. What nobleman could endure the thought that his daughter, a notorious actress on the stage, had been intimate with his friend?

"Well?" he asked.

If she played it carefully, she told herself, she could use Lord Hampden to strike back at her father. Since Lord Hampden would also get what he wanted, her companionship, he'd not be hurt in the process.

With determination, she thrust from her mind the worry of how she'd fool this forceful gallant into believing she'd allowed him to possess her body. "You may call on me, but in three days."

"Two days. That gives you ample time to determine my . . . ah . . . suitability."

His matter-of-fact treatment of the whole matter made her shudder. Was she truly agreeing to take on a lover in the same way a woman chose a seamstress or milliner? She bit back the hysterical giggle that rose in her throat. Perhaps she should ask for written references.

Lord Hampden rounded the chair to stand right before her. "This probably seems cold-blooded to you," he said, as if he'd read her mind.

"Not at all. If you'll send your solicitor over with the proper papers, we can sign a contract and be done with it." She kept her tone light. "What sort of document *does* one write for formal assignations? Perhaps something simple like 'I, the undersigned, do solemnly swear to meet with actress Annabelle Maynard—' "

"Very amusing," he cut her off, the corners of his mouth edging upward. "Perhaps I should impress upon you the depths of my intentions . . . so you won't receive the wrong idea about what our relations to each other are to be in the future." His eyes dropped to her lips, which, to her chagrin, trembled in response.

"Truly, my lord, I don't think that will be necessary," she protested, but it was too late. His arm had already snaked around her waist and his mouth was on hers.

Her emotions immediately became a jumble of fear,

intrigue, anger . . . and some other unfamiliar emotion. Lips supple, yet firm, molded hers into pliancy, causing a pleasant tingling to unfurl in her belly. Struck dumb by surprise, she felt his arms press her tighter, felt his hand slide up and down her back in a caress.

Then he slid the tip of his tongue between her lips and ran it along her tightly clenched teeth. From the other kisses she'd received from men, she knew what he wanted and feared giving it to him, even though she'd given such kisses to other men without a thought. Somehow she knew such intimacy from him would affect her as those other kisses hadn't. Yet if she didn't respond in the accustomed manner, he would wonder how experienced she really was. . . .

So she made the mistake of opening her mouth, thus baring herself to a kiss of such fathomless intensity, it made her body ache. She scarcely noticed the faint scent of leather that clung to him. All she knew was the plunge of his tongue in her mouth, mimicking the act he meant them to share. Her pulse quickened and her eyelids slid shut as one of his hands moved to cup her neck, holding her head still closer while he stole the breath from her.

So this was seduction, she thought as an unfamiliar hunger made her want to arch into him, to pull him into herself. No wonder her mother had succumbed.

When at last he drew back, after possessing her mouth so thoroughly she no longer knew where she was, she stared at him through heavy-lidded eyes, her lips slightly parted. She couldn't have spoken if she tried. His gaze locked with hers. He moved his hand from the back of her neck to cup her cheek, then stroked his index finger along her lower lip.

"Two days," he murmured, almost to himself, as his eyes darkened at the sight of her quickened breath. "How will I wait two days?"

The words sent a ripple of something through her. She feared it was desire. It most certainly was desire. She recoiled from the thought almost as soon as it came to her. Her mother had let desire ruin her life. Annabelle wouldn't make that mistake.

Yet the intimate press of Lord Hampden's lips on hers had enticed her beyond belief. Of the fumbling gallants who'd kissed her in dark corners behind the theater flats, in the tiring-room, and even in her lodgings, none had kissed her quite like this.

What was she doing, allowing this powerful lord to tempt her from her purpose? She'd never be able to control him. Only a fool would believe she could. "This is madness," she whispered aloud, struggling to disengage herself from his embrace.

"Aye." He drew her against him until their thighs, their hips, even their bellies met. "A very pleasant sort of madness, I think."

His lips lowered again. Spurred on by fear, she strained away from him, knowing she couldn't endure another searing kiss that stole her will.

Then Charity burst through the door, Annabelle's costume draped over her arm. The buxom woman quickly turned red before giving a quick curtsy. "I'm so awfully sorry. I—I didn't mean to disturb you. I'll just go—"

"No!" Annabelle practically shouted. Her breath came in quick gasps, try though she did to make it sound normal. "No," she repeated, "don't go. His lordship was just leaving."

She didn't know whose expression looked the more amused and speculative, Charity's or Hampden's. A secret conspiracy seemed to exist between the two of them, and Annabelle wanted to know exactly how much of the conspiracy rested on Charity's side.

At the moment, however, Hampden's wide grin struck her with the most terror, and she suddenly knew she could never meet him alone without disastrous consequences. His hands clasped her waist intimately, holding her flush against him. Her lips were no doubt reddened from his kiss. She knew it and hated it.

"Lord Hampden," she said, annoyed by the breathiness in her voice. She thought of her mother, then lowered the intensity of her tone a notch. "I've changed my mind about your request. You needn't bother me again, though I thank you for your visit today. It's been most enlightening."

He chuckled as he released her. "For me too." He reached for his plumed hat and settled it on his wild mane of curls. Then he added in a distinct tone of command, "Two days, Annabelle. You get two days. Use them well."

"You don't understand—" she began, but before she could finish, he'd stalked from the room, leaving her alone with Charity.

Annabelle whirled on her servant in a fury. "How dare you set up an assignation for me with that man without telling me! How dare you!"

Charity shrugged. "Looks to me like you got on together pretty good. Looks to me like you weren't complainin' about him the whole time he were here."

Charity's remark hit close enough to the truth that it stopped Annabelle short. With a stony expression on her face, she gathered up the tatters of her dignity. "I wouldn't have had to 'get on' with him at all if you hadn't invited him here in the first place."

"If you hadn't wanted to talk to the man, you could've made him leave. I knew you wasn't in no danger with him. I knew you could hold yer own against most gallants."

Unfortunately, Charity was right. If Annabelle had chosen to be firm, she could have. She hadn't had the strength of character to evict Lord Hampden from the tiring-room, so how could she complain about Charity?

The image of herself that rose to her mind wasn't pleasant. "Well, then, you should have told me of your intentions," she insisted as she drew in a shaky breath and tried to regain her composure.

Charity looked a bit sheepish. "I—I didn't tell you because I knew y'd be stubborn about it just like I knew the two of you would suit. I was right, wasn't I? If I hadn't come in—"

"Nothing would have happened," Annabelle retorted icily.

Charity grinned. "Nothing, you say?"

Annabelle avoided Charity's eyes. "I'll admit I allowed him certain . . . ah . . . liberties. What else was I to do?" She shot Charity a faintly accusatory glance. "After all, he had me trapped here. I had to rid myself of him somehow, and the only way to appease these gallants is with a kiss. So I let him kiss me . . . out of pity, of course, but—"

"Judging from the way he smiled, like a cat with a mouthful of sweet milk, 'twere more than a pity kiss he got from you," Charity said with a snort. "Don't try to tell me somethin' else because I won't believe a word of it."

And that was that, Annabelle thought as Charity began to lay out the items of Annabelle's costume, preparing for the performance. She couldn't blame Charity for being skeptical. Lord Hampden had affected Annabelle as no other man had, and Charity was certainly perceptive enough to notice.

As silence descended in the room, broken only by the rustle of rich fabric, Annabelle pondered the very disquieting Lord Hampden. What did he want from her? She touched her hand to her lips. No, what he wanted from her was clear. The question was, why did he want it so badly? Or was there more to his interest in her, more than the typical rake's desire for a conquest?

"Charity," she said idly as she fingered her brooch. "When you and Lord Hampden set up this assignation, did he mention he knew other people named Maynard?"

Charity glanced up from her work with a startled expression on her face. "His lordship knows yer father?"

"I don't know. He claimed to know men with the Maynard surname."

"That's good, ain't it? Perhaps if you treat him right

and proper, his lordship will help you find yer father."
Charity winked, eliciting a groan from Annabelle.

"I don't think the word *proper* figures into it, and
you know it."

"You must admit he's a fine figure of a man."

She fought to erase the image that sprung instantly
into her mind. "Aye, he's fine-looking, but he's not
stupid. He'll guess my game easily, and I can't afford
that. Lord Hampden's eye is far too sharp and his
tongue far too quick to serve my purpose."

"I take it you got a taste of that tongue firsthand."

Annabelle winced. She'd set herself up for that one.
"You're having a pleasant time with this, aren't you?"
she snapped.

Charity hid her face, but not before Annabelle
glimpsed her smile.

Annabelle sighed. If she weren't so worried, she'd
smile herself. She closed her eyes and rubbed her temples. Her headache was returning. "I don't know what
I should do. He plans to come to my lodgings two days
hence and you know what he wants."

"So give it to him."

"Charity!"

"Nay, I mean it." Charity moved behind Annabelle
to her laces. "Let him sniff about your honeypot
a bit, then while he's in the throes of passion, ask him
yer questions. When a man's breeches is open, he don't
much care if his mouth's open too. He'll say anything
to keep you in his bed."

"And you complain about *my* language! You're
worse than I am by far. My 'honeypot' indeed." A
blush stained her face as she busied herself with removing her simple gown.

" 'Twasn't original with me. Riverton says the rakes
are always buzzing about the actresses' honeypots like
flies."

"You shouldn't listen to Riverton." Annabelle
stepped out of her dress. "That man will lead you
astray faster than you can say 'honeypot.' "

"Aye. Well I know it."

Annabelle's head shot up in time to catch Charity with a dreamy smile plastered on her face. "Prithee, whatever do you mean? Surely you're not interested in a thorough scoundrel like Riverton."

"He's not a scoundrel." Charity sniffed. "He may not be a marquis like yer Lord Hampden, but he's still a nice man."

"The marquis is not my Lord Hampden," Annabelle bit out.

"Oh, but he will be, you wait and see. He will be."

Annabelle would have retorted, but Mrs. Norris and Moll Davies entered the room, discussing their latest conquests. Charity flashed Annabelle a grin, then vanished out the door.

Faith, but that woman is cocky, Annabelle thought with a faint smile. *If Charity has her eye on Riverton, he'd best run and hide before it's too late.*

She sobered as thoughts of Riverton led to thoughts of Lord Hampden, of his commanding manner and overwhelming arrogance. Not since she'd faced her mother's death had she found herself in such an impossible situation. She wanted to know his secrets. She guessed he wanted to know hers. But if he discovered hers, then knowing his would do her no good, for her revenge would be for naught. He'd warn her father of her intentions before she could bring her plans to fruition, and then what would happen?

With a shiver, she acknowledged that she knew little about the man whose blood tainted hers, and most of what she knew wasn't good. He'd abandoned his pregnant lover after involving her in some sort of dangerous intrigue where soldiers had lurked about. It didn't make for a pleasant picture.

For the first time, she considered the possible dangers of her plan for vengeance. What if her father discovered her relationship to him before she discovered his identity? What would he do to protect his reputation? *It's foolish to worry about that,* she assured herself. How could he possibly learn of her plans?

Unless, of course, someone tried to discover her

purpose for him. She was playing a dangerous game by toying with this Lord Hampden, who might know her father.

She must stop the game at once, before the man's curiosity got out of hand. Unfortunately, the marquis seemed quite determined to continue. So what on earth was she going to do about it?

Chapter Five

"For secrets are edged tools,
And must be kept from children and from fools."
—John Dryden, *Sir Martin Mar-All*, Act 2, Scene 2

As usual, The Grecian bustled with noblemen and merchants alike. Colin stood in the doorway of the coffeehouse in Threadneedle Street for the first time since his return. Things had certainly changed in the last three years, he thought, and the coffeehouse crowd was certainly an example of that. Although some men had come to participate in scintillating conversation while they sipped at dishes of the exotic strong drink, far too many others were there to vie for a prominent spot from which to display their latest petticoat breeches and brocaded vests. London had become a city of fawning peacocks, and it saddened him to see it.

Then he brightened when he caught sight of a member of the Royal Society. At least the society members were still frequenting The Grecian after meetings. Colin had joined them on several occasions before he'd left for Antwerp.

Today, however, two days after his talk with Annabelle, he had come to the coffeehouse for an entirely different purpose—to find Riverton. As he stood there scanning the dimly lit room, the aroma of freshly brewed coffee and the peculiar mixed scent of unwashed bodies and strong perfumes overtook him. In moments he caught sight of Riverton sitting at a table in heated discussion with another man.

Colin recognized Riverton's companion immediately. A burst of pleasure filled him at the sight of Garett Lyon, Earl of Falkham, and he approached them, the beginnings of a smile on his face.

"Decided to brave city life for a while, have you?" Colin asked Falkham as the smile became a full-fledged grin. Placing his hat on the table, he took a seat on the bench opposite them.

Falkham's broad forehead knitted in a mock scowl. "My wife wanted to spend a few days in the city. You know how women are. Even Mina has the urge to acquire a new gown every once in a while." He shook his head in that way well-loved husbands always do when they're talking about their wives, then gave a rueful sigh. "Besides, she'd heard that one of the theaters was doing *The Tempest,* and you know how she loves Shakespeare."

Colin's own smile slipped as his expression turned pensive. One of the theaters was indeed doing *The Tempest*. And a certain actress had a role in the play.

"Now, that's the face of a man who's been rejected by a beautiful woman," Riverton said to Falkham with a jocular expression.

How on earth did Riverton know about it? Colin wondered. Oh, yes, Charity and Riverton were thick as thieves. No doubt the pretty maid had been amusing herself by telling Riverton about Colin's useless attempts to capture Annabelle, the roving target.

"What?" Falkham retorted. "Hampden rejected by a woman? I can hardly countenance that. I thought he'd perfected the art of seduction. In fact, my poor wife has almost entirely given up on his ever marrying, since there's no need for him to hunt for a wife when women fall all over him wherever he goes."

Colin forced some modicum of nonchalance into his demeanor as he tried to draw the conversation away from the subject of Annabelle. "Mina hasn't given up on anything, and well you know it. She'll keep trying to find me a wife until the day I die a bachelor."

Changing the subject never worked with Falkham.

"I'll warn her to put her plans aside while you pursue your current woman," Falkham remarked, one eyebrow lifted as he dug his left elbow into Riverton's side. The two of them exchanged smiles. "Which leads me to the question—how did you manage to be rejected by a woman?"

Colin sighed. Though he'd been glad to see Falkham, he wished the younger man hadn't decided to visit at this particular moment. Riverton's gibes were bad enough without Falkham paying Colin back for past gibes.

"Riverton hasn't quite got it right," he said with a shrug. "Annabelle's merely avoiding me, but that's a small circumstance I'll remedy shortly."

Amid genial laughter, Colin admitted the situation to be more complex than that. Actually, according to Charity, Annabelle had disappeared from her lodgings at morning's first light before anyone was up. Colin had watched their lodgings half the morning after that, but Annabelle had never returned.

Riverton rolled his eyes. "Can't admit defeat, can you? Come now, Hampden, the woman isn't interested in bold gentlemen like you. She likes simpering fops who'll let her twist them around her little finger. A woman like the Silver Swan can't abide being told what to do. And we both know you can't abide keeping your ideas to yourself." He winked meaningfully at Falkham.

"The Silver Swan?" Falkham interjected.

"She's an actress," said Riverton, leaning toward Falkham confidentially. "One of the duke's players. You'll have a chance to see her later if you attend today's performance of *The Tempest*. She's playing the role of Miranda since Moll Davies is ill."

Falkham's amused expression didn't quite hide the calculating glint in his eye as he shifted his gaze to Colin. "An actress? Not your usual preference, is it?"

"No," came Colin's clipped reply, and Falkham immediately fell silent.

Most of Colin's close friends knew well his opinion

of actresses. Colin's mother Pierrette had been a vain, pretentious French actress and sometime courtesan. Over the six-year-old Colin's frightened protests, she'd eagerly relinquished her son to Marlowe Jeffreys, Colin's father, when the late marquis had come to France in search of his bastard son.

Determinedly, Colin thrust those dark memories from his mind. No, he didn't think much of actresses. But Annabelle . . . well, she seemed different somehow.

"So what are you planning to do about Madam Maynard?" Riverton pressed when Colin wasn't forthcoming.

"Oh, don't worry. Just because she's been avoiding me all day doesn't mean she'll escape me forever." He rubbed his chin. "After all, she can't bow out of the play, can she?"

"Will you abduct her from the stage, then?" Riverton asked.

"I think not," Colin said, his slow secret smile bringing chuckles from the other two. "There are better ways to deal with Madam Maynard."

Like the way he'd dealt with her in the tiring-room, Colin thought. His gut twisted at the memory, desire and suspicion making it doubly painful. Hell and furies, he never would have dreamed the skin on a woman's face could be that soft or that warm to the touch, nor that the bones beneath it could be so fragile, so delicate, like the fine filigree of her swan brooch.

He must get control of these . . . these feelings for Annabelle Maynard. After all, he'd promised Walcester to root out her secrets, and now he believed she indeed had secrets. Until he'd actually met her, he'd thought Walcester overly concerned. But after coming in on her quoting that morbid poem, then witnessing her reaction to his comments about her brooch and her possible family connections, Colin could understand Walcester's concern. Her behavior seemed well worth examining.

Unfortunately, it wasn't her behavior, but her body

he wanted to examine. 'Sdeath, it had been a long time since he'd experienced such a fierce desire. In Antwerp he'd been too busy doing the king's business to spend much time wenching. Since he'd returned to England, he'd fast grown disenchanted with the court's single-minded pursuit of pleasure at the cost of the country. His interest in wanton enjoyments seemed to have waned.

Yet here he was, unable to stop thinking about Annabelle—the faint scent of oranges that clung to her, the way her lush body had curved into his arms. If he didn't watch himself, he'd be sucked into the merry-go-round of the court's sexual abandonment. He'd be nipping at her heels like all the other bucks, without a thought of his estates and his more important concerns.

Don't be absurd, he told himself. He could handle his desire for a woman, if anyone could. He must if he was to help Walcester.

"Well," Riverton remarked, bringing him out of his reverie, "be certain Charity doesn't object to your methods of persuasion, or you'll have not one, but two angry women on your back."

Colin smiled wryly. "I think Charity is my ally. In fact, that's why I came in search of you. I want you to find out—discreetly, of course—if she's still on my side and what Annabelle really thinks of me. 'Tisn't likely Charity will tell me the truth, but she might tell you."

Riverton rubbed his well-shaved chin, his brow furrowed in thought. "Perhaps. It's hard to say. Charity's a woman who mystifies me completely."

"Oh?" Colin asked absently as he reached over to catch the arm of the serving boy passing by and ordered more dishes of coffee all around.

"Aye," came Riverton's studied reply. He planted his elbows on the table's scarred wood surface as he leaned forward. "She's a widow and flirts outrageously with the gallants who swarm about her mistress. Nonetheless, I have it on good authority that

she's refused a number of men who want to . . . ah
. . . deepen the intimacy. Now, why is that?''

"Perhaps for the same reason her mistress puts them
off,'' Colin remarked.

Riverton chuckled and shook his head. He flashed
Falkham a knowing glance. "The man persists in these
strange delusions.'' He turned back to Colin. "I told
you already, Somerset has bedded the Silver Swan,
and God knows who else. If you're looking for a gentle
virgin, then you're looking in the wrong place.''

Colin thought of the way Annabelle's eyes had reflected first shock, then dismay after he'd kissed her.
He remembered her confusion, her nervous agitation
as she'd practically pushed him from the room.

"Some of us hear only the words and see only the
smiles of those around us. But some of us,'' Colin
continued, "read the truth behind the words and the
fear behind the smiles.''

Colin's gaze flitted to Falkham, whose expression
had darkened in memory. Falkham at least understood
how easy it was to misjudge a woman.

"Annabelle Maynard is no wanton actress,'' Colin
continued. "I'd stake my fortune on that.''

Riverton threw up his hands. "Ah, well, these things
a man must discover for himself. Of course, first you
must get the woman alone, and you aren't having much
success with that.''

At that moment the dishes of coffee were served.
Colin stared into the steaming liquid for a moment,
then lifted his dish to his lips and took a long pull. The
pleasantly bitter taste lingered in his mouth as he set
the dish down carefully. "Without obstacles, success is
meaningless. My success with Annabelle will be all the
sweeter for her resistance. And trust me in this, dear
friend, I will have my success.''

"Spoken like a true rake,'' Falkham said, his eyes
thoughtful as he fixed Colin with a steady gaze. "Well,
if anyone knows how to overcome the obstacles in seducing a woman, it's you.'' Then he lifted his dish of
coffee in silent toast before bringing it to his lips.

Riverton glanced from Falkham to Colin. "Aye, that much is true." He laughed, then he too lifted his dish. "Here's to seduction."

"To seduction," said Colin and drank with them, but without fervor.

For he wasn't sure he had only seduction in mind. He wasn't sure of that at all.

As the first act of *The Tempest* ended, Annabelle exited into the wings. The tenor who was to provide the musical interlude between the acts slid past her, brushing her pearl satin gown as if she were invisible. Too bad she couldn't be invisible. This afternoon, she wanted desperately to disappear. Somewhere out there in that audience was Lord Hampden. She hadn't been able to pick him out, but she'd felt his gaze on her even while she couldn't see him, felt him watching her with those assessing eyes.

The awareness of it sent her pulse racing and made her palms dampen with sweat. Oh, yes, he watched and bided his time, as a tiger watches the arc of a bird in flight until the prey settles and the tiger can pounce.

He'd told her to take two days to ask about him, and she'd done so, to her infinite regret. She'd discovered that the Marquis of Hampden was a powerful man with powerful friends. The king held the marquis in highest esteem, as did a number of other influential nobility.

While it flattered her to be sought by such a noble, she grew increasingly alarmed as she discovered how well he was regarded. Lord Hampden was no minor lord like Somerset, whom she could treat with disdain without worrying she'd be criticized for it. He had wealth, respect, and a widely admired wit.

And he wanted her. Or did he? There might be another noble he counted among his intimates . . . like her father. Perhaps he was trying to coax the truth from her. Perhaps not, but she couldn't take the chance.

Thus it was with extreme trepidation that she found the object of her distress standing next to the closed door of the tiring-room, leaning against the wall in complete nonchalance. Taken off guard, she lifted her hand unconsciously to her throat.

Then she forced a smile to her face. "What brings you behind stage today, Lord Hampden? Was the play not interesting enough for you? Have you come to find more pleasurable sport with us wild theater folk?"

The corners of his mouth twitched, but he didn't smile. "You know why I'm here."

Faith, but she did. She swallowed, folding her clammy palms together. "I don't have the faintest idea what you're talking about. I'm afraid I'm not adept at guessing men's thoughts." She pushed her dark curls back from her face and let out a bored sigh. "You men must think we spend all our waking hours trying to anticipate your whims. Some of us have more important matters to concern us."

"Like not missing appointments?" he asked, pushing himself away from the wall.

She tried not to notice how the muscles of his well-formed calves tensed as he straightened, nor how he planted his feet in a decidedly masculine stance. Instead she concentrated on keeping her face impassive. "I believe I told you the other day that I didn't wish to meet with you."

His gaze started at her carefully coiffed hair and traveled slowly down, over her rich gown to her cinched waist to her slippered feet. Then it returned to her now flushed face.

"So you're a coward after all," he said, his voice so soft she could scarcely catch his words over the noise coming from the tiring-room. "One would think that a woman with a reputation for enjoying the finer pleasures of life wouldn't allow such a paltry thing as a kiss to make her turn tail and run."

He had her there. Devil take the rude beast! Somehow he knew what accusations would strike home. She couldn't let him think she was other than another wanton actress. But had he already guessed the truth?

Dear heaven, what was she to do about him? He'd

thrown down the gauntlet. If she accepted the challenge, it would be like trying to cage a fighting tomcat. If she refused it, he might pursue her all the more fiercely.

Then there was a third choice—to bell the cat, treading as carefully as any mouse. Unfortunately, belling a cat wasn't easy when the cat was a sleek and intimidating tiger.

She stood there in thought a moment, trying to block out the bustle backstage, the chatter of the audience members, and the interlude music. Suddenly the door to the tiring-room burst open and an actress sailed out. Through the open door, Annabelle could see Lord Somerset, tapping his foot with impatience as he attempted to fluff out the flounces of his petticoat breeches.

She stifled a wave of disgust and willed him to look her way. Apparently her silent plea worked, for he glanced up through the doorway and saw her. He immediately sauntered out to join her, followed by Sir Charles Sedley, a notorious rake with an almost pretty face who was known for his outrageous exploits, most recently for disporting himself naked on a balcony. Sir John Riverton came behind them both.

"Hello, angel," Somerset cooed in an unctuous voice. "You are captivating tonight as always."

He stank of some strong perfume that nearly made her choke. Nonetheless, when he leaned forward to press a kiss to her cheek, she turned so that his wet mouth met hers squarely. He drew back, his surprise at her response showing in the tightening of his flaccid features and the lift of his plucked eyebrows.

Fighting the urge to wipe her lips, she ignored Hampden's scowl and the amused twinkle in Riverton's eyes as she threaded her arm through Somerset's bent one.

Today Somerset wore three patches on the rouged cheeks of his powdered face. Together with his new periwig of flowing yellow curls, they made him look like a truculent child in costume awaiting Mother's treats.

"I've missed you," she leaned up to whisper in his ear.

Now his surprise became truly full-blown, his thin-lipped mouth pursing primly. "Can't have that, can we?" He tossed his horrible corkscrew curls, then began to lower his mouth to hers again, his intention giving some warmth to his cold eyes.

Hampden cleared his throat loudly. Immediately Somerset drew back to see who stood in the shadows. "Ah, Hampden. What are you doing skulking about there? Decided to have a look at all our lovely actresses, have you?"

"Only one in particular, although the woman has apparently forgotten about our assignation. Such a damnable shame, too, since I very much looked forward to stroking the dear creature's feathers, if you know what I mean."

"Indeed, indeed," Somerset said with a titter, lifting one hand to toy with his flamboyantly tied lace cravat. He slipped his arm around Annabelle's waist and drew her closer, casting her a brief, lascivious glance. "Even this wild creature here is prone to the occasional shy moment."

She didn't know if she liked being referred to as a "wild creature," but at least Somerset hadn't realized whom Hampden was hinting at with all his talk of feathers.

"Oh, yes," Riverton put in. "We all know the Swan hides behind her *feathers* whenever possible."

So Riverton was going to make certain Somerset got the point, was he? Annabelle thought with irritation.

But Somerset was obviously too intent on taking a peek down the front of her dress to pay much attention to Riverton's comment. "Yes, yes," was all he remarked.

Annabelle's hands felt like ice. She dared not meet Hampden's eyes, so she looked instead at Sedley, and that made it worse. The lean, fine-featured rake

seemed ready to explode into laughter, but fortunately
constrained himself. Riverton couldn't, however, and
a strangled chuckle leaked from his lips.

Somerset didn't even notice. He was too busy
smoothing his hand down her backside. He'd certainly
taken her kiss seriously, she thought as she tried gently
to push his hand away. She wanted to point out to him
that he ought to keep his mind on the conversation,
since his companions were mocking him to his face.

"I can scarcely believe Madam Maynard hides from
anyone," Hampden remarked. He wasn't smiling and
had clearly noticed the way she was trying to make
Somerset keep his hands to himself.

"I know," Somerset said with a leering grin,
abruptly bringing his full attention to the conversation.
"She can be a bold little thing at times. Quick-
tongued, you know."

She winced at Somerset's obvious double entendre,
while Sedley seized on it with glee. "Well, not all of
us have had the privilege of receiving the end of
Madam Maynard's tongue."

Annabelle shot Sedley a murderous glance. Normally she made an effort to be good-natured about the
men's bawdy flirtations, but at the moment, she could
scarcely stomach her peculiar role.

"She saves her tongue for me," Somerset said,
preening as he patted her arm.

Sedley and Riverton laughed aloud, making Somerset look all the more pleased with himself for his
wit, but that merely fired Annabelle's anger.

Before she could speak, Hampden said, with thinly
disguised irritation, "Perhaps she saves her sharp
tongue for you, because she enjoys slicing you to ribbons."

Annabelle couldn't decide whether to be grateful to
Hampden for making the subject of tongues innocent
once more or angry at him for baiting Somerset.

Somerset said archly, "As long as she allows me a
thrust or two of my own occasionally, I don't mind her
barbs."

Normally, Annabelle could endure having such matters so flippantly discussed, but not today, not in front of Hampden. While Riverton and Sedley had a loud laugh at her expense, she barely suppressed a groan.

Then Sedley's laugh was cut short when Hampden glared at him. The young rake mumbled something about having forgotten his hat in the tiring-room and fled. Hampden turned his sharp-eyed stare on Riverton, but Riverton merely shrugged and continued to chuckle to himself.

When Somerset, pleased with his wit, drew her close enough to press a kiss against her hair, the marquis visibly stiffened. The edges of his mouth whitened a fraction as cold emerald lights glinted in his eyes. "You know, Somerset, I'm glad to see you enjoying yourself. After the terrible news you received this morning, I would have thought—"

Somerset's head snapped around. "What terrible news?"

Hampden feigned surprise. "You didn't know? Hell and furies, I've spoken out of turn. Of course, perhaps I misunderstood His Majesty. . . . Yes, I'm sure that's it. Never mind. A simple misunderstanding."

Riverton took up the theme with glee. "I believe I heard the same thing you did, Hampden. Could we both have been mistaken?"

Somerset released her, wringing his hands. "Out with it, man! His Majesty spoke of me? What did he say?"

Hampden shrugged, stretching out the moment with calculated nonchalance. He flashed Riverton a knowing glance meant for Somerset's eyes. "Well, I don't know if I should tell you. . . . Perhaps I'm wrong—"

"It's my petition, isn't it?" Somerset broke in, his face paling. "His Majesty has refused my petition."

"As I said before, I may have misunderstood. . . ."

Somerset's colorless, watery gaze darted first from Annabelle to Hampden and then toward the tiring-room. Actors and actresses were already leaving the tiring-rooms to mill onto the backstage area behind the

painted flats, preparing for the second act as the tenor
ended his song.

"Oh, dear," Somerset murmured half to himself,
then turned to Riverton. "You heard it too?"

"It's possible that I misunderstood as well. . . ."
Riverton trailed off meaningfully.

"God-a-mercy!" Somerset's face had turned even
more ashen than normal. He faced Annabelle. "Listen, angel, you won't mind if I go to Whitehall for a
bit, will you? I must find out about my petition. Terribly important."

She stared at him, then swung her gaze to Hampden's, meeting his in a silent clash of wills. She could
see the triumph lurking in his face. How badly she
wanted to drive it out.

She grasped Somerset's arm. "Now, then, my lord.
As Lord Hampden and Sir John say, they may have
misunderstood. Do you have to go off before the play's
even over? If you'd stay awhile, then perhaps after the
play we could go back to my lodgings and . . . well . . ."
She trailed off with a brilliant, seductive smile.

He appeared stricken. For a moment, she thought
he'd change his mind. Then he shook his head, as if
to shake off the power of her invitation. "Later, angel.
I won't be gone that long. You understand, don't you?"

"Of course she understands," Hampden put in. His
voice could have melted solid rock, yet underneath its
ingratiating tone lay a steely quality she recognized all
too well. "Don't worry, Riverton and I will watch over
her to make sure none of the other gallants presses her
for an invitation. After all, my own companion hasn't
yet arrived, so I might as well make myself useful."

The smile of victory Hampden threw her way made
her itch to slap him.

"Thank you," Somerset gushed breathlessly in his
haste to get away. He clasped her hand and pressed a
kiss onto it. Then he was gone.

As soon as he moved out of earshot, she whirled on
Hampden. "You, my lord, ought to be ashamed of
yourself for telling such monstrous lies—"

His eyes sparkled with mischief. "Careful, now. I might be a rake, but I never lie."

"Those weren't lies you told Lord Somerset?"

He shrugged and glanced at Riverton. "Not lies, eh, Riverton? Half-truths perhaps, but not lies. The king does have some terrible news for Somerset. As I recall, it concerned the situation in the colonies or . . . some affairs of state or . . . Oh, what was it, Riverton, that His Majesty said?"

Riverton shook with silent laughter. "I believe His Majesty threatened to exile Somerset to the colonies if Somerset didn't stop boring him with endless tales about his tailor. Yes, that was the gist of it." Riverton began to chuckle again.

"You see?" Hampden told her, a broad smile on his face. "I wasn't lying a bit."

Rage boiled up through her, so intense she wanted to snatch his sword from him and break it over his head. "You are the most despicable, insolent, and monstrous—"

"Devil?" Hampden finished for her, amusement glittering in his eyes. "That I am. Be glad for it. If not for my interference, you'd have found yourself enduring that popinjay's slobbering ministrations all evening."

Annabelle shuddered despite herself, then forced some iron into her backbone when she saw his grin widen. "Better a popinjay than an arrogant brute who presses his attentions where they're not wanted."

She whirled away from him but he caught her arm. When she stared him down, her face full of impotent but chilly fury, he seemed to take note of the other players watching the two of them. With a muttered curse, he jerked her behind one of the painted flats that stood from floor to ceiling in wooden grooves, waiting to be pulled onstage. She could hear Riverton's muffled laughter on the other side.

"The choice is yours, Annabelle," Hampton whispered, his breath hot against her cheek as he pressed her against the painted scene of an idyllic garden.

"Either explain to me why my kiss two days ago so upset you that you suddenly forgot our assignation, or meet me after the play as you'd originally agreed. I won't take anything else."

Devil take the man! Why in heaven's name was he so persistent?

She searched for an explanation of why his kiss had disturbed her, an explanation that wouldn't reveal all her secrets. "Your kiss demonstrated you were far too rough a man for me. I don't like being mauled, Hampden." She smoothed down her skirts with a primness befitting a queen. "It might benefit you to remember that."

His fingers clutching her arm burned her skin. For some reason unknown to her, her knees shook beneath her skirts.

"You don't know what 'rough' is, you little fool," he hissed. "You keep toying with these fops and gallants as you have for the last few months and one day you'll find yourself mired in quicksand. They're not all as easy to manipulate as Somerset."

Her gaze shot to his, then wavered as she saw how sincere he was. "I can take care of myself," she asserted with a stoutness she didn't feel.

"Then why are you so afraid to meet me?"

There it was again. The gauntlet. Why did she let it upset her? What could he do if she refused to meet him? He could voice his suspicions about her to her father, if indeed he knew the man, she thought as a chill stole over her heart. Then she'd never discover his identity. She'd never complete her plan for vengeance.

She could hear the second act beginning and the crowd hushing as the players entered. She had to decide. Why was she being so foolishly reticent anyway? Hampden couldn't possibly have guessed what she was up to. Why *should* he tell her father anything? More likely, he'd lead her to her father and help her determine which Maynard had sent her mother to the gallows.

That settles it, she told herself. She'd not let this chance slip by. She'd handle this arrogant lord as she'd handled the rest, by playing on his vanity and pretending to capitulate.

Feeling more confident, she met his gaze. "As you wish. I'll meet you after the play, though I don't know why you're so determined to pursue me. Any number of actresses would be only too glad to oblige your raging passions." She spoke the words with sarcasm, but the last few stuck in her throat, mocking her.

"I know," he retorted without a trace of conceit in his tone. "Any number of actresses would. They earn little enough money without spurning the honest advances of a wealthy man. So why are you so adamant about avoiding me, eh, Aphrodite? It would almost tempt a man to wonder what you're hiding."

He released her as she stood there, uncertain what to say. Then he took her hand much like Somerset had, but the hard kiss he pressed into her palm bore no resemblance to Somerset's sloppy caress. Hampden's firm lips lingering on her skin made even her toes quiver.

"I'll be waiting for you by the tiring-room after the play," he asserted, enfolding her hand in his for one aching moment. "If you're not there, I'll find you. We made an agreement, you and I. I for one intend to hold up my part of the bargain."

Then, releasing her hand abruptly, he whirled on his heels and left. She stood there a moment staring after him.

So the insufferable beast intended to bed her after the play, did he? Well, he'd find himself in bed, all right. She smiled as she wondered how much of Charity's wondrous sleeping elixir was left. Yes, Hampden would find himself in bed, but alone. If she planned it right, he'd awaken tomorrow with such a horrendous headache, he'd never want to approach her again.

A secret smile creased her face as she went in search of Charity.

Chapter Six

"Words may be false and full of art,
Sighs are the natural language of the heart."
—Thomas Shadwell, *Psyche*, Act 3

Annabelle and Colin waited in the doorway to the Duke's Theater as sheets of rain pelted the road outside, transforming the already muddy thoroughfare into an unnavigable mire.

Of all the wretched luck, Colin thought. All the hackney coaches had left long ago, hired by the theatergoers. He'd waited for Annabelle to change out of her costume, so by the time they'd reached the street, there'd been no coaches left to hire.

Not that it would have mattered. Night had fallen and the road now resembled a marsh, with enough mud to stall even the largest hackney coach. No, the only thing for it would be to keep close to the buildings where the ground was firmer and to take their chances with the bitterly cold rain.

He glanced at Annabelle, silhouetted in the door by candlelight. She'd wrapped herself so tightly in her drab brown woolen cloak that she resembled a humble sparrow more than a shapely swan. The hood hid her raven curls and winsome eyes while the cloak itself disguised her curves. But he didn't need to see them to know what lay beneath that cloak. The knowledge burned deep within his belly . . . and lower . . . a fire that wouldn't be quenched until he'd had her.

Hell and furies, but the woman had thrown him off balance. He must remain aloof in this game they played, so he could ferret out the information he'd promised to get for Walcester. Why, then, had he allowed himself to become so damnably enamored of her that simply thinking of Somerset's leer and Sedley's sly insinuations incensed him?

After all, Colin himself had participated in his fair share of bawdy flirtations in the past. He knew how the game was played, yet here he was, ready to cuff Sedley for all his damnable talk about tongues.

Colin shook his head. Where were his purported cool facade, his calm in the face of danger, his watchful perception? They'd disappeared the moment he'd held the Silver Swan.

'Sdeath, he told himself, the woman's past still remained a mystery. He mustn't lower his guard. He must keep his wits about him. But what man could keep his wits about him with a sweet wench like her pressed against his aching loins?

As if he'd summoned her attention with his thoughts, she peeked out of her hood long enough to cast her triumphant blue gaze his way. "I suppose we'd best stay here for a while, unless we want a thorough drenching." She paused, eyes sparkling. "Of course, you don't have to wait, if the rain doesn't bother you."

He bit back a grin. Did she think it would be as easy as that to rid herself of him? "No need to stay. It'll slacken soon, and then we can take it at a run. Thank God your lodgings aren't far."

Her eyebrows drew together in a frown. "Perhaps *you* can afford to ruin a pair of breeches and a coat in mud and rain and grit, but I can't afford even to ruin my hose. In case you didn't know it, your lordship, clothing is rather dear for us humbler folk."

"Don't worry, I'll buy you more hose," he said without thinking, "and a new gown and a new cloak . . . whatever you want."

She blanched. "I didn't mean . . . I realize what you think, but . . . Oh, fie, must you be so blatant about all this? You have a way of making a woman feel like a trollop."

Her distress gave him a twinge of guilt. "You're the only actress I know who'd regard a simple offer of clothing as a vile insult," he muttered as he scanned the dark street.

It was true. For an actress, she had the oddest scruples. Why did she treat him like an uncaring brute for offering the same gifts Lord Somerset had no doubt offered her? Damned if he could figure out the way a woman's mind worked.

As they waited, he suddenly noticed two urchins, a boy of about twelve and a girl of ten, dashing quickly along the theater wall. They came out of the rain, approached Annabelle, and said, " 'Ave ye any oranges for us today, miss?"

To his surprise, she smiled and dug into her cloak's deep pockets. "I do believe there's a couple here." She drew two oranges forth and put them in the outstretched, grimy hands.

The children's eyes lit up as they tore into the oranges greedily. "Thankee," they muttered as they turned to dart away, but Annabelle caught the arm of the girl.

"Hold up, there, I think I have something else in these big pockets," Annabelle murmured as she stuck her hand in once more and pulled something out. "Oh, look, a cross bun I didn't have the chance to eat." She handed it to the girl, whose eyes filled with tears as she took it.

"Y're an angel, miss," the girl said, then broke the bun in half and handed one half to her companion. Between them, the bun disappeared in seconds. The girl then gave a stiff curtsy and began to leave.

But the boy shifted his solemn gaze to Colin. "Best ye be nice to the orange lady, milord," he said boldly before his friend worriedly yanked his arm. They scampered back out into the rain.

Colin stared after them a moment. "Do you do that often? Give food away to the street urchins?"

Annabelle drew her cloak tighter about her and shrugged, not meeting his eyes. "Once in a while."

Colin rubbed his chin thoughtfully, wanting to point out that oranges weren't exactly cheap. She'd complained about the cost of new hose, but she apparently had no compunction about feeding the street urchins off her modest salary. Yet he couldn't bring himself to chide her for her generosity.

So they stood there in silence until the rain slowed to a drizzle. Then he reached over to clasp her wrist. "Time to spread those wings, Mistress Swan."

He pulled her behind him into the street before she could protest and ran into the wind with her in tow. She kept surprisingly good pace with him. The drizzle misted his face, but her cloak appeared to protect her well. As long as they stayed close to the buildings, the mud was only a small problem, although their feet sunk in deep a couple of times.

They'd rounded the corner into the dark alley where her lodgings lay when the skies opened again. "Hell and furies!" he mumbled as a wave of wind and water whisked his hat from his head and soaked his coat. The same sheet of water whipped her cloak from around her and threw back her hood, exposing all of her to the merciless, cold rain.

Without hesitation, he snatched her up in his arms and strode quickly toward the lit door at the end of the alley. Fortunately, the door wasn't latched, and in moments he'd maneuvered his way into the house with her in his arms.

He didn't set her down right away, but lingered there, intensely aware of the soft weight of her and the clean rain scent that rose from her soaked clothing. Unlike most women in London, she apparently bathed often enough not to need the cloying perfumes often used to cover up the body's stench.

She stared up at him. Her arms still clasped his neck, but he scarcely noticed the interlocked fingers tangled in his hair. Her wet face absorbed his attention far more. Candlelight played over the slope of her pale brow, the fine curves of her cheeks, the slender nose with its pert tip.

For a second, he glimpsed the naked pain glimmering in her eyes. He thought he might even be able to see into her soul, to pluck out the thorn that pricked her spirit.

She watched him behind lashes dusted with tiny raindrops, like honeysuckle nectar, like rain tears. He bent his head, wanting to kiss them away, and perhaps with them, to kiss away that dark hint of pain. Then she blinked and the moment passed.

With what sounded like a sigh, she released his neck. "You can let me down now." Her voice was low and husky. It sent shivers of anticipation through him.

He obliged her, but only because he feared if he kissed her here, they'd never reach her rooms. Water dripped from every stitch of their clothing, forming ever-widening puddles on the wooden floor. She attempted to wring more of it out of her wool skirts, then shot him a helpless glance as she realized it was hopeless.

He removed her cloak and gestured up the stairs. "We'll have to get out of these clothes."

To his surprise, a glint of terror flared up briefly in her eyes. Then the flash of fear passed, and he wondered if he'd only imagined it.

As if she drew her soul into herself, she changed into another creature entirely. Gone was the vulnerable, hurting maiden. Gone was the gentle woman who fed oranges to the urchins. In their place was the remote actress, as unapproachable as the swan she was called.

"My rooms are upstairs," she said haughtily through her shivering. Then she took a brace of candles from beside the door and motioned for him to follow.

He nodded, striding behind her up the rickety staircase. They'd gone only a few steps, however, when a door beneath them flew open and a wizened old man appeared.

"Madam Maynard, what . . . who . . ." the old man stammered.

Annabelle froze on the stairs, then looked down at the man with a brittle smile. "Good evening, Master Watkins. I'm so sorry for the water on your floor. You see, we got caught in the rain and—"

"Ye wouldn't be bringin' the gentleman up to yer rooms, now, would ye?"

Ah, so this was her landlord, Colin thought.

Her smile wavered a fraction. "Oh, but surely you wouldn't mind if my brother visits with me a short while."

Laughter bubbled up in Colin's throat, but he fought it back. He'd used that ploy once or twice himself, but he'd never thought to have a woman use it for him.

"Yer brother?" Master Watkins assessed Colin with a look of pure skepticism.

"Aye. My brother."

"Colin . . . Maynard at your service," Colin put in with a bow, enjoying the masquerade immensely.

Master Watkins now regarded Colin with even greater suspicion.

"Yes, this is . . . er . . . Colin," Annabelle echoed, her disdainful chin tilted in the air. "Colin. My brother."

The landlord turned two pleading eyes her way, clearly unconvinced. "Ye know me wife don't like ye bringin' men to yer rooms. After that last gentleman, she said if ye brought more, she'd toss ye in the street. We run a respectable house here. Can't be havin' talk goin' 'round about us."

After that last gentleman. Somerset? Colin wondered as his eyes narrowed.

Perhaps Riverton had been right after all. Perhaps Annabelle Maynard wasn't such an innocent and Colin would have to eat his words.

Annabelle planted her hands on her hips. "I don't understand why in heaven's name I can't bring my own brother—"

"Yes, yes. Your brother," Master Watkins said with

a sigh, rubbing his hooked nose with the back of his hand. His small eyes glanced furtively around. "Go on with ye, then. But don't let me missus see ye." He cocked his head toward Colin and added, "Ye'd best keep yer 'brother' well out of sight."

Annabelle drew herself up like a queen. "Thank you, Master Watkins." She then continued up the stairs, her back stiff and proud.

Colin nodded to the landlord and followed her up, trying not to notice the way her wet gown clung to her rounded behind.

Once she'd unlocked her room and beckoned him in, she shut the door and whirled on him in a fury. "Now see what you've done? 'Tis hard to find cheap lodgings. Thanks to you, I may find myself in the street tomorrow, if not sooner!"

"Don't blame it all on me. If I understood your Master Watkins correctly, I wasn't the first man to enter these hallowed rooms." 'Sdeath, was that jealousy he heard in his voice? It couldn't be. He'd never been jealous in his life.

She must have heard it too, for suspicion flickered in her eyes. "I told you before that Somerset and I were—"

"Lovers?" He'd blurted out the word before he could stop himself. Oh, yes, he thought with self-disgust. The green-eyed monster had definitely latched on to him.

She continued to meet his gaze, although he thought a touch of a blush stained her cheeks.

"No, you never told me you were lovers," he continued in a more normal tone. "To be honest, I don't care one way or the other. Somerset isn't here now. I am."

That stopped her short. "So you are," she retorted. Her movements rigid, she swept around the room, lighting candles. With a jerky nod that encompassed everything, she bit out, "Welcome to my lodgings. You seem determined to spend time in them, so you'd best make certain they meet with your approval."

Colin could easily see how she'd gained her reputation for being "quick-tongued," as Somerset had put it. The woman had a way of spreading such contempt on her words that any man would think twice before willingly letting her flay him publicly.

Of course, Colin wasn't just any man. Without a word, he scanned the room, beginning with the cold hearth, which had two chairs placed before it. Then his gaze moved to where a crude, lace-covered table sat flanked by two more chairs. He noted the oak cupboard in the corner and the full-length looking glass with gilt edges that stood close to one of the windows and represented the most expensive piece of furniture. His survey ended with the corner of the room containing a daybed and an armchair, clearly the spot where she received visitors.

Overall, despite the cheap materials and rough workmanship of her furnishings, she'd managed to create a pleasant, homey atmosphere. It helped that everything was scrupulously clean. He wondered if the same were true of the bedchamber, which apparently adjoined this room.

"Will it do, my lord?" she asked when he remained silent at the end of his survey. "Or are you already planning to have workmen in to remake it the way you like? Do let me know your plans, so I won't inadvertently be a nuisance." Though she spoke acidly, the faintest trembling of her lips betrayed her anxiety.

"At the moment, my only plans are to remove these wet clothes." He lifted his arm with her cloak draped over it. "Is there somewhere I can hang your things?"

She regarded him with suspicion. "Yes, of course. I'll take it." Then she approached him and added more decisively, "I'll take your wet coat and vest too."

Without hesitation he peeled off his sodden outer garments and handed them to her. For a second, her eyes seemed fixed on the sight of him wearing only his lawn shirt and snuff-colored breeches, the wet cloth clinging to him like a second skin. Then she jerked her gaze away and crossed the room to the hearth, dropping their clothes onto one of the chairs. She knelt to build a fire in the grate.

"Let me do that," he said, moving to her side. He knelt beside her and reached for the bundle of kindling she clutched in her hand. His fingers brushed hers, which were icy cold.

She jerked away as if she'd been branded. "I'll see about your coat." Then she jumped to her feet. Averting her eyes from him, she draped her cloak over one chair and arranged his clothing over the other.

Once the fire had caught, he rose. She stood stiffly beside the chair that held her cloak, plucking at its folds and rearranging it to better catch the heat from the fire.

She was stalling. He knew it, and so did she.

"Annabelle—" he began in a low voice.

"Tea! We must have tea. You need something to warm you. . . ."

"I can think of something better than tea," he ground out.

"No, no," she said as if she hadn't understood him. "It's . . . it's no trouble at all. It'll take but a moment."

She whirled from the fireplace and went to the cupboard. Pulling out a kettle, she then started back toward the door that apparently led into her bedchamber. But before she'd taken two steps, she caught sight of herself in the mirror on the opposite side of the room and stopped short. He heard a sound of distress escape her lips.

"Faith, but I look a sight!" she exclaimed, running her free hand through her now nonexistent curls. "Charity will wring her hands when she sees how I've ruined all her handiwork."

He thought he'd never seen a more fetching sight than her in her wet gown, the woolen skirts plastered around her hips and thighs, but wisely didn't say so.

She pivoted to face him. "Look at you. My curls are completely gone, but yours are still crisp and tight. You should give your secret to Charity. She despairs over my unruly waves every day. No matter how hard she works at it with the irons, she can't train my hair to form perfect ringlets.''

"It helps when the ringlets are natural. I'm afraid that's the secret to my success.''

She planted her hands on her hips and stared at him, her head cocked to one side as if she sought to catch him in a lie. Then she sighed and shook her head. "I should have known it. Every other rake has to work at being fashionable, but you of course were born that way. I suppose if it were the fashion to have green hair, yours would have sprung out green as grass.''

"Now, that *would* be a sight, wouldn't it!'' he said with a chuckle. He sensed her babbling was meant to stave off her nervousness. Why was she so nervous? If she had let Somerset bed her, then why all this reticence? Why the fire and the tea?

And why the heart-wrenching fear lurking behind those silvery blue eyes?

Her drenched sleeves clung to her arms as she stood there.

"You should get out of that gown,'' he murmured. God, how he ached to see her without her gown.

"Yes, of course. I'll get the tea while I'm at it.''

She fled into her bedchamber. With an effort, he let her go and didn't follow, knowing it would do no good to press her. He didn't know what he'd intended this assignation to accomplish anyway. Did he really want to seduce her just to find out what Walcester wanted to know?

Sitting down on the daybed, he rubbed his chin thoughtfully. No, the seduction was for his own benefit. He couldn't help himself. She'd gotten under his skin somehow with her armor of wit and her ability to change roles with the wind. Beneath it all lay a real woman whom he desired with an intensity he'd never thought possible.

He'd find out what Walcester wanted to know, but he'd damnably well do it for his own reasons . . . because he too wanted to know what she was . . . *who* she was. Plainly, she wasn't who she appeared to be. Was she a spy, for the Dutch or the French perhaps? With all the treaties Charles II was juggling at the moment, she could be working for almost anyone. Then again, perhaps her secrets were more mundane.

One thing was certain, the woman herself was far from mundane. Hell and furies, how could one woman be so damnably desirable?

She returned a few moments later, freshly garbed in a low-cut gown of brilliant royal blue with the décolletage well covered by a demure scarf. He had to stifle a groan. Didn't she understand what this was all about? He knew she did. So why was she tormenting him like this?

She was carrying a pouch in one hand and the filled kettle in the other. He watched in silence as she knelt by the fire and placed the kettle on the pothook.

"We should have some tea, don't you think?" she said brightly.

He lifted his leg to rest one ankle on his opposite knee and began to remove his muddy half boot. "By all means, let's have some tea. That will give us a chance to talk."

Her eyes went to his boot, then jerked back to his face. "Yes, yes, let's talk."

"Why don't you tell me where you're from?" he remarked in his best casual tone.

Apparently his question heightened her anxiety. "Where I'm from?" With a quick nervous gesture, she brushed a damp lock of hair back behind one ear. "Well . . . ah . . . the country, of course. I was born and bred in the country."

He dropped his boot to the floor, noting the way she flinched at the sound. "That doesn't exactly narrow it down, Annabelle. At least give me the county. Are you from Yorkshire? Lancashire?" He paused. "Or perhaps not England at all. Perhaps Ireland?"

"No, of course not! I'm as English as you are."

He merely looked at her. The look was one he'd perfected in France as a young man, when he'd gathered and sold information to keep from starving. From experience he'd learned that if he remained quiet long enough and merely fixed the subject of his questioning with an expectant gaze, he . . . or she . . . would eventually tell him something, anything, just to pacify him.

Annabelle was no exception. "Northamptonshire," she remarked after a moment with a defiant lift to her chin, as if daring him to doubt her. "I grew up in Northamptonshire in a small village you've probably never heard of."

"Oh, I doubt that. I roam our fair country a great deal. I'm sure I've been in your part of the woods at some time or another."

"Well, it doesn't matter where I'm from, does it?" Her eyes suddenly narrowed. "What do you care anyway?"

Ah, he thought, the Silver Swan wasn't known for her shrewd perception for nothing. Unfortunately, he must pretend not to be concerned at all about the answers to the questions he asked. Still, she didn't know she was dealing with a master. He'd find out her secrets somehow.

"I *don't* care," he murmured as he removed his other boot. "Believe me, I understand your reluctance to discuss your background. In your profession, you must consider who might carry tales to your family. No doubt your parents would haul you back to the family home and marry you off instantly if they knew you were in London on the stage."

Before she faced the fireplace, he caught a glimpse of acute suffering in her face. With slow, deliberate movements, she drew out the kettle, then poured the hot water into a teapot sitting on the table. She took the pouch of tea she'd been worrying in her hand ever since his questions had started, and she dumped the leaves into the teapot.

"My parents are dead," she replied, "so you see, they don't care what happens to me."

"I'm sorry." A twinge of guilt made his voice gentle.

She stood in silence a moment. When her eyes returned to his face, they were shiny with unshed tears. " 'Tis no matter. At least I can care for myself, which is more than some orphans can do."

He thought of the urchins at the theater, and her kindness toward them. No wonder she felt drawn to them. His gaze locked with hers. Her breath began to come more quickly, and he knew she already anticipated what was to come. He watched the rapid rise and fall of her breasts, the stubborn, defensive set of her mouth, and wondered how on earth she could be a spy.

She can't be, he told himself as she looked away.

Then her next words made him wonder again.

"Since I'm an orphan, I suppose I ought to search out other members of my family. So tell me all about these relatives of mine you seem to know." She moved to the cupboard with studied nonchalance and removed two chipped bowls from among the other pieces of crockery that had seen better days.

He digested her words in silence for a moment, trying to decide what to say. He racked his brains for information about Walcester's family and distant relations. "Let me see," he said at last, crossing his arms over his chest. "There's John Maynard, of course. He's a lawyer and a knight."

"Oh?" She took down a dish of sugar. "A knight?"

Ah, so that was of importance, was it? "Aye, although he was given that honor only recently when he was made the king's sergeant. Before that he was a mere mister."

She looked disappointed.

"Then there's Leticia, his sister. She's a bitter witch with a penchant for tearing apart other women's reputations. Since she married into nobility, she fancies herself a great wit. I've never understood why she thinks one thing has anything to do with the other."

Annabelle didn't even crack a smile at his paltry jest. Clearly Leticia didn't interest her.

"Oh, and Louis, the poet. Let's not forget him. Not that anyone could, since he spends most of his time circulating verses among the pompous old fools at court."

Her brow creased in thought, she took the bowls and sugar back to the table. "He's an older man?" she asked, interest in her tone.

"No, actually he's about my age."

Her interest seemed to fade immediately. She poured the tea into the bowls.

"I almost forgot," he added in as offhand a manner as he could manage. "There's Edward, the Earl of Walcester, a man of about fifty, I should say. Now, that's a relative you should cultivate. His fortune isn't vast, but it's certainly enough to keep a woman like you in gowns and slippers for some time."

He'd hit the target, all right. She froze with a bowl of tea poised midair in her hand.

A shaky laugh came from her lips, but she avoided his eyes. "A nobleman? I hardly think I'm related to nobility."

Nonetheless, she carried his tea to him with hands that trembled ever so slightly.

He took the bowl from her and set it on the floor. "Oh, I can well believe you have connections to nobility." When she started to move away, he clasped her hand. "A woman of your beauty and obvious refinement can't help but move in high circles." Her hand stiffened in his, but he ignored her reaction, pulling her to stand between his thighs. "And now, dear Annabelle, it's time we engaged in a more intimate discussion."

She pushed away from him none too gently and went to sit at the table. "Please, not yet." She seemed to realize how oddly shy that sounded and added, "I just need a bit of tea to warm me. Why don't you drink yours too? It will do you good."

Again with the damnable tea, he thought. He started

to tell her he wanted her, not the tea. Then, noting how she lifted her own bowl to her lips but didn't drink, he lifted his and sniffed as unobtrusively as possible.

Valerian root and tarragon. He couldn't mistake the fragrance of those two herbs, important ingredients in a sleeping decoction. He'd prepared the mixture himself a few times. Mina had taught him and his companions at the Royal Society how to brew the special tea.

He lowered the bowl to the floor without taking a sip. Anger burned within him, slowly at first, then like a raging fire, taking all his discretion with it. Hell and furies, the wench was trying to put him to sleep. He watched her with her own bowl pretending to swallow the tea when he knew not a sip had passed her lips.

What had she hoped to accomplish? Robbery? Murder? Did she detest him that much? Then the truth hit him like a well-placed blow. She feared seduction. Perhaps she'd even used this same ploy on Somerset. She'd drugged him at night, then the next morning . . . Well, he wasn't certain how she'd managed after that, but no doubt he'd know more once he spoke with Somerset. He'd definitely speak with Somerset. Tomorrow.

As for tonight . . . He smiled grimly to himself and rose from the daybed. Her eyes widened; then she set down her bowl so quickly, some of the liquid splashed out.

She jumped up from her chair, nearly knocking it over in the process. "Aren't you going to—"

"Drink my tea?" Sarcasm dripped from his words. "No, Annabelle, I am not going to drink tea right now. I think I'll kiss you instead."

Her mouth fell open as she stepped back and lifted her hand to her throat, but in two strides he stood next to her. The next moment she was in his arms.

He saw her defenses go up seconds before his mouth seized hers, but after that all thought fled from him. The vestiges of his anger gave an edge to his kiss. He held her without remorse, held her knowing she'd not intended this to happen. That realization made him all the more fierce. His arm crushed her tight, his lips ground against hers, and he entangled the fingers of his free hand in her long, damp hair, holding her head still.

Her body lay within the circle of his arms stiff as a sword and just as cold. He knew she clung to her precious shield of detachment. He also knew he'd splinter it into a million pieces if it took him half the night to do so.

His determination wasn't lost on Annabelle either. She didn't know what had set him off, but something had. After the way he'd indulged all her delaying tactics, she'd hoped he would let her wriggle out of this absurd situation.

From the moment he'd set down his tea and come for her, however, she'd known all was lost. Never had a man's gaze stripped her bare as a maple tree in winter. That frightened her almost as much as the whisper of anger in his eyes. But it wasn't her stepfather's anger, not that familiar shattering urge for violence.

Nonetheless, the tenacity in his gaze shook her and made her all the more determined to fight him. She'd fought him from the moment he'd touched her . . . she fought him now. Unfortunately, she was losing, and she knew it.

Now she chanted a litany in her head to keep herself remote from him, a litany of memories about her mother's torments under the squire's sick hands, a litany of her distrust of men. Yet the litany fast grew to gibberish as his lips continued to press hers and his tongue skimmed the line of her teeth, begging entrance.

When his mouth left hers, she sighed with relief, knowing she wouldn't have lasted much longer. Unfortunately, he didn't free her. Instead, his mouth sought out the taut skin of her brow, her closed eyelids, the lifted tip of her nose. Her heart leapt into her throat at the tenderness of his caresses. Then his per-

suasive lips closed over hers again, and devil take her
if she didn't allow him to make the kiss intimate, to
take her in the French way, his tongue filling the deep,
rich hollow of her mouth. She hated herself for the
weakness, for the cracks appearing in her wall of resistance.

But how could she help it? Faith, the man kissed
like a god. Adonis. Adonis had her in his thrall, and
there wasn't a blessed thing she could do about it, not
with her body melting like a snow woman under the
spring sun.

His broad hand clasping her neck slid around to under her ear. His thumb brushed her ear, then slipped
down her slender neck in a caress as potent as the
kisses he now pressed in the corners of her mouth.
Before she even knew what was happening, he'd
yanked loose the scarf she'd tucked in so carefully and
dropped it to the floor. Then his hand slid over her
shoulder and downward, easily taking with it part of
her gown.

The air chilled her shoulder. *Devil take these low-
cut gowns with their wide necklines,* she thought as his
hand covered the bare skin there.

All thought fled her as his fingers brushed the upper
swell of her breast. She drew back, her heart pounding
in her distress. The way he looked at her with those
intense sea-green eyes sent her emotions skittering in
a thousand directions.

"I'd like to see you without your feathers," he whispered.

She closed her eyes, knowing exactly what he meant,
but somehow incapable of resisting him. He slid one
finger beneath the tight edge of her gown and her
smock, running it all along the top, right over the nipples of her barely covered breasts. The tips tautened
into hard pebbles as her eyelids fluttered open. Raw
desire shone in his eyes, sending an answering shudder
of longing through her body.

His other hand at her back stroked upward from her
bottom to pull at the laces of her gown. How adept he

was at loosening her laces, she thought. Though he had to use both hands, he unfastened her clothing with expert ease. Of course, she told herself. After all, he was a rake. No doubt he'd undressed untold numbers of women.

Her hands clenched into fists as she strove to summon back her armor of resistance. Her mouth felt dry as cotton. She couldn't have uttered a word if she'd wished to. Why was she standing there like a statue, letting him strip her of her dignity, of her freedom?

Because his gaze riveted her with its knowledge. He knew her like none of the other gallants had. She couldn't say why she felt it to be so, but the realization paralyzed her nonetheless. No one else had seen beneath the role she played; no one else had glimpsed the real Annabelle.

Somehow she sensed that Lord Hampden had.

Only when her gown loosened did she find the power to speak. "Let go of me, my lord." At first the words sounded more like a caress than a command.

"My name is Colin, remember?" he said, ignoring her request as he pushed her gown down to her waist. Nothing but her thin holland smock covered her breasts now. With a delicacy she hadn't expected, he refrained from looking at them. His eyes remained fastened on her face, but his hands . . . faith, his hand covered one cloth-draped breast.

A sharp pang pierced her chest, and she found it hard to breathe. Her breast filled his hand as if made to fit there. Then he slanted his mouth across hers. His mouth also fit.

Only this time she didn't soften. She refused to acquiesce, refused to succumb. She'd fight him, she told herself, but with the weapons she'd learned would wound him most.

Indifference.

She fell back on the trick she'd used during the squire's beatings, pretending she were someone else. His lips pressed hers apart, but in her mind she was no longer Annabelle being kissed by the closest thing to Adonis, but instead the goddess Diana, wild and free, mocking all men as she hunted alone in the forest.

Diana, she told herself, *I am Diana.* Chanting those words in her mind, she somehow withstood the promise of Colin's body, forcing her own body to remain slack and unmoved beneath his hands.

Sweet Mary, it was difficult. In her mind's eye, she was Diana, but the image kept fading. Only with great concentration could she maintain the role. Colin's thumb circled her nipple through the cloth of her smock, eliciting a sweet ache with each passing. A moan bubbled up in her throat. She closed it off just in time.

I can do this, she told herself. *I can fight him if I try.*

He drew back from her, his eyes hard and searching, his expression taut with unbridled desire. "I won't hurt you, dearling. You need not fear that. 'Tis not my wish to take your pride from you, to bend your will to mine. I want only to give you pleasure."

Where his seductive movements had failed to break through her defenses, his gentle words succeeded. Her lips began to tremble, her chin to quiver. He saw it and caught her fear with his kiss. She tried again to summon up her image of the virgin goddess Diana, but she couldn't think of anything but his reassuring words, his infinitely gentle tone.

Scarcely knowing she did so, she opened to him, her heart slamming in her chest. Such sweet strokes his tongue gave. Such intimate, gentle nibbles his teeth took of her mouth.

He undid the ties of her smock, then slid her smock off her shoulders until it dropped to form a kind of apron over her half-fallen gown. A moan sounded deep in his throat as he filled both hands with the soft weight of her bare breasts, shaping them, caressing them until she thought she'd faint away right there with the pleasure of it. Unconsciously she pressed against his hands, her own hands finally stealing around his waist to clutch at the rock-hard muscle.

Where had all her pride gone? she thought as his fingers worked their magic and his mouth plundered hers with honeyed kisses. How could she have forgotten the lessons her mother had taught her about the dangers of seduction? The question brought tears welling in her eyes. One slipped between her lowered lashes.

Apparently he felt the damp trail against his own cheek, for he lifted his mouth from hers and his hands stilled on her breasts.

His eyes, dark green as a night forest, bore into her, questioning, longing. "I want to coax your body to sing, my beautiful swan," he murmured, brushing soft kisses along the path her tear had taken. "Is that so terrible?"

She fought to regain her composure, to hold back any other wayward tears. "You want a swan song. If I give you that, then I die."

He stiffened, his sculpted jaw becoming harsh and unyielding. She could see him fighting his urges, his brow beading with sweat from the effort.

He lifted his hand to smooth one damp lock of hair from her cheek. "Even swans mate, dearling. And they don't die afterward."

She must tell him something, she realized, must give him some excuse for her hesitation. How could she do so without explaining that her maidenly fears came from being a maiden? She must play this role exactly right if she were to slip from his trap unscathed.

There was one thing she could request without being thought odd, she thought suddenly. It wasn't a part of her role she relished, but if it would protect her . . .

"I'm sorry, my lord," she said, forcing a knowing smile to her lips. "This swan requires more wooing before she mates."

"Wooing?" he asked, suspicion glinting in his eyes.

"Yes. Sweet words, public attentions . . . gifts."

"Ah," he said, the warm light in his eyes fading

slowly to a cold cynicism. He didn't release her, however. Instead he bent his head to kiss her fiercely, almost angrily. She remained stiff and remote. He drew back from her mouth enough to mutter, "I'll bring you all the gifts you want tomorrow, my greedy miss, I promise. But tonight, we shall find another pleasure."

"Nay," she said more desperately, pushing his hands off her breasts. Remembering her role, she forced an expression of bored disinterest to her face. "Nay, I'll find no pleasure with you until I see some material proof of your affections."

He hesitated, his eyes glittering with suppressed anger and the remnants of desire. For a moment, she feared he'd take her anyway, if only to prove his power. But at last he stepped back and drew her smock in place, knotting the ties with quick, jerky movements, as if he feared he'd not be able to do so if much more time passed.

"Material proof, eh?" He arched one brow. "I should have known."

Perhaps she'd gotten rid of him for good with her callous words, she thought.

Then he pressed his body to hers, deliberately letting her feel his arousal. "You'll have your . . . ah . . . gifts, my coldhearted swan, as soon as I find ones to suit your beauty. In the meantime, you'd best accustom yourself to my presence, for I don't intend to relinquish the pursuit."

His words thrilled her, although she hated herself for it. Without another word, he released her and sat down to draw on his boots. Then he rose and strode to the fire to gather up his coat and vest. She stood there numbly watching, only half thanking the heavens for her reprieve.

After donning his still sodden outer garments, Colin went to the door, but he paused there, turning to fix her with an angry gaze. His eyes raked her so slowly, they set her afire again.

"Oh, and Annabelle," he said, a tinge of quiet

menace in his tone. "I don't know who mixes your tea, but I recommend she use prickly lettuce in her sleeping decoction instead of valerian. It's quick, effective, and best of all, the scent is easier to mask."

He actually smiled then, although the smile stopped short of his eyes. His gaze locked with hers, a challenge in its depths. Without another word, he left, slamming the door behind him.

She dropped into a nearby chair, not even bothering to pull up her gown to cover her smock. His words echoed in her mind, over and over. Then she gazed sightlessly at the full bowl of tea he'd left on the floor by the daybed, and fear clogged her throat.

Oh, sweet Mary, I am undone, she thought as she buried her face in her hands. *He knows. Devil take the man, he knows.*

Chapter Seven

"There's beggary in the love that can be
reckoned."
—William Shakespeare, *Antony and
Cleopatra*, Act 1, Scene 1

Annabelle tossed and turned on the down mattress as
images flitted in and out of her sleeping mind. First
came the swan with a flutter of snowy wings. The
graceful bird stepped up to the water's edge. From out
of nothing, a man appeared. The squire!

Annabelle watched as he crept up behind the swan,
a gnarled noose in his hand. She tried to cry out, to
warn the swan, but no sound escaped her mouth.

He threw the noose over the swan's head, then tightened it around its neck before she even knew what was
happening. Once caught, the swan fought like one of
the winged Furies, flailing about at the waterside until
her feathers were caked in black mud. The mud
weighted the swan down pitifully, like quicksand.

The squire laughed his hideous, mocking laugh as
the swan ceased her struggles, exhausted.

Behind the squire another man approached with an
ax in his hand. Annabelle's stomach vibrated, hollow
as a drum, when she recognized the face . . . the smile
. . . the golden mane of hair. . . .

Then the man brought the ax down. . . .

"No!" Annabelle shouted, sitting bolt upright in
bed. Her skin felt too tight for her body, her heartbeat
too loud for her ears. Fleeting images remained . . .
the swan, the squire, the ax . . . Colin.

The dream was an evil portent, that was certain, for it left her chilled and frightened. The squire was dead, she reassured herself. He couldn't hurt her anymore.

But Colin was another matter entirely, she thought as she tried to slow the pounding of her heart. His parting sally proved he couldn't be deceived. The question was, could he hurt her? *Would* he hurt her? Her dream clouded the issue. Had the ax been meant for the swan or the squire? She'd awakened before she'd found out.

Then again, it might be better not to know.

Lying back against the pillow, she surveyed her bedchamber. The gray morning light seeped into the windows like a mist off the Thames, hiding as much as it revealed. 'Twas like her evening with Colin. Every time she'd thought to determine his true intentions, he'd shifted tactics, constantly throwing her off guard.

Last night, his tactics had been particularly effective. She raised her hand to her throat, then let it drift downward to the edge of her smock, following the path of Colin's kisses. Fie, but she'd come close to sharing her bed with him.

The words he'd spoken, the caresses . . . they'd woven a magical veil around her so impenetrable she could no longer see the world in the same light. Last night's events changed everything.

It wasn't merely his kisses that touched her either. It was his willingness to consider her feelings. He'd stopped when she'd asked. What's more, unlike the other gallants, he hadn't mocked her for giving oranges to the urchins. Despite his talk of buying her gowns, he'd not treated her like some doxy to be tumbled at his whim.

In short, he was witty and intelligent and all too attractive. She even had to smile remembering the adroit way he'd gotten rid of Somerset.

The man has bewitched me, Annabelle thought as she shook her head. *His kisses have completely clouded my judgment.*

She touched her fingertips to her lips briefly. They

felt heated, far too heated for a somber winter dawn. The man had a sorcerer's touch, that was certain.

A sorcerer's all-seeing eye as well, she thought. Unfortunately, he used the very intelligence and sensibility she admired to see beneath her roles and discern all her deceptions. She shivered as she remembered his final words last night. He knew about the drugged tea. What would he make of it? Could he hurt her plans by knowing that bit of information?

Suddenly she heard the door from the hallway open, jolting her from her ruminations. For an instant, she feared she'd conjured up Colin with her thoughts. Then Charity appeared in the doorway to the bedchamber they shared, obviously distracted.

"Where have you been?" Annabelle queried, unable to hide the sharpness in her tone as Charity passed by her bed in a dreamy daze on her way to her own bed.

Charity started, her hand flying to her mouth. "Faith, but you frightened the life out of me! What are you doin' up so early when you don't have to be to rehearsal at all today?"

Annabelle's eyes missed not a detail of Charity's distress—her mussed hair, her clothing slightly askew, her reddened lips. "And what are you doing out so late?"

She couldn't mistake the bright red flush that spread over Charity's apple cheeks. Charity's odd expression drove Annabelle's own worries right out of her head.

Charity walked to Annabelle's bed and sat on the edge gingerly, as if her body were spun glass. Though still blushing, she met her mistress's concerned gaze. "I was with John."

"John? Sir John Riverton?" Annabelle clutched her pillow in her arms. "Oh, Charity, not him. You didn't let him—"

Charity got a stubborn look on her face. "I did." Her expression shifted, becoming soft and dreaming. "And I don't regret it for a moment."

Annabelle sighed. Only a fool would misunderstand

what Charity was saying, and Annabelle was no fool. Charity had wanted this all along—to find a kind, wealthy protector in London, preferably a handsome one. Charity had always said she'd tasted respectability with her husband, and now she sought to taste wickedness with a lover.

Annabelle had tried to convince Charity that taking a lover, wealthy or not, would represent a disastrous fall into degradation. But Charity had continued to insist that once Annabelle had herself experienced the joys of bedding a man, she'd not be so keen to leave it behind either.

Annabelle wasn't so sure about that. Charity had told Annabelle long ago about the mechanics of making love. It sounded to Annabelle as if the actual experience would be like so many other things in life . . . more fun for the man than the woman. She couldn't imagine finding enjoyment in having something resembling a hefty sausage stuck up inside you.

Yet Charity kept insisting it was pleasurable. Oh, yes, Annabelle had known all along what Charity wanted. Still, Charity's defection left Annabelle feeling bereft.

"Is Sir John going to . . . to keep you now?" she queried.

Her face expressionless, Charity plucked at the folds of the counterpane. " 'Tis too soon for that. In truth, I don't think he intended this to happen at all." She stared off into space, her brow creased. "The man has always flirted, but I never thought he was much taken with me. Then last night I stayed at the theater to mend some costumes, and he came in search of Lord Hampden. I told him his lordship had left with you, so he talked with me a long while. When it got late, he apologized for keeping me so long without my supper. Then he . . . he asked me to supper at his lodgings."

"So you went."

"Yes."

Annabelle groaned. Men were such sly creatures when it came to finding their pleasure. And Charity was so warm and open, she fell right into the hands of a rake like Riverton.

Charity laid her hand over Annabelle's. "I knew what I was about. I promise you, I wasn't forced."

"No, you were seduced." *As I nearly was myself last night.* That thought made something in her snap. "He didn't even have the decency to offer to keep you."

"Oh, but he did," Charity protested, then clapped a hand over her mouth.

"I thought you said . . ." Annabelle trailed off as Charity refused to meet her eyes. She thought back to what Charity had said. *'Tis too soon for that.* Why would it be too soon for that? The truth dawned on her. "You refused because of me, didn't you?"

"Now, now, dear heart, don't be angry. 'Tis not the time for me to be setting up housekeeping elsewhere, and well you know it."

Annabelle started to answer her, but Charity shook her head, forestalling her reply.

"Besides, I believe in lettin' a man stew." A coy smile flitted over her face. "They say once a man has breached a woman's defenses, he loses interest, but that's not true. It's feelin' sure of her before he knows his own mind that makes a man lose interest. Sometimes a woman's got to help a man know his own mind before she lets him get a glimpse into her own."

Annabelle thought of Colin and his fierce assurance that he'd pursue her to the end. "I only wish Lord Hampden didn't know his own mind quite so well."

"Faith, but I'd completely forgotten! What happened with his lordship? I see the man ain't lying about here. Did you put him to sleep or not?"

Annabelle grimaced. "I tried to get him to drink the tea, but he sniffed out the sleeping potion and wouldn't touch it."

Charity grew thoughtful. "Did he, now?"

"Aye," Annabelle said irritably, "he most certainly did. Before he left, he even had the temerity to suggest that next time I use prickly lettuce."

"Did he, now?"

"For heaven's sake, stop repeating that! He did, he did! He insinuated himself in here, sniffed out my ruse in one evening, and nearly bedded me before I could stop him."

Charity's eyes twinkled. "Oh, did he, now?"

"Devil take you, Charity Woodfield! I don't find this the least amusing!"

Charity chuckled before growing more serious. "I take it his lordship didn't bed you?"

"Nay," Annabelle said, coloring slightly. "But not for want of trying."

"Hmph, if his lordship had wanted to bed you, you would have been bedded, and no doubt more than once."

Annabelle didn't answer. Charity had a point. Colin hadn't struck her as the kind of man to take no for an answer. He'd obviously been furious when he'd found out what she was up to. Most rakes would have bedded her by force at that moment.

But he hadn't. What's more, she'd trusted him not to. It had only fleetingly occurred to her that he might harm her in his anger. She hugged her pillow to her chest. That was the worst of it—he'd already begun making her trust him, the sweet-tongued devil. Dear heaven, but the man truly did have a sorcerer's powers!

"So did he touch you?" Charity broke into her thoughts.

Heat rose in Annabelle at the memory of the many caresses he'd given her mouth . . . her neck . . . her breasts. Her face flamed, and not entirely with embarrassment either.

A sly smile crossed Charity's face. "I figured his lordship knew how to woo a woman."

" 'How to seduce a woman,' you mean," Annabelle said tartly.

"Seducing's part of wooing, if you ask me."

"No one asked you."

Charity threw back her head full of mussed blond curls and laughed. "I see Lord Hampden is a mighty sore subject with you." She shook her head, still smiling. Then she caught her mistress's sober expression and her smile faded. "So what d'ye intend to do now?"

Annabelle shook her head. "I don't know. If he's discovered the sleeping potion ploy, he may eventually determine that I use it for other men as well. Once he knows that—"

" 'Tis of no consequence at all. Even if he guesses that y're giving men a sleeping decoction to avoid bedding them, what good will it do him? All it means is y're afraid to bed men. 'Twouldn't reveal yer deeper purpose."

Her deeper purpose. The Maynards. She'd forgotten all he'd said about the Maynards. And one Maynard in particular. Odd how he'd known exactly who would interest her most. Perhaps he'd simply thought a commoner would be most interested in the exciting possibility of being nobility.

On the other hand . . .

"Charity, how much do you know about Lord Hampden? That is, his friends, his alliances?"

Charity stretched out on the bed, resting her head on her hand. "There's John, of course, and Sedley and—"

"No, no. I mean, aside from the gallants and rakes. Does he have friends among . . . say . . . older nobility?"

Fixing her mistress with a speculative gaze, Charity asked, "Like who?"

Annabelle plucked at the worn threads of the counterpane. "I got him to tell me last night about some of the Maynards in London. He mentioned one, an earl, who'd be the right age—"

"To be your father?"

"Aye. I almost got the feeling Lord Hampden knew him. If Lord Hampden knows this man and the man *is* my father, what if the man put Lord Hampden up to finding out about me?"

The very thought that Colin might be manipulating

her in such a manner nauseated her. She'd allowed him so very close, much closer than any other man.

Charity's lips pursed. "Can't see Lord Hampden being put up to anything by anybody, can you?"

Annabelle tried to shake off her queasy feeling. "No, I suppose not."

"What would it mean in any case, if he did somehow determine who you are?"

"Don't you see? If he determines who I am before I know who my father is, then my revenge is all for naught. How can I unmask my father before all his friends if I don't know who he is? If Lord Hampden ever guesses why I search for my father—"

"He'll not guess if you don't tell him."

"Still, it worries me."

"Actually, if he knows yer father, it gives you even more reason to let him continue his pursuit of you. If you can manage it, you might even open up enough to tell him who y're searching for. As long as you don't tell him what y're after in knowing, he might lead yer father to you."

She considered that possibility. "Aye. If I can get him to sympathize with my quest." She added dryly, "And if his lordship doesn't ravish me before I find out what I need to know."

With a laugh, Charity sat up. " 'Ravish,' eh? Now you sound like the ladies you play on the stage. I doubt it would be so dramatic and awful as all that."

Perhaps not, she thought. Still, she didn't want to be ravished or even seduced. For one thing, she feared ending up as her mother had—with a child in her belly and no one to claim it. Much as she wanted to believe she could keep Colin at arm's distance while finding out what she needed to know, the sad truth was she couldn't even keep the man at a finger's distance. He had this uncanny ability to unmask her and strike where she was more vulnerable. No, she couldn't let herself be tempted by his sweet kisses. She mustn't.

"I think I'd be better off avoiding the man completely," she told Charity determinedly. "He's too clever. He's already given me one name to explore. I should content myself with that and not attempt the harder task of trying to manage his passions and his sly questions at the same time.''

"If you don't mind my sayin' so, I think yer worries are foolish. I mean, the man—''

A knock sounded at the door to the hall, cutting off Charity's words and making them both jump.

"Are you expecting anyone?'' Charity asked.

Annabelle frowned. "Do you think his lordship would return so soon?''

Charity shrugged as she slid off the bed. "John says the man is taken with you. Who knows what a man captivated by a woman will do?''

As Annabelle smiled at the absurd idea that Colin was captivated by her, Charity moved into the other room. Annabelle heard the door open. A low-voiced conversation followed.

Then Charity appeared in the doorway, a young boy of about twelve at her side. He was prettily dressed in a rich burgundy and gold livery.

"We have a visitor from the marquis's household,'' Charity said with amusement in her voice. She didn't need to say which marquis.

The boy bowed solemnly when he caught sight of Annabelle in her smock sitting up in bed. His expression betrayed not a whit of surprise. No doubt he was accustomed to being ushered into the kind of houses where women went about in their smocks, Annabelle thought. In truth, many actresses received guests while they were dressing. Annabelle had become so accustomed to changing gowns in the tiring-room before an audience that she wasn't the least bit modest anymore.

"I wish to speak to Madam Maynard,'' the boy said in a haughty tone befitting the pride he apparently took in his position.

Annabelle smiled as she beckoned him into the room. "You're speaking to her now.''

At Charity's prodding, he came to stand beside the bed. "My master sent me to give you this, madam.''

He held out a package wrapped in gold cloth and tied with a burgundy velvet ribbon.

"Oh?" She took it from him. A gift? From Colin? Suddenly she remembered last night when she'd told Colin he must woo her with gifts. Shame washed over her. She certainly hadn't meant her defensive words. In truth, she hadn't been certain he believed them.

Apparently he had. Dear heaven, but he seemed terribly determined, despite her petty resistance. She remembered with distress the words he'd spoken before he'd left, when he'd vowed to have her, no matter what.

That very persistence could be her undoing if she dallied with him anymore by accepting his gift. Oh, yes, he'd view that as tacit approval of his pursuit. Then, sweet Mary, she might as well have announced, "Come learn all my secrets." The possibility that he might lead her to her father wasn't worth the risk of letting him too close. After all, she couldn't use the sleeping potion on him, and she couldn't avoid him. No doubt about it. She must refuse his gift.

With a sigh, she handed the unopened package back to the boy. "Return this to your master. Tell him I don't want his gifts."

"Madam!" Charity exclaimed, placing a hand on the boy's shoulder. "You can't mean that! Why, you haven't even seen what it is!"

"I don't care what it is. I do not wish to encourage Lord Hampden's advances, and you know quite well why." She jerked her head toward the boy as her eyes met Charity's. "Show the boy out, and give him a shilling for his efforts."

Defiance in her eyes, Charity snatched the package and opened it with deft movements.

"Charity!" Annabelle protested, but the woman ignored her as she removed the contents.

With a sharp intake of breath, Charity held it up to the light. "God in heaven! 'Tis a gold ring with diamonds and rubies! You can't be wantin' to return a gift like that!"

Light glittered off the cut stones, sending a thrill of

pleasure through Annabelle before she could stop it. It took enormous effort to shut her eyes and not stare at the ring. Knowing Colin, it was exquisite . . . and expensive.

A shame she couldn't take it and sell it to support her and Charity. A shame she couldn't play on Colin's affections to learn her father's identity. But last night had taught her Colin wasn't a man to be manipulated. More was the pity.

"There's a note here too," Charity added. She opened it and read, " 'For the fire and ice of my lovely swan. May my paltry gift melt her heart.' " Charity clutched it to her chest with a dreamy sigh.

Paltry gift indeed, Annabelle thought even as the note sent tendrils of excitement twirling about her heart. She squelched that unwelcome sensation with a vengeance. "Charity, give it back to the boy and let him return it as I asked."

"But madam—"

"Give it to him and show him out," Annabelle commanded more sternly.

A moment's silence ensued. Annabelle opened her eyes to stare at Charity balefully, doing her best not to notice the lovely, glittering ring in her maid's hand. With a sudden forced nonchalance, Charity shrugged before complying.

Annabelle heard the outer door open and shut. Then Charity returned seconds later, her doe's eyes alight with anger. "Faith, have you lost all good sense? Don't you think this foolish stunt will draw his attentions more than yer taking the gift would have? His lordship loves a challenge, John tells me. 'Tis like beating a hornet's nest to spurn his gift."

Annabelle rubbed her temples wearily. This game was trying her wits sorely. "Perhaps, but I dare not let him any closer." She attempted a hopeful smile. "With any luck, my refusal will convince him I'm not worth the trouble."

Charity snorted as she neared the bed. "Aye, and wolves may lie down with lambs."

Annabelle sighed. "If he refuses to heed my clear message, I shall simply have Lord Somerset impress upon him that I'm not available."

Another snort sounded from where Charity stood at the foot of the bed.

Annabelle ignored it as a thought occurred to her. "That's it! Charity, you must go tell Lord Somerset of Lord Hampden's overtures to me! Yes, yes, do tell him!" She clutched the pillow to her with a smile of relief, then threw it in the air. "That will solve all my problems. Lord Somerset is a jealous man. He'll warn Lord Hampden off, and then I'll be safe!"

Charity looked at her mistress, blatant disbelief written on her face. "Lord Somerset defend you from Lord Hampden? No offense, dear heart, but if y're thinkin' that a painted coxcomb like Somerset'll stand up for you to his lordship, y're a mutton-headed fool. Even if you are my mistress, y're a fool."

Annabelle leveled her most frosty gaze on Charity. "Thank you for your opinion. I'll keep it in mind while you're at Lord Somerset's."

Unperturbed, Charity bent to pick up the pillow from where it had landed on the floor. "As you wish, madam. I'll fly to solicit Lord Somerset's help this instant, for all the good it'll do." She straightened and rubbed her chin, her eyes narrowing as she tossed the pillow back to Annabelle. "Though I suppose 'twould be amusin' to watch the popinjay crumble into a sodden heap of cowardice."

"Don't provoke him too badly, Charity. I need him, even if he is a puppet of a man."

Charity chuckled and shook her head. "I think y're puttin' yer money on the wrong cock, but I'll do what you say."

Granted, Charity was probably right. Granted, the thought of Lord Somerset calling Colin out was too outrageous to be believed. But she must do something, mustn't she? She couldn't sit here and let the insolent, overconfident Marquis of Hampden dig into her secrets and ruin her plans.

Charity began to leave the room.

"And Charity?" Annabelle called out.

Charity paused in the doorway.

"Find out what you can about a man named Edward Maynard, Earl of Walcester."

"Is that the Maynard his lordship spoke of?"

"Yes. Determine if he has a family. If you can, find out where he was around the time of my birth."

Charity's lips tipped up. "For pity's sake, how am I to do that?"

Annabelle shrugged. "I have no idea. Can't you speak with the man's servants?" She brightened. "Or ask Riverton, perhaps?"

"If I ask Riverton, he'll tell Lord Hampden."

With a groan, Annabelle clutched the pillow to her chest. "That's true. Oh, devil take the marquis, he's been a nuisance from the moment I met him."

Charity smiled enigmatically. "His lordship will no doubt be much more of a nuisance before this business is finished." Then she left the room.

Annabelle sank back onto the bed, closing her eyes and praying that Charity proved to be wrong. The last thing Annabelle needed was the persistent Lord Hampden pursing her.

Not when he offered her the sweetest pleasures this side of heaven.

Chapter Eight

"It holds for good polity ever, to have that
outwardly in vilest estimation, that inwardly
is most dear to us."
—Ben Jonson, *Every Man in His Humor*, Act 2, Scene 3

"What's this I hear about your going to the colonies?"
Sedley asked Colin as they stood in Riverton's drawing
room drinking wine.

Colin glanced at the door, irritated that Somerset
hadn't yet arrived. He and Sedley had come early to
Riverton's supper, having skipped the play. Colin had
hoped Riverton could convince Somerset to show up
before the actresses.

And Annabelle.

"I've been considering the possibility," he answered Sedley, keeping his eye on the door.

"Egad, I can't imagine why you'd do such an absurd
thing."

Colin sighed. How could he explain the change in
him since he'd returned from Antwerp? Where once
he'd enjoyed the games played among the nobility, he
now tired of them. Sex had become a currency among
the nobility and the players. The actresses offered sex
in exchange for a comfortable living, and the rakes
provided sex to their friends' wives to sate their boredom. Now he saw the tawdry schemes for what they
were, empty pursuits with little to commend them. Of
late he found more satisfaction out of his experiments
with the Royal Society than his other dealings with his
peers.

So he'd thought he might travel to explore this fascinating continent of which he'd heard so much from the privateers passing in and out of London. After all, he had no family obligations and enough wealth to begin a plantation.

Of course, Sedley would never understand how appealing the honest hard work of running a plantation might be to a man tired of deceptions and lies, who wanted to begin again. Still, Colin tried to explain. "Those who've been to the colonies say it's filled with new flora and fauna to examine, new lands to conquer, new peoples and new cultures to study. I thought it might be interesting to add something to human knowledge by exploring that abundance of exciting newness."

Sedley shrugged. "I have enough trouble dealing with the new women who appear on the stage weekly to even think of traveling over the sea to a distant land. I should think you would too, with your merry pursuit of the Silver Swan."

Colin scowled as Sedley caught sight of a friend and strolled over to speak with him. Colin hadn't wanted to be reminded of the deceitful vixen who would undoubtedly be arriving at Riverton's as soon as the play was over. Colin might be tiring of London's glittering society, but he couldn't eliminate his interest in the ever-changeable Annabelle.

'Sdeath, he told himself, moment by moment this endeavor grew more exasperating and Walcester's suspicions more plausible. Night before last, a very definite though wary interest had shone in Annabelle's brilliant eyes as they'd spoken of the Maynards. The woman was most assuredly up to something.

Thrusting his hand into his waistcoat pocket, Colin clenched it around the ring he'd sent to her lodgings yesterday. As the jewel-encrusted ring dug into his palm, anger dug into his gut and festered there. Hell and furies, no woman ever refused his gifts. Not a gift of this worth anyway.

Oh, yes, the woman was up to something, all right—up to driving him mad. In all his days of spying, he'd never met a woman he couldn't twist around his finger to discover her secrets. Now here was this actress, paying him back fourfold for all his previous deceits.

Night before last she'd slipped valerian in his tea. Valerian! The damnable chit had actually thought she could drug him without his realizing it! Rage still seared him every time he thought of it. How determined she'd been to thwart his seduction, the little temptress!

Ah, but not entirely determined, he reminded himself. Once or twice she'd melted under his caresses like an icicle under sunlight. Only when he'd nearly undressed her had she iced over again, acting skittish as a virgin on her wedding night.

He couldn't help feeling that her fear of him had been most maidenly. After all, she'd excused her sudden reticence by claiming she wanted gifts, but today she'd spurned a gift of great worth. She was as fickle as fortune's wheel, a chameleon of ever-shifting colors. One moment a wanton, the next as embarrassed as a maid. What damnable game was the woman playing?

Was she an innocent? He mused on that possibility a moment. If she were, then why did so many men seem to have known her intimately?

No, he corrected, one man. Only Somerset's name had actually been linked with hers in that manner. Colin rubbed his chin thoughtfully, wondering again if she'd drugged others besides himself—Somerset, perhaps, who would have fallen for such a ruse.

Yes, but she's an actress, he told himself. *Could she truly be chaste after months treading the boards in London?*

Either way, he didn't care. He wanted her, and he would have her, despite all her tricks. After all, there was his promise to Walcester. It was increasingly apparent that Walcester's concerns were valid, even if they seemed based on a secret he hadn't yet revealed.

No matter. Colin had promised Walcester he'd find

out her secrets. What better way to learn a woman's secrets than to take her to bed?

Nonetheless, he was quickly finding distasteful the thought of using Annabelle in such a scurrilous manner. Something about the glimpses she'd given him of a vulnerable woman who masked a deep hurt behind her many faces made him loath to hurt her more. He thought of the urchin who'd warned Colin to treat her well, and a smile touched his lips. Nay, he wouldn't want to hurt her.

He was still musing about how thoroughly she'd captured his sympathies when a commotion in the hall intruded into his thoughts. Lord Somerset entered the drawing room, followed by Riverton.

Colin smiled. So the game had begun, eh? Somerset had arrived as planned. Now if Riverton had told Somerset the tales he'd been supposed to relate to the fop . . .

Colin waited as Riverton sidled in his direction with a clearly nervous Somerset mincing along beside him. Then Colin stepped forward to confront Somerset. Riverton suddenly found something to do elsewhere. Colin noticed that he took the other occupants of the room with him as he left, leaving Somerset alone with Colin.

"Good day, Somerset," Colin remarked coldly. "Rather a surprise to see you here."

Somerset visibly started, then scanned the room as if searching for a friendly face. Seeing none, he brought his wary gaze back to Colin. "Ahem, good to see you, Hampden. Now if you'll excuse me—"

Colin caught his arm before the man could flee. "I wish a word with you."

With a sigh, Somerset nodded, setting the curls of his ridiculous periwig bouncing. "It's about Madam Maynard, isn't it?"

Now it was Colin's turn to be startled. "How did you know?"

"Her maid . . . er . . . warned me yesterday that you'd been harassing her mistress." Apparently unwilling to meet Colin's eyes, Somerset fiddled nervously with one of the patches on his face.

"Harassing?"

The fidgeting became all the more pronounced. "Oh, you know, man. Paying her attentions and such." He sucked in his breath and met Colin's gaze, though the wariness still lay latent in his eyes. "The woman doesn't want them. Her maid said I should defend her from you."

Colin couldn't help it. He gave a short burst of laughter, heedless of the insult to Somerset. The very thought of this fop defending anyone was absolutely ludicrous.

Somerset looked more pained than insulted. "Look here, now, Hampden," he protested in a high, squeaky voice. "Madam Maynard asked me to defend her, and I shall." He drew himself up like a stuffed goose. "Desist in your attentions at once. Madam Maynard wishes that you leave her alone."

Another laugh escaped Colin's lips. "The woman's name is Annabelle, or haven't you gotten far enough with her to know that?"

Somerset colored instantly, but thrust out his chest nonetheless. "I call her Madam Maynard out of respect. She prefers refined gentlemen, who treat her with consideration." He sniffed, then swept Colin with a contemptuous gaze. "Not beasts like you with base appetites."

"Which means you haven't bedded her," Colin remarked dryly.

"Sir, you go too far!" Somerset tugged at his flowing cravat nervously. He glanced around, clearly torn between bragging of his exploit and holding to his position that Annabelle Maynard deserved respect. Colin's amused expression apparently decided him. "I *have* bedded her, as you so crudely put it. Not that it's any of your affair."

Colin took a stab in the dark. "Have you, now? Did you bed her in your sleep, then?"

"What's that supposed to mean?" Somerset asked in his most haughty voice.

"You and I both know you slept through your entire night with her."

Colin knew he'd hit upon the truth when Somerset went completely red, rage flickering in his cold eyes. "That little trollop tell you such a lie?"

So much for respect and consideration, thought Colin, barely able to restrain a burst of anger. Hell and furies, what had the woman seen in this pompous ass whose only concern was to preserve his own reputation, such as it was?

Colin cast about for a palatable lie that would take suspicion from Annabelle. "Charity told me."

"Another trollop. 'Tis all a lie. Ask Madam Maynard . . . er . . . Annabelle herself. I've given her gifts. She's given me kisses . . . and much, much more. That maid of hers lies." He shot Colin a knowing glance.

Colin was fast tiring of this game. "I care not what you claim she has given you. I want her, Somerset, so find another actress willing to toy with your affections."

A pompous stiffness overtook Somerset. "You would take my leavings, then? Have you no pride, man?"

Colin barely restrained himself from slamming his fist into the fop's delicate chin. Leaning close, he gripped Somerset's arm. "If I thought for one moment that you'd truly possessed any part of Annabelle Maynard's heart or body, you'd be welcome to her, I promise you that. But she's too much of a woman to have any interest in you. Annabelle could never be your 'leavings.' It's that which saves you from having your face smashed in."

Somehow Somerset managed to appear both peeved and fearful at the same time. Colin thought of the exaggerated tales Riverton had been instructed to tell Somerset of Colin's unpredictable temper and tendency toward violence. Apparently they'd had an effect. When Somerset glanced down at Colin's fisted hand, his face went as white as his snowy silk cravat.

"She makes a fool of you with others, whether you know it or not," Colin persisted. "Despite her game in sending her maid to you, I tell you she is as enamored of me as I of her and has given me kisses to prove it."

Colin felt a twinge of guilt at revealing any part of his intimacy with Annabelle, but rationalized it was the only way to keep the other men from her. He would claim her, whether she liked it or not. Perversely he had this desire to protect her from the fops and gallants who would treat her as a toy, then toss her aside.

You're not planning to do the same after you've uncovered her secrets? his conscience whispered.

Nay, he told himself. Not this woman. Not unless she proved to be a treacherous villainess. He wondered if he wouldn't want her even then.

Somerset, however, was apparently having second thoughts about his alliance with Annabelle. He kept glancing at Colin's coat, strained tight over muscular arms and shoulders.

"God-a-mercy, I hate to give her up. She's a pretty wench," Somerset murmured, but his gaze fixed on Colin's iron fingers digging into his arm.

"And you, sir, are a pretty man. If you want to stay that way, relinquish your interest in her. Unless, of course, you want to 'defend' her on the field of honor."

Reeling back a step, Somerset's face suffused with horror. "No, no! I—I wouldn't wish to fight you, sir, and certainly not over some actress. I—I'm not a man of violence."

Colin bit back a sarcastic retort. Somerset wasn't a man of violence because he dared not be. The fop was known to be a wretched swordsman. On the other hand, thanks to Riverton, Somerset had now been told that Colin hadn't lost a single one of the duels he'd fought in the past.

Content that he'd made his point, Colin released the

stricken man before him. "Well, then. I see we have an understanding. You'll cease your pursuit of Annabelle Maynard, and I'll overlook your previous association with the woman."

Regret tinged Somerset's face for a moment. Then he attempted to draw the shreds of his pride about him. Waving his hand in an affected gesture of nonchalance, he remarked, "You're welcome to her, sir. In truth, the woman has cost me a pretty penny. I don't envy you the expense of buying her affections."

Colin bit back a smile. The expense didn't bother him nearly as much as the apparent difficulty he was having in making the transaction. "Good day, then, Somerset," he said coldly.

Apparently relieved to be dismissed, the man fled the room with unseemly haste, no doubt going in search of less forbidding company.

Colin watched him go with amusement . . . and a peculiar trace of pity. There'd been a time when he would have delighted in baiting a fop like Somerset. Now it merely saddened him to see a full-grown man with so little concern for his pride that he would rather fawn and preen . . . and sully the reputation of a woman he supposedly cared for . . . than chance being taxed in a fight. How vain the courtiers in London had grown under Charles II, how very caught up in their clothes and their wigs and their appearances. These days he couldn't tell the actors from the real people. Everyone seemed to be in costume.

Including Annabelle, he thought suddenly. She was playing a double role—he felt sure of it after his conversation with Somerset. After all, the Silver Swan, widely acclaimed and freely admitting to being a passionate lover, had drugged at least one man to keep him from bedding her.

Why create such an elaborate scheme? To protect her virtue? Such an odd concern for an actress.

Then again, Annabelle Maynard was an enigma from head to toe. Once more, he clenched the ring in his pocket, thinking of Somerset's peculiar assertion that she'd bled him for expensive gifts. If that were the case, why had she spurned Colin's gift? If the woman were a greedy temptress, why did she avoid him, when he'd agreed to meet her terms?

Her resistance pricked his pride and heightened his suspicions. Hell and furies, but he couldn't figure her out. He would, however. He lifted one eyebrow. If his lovely swan maiden thought spurning his gifts and sending Somerset to defend her would send him running in terror, she had a surprise in store. He fully intended to follow this intriguing game wherever it led.

And in the end, whether she liked it or not, the game would lead to her arms. He'd make certain of that.

Surrounded by half a dozen other chattering actresses, Annabelle and Charity swept into Riverton's town house for the supper to which he'd invited them. Annabelle surveyed her surroundings, astonished at the wealth before her. Charity had told her Riverton had a secure income, thanks to his investments in shipping, but she hadn't guessed how secure. Riverton might only be a knight, but he surpassed many a nobleman in wealth, judging from the spacious hall decked with Italian paintings of the first quality. No doubt his 'informal supper' would be a seven-course affair with music and dancing.

Good, Annabelle thought as she handed her cloak to Riverton's housekeeper. After her long afternoon, she was ready to eat fine food and be entertained for a change.

The play had gone badly, for Henry Harris and Thomas Betterton had made a mistake in their scene that had sent them both into uncontrollable fits of laughter. It had been hard for any of the other players to hold a scene together after that.

Nor had it helped that throughout the play she'd been preoccupied with thoughts of a certain dangerous lord. As she entered the drawing room, she surveyed it quickly, relieved to spot Lord Somerset in one corner. Although Riverton had said Colin was out of town and wouldn't attend, it reassured Annabelle to see Lord Somerset there.

Their host was also standing in the drawing room, Annabelle noted. She glanced at Charity, but the other woman had already noticed him and was smiling. Annabelle scowled. 'Twas a shame Riverton had to be the one to capture Charity's heart. A wealthy man of his flirtatious nature no doubt had a string of mistresses as long as the Roman road.

Yet when he turned and his eyes locked with Charity's, there was no mistaking the expression of pleasure transforming his face. Rapidly he came toward them, his face all smiles. He took Annabelle's hand first, pressing a perfunctory kiss to the back of it, but when he captured Charity's hand, he took his time about the hand kissing.

Annabelle could take a hint. She left them to their cooing, wryly acknowledging that Charity's involvement didn't seem to be completely one-sided.

Gazing about once more, Annabelle noted that Somerset had passed into another room. She wondered if she should follow and thank him for the generous assurance he'd given Charity earlier that day that he'd defend Annabelle from Lord Hampden, no matter what. It was odd to have to seek him out at all. In the past, he'd always rushed to her side whenever she'd entered a room. But he'd apparently not noticed her. Perhaps he hadn't heard the commotion when they'd all come in, she told herself.

Well, if the fool wouldn't take the initiative, she'd do it herself. She wandered through Riverton's well-appointed town house, searching for Somerset. At last she found him in a small ballroom that adjoined the dining room. His face paler than usual, he was speaking with Sir Charles Sedley.

As she approached the two men, Sedley halted his conversation, an amused smile crossing his lean features. She slid her hand in the crook of Somerset's arm.

"Good day, dear," she murmured, and placed a quick kiss on the fop's heavily powdered cheek.

He jerked back, a haughty, distant expression on his face. "Madam Maynard, so good to see you."

This grew more and more curious by the moment, Annabelle thought. "I would speak with you privately a moment," she said, not wanting to give him her thanks in front of Sedley. "Perhaps we could step into the next room?"

Somerset's eyes avoided hers. He whisked his hand in a dismissive gesture. "Afraid that's impossible. I was just this moment leaving. Another engagement, you see."

Dear heaven, but the man seemed very agitated, even for him. She glanced at Sedley for an explanation, but Sedley merely shrugged.

"Another engagement?" she asked.

"Yes, yes. I'm dining with a friend. A good friend. Afraid I have to go. So good to see you." He whirled away from her, striding toward the door in an unusual hurry.

"Wait!" she called, but he'd already slipped out. How very peculiar, she thought. Normally a kiss on his cheek kept him docile. It certainly never sent him running from the room to another engagement.

"It seems you've lost your . . . ah . . . friend this evening," Sedley remarked, a wicked gleam in his eye.

"It does seem so." She frowned. "I wonder what that was all about."

Sedley folded his arms over his chest as he leaned against the wall. "Perhaps he's tired of fighting the others for you."

It took a moment for Sedley's words to sink in. "The others?"

"Yes. Surely you realize that a number of men have been vying for your affections."

"It's the same with all the actresses," she protested,

still staring off in the direction that Lord Somerset had gone, her brow creased in a frown. "Besides, it's never bothered Lord Somerset before."

"Lord Hampden wasn't pursuing you before."

She swung her gaze back to Sedley instantly. "Prithee, what does that mean? Did Lord Hampden have something to do with this? I swear, if that scoundrel has been telling Lord Somerset lies about me—"

"No lies, I assure you," a voice broke in behind her.

Annabelle whirled to find that the scoundrel himself had come up behind her. "You! What are you doing here? What have you been telling Lord Somerset?"

With his usual arrogant smile, he quipped, "To answer your first question, I was invited."

As she simmered, both Sedley and Colin grinned. No doubt they were both in on this, as well as Riverton and even Charity, perhaps. Oh, when she got her hands on whomever had lied to her about Colin's being out of town, she'd strangle them.

"To answer the second question," Colin continued, amusement glinting in his eyes, "Somerset and I had a very intriguing conversation. We compared notes about your tea. I believe he actually had the chance to drink his, but he couldn't tell me much about it."

She snapped open her fan, fluttering it in front of her face to cover her confusion. Sweet Mary, she'd been afraid of this. It was bad enough that Colin had realized she'd drugged him, but now he'd figured out that she'd also drugged Lord Somerset.

What's more, judging from Lord Somerset's cold reception of her a few moments ago, Colin had said something to the poor fop to make him relinquish his pursuit of her. Fury swelled within her breast, both at Lord Somerset for giving up so easily and at Colin for pursuing her. Did the man never stop?

"What? No barbed denials?" Colin asked at her continued silence, triumph apparent in his expression. "No protestations of innocence?"

After a wary glance at Sedley, she met Colin's gaze,

forcing a faint, bored smile to her lips. "What is there to deny? I offered you both . . . er . . . tea when you came to my chambers." Her tone was honey-sweet as she gave the word *tea* another meaning entirely. "Is that so unusual? Then again, perhaps you're complaining about the tepid condition of what I offered you in particular." She flashed Sedley a knowing smile, then shrugged. "I suppose the warmth of it depends on the congeniality of my visitors." She added in her most seductive tone, "I can assure you, the 'tea' I offered Lord Somerset was steaming."

Sedley grasped her meaning immediately and chuckled.

Colin didn't laugh. His eyes narrowed. "Was it? Perhaps that explains why he isn't returning for another serving. Perhaps you heated his tea too much, and he scalded himself. I'm not so foolish. I know how to deal with hot tea." He let his gaze trail meaningfully down the length of her, reminding her that he'd tasted more of that "tea" than she cared to admit.

She colored and snapped her fan shut. "Yes, but it would have to be offered to you, wouldn't it? And there's little chance of that occurring. All I can offer you is tepid tea, Lord Hampden, and I doubt that would satisfy you."

He opened his mouth to retort, but voices sounded behind them, forcing them to break off their conversation. "There you are," said Charity breathlessly as she hurried to Annabelle's side.

Annabelle regarded her maid with an expression of profound relief.

"We've been looking for you," Riverton told Colin.

Thank heaven someone had joined them, Annabelle thought. Despite her protestations to Colin, another minute or two of sparring with the wily marquis would have seen her offering him a good deal more than tea. The man had a way of speaking to her that made her weak in the knees.

Charity and Riverton were accompanied by others of the party. "We were talking about the rumors of a treaty with the Dutch against the French,'' Charity said brightly to Colin, ''and Riverton here says you know the most about it, since you came from Antwerp a few weeks past. He says you were seeking out news for His Majesty. Tell us what y've found out.''

Annabelle flashed Charity a grateful smile, reminded once again of how adept Charity was at rescuing her mistress from unwanted male attention. Charity had never had an ounce of interest in political matters, but she kept her ears open enough to show an interest when necessary. At the moment, Annabelle welcomed any discussion that would keep Colin and her apart.

''Yes, do tell us about the Dutch,'' Annabelle said, moving away from Colin, ostensibly to give him center stage, but mainly so she could escape his disturbing presence.

She wasn't to be let off so easily. With a smooth, leisurely grace, Colin followed her until once more he stood at her side. Then he remarked with some irritation to the crowd around them, ''I can't speak a word about that, you know. What I heard and saw in Antwerp is for the Crown's ears only.''

''Oh, do tell us something,'' Charity pressed, noting the looks of distress her mistress was sending her way. ''Are we really to be allied with the Dutch?''

''You're wasting your time badgering Hampden,'' Sedley put in. ''The fool has already left His Majesty's service, and now he's talking of sailing off to the colonies.''

Annabelle's startled gaze shot to Colin's eyes as her stomach inexplicably sank. He met her gaze with amusement.

''Why would you go to the colonies?'' Charity asked. She'd often spoken to Annabelle of the colonies, of the barbarian jungle they were rumored to be.

Annabelle felt a hand rest in the small of her back and knew instantly whose it was. She tried to shift away from Colin again, but he hooked two fingers in the laces of her gown. Short of engaging in a tug of war, she couldn't move.

Colin smiled at her as he answered Charity. "I'd like to experience living in a country of unlimited potential, where a man can create a new world from the earth's bounty."

"You would be a farmer, then?" Riverton asked in amazement.

Colin shifted his gaze to his friend. "Perhaps. I could run a plantation. I hear the land's more fertile than any in England."

Sedley snorted. "I can hardly imagine you beating your sword into a plowshare, Hampden." He glanced knowingly down at Colin's breeches. " 'Twould be a waste of a good sword."

Catching Sedley's jest, Riverton slid his arm around Charity's waist. "Aye. A deft sword can prove much more amusing to a lady than a clumsy plowshare, wouldn't you say, Charity?"

To Annabelle's amusement, the normally unflappable Charity blushed as the entire company laughed.

Though his laugh rang out with the rest, Colin seemed far more absorbed with working his two fingers farther inside her laces. Thank heavens he and she stood with their backs to a wall, Annabelle thought, unnerved by the liberties he was taking.

She pulled away. He jerked her back. She cast him a scathing glance. He merely grinned as he tucked his fingers down deep beneath the laces.

With a sniff, she turned her gaze to the group around them. "Perhaps Lord Hampden prefers the plowshare, since his sword spends so much time lying useless in its scabbard, wasting space."

She got a laugh from the others for her attack on his virility, but if she'd thought to anger him, she didn't succeed.

"I might indeed prefer the plowshare," he said boldly. "I have to admit, plowing a fertile field can provide its own sort of amusement."

The men all laughed, annoying Annabelle. These

gallants would always find the double entendre in any comment. "What if the field is full of thornbushes?" she shot back.

"Ah, then, I'll have to return to my hapless sword and chop down the thornbushes," Colin said behind her, to the general amusement of the company. Then he twisted the laces of her gown in his fingers, drawing her even closer, until her backside pressed against his body. She could feel his hard thigh against her, sending delicious sensations coursing through her body despite her determination to ignore him.

Then his words sank in. Devil take the man if he thought he'd chop down *her* thornbushes! "So you think your sword, your plowshare, your whatever will always conquer, do you, even if your foe fights mightily?"

"If the reward is enticing enough, my sword will conquer any foe, madam." The words, spoken with a wealth of sensual meaning, made her belly tighten.

Fighting the unwanted desire hurtling through her, she said nonchalantly, "I say it takes a man of strength and skill to manipulate his sword well enough to conquer an unwilling foe."

Everyone laughed. Before Colin could retort, the steward stepped into the room to announce it was time to go in to supper. The rest of the company paired off, chattering as they headed into the dining room, which adjoined the ballroom. Colin still had Annabelle trapped with his fingers in her laces.

He leaned close to whisper, "Is it my strength you doubt, madam, or the extent of your willingness?"

Her gaze shot to his. His eyes sparkled with mischief, and his slow, seductive grin made her blood run in frenzied circles through her body.

"I know quite well the extent of my willingness," she retorted, wishing fervently it were true. "As for your strength . . . well . . . I'm certain you can unsheathe your sword, Lord Hampden, but I don't know if you have stamina enough to conquer your most unwilling foe."

They were alone in the room now. She reached back to pry his fingers loose from her laces, but he loosened them himself only to catch her hand in his, lifting it to his lips for a brief kiss.

"Ah, then I must coax my foe into surrendering," he said in a low, vibrant voice.

Time stood still then. Dimly she heard the clink of silver and pewter in the next room. Dimly she realized she and Colin should be joining the others. She should pull her hand away, make some offhand comment, and go in to supper. Unfortunately, she felt incapable of doing anything but staring into his emerald eyes, dark with desire.

"H-how do you propose to . . . to coax your foe into surrendering?" she heard herself ask through a mouth gone dry.

With one eyebrow raised, he stroked her hand, running his thumb over her trembling fingers. His gaze pinned her. "In truth, I don't know, madam. I've tried gifts, but that didn't work. Have you a suggestion for how I should proceed?"

Trying to regain her role of witty actress, she shook her head with mock sorrow. "Alas, no. 'Twould seem that your foe would rather die than surrender."

"Or run from the battle like a coward."

Oh, he knew her well. Fixing him with a cold stare, she put scathing contempt into her voice. "Wasn't it Shakespeare who said, 'Discretion is the better part of valor'? I would merely be discreet in my choice of companions, my lord."

At the moment, she realized, running was absolutely essential to her sanity. It would no longer do to go in to supper, where she'd no doubt be seated beside Colin and be forced to battle her wayward desires throughout an entire meal.

No, she must leave completely and rush back to the safe haven of her lodgings. She tried to remove her hand from his, but he gripped it fast, refusing to let her move away.

"Why did you return my gift?" He said the words

nonchalantly, as if he didn't care what her answer might be. Nonetheless, the spark of interest in his eyes showed he was more than mildly curious.

She tossed her head, shifting her gaze away from his unsettling one. "I don't like small gems. You'll have to do better than that if you want to win my favors." Maybe *that* would put him off, if nothing else would.

He surprised her by chuckling. "I suspect you'd have rejected my gift even if it had been a diamond the size of a pear."

Faith, but the man was perceptive. She tried for a tone of bored sophistication. "Ah, but you won't know that for certain until you try, will you?"

"Why try when I know what the outcome will be, when the only thing of real value you wish from me is information?"

Her gaze snapped back to his. She stood there shaking. "Wh-what do you mean?"

"You want to know about your relatives, the Maynards, don't you?"

Her pulse quickening, she stared at his implacable features, trying to determine how much he'd guessed of her true purpose in coming to London. Had she been so transparent? Or had he found some other source of information about her? Like her real father, perhaps?

She forced her eyes to widen innocently, even as she tried to still the frantic fluttering of her heart in her breast. "What makes you say so?"

"Come, now, my secretive swan, don't be evasive." His easy grin didn't quite reach his eyes. "I'm vastly more experienced at hiding my purposes than you are. I don't know why you're so interested in the Maynards of London, but I promise to tell you all you wish to know."

Charity had told Annabelle before the play that she'd had little success in questioning Edward Maynard's servants. They'd been closemouthed and suspicious of an actress's maid. Yet here was Colin offering to tell her everything. Did that mean Edward Maynard was indeed her father? Did Colin know her father better than he said? And why was he so certain that knowledge of the Maynards would interest her?

The more she thought about it, the more alarmed she grew. She twisted her fan nervously in her hand. Colin, she reminded herself, had been an accomplished spy for the king, or so she'd gathered from the conversation tonight. Who knew what other people he might spy for?

He couldn't be trusted, that was certain. No matter what his intentions, she didn't think they were limited to making her his mistress. He might offer to give her information, but he would no doubt try to guess her secrets before he'd tell her anything of substance. If he did figure out what she was up to, he'd warn her father off. Then she'd never find out who her father was and never have the chance to wreak her vengeance.

And her mother's death would have been meaningless, a mere hollow cry in the wind.

That decided her. She must get rid of Colin once and for all. He'd gotten far too close, and she'd let him toy with her far too long.

Making a quick decision, she shouted as loudly as she could manage, "Sir John!"

The conversation in the next room stopped. A moment of silence passed during which she and Colin stood frozen, though his face showed a barely masked surprise.

Riverton appeared at her side. "What's going on? Why aren't the two of you coming in to supper?"

The only way to deal with these gallants was to wound their pride before their friends, she told herself. She set about to do it quite diligently. "This rude coxcomb is bothering me, Sir John. He is making indecent proposals and refuses to unhand me."

Fury shone in Colin's eyes and he dropped her hand as if he'd been burned. He cast her a look so contemptuous and hostile that she instantly wished she could take back her words. But she dared not. It was the only way to stop his pursuit.

The unspoken rule among actresses and rakes was that the rakes pursued and the actresses played coy. Never, never did they take it seriously. Never, never did they make their sparring publicly uncomfortable.

Riverton's embarrassment demonstrated that. Of course, Riverton didn't give a farthing for her reputation or her feelings. After all, actresses were considered little more than whores. If a gentleman insulted one, who would care?

Still, she was making a scene, and neither Colin nor Riverton would deal well with that. Good, she thought. The sooner she became unpopular with *their* circle, the better.

"Will you throw this insolent brute out, Riverton?" she persisted, playing the role of injured lady to the hilt, though she found the role more distasteful as she went on.

Riverton muttered a low curse. A few of those in the dining room had now come to stand in the doorway, watching curiously what was taking place. With a glance at them, he said placatingly, "Now, Annabelle, I'm sure Hampden didn't mean to—"

"So you will allow me to be insulted by an unmannerly bastard in your home, will you?" The word *bastard* made both men stiffen, but she went on relentlessly, "If you won't throw him out, then I shall leave."

Riverton's face grew flushed. He'd never throw Hampden out. That was what made the situation so galling for both men. One thing you didn't do to a gentleman was embarrass him before his friends.

She was taking a chance, for Riverton might call her a strumpet and tell her to leave if she couldn't handle the rakes. She didn't think he would, however—not with Charity there.

In any case, he was saved from making the decision. Colin swore under his breath, his implacable features thinly masking the wounded pride that glinted in his eyes. He seemed unaware of those staring from the next room, although she knew he wasn't.

He glanced at Riverton. "No need to throw me out. I find I have no stomach for supper all of a sudden. Good evening."

Whirling from her, he stalked from the room without another word or glance her way.

Her heart plummeted as she watched him leave, his spine rigid and his fists clenched. She'd succeeded at last in driving him away. He'd certainly never come near her again.

So why did she feel so wretched?

"You're a heartless woman, Annabelle," Riverton muttered beside her as the front door slammed in the hall. "Hampden's not like the others, you know, and doesn't deserve your sharp words. He'd show you more care than any man I know. You had no cause to spurn him before his friends like that."

His other guests, deprived of the spectacle, were drifting back into the dining room, leaving them alone.

"He'll recover," she managed to say through the odd lump of guilt forming in her throat.

"No doubt he will. He's used to treachery from actresses." He said the word *actresses* with such contempt that she cringed. "His mother was an actress, and the cruel creature gave him up to his father without so much as a protest."

Riverton's statement startled her. "But Lord Hampden . . . I mean . . . I thought he was—"

"A nobleman? He is. He's a nobleman's bastard who inherited the title because his father chose to recognize him. He's become powerful enough that most ignore his origins. Unless someone reminds them of it, that is."

Guilt ripped through her, cold as a knife blade. She hadn't known. . . . She'd never heard that about him. Dear heaven, and she'd called him a bastard before everyone, not meaning it at all the way he'd undoubtedly taken it. Oh, how she wished she could take those words back. She knew all too well what it was like to be mistreated for one's bastardy.

"You'll never snare a man as fine as that again, I assure you," Riverton added, heightening her chagrin. He fixed her with his condemning gaze. "Then again, maybe you truly do prefer strutting cocks like Somerset."

He turned toward the dining room and his other guests, then paused. "If so, then Hampden's better off without you. And you're a woman to be pitied."

In more ways than one, she thought, hating herself for what she'd done. Oh, yes, she'd stopped Hampden before he could destroy her. But she hadn't thought it would hurt so much to do it.

Chapter Nine

"Whilst we strive
To live most free, we're caught in our own toils."
—John Ford, *The Lover's Melancholy*, Act 1, Scene 3

Annabelle stood in the tiring-room alone, cursing as she struggled to remove her gown. Where in heaven was Charity? Act 3 was to begin any moment, and Annabelle had to change her costume.

This week, D'Avenant had given Annabelle her first major role, the one of Selina in *The Schoole of Compliments*. Though she'd been thrilled to have the role, she still hadn't gotten over her nervousness, even though it was her third night to play the part. She glanced ruefully at the shepherd's disguise she was ready to wear for the remainder of the play. At this rate, she'd never get it on.

"Dear heaven," she muttered as she tried again to reach the laces of her gown. "Somebody help me!" she shouted, loud enough, she hoped, to attract someone's attention.

"I've got it, I've got it," a voice called and Charity rushed in.

"Where have you been?" Annabelle bit out as Charity pulled the laces loose.

Ignoring the question, Charity said in a rush, "You'll never guess who's in the audience tonight!" Her face looked flushed and her eyes wide.

"Colin? I—I mean, Lord Hampden?"

Charity rolled her eyes. "That's not who I meant, but aye, he's here, though I'm surprised to see him after the miserable way you treated him at Sir John's. Lord Hampden told Sir John he wouldn't be coming back to this theater for a while, that you'd driven him to the King's Theater, where he could watch a more congenial woman flaunt her charms.''

They both knew of whom he spoke—Nell Gwyn, who had all the gallants captivated these days. Hiding the mixed emotions Charity's words evoked, Annabelle forced nonchalance into her tone. ''I suppose he changed his mind.''

''Yes, though I don't think you need worry about his bothering you,'' Charity quipped sarcastically as she yanked the gown over her mistress's head. ''He's sitting with a lady of quality.''

''Good.''

A shame she couldn't convince herself of her good fortune. Three days had passed since she'd called Colin a bastard to his face, and she still felt wretched. Riverton absolutely refused to talk to her, and though Charity, as always, stood by her mistress, Annabelle could detect a coolness where once there'd been warmth.

Still, it wasn't their behavior that disturbed her; it was the thought of what she'd said, of how she'd sent Colin away. Couldn't she have found a better way to be rid of him, one that wouldn't have shamed him? One that wouldn't have left her feeling like a horrible shrew?

''Anyway, 'tis not Lord Hampden I came to tell you of,'' Charity said. '' 'Tis His Majesty, Old Rowley himself.''

Annabelle stopped in the midst of pulling on the breeches of her shepherd's costume. ''What? The king? Here? Tonight?''

''Aye. Here tonight.''

''But the royal box was empty.''

Charity gave her a secretive smile. ''Aye, it was. He's what Moll Davies calls 'incognito.' ''

''You mean he's in disguise?''

''Moll says he likes to do that at times—put on common clothing and go about the town. She's seen him before, when he's come to watch her on the stage. Tonight she spotted him in one of the other boxes, sittin' with the Duke of York.''

Clutching Charity's hands, Annabelle whispered, ''Is she sure it's His Majesty she saw?''

A cynical smile briefly touched Charity's lips. ''If anyone's sure, it's our Moll. As many times as she's graced his bed, she ought to be familiar with his countenance.'' With malicious glee, Charity added, ''She's none too happy y're to dance tonight, especially in those tight breeches. Mrs. 'Put-on-Airs' tried to cozy up to Sir William to convince him she would do better in the part because of the dance, but of course, he's used to Moll's petty jealousies and he ignored her.''

Annabelle groaned at being reminded of her dance. A pity Moll hadn't succeeded in convincing Sir William. ''Sweet Mary, I wish you hadn't told me.'' Annabelle stared around the room in dazed amazement as Charity helped her put on the shepherd's smock and button it. ''Now I shall be nervous and become a laughingstock before the king himself.'' And Colin, she thought despairingly.

''You will not! Stop talkin' such nonsense. You'll dance and kick up yer pretty heels, and they'll all be mightily impressed.''

Although the thought of performing a dance before the king would have made anyone nervous, it didn't disturb Annabelle nearly as much as the prospect of dancing before Colin, of having him see her blunder. She'd been tense enough about the dance without being told Colin would witness it.

Don't brood on it so, she told herself as Charity put the finishing touches on her costume.

It was neither here nor there if Colin saw her dance. After all, he could hardly think worse of her. She couldn't take back the words she'd spoken at Riverton's, and shouldn't take them back in any case. It was better to leave matters as they were, to forget about Colin with his sly hints and acute perception.

Yet as she left the tiring-room, she couldn't stop thinking of him. Even after she took the stage, she found herself speaking every line differently, conscious of his presence somewhere in the theater. Performing for the king became an everyday occurrence next to the thought of performing for Colin. Because she knew he would appreciate the nuances of her role more than anyone else, she performed for him and him alone.

When it came time for her dance in the fifth act, she no longer thought of His Majesty, King of England, Scotland, and Wales, nor of his brother, the Duke of York, who sat disguised in the shadows. Instead, she pirouetted and swirled for Colin, for the man she could never have, the one whom she feared and the one whom she wanted.

She scarcely noticed that the gallants were cheering when the dance ended. Nor did she do more than drift through the last few moments of the play. All she could think of was what Colin would say about it . . . if he were speaking to her, that is.

Stop this, she admonished herself as she left the stage at the end of the last act. *Colin is the most dangerous man you could ever take up with, and you're better off without him.*

Ah, yes, she thought with a sigh, better off without his wit, his kindness, his kisses. Impatiently, she pushed that thought from her head. The last thing she needed was to think about Colin's kisses.

Sir William hurried along in the wings, pausing to compliment her profusely on her dancing before he shooed them all onto the stage to take their bows. The man Charity had pointed out to her as the king glanced down and smiled at her briefly before slipping out the doors with his companion, but she did little more than nod in return. She was too busy scanning the theater for Colin.

As they filed offstage, she caught sight of him in a far box, a beautiful woman with honey-blond hair at his side. He wasn't even looking at the stage, but was instead whispering something in the woman's ear, to which she responded with a laugh.

Annabelle fought down the ache in her belly. This was what she wanted, she reminded herself, to be rid of him. Nonetheless, her steps were heavy as she left the stage. Even the orange girl with her ready smile couldn't lighten Annabelle's steps as she approached the tiring-room.

A young man waited there, an envelope in his hand. She knew him. It was John Wilmot, Earl of Rochester, one of the most notorious blades in London, even at the age of twenty-one. She'd seen the fair-haired rake often backstage, lounging among the actresses. She started to go by, assuming he was waiting to see Moll Davies, whom he'd reputedly bedded. But when he caught sight of Annabelle, he strolled up and thrust the envelope at her, a typically mocking smile on his full, sensual lips.

Curious at who would have written her a note to be carried by so important a personage as Rochester, she opened the envelope. The seal at the top of the page stopped her cold.

Her face growing pale, she read the cordial message: "I enjoyed your dance tremendously. Would you give me the honor of supping with me at Whitehall this evening? I'll send a coach for you at nine. I do hope you'll come." It was merely signed "Charles," but she knew exactly who'd signed it.

She'd forgotten about Rochester standing there observing her with his heavy-lidded gaze until he asked with faint sarcasm, "What is your reply, madam?"

Charity had come out of the tiring-room. Stunned, Annabelle handed her the note. Charity read it, then exclaimed under her breath.

"I suppose I should give you time to compose yourself," Rochester remarked snidely, "but I must return a reply, although I'm sure I know what it will be."

"She'll be ready at nine," Charity answered as Annabelle continued to stand fixed. "You tell His Majesty she'll be waiting."

Rochester made a sketchy bow, then vanished back into the theater.

"Odsfish, His Majesty," Charity said in wonder beside Annabelle. "You know what this means, don't you? When His Majesty asks a woman to sup, he has only one intention, and that's to bed her."

Annabelle trembled as she faced Charity with horror in her expression. "Charity, I can't go! You know I can't go!"

"Whyever not? Dear heart, here's your chance to be His Majesty's latest mistress. Barbara Palmer is not much in favor with him these days, and we both know you'd be more apt to keep his attention than that snooty Moll Davies he tumbles."

Annabelle glanced furtively around, relieved when she saw that no one had witnessed the encounter between her and Rochester. She yanked Charity into an alcove.

"I don't want to be the king's mistress," she hissed. "Dear heaven, I didn't come to London to become the king's whore."

In frustration, Charity clasped her mistress's hands, squeezing them tightly. "Now, I know the thought of lying with the king might frighten you a bit. After all, you're a virgin, and rumor has it that Old Rowley is . . . well . . . rather large in his privates. But for pity's sake, madam, do you know how many women wish to lie with His Majesty?"

"And how many have already," Annabelle retorted in a tense whisper. "I can't do it, I tell you." She could hardly explain that after being touched intimately by Colin, she could never let another man touch her so, and certainly not bed her.

Nor had her other reasons for wanting to protect her virtue changed, reasons Charity might understand more. "Every time His Majesty beds a woman, she bears him a child. He's as fertile as a rabbit. I won't do it! It's all very fine for women like Barbara Palmer, whom he treats with almost as much respect as the queen herself. But from what I've heard, the actresses he beds are whores to him! 'Tis one thing to shame my father with my exploits, but 'tis another to bear a child in the doing of it! I won't bear a bastard and subject him or her to such humiliation. I won't!''

Charity looked at her askance. "All right, then, so what will you do? It isn't politic to refuse His Majesty. 'Tis not as if you can drug him with yer tea as y've done yer other gallants.''

Annabelle gazed distractedly about her. "That didn't always work anyway. Lord Hampden, for example, saw right through that ploy.'' She wrung her hands. " 'Tis a shame I'm not as wily as he. If he were here, he'd come up with some great stratagem to fool the king.''

Suddenly her eyes widened as she thought of Colin and the way he had rid himself of Somerset with ease. Colin was an expert at such maneuverings. If anyone could help her out of this mess, he could.

Of course, it would be galling to have to ask him for the help. If he didn't ignore her pleas outright, he'd listen to them with triumph in his face. She stiffened at the thought, but knew she'd have to swallow her pride and at least ask him for aid. Otherwise, she'd find herself deflowered by the king before morning.

"Charity, do you think Lord Hampden has left the theater yet?'' Annabelle asked.

"Fie, madam, there's no telling. The play has just ended, and there will be a crush of people at the front. He may still be here, he may not. Anyway, I don't see—''

Annabelle gathered her skirts and started to make her way through the wings. "I know Colin can help me. He's a friend of the king's. He'll know what to do.''

With one soft hand, Charity stayed her. "An' why should he help you? Y've spurned his gifts, spurned the man himself publicly. Not likely he'll do yer biddin' now.''

Wrenching away from Charity's arm, Annabelle muttered, "I have to try, don't I?'' She leveled a pleading gaze on the maid. "Don't you see? I—I can't lie with the king. 'Twould make me a wanton in more than just name.''

Charity's expression softened. "Aye, dear heart, I know. But if you go runnin' after his lordship, he'll take one look at you and run t'other way. Let me talk to him. I'll see if I can't convince him to help you."

A wave of relief flooded Annabelle. She hugged Charity fiercely. "Thank you, thank you! Please, Charity, do catch him and bring him back here!"

"Go now. Wait in the tirin'-room for me. If I'm not back in a few minutes, go on home and I'll meet you there, for I may have to track him down."

"We've got a few hours yet." With the play over, it was only about five o'clock. "Hurry, Charity, please hurry." She paused, then added in a quavering voice, "Tell his lordship . . . tell him I'll do anything . . . *anything* . . . not to 'sup' with the king."

Charity raised one eyebrow as she gave her a piercing stare. "I'll not be makin' promises you don't intend to keep. But I'll get his lordship back here, come what may."

Then she was gone, leaving Annabelle alone to realize she would indeed do anything to keep from supping with the king. Because, in truth, the only man she wanted to "sup" with was Lord Hampden.

" 'Sdeath, Mina, where is that damnable coach?" Colin exclaimed as he and the Countess of Falkham waited outside the theater. He scanned the road, but saw nothing but a sea of unfamiliar coaches. "I swear, Falkham ought to boot your coachman out the door the first chance he gets."

"Why?" Mina responded, an amused smile on her face. "Because he doesn't drive fast enough to suit you and because he doesn't appear in the twinkling of an eye when you want him?"

He softened his expression. "No. Because he keeps you waiting in the bad weather."

She slapped at his arm with her closed fan. "Hampden, you're the worst rogue I've ever seen. You've spent all night frowning and complaining and now you think to redeem yourself with one chivalrous statement. You should be ashamed of yourself. I'll tell Falkham you've lost all your wit.''

Falkham would laugh to hear that, for he was generally the one accused of being a grouch. But in truth, Colin *had* been a bear this evening, and it was all because of Annabelle, damn the woman. He'd vowed to avoid the Duke's Theater, no matter what Walcester asked of him. Then he'd foolishly allowed Mina to talk him into accompanying her to the play. Now he regretted it.

Involuntarily, he closed his eyes, seeing again the Silver Swan dancing gracefully in that alluring shepherd's costume, the tight breeches accentuating her fine hips and thighs. It had made him ache all over to watch it. It did no good to remind himself of what a sharp-tongued witch she was, of how heartless she'd been. Her soulful expression as she'd danced had reminded him of the other Annabelle he'd glimpsed, the frightened, wary one with skin of silk, the one who gave oranges to urchins. She'd tugged at his sympathies with each lowered glance, each sad smile.

Hell and furies, but he'd sunk far. He'd always said he'd never let a woman under his skin like this, and here he was brooding over a deceitful witch like Annabelle Maynard.

''She was very beautiful,'' Mina commented beside him.

Colin's eyes shot open, and he eyed Mina with suspicion. ''Who was very beautiful?''

''That actress. The one who danced.''

He groaned. ''I suppose Falkham's been telling you of my exploits again.''

''Of course. He tells me everything. Then when one of the gallants pointed out the Silver Swan, I had to take notice.'' A grin tugged at her lips. ''After all, 'tis not often I see you truly enamored of a woman, and especially not an actress.''

''I'm not enamored of her,'' he ground out, then

realized he sounded like a petulant schoolboy. "Trust me, the chit is even more sharp-tongued than you are and hates me besides."

"Oh, I don't think so. As the actors and actresses left the stage, I watched her. She cast you a look of such longing, I almost pitied her. I swear, if she'd seen the way you'd watched her throughout the play with that intent, hungry expression, she'd have raced through the theater to be at your side."

"You're seeing things, Mina, I assure you," he said irritably. Then he spotted the Falkham coach at the end of a long line and abruptly changed the subject. "Do you think Falkham will keep up his pretense of being sick once we return to your town house?"

She laughed low, not at all fooled by his blunt refusal to speak of Annabelle. But she humored him. "Oh, yes. He'd rather die than admit his mistake. I believe he truly thought that if he claimed to be deathly ill, I'd not go to the play. This is the third time he's tried to put me off. I was getting very tired of it."

"I'll admit Falkham isn't much interested in theater."

She slapped her fan into her palm a few times, her brow creasing in a frown. "Yes, but he doesn't want me to go unaccompanied either, which is silly, of course, but typical. He thought to outsmart me, but I've demonstrated that I can't be outsmarted. I'm so glad you agreed to take me, Hampden. He couldn't very well refuse to let me go when you'd so generously offered to accompany me, and he was . . . ill."

Colin smiled at the sarcastic way she spoke the word *ill.* "Yes, well, I'm sure he's cursing himself now."

She laughed. "Oh, yes. He might not be jealous of you, but he's surely pacing the floors at home, thinking that half the gallants in the theater are flirting with me."

Colin wisely kept his mouth shut. Falkham might be his good friend, but the man wasn't above being jealous even of Colin. Falkham was no doubt more than a bit mortified at the thought of his wife being out with a rake, even one whom he could trust. Of course, it served Falkham right for not taking Mina to the theater for one damnable night, while at the same time insisting she shouldn't go alone.

Then again, he mused, perhaps Falkham was wiser than Colin gave him credit for. The theater had become a gathering place for all the false creatures in London society, particularly the court, with its base gossip and petty intrigues. No man with a life of purpose would waste his time at the theater.

So what was Colin doing there? He'd thought he was fulfilling his purpose. He'd been repaying a debt to an old friend while keeping abreast of any intrigues that might be of use to him later. Now he wasn't so sure.

His experience with Annabelle had heightened his desire to find some more meaningful purpose in life than spying, than intrigue and gossip. Court machinations disgusted him increasingly every day.

The coach rumbled up then, putting an end to his ruminations, but before the coachman had even leapt from his perch, Colin heard his name called from behind. He turned to find Charity Woodfield headed his way, her pretty cheeks flushed.

"Lord Hampden," she repeated as she rushed up, all out of breath. She cast Mina a wary glance, then returned her attention to Colin. "I . . . I must speak with you."

Just what he needed—Annabelle Maynard trying to sink her claws into him again. "I'm afraid that's impossible. I'm leaving," he snapped.

"Please, milord. 'Twas not I but my mistress who insulted you. Give me a moment of yer time. Please."

A faint sigh escaped his lips. He felt Mina's eyes on him, shining with curiosity, but he didn't enlighten her.

"Yes, all right. What is it?"

Charity glanced at Mina.

"This is Lady Falkham, the wife of my dearest friend," he explained. "You can speak in front of her."

Charity gave a quick curtsy, then twisted her hands with uncharacteristic nervousness. "Begging your pardon, milord, but it's about . . . about my mistress."

He tensed. "Of course. What does your mistress want with me now that she's done her best to flay me publicly?"

Charity colored, but drew up her shoulders with a burst of pride. "She needs yer lordship's help with a private matter."

"Tell her to call Somerset. I'm sure he'd be willing to do her bidding."

He started to turn away, but Charity grabbed his arm. "Oh, please, milord, I know you have good cause to be angry with her after what she called you at Sir John's. But she thought she had no choice. In any case, she's full of shame for it. She truly is. And she needs yer help. Please. Come back to the tirin'-room with me for one moment and hear her out."

"If she's so desperate for my help, why didn't she come herself?" he bit out, hesitating despite himself.

"Because I told her not to. I feared you'd run away before she had a chance to speak."

He stiffened. "Your mistress may be a coward, but I'm not."

"That's true. So will you lower yourself to speak to her . . . if only for a moment?"

Charity's pleas affected him, despite his attempts to remain unaffected. No matter what Annabelle had said at Riverton's, she wasn't the kind of woman to toy with him. If she needed his aid so badly that she'd swallow her pride and send her maid to ask for it, then she must be desperate indeed. But damn the woman, what right had she to ask at all?

"Go on, Hampden," Mina said in a low voice beside him. "What can it hurt to speak to the poor woman?"

"Believe me, Mina, the Silver Swan is *not* a poor woman," he ground out. "She's quite capable of taking care of herself."

"Appearances can be deceiving. Go on. I'll wait here in the carriage. I'll be perfectly safe until you return."

Colin sighed. What a fool he was for these sweet-faced women. Hell and furies, he might as well go. If he didn't, he'd spend his nights worrying about what trouble she was in instead of damning her to hell as he had been. That could be far more dangerous to his peace of mind.

"All right, then," he growled. "But this had better be worth it."

Chapter Ten

"Errors, like straws, upon the surface flow;
He who would search for pearls must dive below."
—John Dryden, *All for Love*

Time passed far too slowly for Annabelle as she waited in the tiring-room alone. A few actors had come and gone, but no one was around now. They'd all left to pursue the evening's amusements.

It reminded her of the day she'd met Colin, when he'd kissed her so temptingly. She touched her fingers to her lips. Would he ever kiss her again? Dared she let him? And what if he insisted on more than a kiss?

Ah, but she had little choice now, she told herself. It was either him or the king, and at the moment, Colin seemed a far less dangerous choice. Perhaps, she thought idly, he'd help her out of the kindness of his heart.

A mirthless laugh escaped her lips. After the way she'd shamed him publicly, she'd be lucky if he helped her for a price.

Suddenly a knock sounded at the door. As Annabelle whirled toward it, Charity peeked around the edge, her eyes scanning the room. "I see no one's here. Good. I brought his lordship."

"Thank heaven," Annabelle breathed, then caught her breath again when Charity stepped aside to let Colin enter.

Never had he looked so handsome. His hair gilded his shoulders like a mantle of gold chain mail, and every muscle of his calves was outlined by his tight hose. She'd forgotten what a wonderfully attractive figure he cut.

If only his eyes weren't so terribly cold as his gaze fell on her, she thought.

"Leave us," he commanded Charity.

The maid did as he bid, leaving Annabelle alone with him.

"So, madam, what leads you to ask my help?" he said in cutting tones. "Do you need advice on your recipe for tea? Or perhaps you're short of funds and you'd like my ring back."

She forced the hurt down as best she could. "I know I deserve that. I had no right to call you a bastard there before God and everyone, but Colin, I didn't know you actually were— Or I would never have—"

"Spare me your tender pity. I've long accustomed myself to being a bastard. That's not what angered me. 'Twas merely the final straw in a long line of offenses, beginning with the tea you tried to force on me. But that's neither here nor there. Tell me what you want, so I can leave."

Wishing he weren't standing there with such implacable unconcern on his face, she nonetheless handed him the envelope Rochester had given her. Casting her a suspicious glance, he opened it and read the contents. For a brief moment, he went rigid.

Then his gaze swung back to hers, even colder than before. "What do you need me for? To help you decide what to wear?"

She winced as his words knifed through her. It took a tremendous effort to withstand the scorn in his face, but she faced him as bravely as she could manage. "I don't want to go, Colin. I—I can't go. Please, you have to get me out of it."

He looked startled for a moment; then interest flickered in his eyes. "You don't want to go? Why not? Half the actresses in London would give their eyeteeth to warm the king's bed, and you want to get out of it?"

She lowered her gaze to her hands, which twisted a

ribbon on her skirt with increasing agitation. "I—I
know it sounds unusual, but yes, I do."

"Why?"

The simple word struck terror into her. Now she'd
have to explain. Yet how could she without sounding
like a frightened virgin before her wedding night?
Which, in a sense, she was.

Instead she told him another thing entirely. "I don't
want to be involved in these court intrigues. They
worry me. I don't understand all the machinations,
and I—"

"Don't be absurd, Annabelle. He wants a quick
tumble, not a woman spy. He doesn't give a fig for
your behavior in court. Unless he makes you his mistress, which isn't likely at the moment, he'll have his
way with you, send you off with a piece of jewelry or
some gold, and not trouble you for anything else."

She flinched from his description of what sounded
suspiciously like the transaction between a whore and
her customer. Nonetheless, Colin more than likely
spoke the truth.

Still, she couldn't give him her real reasons for hesitating, for then he would want to know it all. So she
tried another tack. "I don't think I could please His
Majesty."

His jaw tightened. "Well, then, I can't help you
with that. I draw the line at giving lessons on that sort
of thing when another man plans to benefit from
them."

Stung by the apparent calm with which he said it,
she bit out, "Devil take you, Colin, do you *want* me
to lie with His Majesty?"

With a curse, he shifted his gaze away from hers.
He clenched his hands into fists, crumpling the note
from the king. "No. In truth, I don't want you anywhere near Charles II. It's probably just my stung
pride, afraid to discover that he might succeed in melting your heart where I failed, but still, I don't want
you to go."

Ah, so then he did still feel something for her.

"Then help me. I know you can find a way out of this. I have but three hours or so to come up with a plan that will work. You've got to help me!"

His expression softened, and his gaze swung back to her. He stared at her a long moment, at the frightened heaving of her breasts and nervous twisting of the ribbon. "I wish you'd simply admit the real reason you don't want to 'sup' with His Majesty."

Her eyes widened. "Wh-what is that?"

"It's not that you're afraid you won't please him or you're wary of involving yourself in the court's political intrigues. It's because you're a virgin. And that's an explanation even I can understand."

Annabelle froze. "What do you mean?" She tried to draw on her acting skills, to become the coquette she was coming to loathe. Yet she couldn't quite manage it. "I'm not a virgin any more than you are," she protested weakly.

"We're not talking about me. And don't think you can play your 'wanton' role with me. It won't work." His eyes narrowed. "You smile like a virgin, you walk like a virgin . . . in every way, your innocence shows. It's a beacon to all the debauched rakes in London." His tone harshened. " 'Tis why they flock to you, wanting to wipe their grimy paws all over your sweet body. Our king apparently is no exception."

She fought to keep her composure, though she couldn't meet his eyes. With forced flippancy, she remarked, "You obviously pay no attention to the gossip whatsoever, or you'd know I'm rumored to be quite free with my favors."

For the first time since he'd entered the room, a ghost of a smile crossed Colin's lips. His green eyes glimmered, fathomless as the ocean they mirrored. "Indeed. For the love of God, you should have learned by now I'm not like the other witless fools at court. I'm the master of rumor and innuendo." His voice grew a bit sarcastic. "I honed my skills very well in France and Holland, and I can detect a false tale hidden beneath beds of roses. That one is certainly a false tale.''

"Why would anyone tell such false tales about me?'' she whispered, trying to hold on to the role as long as possible.

"Obviously, someone started the rumor for a good reason.'' He crossed his arms with nonchalance. "Someone like you, perhaps.'' Her startled expression elicited another smile from him. "Of course you started it. Why else would you be drugging gallants to maintain the facade? Or associating with fops like Somerset? As for why . . . well, that I don't know.''

Devil take the man for being so discerning! she thought. She attempted a bored, stiff tone. "You may believe what you wish about my virtue. My reasons are my reasons. I still don't wish to meet with His Majesty.'' She lifted her gaze. "Will you help me or no?''

She could see the indecision on his face, the terrible struggle between his pride and his sense of fairness. She held her breath.

At last he muttered an explosive curse. "I'll help you, damn my soul. I can't very well send a virgin off to be sacrificed to our regent god, can I?''

Her breath escaped in a whoosh. "Thank you, Colin.'' She wanted to rush to press a grateful kiss to his cheek, but knew it would annoy more than please him at the moment.

But he wasn't through yet. "Don't be so hasty in your thanks. My help comes with a price. You know that, don't you?''

She sucked in her breath, an unwarranted thrill coursing through her even as she cursed him inwardly for being such a rogue. "Anything you ask,'' she replied in a whisper, her pride making her incapable of saying more.

His eyes narrowed as her meaning became all too clear to him. He assessed her, allowing his gaze to linger over her body insolently before he searched her face once more. "I must admit your offer is tempting.

But I'm afraid I must refuse it. 'Tis not your damnable virtue I wish to exact from you.''

Surprise kept her speechless a moment. "Then . . . then what do you want?''

"The truth. If I'm to succeed in keeping you out of the king's lecherous clutches, then I expect you to tell me everything—why you pretend to be a wanton when you aren't one . . . why you came to London . . . and why my advances so frighten you.''

Hugging herself tightly, she turned from him. Then she said in a small voice, "I'd rather you take my virtue, my lord.''

She heard him chuckle. "No doubt you would. And perhaps I will have that too.''

She whirled to face him again, outrage on her face, but before she could speak, he continued, "However, I'll not take your virtue in any payment, dear lovely swan, or in gratitude for any service. I'll bribe you no more to win your passion. I've discovered 'tis only of value if freely given.''

The burning awareness deep in his eyes seared her, challenged her . . . and frightened her sorely. "You think I will give it to you?''

"We shall see, shan't we?'' With a rakish grin, he leaned casually back against the wall, then lifted one eyebrow. "So, dear Annabelle, do we have a bargain? My help for your secrets?''

She stepped to the window and stared out at the streets below, her lips pursed as she considered his proposal. She daren't tell him all, not until she knew where he stood. But perhaps she could tell him some things that would assuage his curiosity while keeping the most important of her secrets safe.

With a sigh, she acknowledged she had no choice in any case. "Aye, we have a bargain.''

"Good. Then I have a plan. But we must work quickly. My friend Lady Falkham awaits me in her carriage. I think I can persuade her to take us to your lodgings and help us with my plot to thwart the king.''

Through the window she could see a lone carriage

waiting at the end of the alley, though she couldn't make out its occupant. "Lady Falkham," she said, wanting to sound nonchalant, but sounding biting instead. "Is she the new woman in your life?"

Colin's low chuckle raised her ire. "Don't tell me that my coldhearted swan is jealous."

She tossed her head, still refusing to face him, afraid he would indeed read the jealousy in her face. "Nay. I merely thought it interesting that you waited so little time after relinquishing your pursuit of me before engaging in the pursuit of another."

Before she could even say more, he'd crossed the room to her side and, with a swiftness that took her off guard, had clamped his hands down on her shoulders, forcing her around to face him. "Listen to me well, my sharp-tongued beauty. Lady Falkham is the wife of my dearest friend, the Earl of Falkham, and I have never so much as touched her hand without her husband's express permission. She's a gracious lady who will most likely help you this evening, so I suggest you be civil to her. I won't have you scoring her with your cutting words."

The truth of what he spoke shone clear in his face, filling her with a quick shame. She glanced away from the fury in his eyes, hurt by the obvious respect he felt for this lady and the comparative contempt he held her in. "I'm sorry," she whispered. "I'll be more than courteous, I assure you."

He glared at her for a long moment. Then slowly the anger drained from him. As he continued to stand with his hands on her shoulders, a different expression replaced the anger, one of desire and the barest trace of yearning. It was the first time he'd touched her since she'd insulted him before his friends. Both of them were intensely aware of it.

After sliding his hand with sensuous meaning along her shoulder, he cupped her cheek. His fingers were cold iron against her flushed skin, but his eyes burned hotter than any smelting furnace. "You twist my heart when you stare at me that way. Did you know that? I only wish I knew what terrible storm lies beneath those wide, sad eyes.''

She swallowed. ''Sometimes 'tis better not to know these things.''

He probed her face, as if he could gain her secrets simply by devouring her with his eyes. At last he sighed and released her, turning toward the door. ''Perhaps,'' he muttered. ''Perhaps.''

Somehow she knew he didn't believe it.

To Annabelle's vast relief, Lady Falkham proved to be a woman of wit, with a soft heart and no apparent scruples about associating with an actress. During their short ride, Colin acquainted Lady Falkham with the problem facing them. Once they reached Annabelle's lodgings, Annabelle listened in silence as the others discussed Colin's plan for rescuing her, which involved making her appear to be ill.

''I'll use a balm of oxeye daisy to make her skin flush,'' Lady Falkham told Colin, her petite form a bundle of energy as she paced the floors of Annabelle's front room. ''Rubbed all over her body, the balm will simulate a fever nicely. If it's made properly, it won't hurt her.''

Colin's eyes narrowed. ''If it's made properly, Mina?''

Lady Falkham went on as if she hadn't heard him. ''It will warm her skin for a bit, but it won't last. And we can achieve a rather dramatic effect if we use an emetic to make her vomit—''

''No,'' Colin interrupted, with a glance at Annabelle, ''I don't think we should do anything that will be uncomfortable for her.''

''Won't be nearly as uncomfortable as beddin' the king would be,'' Charity put in.

Colin scowled in response.

''The discomfort doesn't bother me,'' Annabelle broke in, tired of hearing them discuss her as if she weren't there. ''I'd be willing to have a real ague if it would save me.''

Lady Falkham put one finger to her chin. "No need for a real one, but we can certainly have a pretend one. We can manufacture the fever and the vomiting. The rest—the coughing, the aches, the shaking—will simply be good acting." Lady Falkham smiled at Annabelle. "From what I saw at the theater, you'll have no problems with that."

Annabelle blushed at the compliment.

"Oh, no," Charity put in proudly. "My mistress can play a role to perfection when she wishes."

Colin's gaze locked with Annabelle's, and Annabelle knew he was thinking of the last time he'd been in her lodgings. "I can attest to that," he commented dryly. "Annabelle is one of the most accomplished actresses I know."

Squelching her urge to retort, Annabelle shifted her gaze from him to Lady Falkham. "I believe I can carry it off."

Lady Falkham stopped her pacing and lifted her chin. "Then it's settled. Annabelle will have an ague." She added, with a glance at Colin, "And we'll use the emetic. 'Tis the best way. After all, suppose it isn't some servant His Majesty sends? Annabelle told us 'twas Rochester who gave her the note. Who knows who'll come to carry her to Whitehall? It must be convincing."

"That's part of the reason I wanted you to help," Colin interjected. "You're well known among the nobility as a healer, so His Majesty is more likely to believe Annabelle is truly ill if he hears you're attending her. Remember, there must be no doubt left in the mind of the king's messenger that Annabelle is truly too ill to sup with him. If the king even hears a hint of this deception, he might find it amusing, but more likely he'll be insulted and have her discharged from the duke's company. I don't think she'd want that."

"Nay," Annabelle put in, "I could ill afford it."

His eyes met hers, mocking and distant. "True. Where else but in our wild theater could you find ready entertainment and a host of fops slobbering at your heels?''

When Annabelle drew herself up to give him an angry retort, Lady Falkham interrupted with, ''Pay Colin no mind, dear. He's become tedious these days, I'm afraid. He probably thinks men should be allowed to dance and sing and sow their seed freely, but women should sit prettily at home waiting for their poor drunken lords to show them some attention.''

''That's a lie, and you know it,'' he protested. ''Besides, when did you become so free-thinking, Mina? I don't see you allowing every gallant in London to follow you about.''

''Ah, but that's because I don't have a poor drunken fool for a husband. Garett is—'' she paused, a smile playing over her lips, ''a fine and faithful man.'' Annabelle immediately got the sense that Lady Falkham was understating rather than overstating the case. ''I assure you, if I ever found him sowing his seed anywhere but in *my* field, first I'd crush his plow, and then I'd not waste one moment in finding myself a string of gallants.''

''A ruthless woman,'' Colin said with a laugh. ''Well, if the time ever comes for you to seek interests farther afield, pigeon, do remember me.''

Lady Falkham rolled her eyes. ''Oh, of course. I could join the other fifty women who've tried to capture your heart.''

He scowled and cast a glance at Annabelle. ''It hasn't been so many,'' he muttered, rising from his chair and going to stand by the window.

It was Lady Falkham's turn to chuckle. ''Gossip has it to be a hundred. Be glad I've allowed for some exaggeration.''

Charity smothered a laugh, although Annabelle oddly enough had trouble smiling at Lady Falkham's jest.

''Well, that's neither here nor there,'' Colin growled. ''We should be discussing our plans to save

Annabelle from a rogue who truly has had a hundred women. Or more.''

Annabelle met Lady Falkham's gaze and the woman gave her a knowing smile. In that moment, Annabelle realized she liked Colin's friend a great deal, more than she'd expected. Anyone who could parry Colin's witty comments word for word drew her total admiration.

She did, however, envy Lady Falkham her easy friendship with Colin, the regard with which he held the countess even when she teased him mercilessly. Annabelle would have given everything to have him consider her in such high esteem. Alas, Lady Falkham was nobility—a countess, no less—and . . . and . . .

That wayward thought stopped her short. *I'm nobility,* she reminded herself.

Her mother had been a knight's daughter and her father a nobleman. Yet she no longer felt like a noblewoman or even a gentlewoman. The theater had broken down the class distinctions she'd once known so well and made her uncertain of who she actually was. Squire's stepdaughter? Earl's daughter? Actress? Wanton? They all seemed like so many roles, disguising a woman who was just Annabelle of Norwood.

Someday she hoped she could be simply Annabelle of Norwood again.

"Well?" Colin queried impatiently from the window. "If we're to succeed, we must work quickly. What are you three waiting for?"

Instantly Lady Falkham sprung into action. She sent Charity to the apothecary's for the oxeye daisy she needed for the balm and the black alder for the emetic. Meanwhile, Colin went in search of a boy to send a message to the Earl of Falkham about his wife's whereabouts.

He returned an hour later as Lady Falkham had finished mixing up the balm. Annabelle couldn't help noticing that he seemed more tense than before.

"I suppose Garett will be furious with me when I

arrive home,'' Lady Falkham commented when Colin entered.

''No doubt. But I'm sure you can sweeten his temper with one kiss, pigeon.'' Colin sat down at the table where Lady Falkham was working, although his eyes were on Annabelle, who was spooning soot out of the fire grate to use to blacken under her eyes. ''Where's Charity?''

''She's gone down to tell the landlady about how ill her mistress is feeling,'' Annabelle told him. ''It wouldn't do to have the woman give the lie to our tale.''

''Well, it's done,'' Lady Falkham announced, wiping her fingers on a rag. ''Are you ready, Annabelle, to have this ghastly mess rubbed in?''

Although Annabelle didn't relish the thought, she gave a quick nod. ''I suppose we'll have to put it all over.''

''Certainly anywhere that might be exposed when you leap out of bed to vomit. Your back, neck, legs, arms, upper chest . . .''

That got Colin's attention. A sudden grin crossed his face. ''Can I watch?''

''No, you may not!'' both women retorted hotly. Then Annabelle told him, ''You may sit here and behave yourself until it's done.''

Both women rose and went into her bedroom. Annabelle disrobed until she wore only her smock. A bit embarrassed, she slid quickly into bed.

Lady Falkham appeared to be embarrassed as well. ''If I could let you rub it on yourself, I would,'' she said softly, ''but in truth, I worry about the amount. Too much and I might blister your skin. Too little and there will be no effect. I feel more secure doing it myself.''

''It's all right.'' Annabelle managed a faint smile. ''In the theater, I've grown used to being seen half dressed.'' She admitted to herself, however, that she'd never been seen completely naked by anyone but Charity before.

To Lady Falkham's credit, she managed by moving the smock about carefully not to expose much of Annabelle's skin at a time. Her matter-of-fact chatter as she worked put Annabelle at ease. Then Lady Falkham had Annabelle turn onto her stomach.

Just as it occurred to Annabelle that she shouldn't let Lady Falkham see her back, the noblewoman drew down Annabelle's smock and gasped quite loudly.

Colin rushed in from the other room at the sound, and Annabelle twisted over onto her back, knowing exactly why Lady Falkham had gasped. Annabelle had long become so accustomed to the scars on her back from her stepfather's whippings, particularly from his final whipping, that she hadn't even thought to prepare Lady Falkham. One glance at the noblewoman's white face, and she could tell Lady Falkham had seen the scars.

"What is it?" Colin demanded, glancing from Annabelle to Lady Falkham. " 'Sdeath, Mina, you haven't hurt her with that concoction, have you?"

Annabelle's fearful gaze met Lady Falkham's, silently begging Lady Falkham not to speak. She didn't want Colin to know, or he'd ask a million infernal questions.

Lady Falkham apparently understood her wordless plea. A forced smile crossed her face. " 'Tis nothing. Get out, Hampden, so I can finish. I . . . I merely knocked my knee against the bed when I moved closer."

Colin watched them both a moment, then shrugged and left.

"Thank you," Annabelle whispered in as low a voice as she could manage.

Lady Falkham gave a terse nod, jerking her head toward the open door to remind Annabelle that Colin was listening. Annabelle could see the questions in the woman's gaze, but knew she could never answer them. Although Lady Falkham was undoubtedly a woman who could be trusted, Annabelle dared never take the chance. Lady Falkham was, after all, Colin's friend.

It took them only a few more minutes to prepare everything else. Colin banished himself to Lady Falkham's carriage across the street, planning to watch for the messenger from the relative secrecy of the carriage. Charity bustled about Annabelle's bedroom as she tried to make it appear more like a sickroom. Lady Falkham held the emetic ready to give Annabelle as soon as the messenger came.

Then they settled down to wait.

Chapter Eleven

"Age cannot wither her, nor custom stale
Her infinite variety; other women cloy
The appetites they feed, but she makes hungry
Where most she satisfies."
—William Shakespeare, *Antony and Cleopatra,*
   Act 2, Scene 2

Colin tried to center his thoughts elsewhere as he waited in the carriage, but all he could think about was Annabelle and their ruse. What if it didn't work? What if she either made a fool of herself and Mina or found herself bound for Whitehall despite it all?

If she made a fool of Mina before whomever the king sent, Falkham would never forgive him. Mina had enough problems with her reputation as it was, since people would always be suspicious of her abilities as a healer and her half-Gypsy blood. Colin didn't even want to think how Falkham might react to hear that his wife had been involved in some scandalous actress's scheme.

Then again, Mina was glad to do it, and what other choice had they had?

You could have refused to help Annabelle, he told himself. Yes. Then he'd have sentenced himself to the torment of imagining her in the arms of the king. Hell and furies, but that would have haunted his nights for certain. He didn't know why or how, but this one woman roused in him an unfamiliar possessive instinct. No doubt about it, the Silver Swan had bewitched him as no other woman had.

Then he thought of Annabelle's evasiveness when she'd asked his help, of the silent sadness in her eyes.

He thought of how his cutting words that afternoon had appeared to wound her. Most of all, he thought of her grateful smile when he'd agreed to help.

Thinking of that smile undid him completely. What else could he have done? he told himself. Who could have resisted an appeal as desperate as Annabelle's?

The sound of a carriage drawing up across the street interrupted his thoughts. He leaned closer to the window of Mina's carriage, pushing aside the velvet curtain a fraction. The coach that halted at the foot of the alley bore Rochester's livery.

Colin clenched his jaw, well aware of why Rochester had come. He watched with increasing trepidation, his heart hammering as Rochester climbed from the carriage and sauntered in.

Damn the man! Colin hated to think of Rochester going within two miles of Annabelle in her smock. Nonetheless, Colin should have expected the king to use someone like Rochester, for the young earl undoubtedly thought the whole thing a grand lark.

So Colin waited. And waited. And waited more, his pulse quickening by the moment. He could see Annabelle's window and the light on in her rooms, but that was all. After what seemed an ungodly long time, Rochester came out of the lodging house with a frown on his face, looking quite green.

He was alone.

Relief flooded Colin, so intense he marveled at it. He hadn't realized until now how fearful he'd been that they wouldn't pull it off. Impatient to know what had happened, it was all he could do to wait until Rochester's coach had turned the corner. Then he leapt from Mina's carriage and strode back into Annabelle's lodging house.

He'd made it halfway up the stairs when he heard peals of laughter coming from Annabelle's room, followed by the buzzing of loud chatter. Damnable women! Didn't they have enough sense to keep up the pretense until they were certain Rochester wasn't returning? They should have delayed their celebration a few moments longer, he told himself testily.

Determined to pay them a lesson, he took the remaining steps two at a time, then rapped on the door with imperious insistence. Everything went silent.

Charity's voice asked, "Who is it?"

In his best approximation of Rochester's bored tones, he said, "Lord Rochester."

"One moment, milord," Charity called out.

He could hear them scurrying about inside. Then the door swung open and Charity faced him. Mina stood behind her with her face flushed, and Annabelle was nowhere to be seen.

Charity's expression was almost comical in its relief when she saw who was really standing there. Then her brow lowered and her eyes shot sparks.

Before Charity could even say a word, Mina said, "For shame, Hampden! Scaring us like that! You're no gentleman, that's certain, to play such a trick on us."

He entered and shut the door behind him, regarding them both sternly. "I could hear you hens cackling all the way down the stairs. 'Sdeath, didn't you realize Rochester could come back? He could have decided to return for . . . for—"

"For what?" Annabelle's voice came from the door to her bedchamber. She still wore only her smock and although her face was flushed, he thought her the loveliest woman he'd ever seen. Only Annabelle could fake an illness and come out of it looking ravishing.

The thought that Rochester might have noticed any of it made him tense. "For another look at you in your smock," he grumbled before he could stop himself.

Annabelle and Mina glanced at each other, then burst into laughter.

"Me in my smock?" Annabelle said between gasps. "I don't think he was noticing my smock. He was too busy recoiling from my vomiting."

"Oh, I assure you, Hampden, he hadn't a thought in his head about Annabelle's attire," Mina interjected, her face bright with humor. "You should have seen this pair. Annabelle moaned like a woman on the threshold of death. Then when she emptied the contents of her stomach in the chamber pot, Charity set up a pretend wailing for her poor mistress that would have awakened the dead."

" 'Tweren't all pretend, milady," Charity said with widened eyes. "I tell you, I never saw anyone toss up her supper so violently in my life."

Annabelle grinned, infected by Mina's exuberance at their success. "I'll admit some of that was exaggerated. But not all of it. That wretched emetic worked amazingly well. Rochester couldn't wait to get out of here and away from the smell."

Mina twirled around in her excitement. "Everything turned out splendidly, didn't it? Hampden, it was delightful fun—for me, at any rate. I only wish you could have seen it."

Colin shook his head in exasperation. Obviously, he wouldn't put a damper on their spirits with his worries. They were quite pleased with themselves.

"I had to force Rochester to put his hand on Annabelle's head to feel her 'fever,' " Mina was saying. "He wanted to bolt the moment she swung her head over the side of the bed. But we kept him here a bit longer, lamenting the sad and sudden illness of our dear Annabelle." Her eyes twinkled. "All the while, he edged toward the door. I swear, it'll be a long time before Lord Rochester agrees to play messenger for His Majesty again."

At Mina's mention of the king, Annabelle's smile faded. She went to sit at the table, her brow knitting in thought. "Aye, I doubt Lord Rochester will return." She stared up at Colin, worry in her face. "Still, the king can always send someone else, can't he? I don't think we could manage this ruse twice."

Colin's temper rose at the thought that His Majesty could do the same thing again tomorrow. "We won't have to. I'll make sure of that."

All three women looked at him quizzically.

"How can you manage that?" Annabelle asked.

He tucked his thumbs in the sash hanging low on his hips and tried to convey a confidence he didn't feel. In truth, he wasn't sure how to protect Annabelle from His Majesty's advances in the future. But he had a few ideas, which would require Annabelle's approval and cooperation. "We'll discuss that later," he said, directing his statement to Annabelle.

The seriousness in his voice seemed to affect them more than his worried admonitions had. A heavy silence descended on the room.

Colin's eyes met Annabelle's, and something passed between them. He could tell she knew it was time for her reckoning, time to tell him what he wished to know. He saw the hint of fear in her eyes, but forced himself to ignore it. He'd done as he'd promised to gain her secrets, and now he damnably well deserved to have them.

As if she could read both their minds, Charity announced, "I'm off, then, if none of you have further need of me. I have a supper engagement."

"Oh, yes," Annabelle said dryly, with a faint smile. "Do enjoy yourself."

Colin knew exactly whom Charity was meeting. He couldn't resist tormenting her. "Tell Sir John I said you deserve a reward for your service to your mistress this day."

Charity stopped short and fixed him with a haughty stare. "For all you know, milord, I'm meeting someone else. Another man, perhaps, or even a woman."

He merely chuckled. That was all the excuse she needed to hurry from the room, her face scarlet.

Mina was busy tidying up, although he noticed she kept watching him and Annabelle. Well, he'd put a stop to that. This was one discussion he intended to have without an audience. "I think it's time you go home, Mina. Falkham will be beside himself with worry by now, despite my note. The carriage is waiting at the end of the alley."

Mina stopped wiping the table with a rag, a speculative expression crossing her face. "You're not coming with me?"

"I'll walk you to the carriage, but I think you'll be safe once you're inside it." His eyes locked with Annabelle's. "Annabelle and I have some unfinished business to take care of."

Annabelle continued to meet his gaze steadily, although he noted that she lifted her hand to her throat self-consciously. She gave him the barest nod, as if to acknowledge that he'd earned his payment and she would give it to him.

Mina's gaze swung from him to Annabelle and back. She hesitated a moment, as if about to say something. Then she seemed to think better of it. "Let's go, then."

With a regal air, she walked to the door Charity had left standing open. Colin let her pass, then said to Annabelle in a low voice, "I'll be back in a moment."

Once again, she nodded tersely.

Then he and Mina walked out. They descended the stairs in silence, but as soon as they'd passed through the front door of Annabelle's lodgings into the night air, Mina stopped short in the alley and faced him, concern evident in her expression.

"You listen to me, Hampden. I don't care what Annabelle has done or said to you. She's not the kind of woman you think she is."

Her fiercely protective air irritated him. "How do you know what kind of woman I think she is?"

"You think she deserves your censure—I can tell by the way you treat her like a woman who can't be trusted." She tipped her chin up. "Perhaps she can't. I don't know."

"No, you don't."

She ignored his acid comment. "No matter what she's done, she deserves more consideration from you. That woman has a gentle manner and noble bearing, yet she has also suffered. I don't think you should make her suffer further."

Mina had obviously become attached to Annabelle. It would do him little good to try to convince her that Annabelle had a treacherous side. Still, it annoyed him that Mina should presume so much about his and Annabelle's relationship.

"When did you become so concerned about the private affairs of an actress?" he snapped.

"When I discovered that the actress was intelligent, witty, and interesting. Not at all like the other ordinary, barely educated women they pull out of the workhouses and throw into the theaters these days."

Her eyes were stormy as she glared at him with a familiar stubborn expression. Unable to meet it, he glanced away. "You're right about that. Annabelle is anything but ordinary."

"If you realize that, then I hope you admit she should be treated with care."

Stung by her lack of faith in him, he returned his gaze to her, his eyes glittering with barely suppressed anger. "Have I ever treated a woman otherwise?"

"Nay." She paused, placing a hand on his arm. "But I've never seen you react this strongly to any other woman. I suspect this one is capable of rousing your anger more than any."

'Sdeath, but the woman could read minds, he thought. "What lies between Annabelle and me is none of your business," he growled, unable to keep the harshness from his voice.

She didn't even flinch. "When you brought me here to help her, it became my business."

A muscle worked in his jaw. "Annabelle would find that amusing, I'm sure." He tried for a flippant tone, but managed only to sound bitter. "She considers herself quite self-sufficient and capable of fending off any unwanted attentions."

"She hasn't fended them all off successfully, I assure you."

Something in her expression raised a cold chill within him. "What do you mean?"

A sudden flush suffused her face. She glanced away,

concern marking lines in her pretty young brow. "I shouldn't tell you. She wouldn't have wanted me to."

"Has she told you something of her past?" he prodded, trying to keep the interest from his voice.

Shaking her head, she looked down at her hands. "I saw something."

He remembered the gasp Mina had given while she was spreading the balm on Annabelle's back. "What? Mina, tell me what you saw."

She raised eyes filled with pity to meet his gaze. "She . . . she has scars on her back from where someone whipped her . . . rather mercilessly, I suspect. Some of the marks were recent, but some were faint, probably done when she was a good deal younger." She tightened her hand on his arm, her voice earnest. "Someone has mistreated that poor woman from the time she was merely a girl. Remember that when you . . . you take care of your 'unfinished business.' "

The bile rose in his throat at the thought of Annabelle being whipped. He stared at Mina in numb disbelief, his hands forming fists at his sides as dark rage surged through him. "Hell and furies, Mina! What black devil would . . . could do such a wretched thing?"

"I don't know." Mina shuddered. "We didn't discuss it. But I think she wishes you not to know, so don't tell her I told you."

He thought of Annabelle's defensiveness, of the way she shied from him sometimes. It was a wonder she allowed anyone close to her at all. To think that she'd held such a terrible secret inside her all this time, holding the hurt to herself and never daring to trust another with it. It made him want to murder whoever had abused her so foully.

He must find out who'd hurt her and why, so he could exact justice upon the person. Yet he dared not ask her about it right now if he wanted answers to his other questions. Still, it tore at him to think of what she'd gone through. It sickened him to the core.

"One more thing," Mina said, jerking him from his unpleasant thoughts. "She may react later to the balm or to the other herbs. If she does, she'll have trouble sleeping.''

He scowled. "I thought your balm was supposed to be harmless.''

"It is, it is. But if . . . it should happen to cause her problems later . . .'' She pressed a pouch into his hand. "Here's a powder to help her sleep. Tell her to use it if she should feel uncomfortable. All right?''

Still frowning, he tucked the pouch under his sash. How ironic that Mina should offer Annabelle, of all people, a sleeping potion.

Mina's hand still lay on his arm. Apparently she wasn't finished with him yet. He raised one eyebrow, and she colored, then glanced away.

"You'll be . . . gentle with her, won't you, Hampden?'' Her hazel eyes glimmered with sympathy for a woman she'd just met.

Her concern touched him. Obviously, Mina had made some definite assumptions about what he planned to do to Annabelle. Coming from any other noblewoman, her bluntness would have shocked him, but he'd long ago come to admire Mina for her straightforwardness.

"Don't worry.'' He laid his hand over hers. " 'Tis not my intent to hurt or force her. I merely wish some questions answered.''

She searched his face, then smiled, apparently satisfied. "I've always thought you a good man. Now I know it.''

As they walked on to the carriage, he held her words close in his heart, hoping she wasn't mistaken. After all, good men didn't spy on young women with tragic pasts unless they were prepared to take responsibility for dealing with what they learned.

He was beginning to think that in Annabelle's case, that might be a large responsibility indeed.

Chapter Twelve

"For one heat, all know, doth drive out another,
One passion doth expel another still."
—George Chapman, *Monsieur D'Olive*, Act 5, Scene 1

Annabelle waited in her rooms, with clammy hands and pounding heart. She tried to take her mind off the coming ordeal by removing the remaining traces of balm on her skin. Then she donned her only mantua, a silk wrap that well covered her smock once she tied it tightly with a sash.

Feeling better prepared, she tidied the room, opening the windows wide to the chilly air. Yet when she heard Colin's footsteps on the stairs as he returned, she found herself far more tense than she'd been while awaiting the king's messenger.

Colin walked in without knocking, as if he belonged there. She didn't turn from her spot at the window. She heard him shut the door, but she merely went on to open another window.

Aware of the silence behind her, she tried to make light conversation. "I decided to open the windows to get rid of this ghastly smell. It'll be some time before my poor rooms are back to normal. And my body, too, I suspect. I thought I'd never get the bad taste out of my mouth. Fortunately, I still have an orange left in my cloak pocket."

"How are you feeling? Do you itch or anything? Is your stomach still roiling?"

The concern evident in his voice touched her. She faced him with a wan smile, which faded a bit when she noticed he'd removed his coat and sash and slung them over one of her chairs. She tried not to notice how handsome he looked in his sleeveless vest and white shirt. And how dangerous.

"No, my skin is still a bit flushed, but I've removed most of the balm, so it should return to normal in a short while. My stomach has finally settled as well." Then she couldn't resist adding, with a burst of defiance, "I'm quite capable of withstanding your inquisition now, my lord, if that's what you're asking."

Not even a raised eyebrow betrayed his thoughts. He simply continued to regard her with an odd, almost palpable curiosity. " 'Tis not an inquisition, Annabelle. I don't think it's unreasonable to want to know why we've just gone through an elaborate scenario that risked the reputation of my best friend's wife and caused you no little discomfort."

His words reminded her how much Lady Falkham had chanced by involving herself with the affairs of an actress. A sudden stab of guilt made Annabelle drop her eyes from his. "You're not being unreasonable. Nay, not unreasonable at all."

"Then let's begin with the most obvious question. Do you want me to continue to protect you from the king's advances?"

Something in the way he surveyed her, as if she were a prize to be won, made her pull the edges of her wrap more closely over her chest.

Did he wish to protect her? she wondered. If so, what would it entail? "If . . . you can find a way to protect me that I can accept . . . I'd welcome your aid."

He rubbed his chin as his gaze trailed over her. "All right." Settling his hips against the table, he crossed his arms over his chest. "If I'm to help you, I must know the reasons for your reticence. Why do you fear lying with the king? The truth, Annabelle."

Ah, so that's how the questioning is to begin, she thought. A tight smile crossed her face. "I thought you'd already answered that. I'm a virgin, remember? Or so you claim.''

His eyes flashed. ''Yes. But even a virgin actress would lie with the king. 'Tis every actress's aim to bed His Majesty, in hopes that she may gain his affections and perhaps even bear him a child.''

Even as she recognized the truth of his words, she recoiled from them. She turned her back to him, rubbing her hands over her thinly clad arms, which were chilled from the night air wafting in through the open windows. '' 'Tis not my aim,'' she said softly.

She could hear him leave his perch on the edge of the table and move closer. ''Why not?'' His voice, steely and exasperated, probed deep into her thoughts. ''That's what I keep asking myself. Why not lie with the king?''

Hugging her body close, she shook her head wordlessly. How could she tell him the truth? How could she tell him what it was like to be beaten for having been a bastard daughter, to have one's entire life filled with torment because of one man's insanity? How could she tell him without also revealing that her past was what made her seek revenge against her father, who might be Colin's friend?

Yet she'd promised to tell him something, and he had indeed fulfilled his part of the bargain.

As she hesitated, uncertain what to do, he spoke again, his voice sharper this time. ''If you're worried about the pain, you shouldn't be. Once you've made His Majesty aware of your innocence, he will be more than gentle with you.''

The faintest hint of contempt in his voice made her stiffen. She whirled around, her eyes bleak as she blurted out, ''Aye, and then I'll be bearing his bastard nine months hence, won't I, like all the other women he's bedded.'' Then she realized what she'd said, and how he would take it. In horror, she clapped her hand over her mouth, wishing she could take back the words.

He went very still, his eyes hard. She could tell he

remembered the last time she'd spoken of bastards. "I see I misunderstood your reasons entirely."

"Yes . . . no . . . Oh, devil take it. . . . Colin, I'm a bastard myself. I don't know who my real father was, and I suffered . . . for being what I am. I won't do that to a child of mine. I won't!" She broke off with a sob, wheeling away from him to hide the tears that streamed freely down her cheeks.

As she stood there shaking, fighting violently the sobs that showed her weakness, she felt his hand on her shoulder. Next thing she knew, he'd encircled her waist with his other arm and had drawn her unyielding body up against him. Her back rested against his chest, her hips against his groin. She wanted to pull away, but after what she'd been through that day, it was all she could do not to turn to him, to let him comfort her.

He seemed to understand her struggle. With an infinite gentleness, he stroked the hair back from her face. "Hush, don't cry. Hush, now, hush."

He was so kind, so caring. Why was the one man she could consider losing her virtue to also the one man she feared she couldn't trust?

Yet she wanted to trust him so badly. Hardly thinking of what she did, she curved her damp cheek into his palm. "I'm sorry, Colin, for . . . for saying it so harshly. 'Tis something I've only come to know of late. It still affects me sorely."

"If anyone understands that, 'tis I." He nuzzled her hair, sending a thrill through her that she tried to squelch.

She twisted in his arms until she faced him. "Then you understand why I fear lying with the king . . . and . . . lying with any man. You're right. I'm a virgin. And like a virgin, I worry about the pain, the humiliation, and most of all, the possibility that I could find myself with child. You do sympathize with that, don't you, having been a bastard yourself?"

He nodded, then traced the line of her tears with the tip of one finger. "You know," he said after a moment, his finger moving to stroke her lips, "there are other ways of making sure one has no child."

Her stomach sank, for she thought she knew of what he spoke, and it hurt to think he'd suggest it. "Yes. There are herbs that will kill the unborn child. I know other actresses use them, but I . . . I just couldn't."

A faint smile played over his lips. "Nay. That's not what I meant. There's a way to prevent the conception from occurring . . . inside the womb."

She drew back from him to stare incredulously. "What do you mean?"

" 'Tis a device made of sheep's gut. His Majesty uses it to protect himself from disease, but I use it to keep from siring children. Like you, I have an aversion to bringing a bastard into this world."

Searching his face for signs of duplicity, she found only a hint of his humor at her naïveté. Without any scruples about the delicate nature of their subject, she asked, "But . . . but how can sheep's gut keep a man from siring a child?"

"The device is like a sheath, which the man puts over his member to contain his seed."

She blushed, but her curiosity wouldn't let her change the subject. "A—a sheath? Does it work?"

He shrugged. "For the most part."

Still a little skeptical, she asked, "Why haven't I heard of it among the actresses and gallants?"

He glanced away from her, suddenly looking extremely uncomfortable. "Many men don't know about it. I learned of it while I was . . . er . . . gathering information for the king in France." He paused, then added, "The men who do know don't like to use it. It limits their enjoyment."

It took only a second for his words to sink in. Then a slow-burning anger made her nod bitterly. "I should have known. Isn't that the way it is with everything? If something limits men's enjoyment, then they certainly don't tell women about it."

She left his side to pace the room in growing agitation. "Never mind that women suffer through uncomfortable pregnancies every day. Never mind that women die in childbirth, whether they want children or not." She whirled to face him. "If something limits the enjoyment of men, then by all means, keep it a secret, and let the women suffer."

He seemed stung by her sarcasm. "Yes, there are men like that, selfish, inconsiderate men. But not all of us are engaged in a conspiracy to make women miserable. After all, *I* told you about the device. Even if I didn't tell you in enough time to help you with the king, I did tell you about it."

The defensiveness in his words brought her up short. She gave him a considering look. For a moment, he actually appeared vulnerable, and it made her anger drain slowly away.

"Aye, you did tell me," she murmured. She thought of all the ways he'd given her the benefit of the doubt in the past few days. "You're certainly not like other men, Colin. I'll give you that."

With a curt nod, he acknowledged her thinly veiled apology. "I hope you're not going to use your new-found knowledge about this sheath to cut a wide swath through London's gallants."

She couldn't miss the bare hint of jealousy in his tone. "As if I could. Since this device must be worn by the man, I'd have a problem, don't you think? I can't see many of London's gallants 'limiting their enjoyment' by donning such protection, and certainly not for my sake."

That brought a grudging smile to his lips. "True. No man in his right mind would wish to limit his enjoyment of you."

Her mouth went dry at the blatant desire that suddenly flared in his face. She took a step away from him, aware that she skated on thin ice.

He stepped forward, refusing to allow her to put distance between them. "Why do you play the wanton with half the rakes in London, Annabelle, when you shy from me like a newborn colt? You said you'd tell me if I helped you. I held up my end of the bargain. Now I want the truth.''

Devil take the man! Couldn't she ever escape his questions? She forced herself to meet his eyes, searching for some half-truth that might pacify him. ''What else does a virgin do if she wishes to protect herself? You know what it's like for an actress on the stage. Only last week, Rebecca Marshall was violently assaulted because she dared to resist a nobleman's advances. And she received no help from any quarter.''

''Rebecca doesn't play the wanton. She *is* a wanton.''

She nodded. ''That's true, but it's not the point. She became a wanton because she had few other choices. The rakes make whores of the actresses, one way or the other, and delight in deflowering innocents most of all. The only way I could see to escape their advances was to pretend to be thoroughly scandalous with certain companions, whom I chose for their vanity and pliable natures. My ruse at least kept most of the gallants under my control.''

He appeared to consider her words. ''Most. But not all. Not the king . . . or me.''

''Indeed.'' Her eyes dropped to her hands. ''I didn't count on His Majesty's becoming enamored of me. Nor you either. Both of you seemed . . . seem quite intent on stripping me of my innocence.''

He stepped closer until he stood mere inches from her. ''If you're so intent on saving your innocence, then why are you an actress at all?''

She sucked in her breath, cursing him for being so astute. His questions circled nearer and nearer to the truth. Still, she thought she could answer him without giving away too much. ''My parents died recently, leaving me penniless. Charity had a friend here on the stage and suggested that we could at least earn a living here. So we came. After a time, I—I found that I enjoyed the work and was good at it, so I continued in it. The theater was a haven for me.''

''Until now,'' he remarked dryly.

She nodded. "Until now."

She started to draw back from him, but he clasped her waist, pulling her stiff body against his. "Why are you so afraid of me?" he whispered, his breath ruffling the curls at her temple. "Is it because you fear I'll give you a bastard child?"

No, she wanted to shout, *it's because you know my father and might tell him of my purpose.* But she couldn't say that.

"I don't want you to reveal my ruse to the other gallants," she whispered instead, her head lowered. "If they know what you know, I'll be hounded endlessly by them."

He shook his head, then slid his hand to cup her cheek. "You'll not be hounded again, I promise you that. Not after I make our liaison known. And I will make it known, as soon as I can. Because the only person who'll hound you in the future is me."

His voice was husky, cocksure . . . and incredibly tempting. Like a mating call, it drew her to raise her head and look at him. What a mistake that was. He smiled the way a tiger smiles before it pounces. Then he tipped her chin up and lowered his lips to hers.

She truly wanted to draw back. She didn't want the excitement building in her as his mouth covered hers. She didn't want her heart pounding in anticipation or her body straining against him when before it had strained away.

But somehow what she thought she wanted and what she actually did were two different things. She let him kiss her.

Oh, what a kiss. Firm, warm lips molded hers. Firm, warm hands pulled her closer until her body met his, soft thigh to hard thigh, soft belly to hard belly.

It began as a gentle coaxing, his lips caressing her closed ones, but when she continued to offer a token resistance, it became a blatant sparring of two strong wills. He sought to overcome, and she sought to keep part of herself separate, protected.

The trouble was, he was winning. His hands unknotted the sash that held her wrap, then slid inside the loosened robe to clasp her waist, with only the thin muslin of the smock separating his skin from hers. She gasped at the intimacy of it, giving him the opportunity to plunge his tongue deep into her mouth. As his tongue invaded her with long, sensuous strokes, one of his hands covered her muslin-covered breast and began to entice it with incredible touches and caresses.

It was too much pleasure all at once. With a low moan, she entwined her arms about his neck, kissing him back with all the fire that had long lain banked within her. A wondrous desire roused her blood, making her skin tingle all over with sweet urges.

As if he read her mind, he obliged her in her half-named desires. He rubbed her breast with the heel of his palm until it burned and ached for more. All the while his lips dropped feather kisses along her jawline to her throat, where he ran his tongue over the spot where her pulse beat.

Dear heaven, she shouldn't let him touch her like this, she thought as he thumbed her nipple into a hard, aching knot. She should take on some role to protect herself from the desire flooding her.

Yet no role fit her anymore—injured virgin . . . wanton actress. Truth was, she didn't want to play any role at the moment. She wanted to be Annabelle. And Colin seemed to be the only man who'd let her be Annabelle.

Tired of thinking about it anymore, she gave herself up to the delights he was offering with hands, lips, tongue. All she wanted was to touch him and be touched, to taste him and be tasted.

Her hands left his neck and slid down the front of him. He'd raised a craving in her to caress his bare skin the way he caressed hers. A pity that men wore so many unwieldy garments, she thought, trying with increasing frenzy to unfasten the long row of buttons on his vest, but succeeding only in undoing a few.

Seizing her mouth again with his, he brushed her

hands away and worked the buttons loose himself. Then she yanked at his vest, and he let her remove it, reciprocating by sliding her wrap from her shoulders until she stood only in her smock. Her fingers were already nimbly working loose his shirt buttons, which were far easier to manage than his vest buttons.

When at last she slid her hands over his bare chest, marveling at the hard expanse of skin over iron-strong muscle and sinew, he groaned.

"Hell and furies, dearling, you'll kill me yet," he muttered, and swept her into his arms. His face was a mask of suppressed emotion; his eyes gleamed as he strode toward her bedchamber with her in his arms.

She caught at his neck to keep from falling. "What are you doing?" she whispered, although she knew.

He glanced down at her, a strange smile curving his full, sensuous lips. "Taking you to bed. You've haunted my nights once too often. Time to put an end to both our miseries."

"But Colin—"

He stopped her mouth with a fierce kiss, though he barely slowed his steps. When at last he ended the kiss, they were in her bedchamber.

He laid her on the bed, then sat beside her and began to remove his boots.

Alarm skittered through her as she rose to kneel on the bed, dragging the crumpled counterpane up to her neck. "Colin, you mustn't do this," she said in a whisper, though she watched with frightened fascination when he dropped the second boot, then stood and unbuttoned his breeches.

His eyes locked with hers, wickedly taunting. "Why not?"

With quick movements, he slid off his breeches and then his drawers. Though his unbuttoned long shirt still clung to his shoulders, he was completely bare from the waist down. Her protests died in her throat as she heeded the demands of her curiosity and gazed at his chest. Her eyes followed the line of whorled hair that began there, then passed over a firm belly, and then ended at . . . at . . .

Annabelle couldn't help it. Not even conscious that she dropped the counterpane to her lap, she stared at him with blatant curiosity. It had been one thing to laugh and joke with the rakes about "staffs" and "swords" and "plows" and all the endless euphemisms they had for the male anatomy.

It was another thing entirely to see the much-discussed male part in the flesh. She ought to be shrieking and covering her face, but instead she couldn't stop gazing at it.

"You stare like a virgin amazed," he said with a rumbling chuckle. "I take it you not only have never been bedded, but you haven't even seen a man naked before."

She knew a man's member grew with his desire, but somehow she hadn't imagined this . . . this . . . "I've seen statues, that's all," she admitted in a voice hardly a whisper. "But on a statue, a man's . . . I mean, yours is so . . . so . . . big."

"You've roused it from its sleep," he murmured. His low, husky tone sent tremors of desire through her. He swept the counterpane aside, then knelt on the bed in front of her. "Would you like to touch it?"

With a groan, she jerked her gaze away. "Dear heaven, no!" Yet she had to admit that the thought of touching him there stirred a strange hunger in her.

That wayward thought jolted her out of her apparent lassitude. What in the name of heaven was she doing? She was kneeling on a bed with a naked man, for heaven's sake! Even worse, she was gawking at his private parts like a . . . like a true wanton.

Still, she told herself reluctantly, it was very fascinating.

"Are you sure you don't want to touch me?" His voice was teasing. "I can see curiosity burning in your face, Annabelle."

When she shook her head quickly, then attempted to slip from the bed, he caught her at the waist. He stroked the tumbled locks of her hair as she flamed with embarrassment.

" 'Tis nothing to be ashamed of. I'm equally curious to see what lies beneath your gown . . ." He lowered his head to kiss her cheek, then downward to her throat. "To touch your slender belly . . ." He undid the ties of her smock, then pushed one sleeve off her shoulder. "To taste the honey between your legs . . ."

Her shocked gaze flew to his. How did he know about the dampness she felt there?

But it was clear how he knew. She might be inexperienced. He was not.

"Aye, that too, my shy swan maiden," he said. "There are sensual delights awaiting us that you've never even thought about. And we have all night to relish them."

His words took her breath away. She watched, curious, terrified, as he slid her smock completely off her shoulders. The thin material dropped to her waist, baring her breasts to his gaze. As her eyes remained riveted on his face and his on hers, he put his finger in his mouth, then took the dampened fingertip and circled her nipple with it.

Sucking in her breath sharply, she stayed very still, afraid that if she moved, the delicious feeling would leave her. When he repeated the entire operation with her other breast, she sighed and closed her eyes, giving herself up to the piercing pleasure.

After a moment, during which he fondled her senseless, he took her hand and sucked the tip of one of her fingers. He lowered her wet finger until he'd placed it on something smooth and hard and long.

Her eyes shot open. He released her finger, but she didn't jerk it away. Fascinated, she slid it all along his shaft, marveling at the tight, silky skin. Half in a wondering daze, she wet her finger herself, then rubbed it over the tip. She looked at his face, taking a perverse delight in seeing his smiling, knowing expression slip.

Some vague instinct made her close her fingers around the firm length and pull gently. An explosive curse escaped his lips. He jerked her hand away, then pushed her back onto the pillow and covered her with his body.

Not sure why he'd reacted so violently, she whispered, "I-I'm sorry. Did I hurt you?"

"Not exactly." His mouth was beside her ear. He breathed hard and heavy a moment, his body lying still on top of her. Then his mouth closed over her ear, his tongue laving the inside. "But I do hurt with wanting you. 'Sdeath, dearling, you do things to me that no woman ever has."

She took a very feminine pleasure in hearing that. "Does that mean you like me to touch you?" She worked her hand between their bodies to stroke his muscled thigh, inching her hand closer to his shaft once more.

He groaned. "Yes, but right now if you touch me like that, this will be over before it's even begun." He raised his head to look into her face with eyes that glittered like emeralds. "It has begun, hasn't it?"

She knew what he meant. Her mind searched through all her reasons to keep herself pure, and only one made her hesitate. "Do you . . . do you have with you one of those sheaths you spoke of?"

Her question seemed to startle him. Then he dropped his head onto her shoulder, a sigh escaping his lips. "I should have known my honesty would come back to haunt me."

"Well?"

Shaking his head, he muttered, "Of course not. I don't carry them about with me everywhere I go. I'm not that much of a libertine."

"I see," she said in a small voice. She liked his heavy weight on top of her, and she couldn't deny that he'd made her want more of those wanton, extravagant delights his touch had hinted at. But she wouldn't risk having an illegitimate child. "Colin, I . . . I just can't—"

"All right, Annabelle," he gritted out with barely

disguised irritation. He pressed a kiss into her neck, then sighed again. "I won't force you."

They lay there quietly a moment, before he stirred and took her chin in his hand, turning her head toward him. The speculative gleam in his eyes gave her pause. "You may not know this, dearling, but men and women can pleasure each other in ways that won't result in conception."

She eyed him with suspicion. "Oh?"

He grinned as he trailed his hand down past her breasts and over her belly. Slipping her smock over her hips, he then tossed it to the floor. "Yes. Do you wish me to show you?"

Her breath caught in her throat as his eyes greedily drank in her naked form. "I—I don't know."

His hand roamed lower, then lower still until it slid between her legs to cover her mound. He rubbed there with his palm, and she gasped from the intense ache he both created and soothed at the same time.

"You like that, don't you?" he whispered with a cunning smile, eyes dark and mischievous.

One finger probed her silky folds, then darted into the slick, hot passage. A quick throb of delight shot through her, making her shiver deliciously.

"Don't you?" he prompted as he began to stroke, gently at first, then harder and faster.

"Oh, yes," she whispered. Her hands clutched his brawny shoulders. "Oh, sweet Mary, yes."

When Colin slid another finger inside her, she found that the sensation of tight invasion was actually quite enjoyable. In fact, she thought, as he continued to plunge his fingers deftly inside her, it was near to being perfect.

She threw her head back and closed her eyes, scarcely conscious that he'd moved his head from her shoulder, until his mouth closed over her breast.

Ah, such warmth, such . . . such strange, fierce sensations flooded her, barely quenching the feverish thirst he was raising in her. She drank in each delectable pleasure, marveling that he could make her feel this . . . this extraordinary bliss with only his lips and his fingers.

After a moment, his mouth left her breast. Without thinking, she threaded her fingers through his hair, meaning to pull him back, to have him do more of those wonderful things, but he was kissing his way down her belly to . . . to . . .

Her eyes flew open as his tongue darted out to join his fingers in their dancing forays inside her. "Colin," she whispered in rapt amazement as he flicked his tongue over one soft, fleshy petal. Her fingers gripped his glorious hair as she arched up against his mouth. "Oh, Colin!"

"That's it, my swan beauty," he lifted his face from her to murmur. "Let it take you where it will take you."

His tongue and his fingers were driving her mad, she realized as she dropped her hands from his hair to clutch the counterpane so she wouldn't tear his hair out. She writhed against him, wanting yet not wanting to escape that warm, taunting mouth.

As he continued to probe deeply with his fingers, to tease her with his tongue, her body strained toward some mysterious treasure that lay glittering, shimmering just behind her reach. As if he knew what she felt, he quickened the pace of his strokes until she thrashed mindlessly beneath him, wanting . . . reaching . . .

Then everything exploded into brilliant shards of diamonds, glittering with delights and pleasures she'd never known. She cried out, scarcely aware that she did so. She bucked against Colin, her body shaking with wave after wave of glorious enjoyment.

Slowly, she sank into the down mattress. Slowly, she became aware that Colin had stopped his sensuous torment and was resting his head on her belly.

She looked down at him. He wore a taut expression of passion suppressed, and his eyes stared off, remote, as if he fought a battle within himself. She gazed at him, feeling suddenly bereft. He seemed so pained, so apart from her.

Then she realized that though he'd given her bliss with his mouth and his hands, she had given him . . .

Nothing.

While he'd been pleasuring her, she'd been doing nothing to pleasure him. Suddenly she wanted to pleasure him. She wanted to make him feel the way she was feeling.

More than that . . . she wanted him to take her completely, totally. The thought struck her with painful force. She didn't care about her fears; she didn't care what might come tomorrow. The man who'd known how to bring her such wonderful fulfillment was the only man she'd ever want to make love to.

"Colin?" she whispered, laying her hand on his head, on his springy, lush hair. "Colin . . . I want you."

He lifted his head to stare at her with suspicion.

"I want you to . . . to make love to me."

"I just made love to you, dearling," he said softly, a half smile playing over his lips.

She shook her head. She hadn't counted on how utterly embarrassing it would be to make this admission. Her mouth dry, she said, "No, I don't mean like that. I don't care about the sheath. I want you to . . . to . . ." She faltered, unable to say more.

He looked startled at first. Then a dark, seductive gleam shone in his eyes. "To show you the full range of sensual delights?" He began to kiss his way up her body. "Is that it, Annabelle? Haven't I satisfied you enough tonight?"

When he tugged on her nipple with his teeth, she moaned deep in her throat. "Oh, dear heaven, yes . . . I mean . . . no . . . I . . . I . . ." Now he was rubbing his thick shaft over her thatch of hair, arousing her blood again.

"I like it when you're speechless, dearling," he murmured. "You know, if I take you now . . . unprotected, as it were . . . there's always the possibility—"

"Oh, hush," she whispered, arching up against his hardness, which was already beginning to make her feel hot and bothered all over again. "Please . . . Colin . . . please . . ."

"You need not ask twice," he whispered with a blazing smile before he slid between her legs and eased himself into her.

She gasped at the sudden tightness, the uncomfortable thickness pressing farther and farther within her. Unthinkingly, she pushed at his shoulders, now wondering if she'd made a mistake. He'd surely cleave her in twain if he continued.

"You're so tight, so very sweet and tight," he murmured. " 'Twill be uncomfortable at first, dearling. You must relax."

"How can I relax?" she hissed as he inched farther, pressing against some part of her inside. " 'Tis very u-unpleasant."

He stopped his movement, his face hard and drawn as he encountered the barrier of her innocence. Not even a flicker of surprise crossed his face. "Aye. But not for long."

Slipping his hand between their bodies, he found her secret places again and began to stroke the soft buds once more. Despite her awareness of his shaft inside her, she responded almost immediately to the liquid fire his manipulations sent pouring through her.

"Is that better?" he asked.

"Yes . . . oh, yes . . . oh, Colin . . ."

"Now I must hurt you," he warned again, "but 'tis best to get it over with quickly."

Then he plunged through her virginal barrier. Pain shot through her. She arched up, trying to buck him off, but his weight was too great for her, as was the strength with which he pulled her thrashing arms to her sides. He lay motionless within her a moment, allowing her to adjust. A tear escaped her eye, which he rubbed away with his lips.

"The bad part is over," he whispered as he nuzzled her cheek, her temple, her hair. "Now there is only delight for you, I promise."

At first, she didn't believe him, for his movements

as he stirred again inside her left her feeling invaded
and sore. Then gradually the soreness gave way to a
kind of heat, and the heat gave way to licking flames,
and the flames to a raging fire that threatened to con-
sume her in one great conflagration of joy.

"Hell and furies," he muttered as he thrust into her
with increasing rhythm, rocking her body in a dance
more sensual than any court minuet. "Hell and furies
. . . Annabelle . . . ah . . . Annabelle . . ."

Then he caught her face between his hands and
seared her with his kiss, plunging his tongue into her
mouth in ever-quickening strokes that mirrored the ca-
dence of his hips. Despite the slight discomfort, she
writhed beneath him, once again straining to reach
those mystical delights he dangled before her.

As he pounded into her, his mouth devouring hers
as his hardness invaded and plundered, any lingering
pain faded into sweet, sweet oblivion, and there was
nothing left but him and his thunderbolt strokes within
her.

Colin caught her up like a hawk carrying its prey
into rich blue skies, and she soared with him, wheeling into ever more lofty heights. As she dug her fingers
into his muscled shoulders and reveled in his glorious
strength, he transported her farther, faster, higher. . . .
His body carried her with lithe power into the bril-
liance of sunlit sky, into that private space where there
was only him, him and his gift of pleasure hurtling her
upward.

"Colin!" she cried out as she reached the golden
peak where all thought was driven from her mind.
"Oh, Colin!"

He gave one mighty thrust, then spent himself inside her with a roaring cry of his own.

It was some minutes before either of them could
move or speak. Their bodies shook together, their
hearts raced equally fast, and their breathing was
quick.

After a moment, he rolled off to lie on his side next
to her, throwing one arm across her belly. Propping

himself up on one hand, he lazily stroked her skin, then spread her hair down over her chest until it fanned over her breasts, tickling them.

She sighed in contentment, and he leaned over to kiss her shoulder. "When I first saw you at the Duke's Theater, I was told you were haughty and cold onstage, but fire itself in bed. Now I see that even unfounded rumors can have truth in them."

She turned her flaming face into the pillow.

"Annabelle," she heard him whisper.

"Yes."

"You're mine. You have no need to keep up this silly pretense of wantonness with the other gallants now that you're under my protection."

No, she thought sadly, she truly didn't. So what was to become of her vengeance? Was she to become Colin's mistress and abandon all her plans?

"There will be no other gallants now. Agreed?" he said, more sternly.

The possessive tone in his voice worried her, even while it thrilled her. He was sure of her already, wasn't he? she thought. Wanting to prick that assurance, she said, "How can you be so certain, my lord? I mean, now that you've shown me how wonderful it is to lie with a man, I may wish to experiment—"

He cursed, then turned her to face him. His expression softened when he saw the uncertainty in her eyes. She didn't know where to go from here, and he seemed to realize that.

But it didn't change his purpose any. "I'll castrate any man who tries to bed you, Annabelle," he vowed. "That's how I can be certain you'll stay faithful to me."

"Even the king?" she said with a raised eyebrow.

He nodded. "Even the king, damn his soul to hell." He lowered his mouth to hers, then stopped an inch away, his breath hot and heavy against her trembling, waiting lips, already parting to receive his kiss. "Promise me there will be no others, Annabelle. Promise me."

It was hard to think when his hands had begun stroking her in the most intimate places.

"Promise me," he whispered, then ran the tip of his tongue along her full lower lip, enticing her. His fingers were filling her below once more, stroking her until she scarcely knew where she was.

"I promise," she whispered, a renewed ache for him making her willing to promise almost anything.

Then with a growl of triumph he made sure he wiped all thoughts of other gallants quite out of her mind.

Chapter Thirteen

"No mask like open truth to cover lies,
As to go naked is the best disguise."
—William Congreve, *Love for Love*, Act 5, Scene 4

Colin and Annabelle lay spoon fashion on her bed after their second tempestuous bout of lovemaking. Beneath the heavy counterpane that covered them, Colin ran his hand over the smooth curves of her waist, down her hips to her thighs, then back again.

He felt languid and satisfied and oddly content. Never had he found such absolute enjoyment with any other woman. Riverton would have said it was because Annabelle was an innocent, but Colin knew better. If anything, a virgin should have given him less pleasure than a more experienced woman.

Nor was there any doubt that Annabelle had been a virgin. Her blood stained the sheets that lay crumpled beneath their bodies. He'd claimed all along she was pure, and it pleased him absurdly to know he'd been right, to know that only he had entered the fortress of her disguises.

At last he'd uncloaked her to find a woman who was neither aloof nor indiscriminate with her favors, but open, giving, and thoroughly, beautifully enchanting.

He couldn't stop touching her. Anyway, why should he? She was his now. She'd promised to be his, and he'd make her keep that promise. Though he doubted it would be so very hard. He pressed a kiss to her barely exposed shoulder, relishing the way her body leapt to life. Ah, yes, he had her now. He'd caught the elusive swan.

"Mmm," she purred as he continued to drop warm kisses along the curve of bone leading to her neck.

He drew the counterpane down and pushed her heavy mass of hair aside, intending to kiss her neck. That was when he saw them—the marks Mina had spoken of, long lines of white crisscrossing her upper back, a few of them apparently done in the last year or so. His breath stilled as he closed his eyes, his stomach lurching. Mina hadn't been wrong. They were certainly the marks of a whip or perhaps a crop.

He tried not to think of what they'd looked like when they were fresh, but he couldn't help it. Rage against whoever had hurt her sparked quickly in him like a brushfire. Grimly he traced one of the marks.

Annabelle stiffened beneath his touch, then tried to pull the counterpane up over her back.

He stayed her hand, barely able to control his anger enough to speak. "Who did this to you? For the love of God, who beat you so cruelly?"

A tremor shook her. She remained quiet a long time. He propped himself on his elbow to peer over her shoulder at her face, noting that her eyes were sad as she stared off across the room.

"I want to know who, Annabelle," he murmured, drawing her more closely against his body. "Tell me who so I can find and murder the wretch."

A bitter smile crossed her face. "You can't. He's dead."

"He?" He hesitated, his mind racing. "It couldn't be a husband, for I know as well as anyone you were chaste until tonight. An employer, perhaps? The master of a house where you were servant?"

"None of those." She sighed. "My stepfather. I— I told you I recently learned I was a bastard. Well, I didn't know it when I was younger, but my stepfather did. Apparently, my—my mother married him when she found herself with child by another man."

"And he punished you for it," Colin bit out, his hand forming a fist where it rested on her back.

She nodded. "He punished my mother too, until I grew old enough to take her punishments for her. I suppose he couldn't stand the thought of having a child not his own. He was a . . . a very proud man."

"No," he exploded, "he was a cruel man to use you thus."

Twisting her body so she faced him, she gave him an odd, searching glance. "Some men would say he had every right to beat me." Her tone contained all the hurt in the world. "He raised me as his daughter. It was his duty to discipline me."

He trailed his finger over her cheek and knew she asked a question of him. "Discipline doesn't require cruelty or even physical violence. He had a right, a duty to discipline you as a father would. But his cruelty served no purpose but to make you distrust men."

Her eyes filled with tears, and a low cry escaped her lips as she turned to hide her face against the pillow. With a shudder, she drew the counterpane over her scars. He let her.

"It doesn't matter now," she choked out. "He's dead. The past is past."

No, he thought. The past wasn't at all past for her, for she still didn't quite trust him. He sensed it instinctively. But how to make her trust him when she'd suffered so at the hands of men? No wonder she'd been so vehement about her bastardy, about the way men used women. He slid his arms around her, feeling helpless to make her see that all men weren't alike, that she didn't have to face everything alone.

Apparently she'd spent many years facing the world alone. Hell and furies, what kind of mother would let her daughter suffer so at the hands of a brute? Ah, but that was easy to answer. He knew only too well about mothers who cared little for their children. He thought bitterly of his own mother, who'd allowed him to be wrenched away from her by the wild-eyed lord who was his father. His mother had remained unaffected by

Colin's humiliating sobs. He'd already been a nuisance to her, she'd told him. They'd both be much better off if he went peaceably to England with his father.

Now that Colin looked back on it, he realized his mother had been right to let him go. His father, a dashing, hotheaded man who'd been prone to fighting duels and provoking Cromwell's men whenever possible, had nonetheless taught Colin a great deal about honor and family. He'd claimed Colin as his legitimate heir and done his best to provide his son with a decent education. Perhaps the old marquis had only done so because he needed an heir, but Colin didn't think so.

Years later, when Colin had fled into exile with Charles II, his father having been killed in the civil war, Colin had searched for his mother. Any illusions he'd harbored about her character had been finally destroyed when, at the age of sixteen, he'd found her in a respectable old chalet in the country, the kept mistress of an ancient *duc*. Her prettiness still intact, though now become more brittle, she'd accused him of wanting money from her and had tossed him into the streets.

Yes, Colin's father had proven to be a godsend. But where had Annabelle's own father been while she was being mistreated? If Colin's father had ever thought Colin's mother was beating him so, he'd have laid claim to Colin sooner than he had.

"What of your real father?" he couldn't help asking. "Did he know about this?"

She hesitated. "N-no, no, he didn't, at least I don't think he did." She trembled ever so slightly. "I didn't know my real father."

The faint wariness in her voice gave him pause. With narrowed eyes, he began to sort through the things she'd told him before. Her surname was Maynard. Her stepfather's name? If so, then why had she expressed so much interest in the Maynards of London? Had she thought her dead stepfather might have relatives in London to whom she could turn? Or was it another relative entirely she sought?

And why did she go by the nickname the Silver Swan? It couldn't be mere coincidence that it was the same as Walcester's code name. Colin had learned long ago to regard suspiciously anything that masqueraded as chance.

Gently he pressed her shoulder down until she lay beneath him. Her eyes widened as she stared up into his face.

"Was your stepfather's name Maynard?" he asked softly.

A hint of fear leapt into her eyes. "Why do you ask?"

"You've been very interested in my friends the Maynards from the day we met. Are you searching for someone—a relative, perhaps?"

She tried to move from beneath him, but he held her pinned fast. "Tell me," he whispered. "Where did you get the name Maynard—from your father or your stepfather?"

"My stepfather, of course," she said, too quickly, and glanced away from him. There was genuine alarm in her face now.

"Please don't lie to me, Annabelle." He forced a gentleness into his voice that he wasn't at present feeling. "After what you and I have just done together, you should trust me a little."

He knew that was a wretched ploy to use. In the past, he'd used it on many women, but suddenly he wished he hadn't used it on Annabelle.

Yet it was apparently most effective. Paling to an unearthly white, she whispered, "Hush, Colin. You ask too many questions."

A faint smile touched his lips. "Aye. I like to know about the women I care for. 'Tis an odd habit I have."

"Do you care for me?" she asked, her lower lip trembling.

He brushed his mouth against hers. "More than I should, dearling." Between bestowing kisses on her lips, her cheeks, her bare neck, he murmured, "Is Maynard the surname of your father, Annabelle?"

She averted her face from him, but he tugged at her earlobe with his teeth, making her gasp.

Her breath was quickening. "Has anyone . . . ever told you you're a rogue?"

"Is Maynard your father's surname?" he repeated, running his tongue along the outside of her ear.

"Yes, devil take you. Or so my mother told me before she died."

As she realized how much she'd admitted with that one answer, she jerked her head away from him, eyeing him with a mixture of fear and suspicion. Her confession stunned him. This wasn't at all what he'd expected. Nor Walcester, apparently, either.

He wanted to know so much more. How her mother had died, why Annabelle had endured her stepfather's cruelties for so long. . . . Yet he must be very careful with her if he wanted all the truth. He laid a hand on her shoulder, but she flinched from him. Then he saw the tears welling in her eyes.

Her distress struck him like a sword in the belly. "It's all right, dearling. I understand. You came to London in search of your real father, didn't you?"

For a moment, she appeared indecisive, uncertain whether to trust him or not. Then she nodded, her words coming out in pained, curt sentences. "I was all alone in the world. I thought . . . I'd at least look for him. Mother had told me he was a nobleman from London with the surname of Maynard. That was all. Then Charity and I got here. We—we didn't know where to begin. So we found work in the theater, as I told you before."

He felt instantly contrite for pressing her so sorely. Her story made perfect sense, and he could hardly blame her for wanting to seek out her real father. He'd have done the same in her place, if his father hadn't found him first. Slowly, he slid off to lie beside her. She curled her body into a ball, her breath coming in quick gasps.

Why had she been reluctant to tell him this before if she'd been so interested in the Maynards? he wondered. The cynical part of him speculated that perhaps she'd wanted to find her father to wrest a fortune from him in exchange for her silence. That would explain her refusal to confide in him.

Yet he could hardly bear to think her such a schemer. "Have you had any luck with finding your father since you've been here?" he asked, trying to sound nonchalant.

She shuddered, then said in a whisper, "You mentioned an earl a few days ago. That's the only lead I've had."

Could Edward Maynard really be her father? She didn't appear to resemble the earl much, except for her blue eyes, but then, that proved little. "I see."

She faced him, her eyes alert and watchful. She appeared to be toying with some idea in her mind. "Now that you know the truth," she continued hesitantly, twisting a length of sheet in her hand, "maybe . . . maybe you could aid me in my search."

He searched her face. "Maybe."

The tension seemed to leave her body. "Would you help me, Colin? It would mean so much to me."

He suddenly wondered who was manipulating whom. "I don't know. Do you have anything concrete I can use to find this father of yours or at least prove that the Earl of Walcester is your father?"

She averted her eyes from his. Under her nervous fingers, the sheet became a tight rope as she considered his statement. At last she nodded. "Yes, I . . . I do have one thing that would prove my father's identity if I could find him."

"Oh?"

With trembling hands, she wrapped the counterpane around her and slid from the bed. She went to her bureau, the ends of the counterpane trailing behind her. Opening a drawer, she took out a box of inlaid ivory. Then she blocked his view with her body, but he could hear the sound of her setting the box down and then a faint click as she apparently unlocked it. He sat up and tried to see what she was about, but he could see nothing. He heard the faint click again as she locked the box.

When she returned to the bed, she held an object in her hand. Solemnly, she handed it to him. It was a man's signet ring of solid gold, rather ornate and bearing a coat of arms.

"Do you recognize the insignia?" she asked as she sat down beside him, observing him with wary interest.

Though the etching was small, Colin easily detected the quartered shield with four running greyhounds. It was the coat of arms of the house of Walcester.

So the truth was finally out, he thought. He fingered the ring a moment longer in silence. What was he to do? Tell her who her father was? He couldn't do that without first speaking to Walcester, but the yearning in her face made his gut twist. 'Sdeath, but she'd had a hard life. She deserved to know her father.

Then he brought himself up short for his soft thoughts. After all, there was still one thing her story hadn't explained. "What has the Silver Swan got to do with all this?"

She looked startled at his sudden change of subject. "What do you mean?"

"Why do all call you the Silver Swan?"

" 'Tis a nickname, that's all."

No, it wasn't all, and he knew it by her defensive tone and the faintest flicker of fear in her eyes. That one bit of information she was certainly lying about. Why?

He wanted to rail against her, to make her tell him the truth. It wounded him to realize she could still keep something from him after the honest way she'd given him her body.

Aren't you keeping something from her as well? his conscience whispered.

Yes, he thought soberly. He couldn't blame her for distrusting him when he distrusted her nearly as much. Besides, perhaps he was being hasty in attributing suspicious motives to her when she might simply be anxious talking about her absent father.

"Do you know whose ring it is, Colin?" she asked, interrupting his dark thoughts. "I do wish to find my father."

His gaze locked with hers. "Why?"

She shifted her eyes from his. "That . . . should be obvious. Everyone wants to know who her real parents are."

"Do you wish him to acknowledge you, to give you a portion since your stepfather and mother left you penniless?"

"No!" The sharpness of her answer took him aback. "No, I don't care about money."

Yet she cared about something, he could tell that. She cared very much. That decided him. There was another who depended on Colin's discretion, a friend he'd made a promise to. He dared not tell her more until he knew more.

He continued to finger the ring. "I'm not sure about the crest, but I might be able to identify it if I ask the right people."

A relieved smile creased her face. "I knew you could help me! I knew you could!"

Then why didn't you ask for my help before? he wanted to say, but didn't think he should put her on her guard by asking too many questions. Somehow he would get his answers, however.

He glanced briefly at the box on her bureau and wondered what secrets she kept so carefully locked away from him. Could he get a peep inside without arousing her suspicions? Perhaps once she slept . . .

Suddenly he remembered Mina's sleeping powder. An idea formed in his mind.

He forced himself to set the ring on a nearby table and gather her in his arms. "Let's not talk any longer about matters that make you sad."

She accepted his embrace quite easily. "No, let's not."

He drew her down on the bed, and she curved her

body against his, resting her head on his chest. Hell and furies, but despite all her suspicious ways, she could still make him want her more fiercely than any woman he'd ever known. It took all his will to fight the stirring in his loins. Nor did it help when she started planting soft kisses over his chest.

"I don't think that's such a wise idea," he ground out.

"Why not? Have you exhausted your strength?" A coy smile gilded her rose-red lips, tempting him to taste of them once more.

He resisted as best he could. "Nay, but your body has had plenty of excitement for one day. You'll be sore enough as it is in the morning." Nonchalantly, he added, "Tell me, do you think you feel quite normal now after enduring all of Mina's physic?"

"Not exactly normal," she whispered as she caught the nub of his nipple between her teeth. "But it has nothing to do with the physic."

His loins instantly responded to her teasing. Oh, yes, he'd transformed her into a temptress worse than she'd ever been before. He tried to think of anything other than what lay beneath the counterpane that she still held wrapped around her seductive little body.

"I ask," he said in a strained voice, "because I almost forgot to give you the physic Mina left for you. She said you might feel aftereffects, and this would counter them."

Her attention effectively diverted, Annabelle propped her chin on his chest and frowned. "Really? Aftereffects?"

"Yes. In fact, I think you should take the physic now. I wouldn't want you to wake up ill in the morning simply because I forgot to give it to you. Mina would chasten me sorely for my omission. Shall I get it?"

She sighed and then shrugged. "All right, but I certainly tire of filling my body with medicines."

Quickly he left the bed, before her beautiful body could tempt him into changing his mind. He found the pouch of powder where he'd left it on the table. Filling a cup with water, he mixed in the powder, then brought the cup to her.

He watched as she drank the physic in slow sips. "Annabelle, is there anything else you think I should know before I go off on this quest for your father?"

He had to give her the chance to tell him the whole truth.

For a moment, he thought she might. She concentrated on the contents of the cup, a frown on her face. At last she muttered "No, not that I know of" and drained the cup.

He noticed she avoided his eyes. As used to lying women as he'd become, he'd thought it would never hurt him again to have one lie so blatantly. But it did. It cut him down deep, in the part of his heart he'd protected all these years.

Wiping her mouth with the back of her hand, she said, "That's nasty stuff Lady Falkham is giving out."

He nodded, his heart heavy. "Aye, but she says it works."

A few moments later, when Annabelle's head dropped onto the pillow and her eyes drifted shut, he grimly acknowledged that Mina hadn't lied. The damnable powder worked like a charm. He lay beside Annabelle several minutes, to be sure she was thoroughly asleep. Then he left the bed.

Pulling on his shirt and breeches, he headed toward the bureau. Like so many people, Annabelle wasn't terribly imaginative when it came to hiding places, and he found the hidden key to her box quite easily, tucked inside the binding of a book of poems on her bureau.

Glancing back at her to make certain she slept soundly, he opened the box. Inside he found the usual trinkets a woman kept—a pressed flower, a thin silver neck chain, a few small rings, the swan brooch she'd worn before. And a piece of rolled paper with a broken seal and a faded ribbon tied around it.

Carefully, he removed the ribbon and unrolled the paper. A spidery script filled the page, and he realized after reading it that it was a poem. He thought it an odd poem until he read the inscription at the bottom: "The Silver Swan."

Quickly he scanned the poem again. This was no ordinary poem, but a coded one of the kind spies often used to pass messages. Walcester had undoubtedly written it. Judging from the yellowing of the paper, it had been penned some time ago, possibly during Walcester's days spying for the Royalists.

Colin squeezed his eyes shut as a terrible hurt tore at his heart. Annabelle had lied about the Silver Swan, and Walcester hadn't been wrong to suspect her. Clearly, she knew far more about Walcester and his political activities than she'd let on to Colin, and obviously she had no intention of revealing any of it to him.

He'd been duped by her sadness and her tale of woe. "Damnable lying actress!" he hissed. He pivoted to glare at her sleeping form. A seeming innocence lit her face, her eyelashes feathering her cheeks and her hair lying in a tangle over her shoulders, making his emotions clamor riotously within him. Hell and furies, how could she affect him so fiercely?

Had her story of her fiendish stepfather and her quest for her real father even been true? She did have Walcester's signet ring in her possession, which was admittedly a sign of something, and she was the right age to be his daughter.

Colin's throat tightened. Moreover, there was no doubt she'd been beaten by someone.

Well, if he couldn't get any answers from her, perhaps he could get his answers elsewhere. Quickly he read the poem again, memorizing it as he had so many other similar messages. Then he locked it up in her box and replaced the key in its hiding place. Picking up the signet ring from where it lay on the bedside table, he slid it on his finger, then donned the rest of his clothes.

If he hurried, he could visit the earl and be back before she awakened. The hour was late, but Colin didn't care. He wanted answers, and he suspected Walcester could give them to him.

With a parting glance at the woman lying in such glorious splendor on the bed, he strode from the room, his jaw clenched. Yes, Annabelle, sweet lying Annabelle, had made him want answers. A great many answers. And he'd get them if he had to shake them out of the earl.

With impatience, Colin watched the earl enter the drawing room of the Walcester town house. It had taken some talking to convince Walcester's steward to disturb the man, but once he'd done so, the earl hadn't kept Colin waiting long.

Walcester stood uncertainly inside the doorway. He'd dressed in a hurry, judging from his unbuttoned vest and shirt only half tucked into rumpled breeches.

" 'Tis late, Hampden," he grumbled in his gravelly voice, and scratched his balding pate. "I hope you have a good reason for wrenching me from a warm bed in the middle of the night."

"A good reason, I think. I have something to show you." Colin slid the signet ring off his finger, then handed it to the earl.

A frown crossing his face, Walcester took it. The lines etched in his brow deepened as he studied the ring. "Where did you get this?"

"Is it yours?"

"Of course it's mine. You can see my coat of arms on it. Now tell me where you got it."

Colin watched the earl carefully. "From the actress. Annabelle Maynard."

Colin hadn't been sure what to expect, but it wasn't the expression of shock on the older man's face. The earl sat down rather suddenly in a nearby chair, his eyes riveted on the ring.

"Where did she get it?" He lifted sharp eyes to Colin. "Where, man, where?"

"From her mother. She claims it belonged to her father."

The blood drained from the earl's face. He stared past Colin, his eyes bleak and his face suddenly very worn. "What town is . . . the actress from? Do you know that?"

"No. But 'tis in Northamptonshire, that much I know."

"Norwood," he said in a whisper. He shook his head, over and over. "I can't believe it. 'Tisn't possible."

"What isn't possible?" Colin demanded. "That she's your daughter?"

"I don't know." Walcester rubbed his stubbled cheek with one hand and with the other fingered the ring in almost wild distraction. He stared up at Colin helplessly. "A pox on it, Hampden, I don't know."

No, Colin thought bitterly. Half the time the damnable men didn't know they'd sired children, did they? No wonder Annabelle had been so insistent about his using a sheath. The acid of guilt ate away at his insides.

"Is there any chance you are her father?" he gritted out. "Any chance at all?"

"There's a chance. There's always a chance. My God, Hampden, you should know that a man on the run takes his pleasure where he finds it."

"So she may or may not be your daughter, born of your union with . . . whom? A milkmaid? A cook? A tavern wife you tumbled as you passed through this Norwood you mentioned? All of these?"

Hampden's harshly asked question struck Walcester speechless for a moment. He buried his lined face in his blunt-fingered hands and groaned. "Nay. If she's of Norwood and bears my ring, then only one woman could be her mother, and that woman was neither milkmaid nor tavern wife."

"What was she? Come on, then, you asked me to seek out the truth, but you've apparently told me none of it yourself. Who was Annabelle's mother?"

The soft glow of candlelight lit Walcester's tortured face as he lifted his head and breathed deeply. "*If* the chit is truly my daughter, then her mother could only be Phoebe Harlow, the daughter of Sir Lionel Harlow.''

Colin stared at him in amazement. *Sir* Lionel Harlow? So Annabelle's mother was not some chambermaid or doxy. No wonder Annabelle could play a lady to perfection. She *was* a lady.

The ramifications of that struck him numb with anger. ''You lay with a gentlewoman and left her with child? Had you no care at all for what you were doing?''

Walcester visibly bristled at the condemnation in Colin's voice. ''I never knew of the child. After I left there, I heard that her family had arranged a profitable marriage between her and a powerful squire named Taylor. Even if I could have returned for her—and this was during the height of the civil war, you realize—I couldn't have had her. She'd married.''

''Aye. Because you left a child in her belly.''

Rising stiffly to his feet, Walcester stared at Hampden with a haughty expression. ''You have no right to speak to me like that. You've no doubt left a trail of your own bastards across the countryside. I merely sired one.''

Colin wanted to drive his fist into the earl's face for that. Only with extreme difficulty did he rein in his temper. ''To my knowledge, I've sired none. If I had, I would have made certain they were well provided for.''

Walcester didn't even flinch. ''My daughter—if she is my daughter—was raised in a wealthy squire's home. Is that not 'well provided for'?''

Colin stepped nearer. ''That wealthy squire beat her—quite often, apparently. I saw the marks of his crop on her back.'' He added, when Walcester paled, ''He also beat her mother. No, I don't think either of them was 'well provided for.' ''

Walcester's face registered surprise for a moment. Then, whirling from Colin, the earl went to stand at the window, gazing out into the cold, dark night. ''You're a damned insolent pup, Hampden.''

"Aye. You knew that when you asked this favor of me."

The older man's fingers curled into fists. "What of her mother now?" he asked breathlessly.

"Both she and the squire are dead, or so Annabelle says."

He whirled around. "Dead? But the woman would only be about forty by now."

"Annabelle said no more about it than that, but I believe her when she says they're dead. She says she came to be in the theater because they left her penniless."

Walcester's expression shifted, hardened. "Ah, yes, the theater. You've done your work well. You've unearthed my dark past only to present me with a whoring daughter. Thank you for that fine favor."

Struck dumb by the vehemence in those words, Colin balled his hands into fists, then strode up to Walcester. "Haven't you been listening at all? Your daughter, your own daughter, grew up being beaten by the man to whom you abandoned her. Knowing that, all you can say is that I've presented you with 'a whoring daughter'?"

"No doubt the wench deserved beating if she acted as she has these past months in London. From what I hear, she's taken more lovers than anyone can count." He glared at Colin. "Can you truly tell me I should rejoice at such a daughter?"

Colin wanted to throttle the man for his cruel unconcern. Then he wanted to set him straight about a few things concerning Annabelle. Yet would it do any good? As far as the earl was concerned, his daughter had shamed him publicly by pretending to be a wanton. What did it matter if she hadn't in fact performed the act?

Besides, to set Walcester's mind at ease about his daughter's innocence would require giving the man proof, and that would mean Colin would have to admit he'd bedded Annabelle. He wasn't certain how Walcester would take that.

"So what does the chit want from me?" Walcester bit out. "Money? Blackmail money? Is that her game?"

With rapidly dwindling patience, Colin ground out, "She doesn't even know who you are. She says she came to London to search for you simply because she wanted to know who her father was."

Walcester's acid laugh chilled Colin. "Oh, of course. That's why she's using my code name from the war. It has nothing to do with blackmail at all."

That comment stopped Colin short. Walcester had a point. Why *was* Annabelle using Walcester's code name? Why had she kept that coded message hidden? If her mother had passed it down to her, then that meant her mother had been part of the earl's spying schemes. But Walcester hadn't yet mentioned such a thing.

Nor did Walcester's worries about blackmail put Colin's mind at ease about either the earl's or Annabelle's motives. His suspicions made him hesitate to mention the coded message to Walcester. "How could Annabelle use her knowledge of your code name to blackmail you?"

Walcester stiffened so imperceptibly that anyone else would have missed it. Not Colin.

"I don't know," Walcester muttered gruffly. "Yet you must admit she has no reason for using it otherwise."

Colin shrugged. "Perhaps her mother told it to her. She came here to seek you. How better to draw you out than to use your code name?"

"Her mother didn't know my code name," Walcester said, a shade too quickly.

Something was certainly wrong here, Colin thought. Obviously Annabelle's mother did know, unless the woman had stumbled upon the coded message by accident after Walcester had left Norwood. Yet what self-respecting spy left such clues lying about?

'Sdeath, but between Annabelle and the earl, a veritable treasure of lies mixed with truth lay before

Colin to be sorted out. He didn't know if he should mention the coded message to Walcester or to Annabelle. If Walcester was lying to him about the code name, then what was the man hiding?

What in the name of God was going on?

"What do you wish me to do now?" Colin asked, although he was forming his own plans in his mind.

"I don't know. I'll have to think on it. If you have any loyalty to me at all, however, you'll keep my secret awhile longer until I can sort out what to do."

"You mean, keep it secret from Annabelle."

Walcester nodded curtly.

Colin sighed. He owed Walcester his life but at the moment that indebtedness hung about Colin's neck like a lead weight. "What will you be doing in the meantime?"

"Perhaps I'll take a look at this actress myself."

Colin thought that was a good idea, although it worried him that Walcester was so contemptuous of her. "Will you speak with her?"

Walcester shook his head jerkily. "Not yet."

That eased Colin's worries some. As much as he resented Annabelle's deceiving him, he hated to think of her being exposed to her father's vitriolic temper. "She's asked me to seek you out for her. What shall I tell her to put her off?"

A startled expression crossed Walcester's face. "You've gotten quite close to her, then."

"Of course. 'Tis what you wanted, isn't it?"

Walcester pondered that a moment, rubbing his shiny pate as he did so. "Did she mention anything about the Silver Swan? Had she no reason for wearing a swan brooch?"

The man was obsessed with Annabelle's knowledge of his code name, even now that he seemed to believe she was his daughter. "No, she had nothing to say about any of it. She claimed the Silver Swan was nothing more than her nickname."

"She's lying. You must find out what else she knows."

Colin agreed, but he was beginning to think he also must find out what the earl was hiding. Both father and daughter seemed determined to keep their secrets. Still, perhaps he could glean the truth another way.

Stroking his chin, Colin thought about that. "All right. I'll do what I can," he said absently.

He didn't tell Walcester that he'd do it outside of London. Oh, yes. He'd dealt with his duplicitous mistress and his equally duplicitous friend long enough. He was tired of hunting between their words for the fragments of truth they chose to feed him.

It was time to change tacks entirely. It was time to travel to Norwood.

Chapter Fourteen

"Is this her fault or mine?
The Tempter or the Tempted, who sins most?"
—William Shakespeare, *Measure for Measure*,
  Act 2, Scene 2

Light was streaming in through the window when Annabelle opened her eyes a crack. She shut them with a groan. Her head pounded like a pestle in a mortar and her lips felt cracked and dry. Then she shifted onto her side, and the stickiness between her legs made her eyelids fly open again as last night's events flooded her memory.

Dear heaven, she thought, *Colin made love to me.* Ignoring her headache, she lifted her head from the pillow to survey the room. Colin wasn't there, but evidence of their lovemaking remained. Her clothes lay scattered on the floor, and the cup from which she'd drunk Lady Falkham's medicine was sitting beside her bed.

Probably the splitting headache came from that very medicine, thought Annabelle, although she'd assumed the medicine was meant to make her feel better, not worse. Then again, after all the herbs Lady Falkham had given her yesterday, there was no telling how she should feel.

Suddenly she caught sight of something on top of her bureau that glittered in the sunlight. She slid from the bed, found her smock and put it on, then wandered over to the bureau, each step a torture. The ring Colin had given her before lay on top, its diamonds and rubies winking like a dozen small lights.

Pinned beneath it was a note which read, "I've gone to get us food. Be back soon."

No signature, but of course Colin had known there was no need. Nor was there a need to mention the ring. Its presence on her dresser was message enough.

She lifted the heavy, jeweled band. It jolted her unwillingly back into the realities of her situation. Her shoulders slumped. There was no going back now, was there? Colin had bedded her. He would expect their relationship to continue.

Closing her fist around the ring, she stared out the window at the streets of London, bustling with activity. So many people, and of them all, she'd had to take up with Colin. She'd had to meet a charming rogue who thought to buy her virtue with a ring.

Now, now, you're being overly dramatic, don't you think? she told herself. *You knew this would happen if you let him close. You wanted it to happen; you know you did.*

Had she? Had a part of her hoped for this all along? After all, an alliance with Colin could give her much, and not simply financial security either. She'd no longer have to fight off the gallants. She'd have an ally in her search for her father. She hadn't wanted to tell him about her father, but after they'd made love, it had seemed like the best thing. If she couldn't hold him at arm's length anymore, then she could at least have his help. She knew Colin would uphold his promise, since he'd proven, despite his secretive ways, to be a man of his word.

Besides, if Colin was indeed her father's friend, she'd have another weapon in her plan for revenge. The thought struck her hard, like a physical blow, and she sat down suddenly at her bureau, burying her face in her hands.

Sweet Mary, she couldn't use Colin like that. Never. Their lovemaking had been too precious to hold up before her father as evidence of her debauchery. Besides, it would hurt Colin, even perhaps shame him before his friends. No, she couldn't do that. Not again.

Yet she couldn't bear to relinquish her plan for vengeance. And her plan for vengeance required that she make a public spectacle of herself, that she confront her father before all his friends and peers, the very thing that would cause Colin pain.

Oh, but how could she cause Colin pain? She held Colin's ring against her cheek, the cool, hard stones oddly enough reminding her of Colin's generosity, his kindness . . . his determination to have her. That brought her to thoughts of the night before.

Soft caresses, sweet kisses . . . dear heaven, he'd been magnificent as he'd taken her. She could almost feel again his deft hands kneading her breasts, his lips teasing her in private places until she'd thought he'd drive her mad . . . and at the end, his taut body around, over, inside her, all thunder and storm and wild male heat.

Charity had been so right when she'd extolled the virtues of lovemaking. Being bedded was a singularly wonderful experience, especially when the man doing the bedding had the looks of Adonis, the grace of a tiger, and the touch of a sorcerer.

Not to mention the kindness and caring of a friend. That thought sent emotions churning within her. Ah, but he wasn't simply a friend, was he? He required more of her than any friend would. He wanted her heart, her trust, her very soul. And her loyalty. He wanted her to be his mistress. What's more, he saw no reason why she shouldn't.

The problem was, she saw exactly why she shouldn't. If she became his mistress, she'd be no better than the other actresses who sold their favors to the highest-bidding protector. Worse yet, she'd give up her independence and any prospects for the future.

Prospects for the future. She'd always known that once her vengeance was complete, she'd be unable to marry, at least in London. No man who knew her reputation on the stage would wed her. Nonetheless, she'd harbored dreams of going somewhere else . . . to the Continent, perhaps, where she'd be unknown. There she'd intended to start all over, maybe even find a man to marry, who'd love her as she wanted to be loved, someone she could love in return. She'd intended to protect her virtue until that day. Now that endeavor was fruitless.

Yet she couldn't say she regretted last night. Colin was the first man she'd ever cared for. She could almost imagine spending her days making him happy, being a different sort of companion to him than her mother had been to her stepfather—a woman who shared her lover's life totally, who feared him not.

She bit back a sob of despair. Nay, if she were truthful with herself, she'd acknowledge that she didn't simply want to be Colin's lover. She wanted to be Colin's wife, the beloved companion of his old age, the one to whom he confided his dreams, his hopes, his cares. When a woman dreamed of a future with a man, she didn't think in terms of the temporary servitude of a mistress. She thought of matrimony. Annabelle was no different from any other woman in that respect.

Oh, yes, painful as it was to admit it, she would choose to be Colin's wife, given the chance. She closed her fist around Colin's ring and pounded the bureau. Faith, but she must stop tormenting herself. The fact was, she would *not* be given the chance. A marquis, even one born on the wrong side of the blanket, didn't offer marriage to an actress of dubious origins.

No, he was offering to be her lover, plain and simple. She mustn't harbor dreams of more. Besides, she reminded herself sternly, could she truly want to be his wife when he still held so many secrets from her? Or was this simply the mooning of a woman who'd had her first experience with lovemaking?

After all, she told herself, nothing had changed since last night except her virginal state. Colin was no more to be trusted than before, even if he had agreed to help her find her father. That thought made her glance at her bedside table in alarm, but the signet ring still sat there from the night before.

She relaxed a fraction, though her heart lay heavy in her breast. No, her situation remained the same. She still didn't know how closely entangled Colin might be with the Maynards, nor why he kept mentioning the surname to her, like a hunter laying bait, nor why he seemed so inquisitive about her past. Why did Colin keep pressing her about the Silver Swan? Why would he care about her nickname unless he knew something about it? She didn't want to believe he'd been pretending to care only to get information from her, but she couldn't ignore the possibility.

Faith, what was she to do? What was she to think? Was Colin merely toying with her, his true intentions veiled, or had he meant it when he'd said he cared for her? And was his caring enough?

Suddenly she heard the door in the other room open. She started, then sat frozen, silent. The door to her bedchamber opened, and Colin sauntered in. He stopped short when he saw the empty bed, but released a breath as he caught sight of her sitting beside the bureau.

He smiled, but his smile touched only his lips, not his eyes. Did she imagine it, or was his gaze less warm than it had been before?

"I see you've awakened at last," he said in matter-of-fact tones.

"Yes." A sudden shyness overwhelmed her. So much had passed between them last night, yet she felt as if she were in the presence of a stranger.

It didn't help that he was fully dressed and looking splendid in his noble finery, accentuating the difference in their stations. Self-consciously, she glanced down at the rumpled muslin of her smock, wishing she'd had time to dress before he'd returned.

He didn't seem to notice her discomfort, but jerked his head toward the other room. "I've brought some bread and cheese. Are you hungry?"

"Yes." But she didn't move from her perch on the

chair by her bureau and merely toyed with the ring in her hand, her head bent and her eyes averted from his.

He stepped closer. "I see you've found my gift. Are you contemplating returning it once more?"

Something in the harshness of his words made her look up. He stood in an attitude of defiance, legs splayed and his thumbs tucked into his sash, daring her to toss his gift back to him and prove once more that she had no heart.

She stared at him. "What does it mean? Your gift. What is the significance of it?"

A dry, hard laugh escaped his lips. "It means whatever you want it to mean."

He sounded so flippant—insolent, even—though for a second she glimpsed the vulnerability behind his tone, and it saddened her. "I'm not trying to insult you for your gift, Colin. 'Tis quite lovely. Any woman would be happy to wear it on her finger."

"But not to take the strings attached to it. Is that it?"

She winced. "I—I never intended to be any man's mistress."

With a muttered curse, he stepped up to her, took the ring from her, then placed it on the ring finger of her right hand. He closed his hand around hers and bent to place a cool kiss against her forehead. " 'Tis a gift, Annabelle, that's all. A sign of my . . . my affection, if you will. Perhaps it will remind you of me while I'm gone."

Her head shot up. "Gone?"

He glanced away from her. "Aye. I've been called to my estate in Kent. It appears there's been some trouble with the steward that needs my management. I leave today."

She noted that he didn't mention having her accompany him. Then again, why should he? She had her work at the theater, and it wasn't as if he'd made any vows to her. That thought sent her emotions churning once more.

"When . . . will you return?" she managed to ask.

His gaze flitted to her, his expression softening for a fleeting instant. He lifted his hand to cup her cheek. "I can't say, but I won't be gone long, I suspect."

Though her pulse quickened at his feathery caress, she forced herself to remain detached, unconcerned, as if he'd just told her he'd be going out for a midnight jaunt. "It shall be dull here without you."

"It will be more dull for me in Kent, I assure you." His voice sounded strained as he stroked his thumb over her cheekbone.

Abruptly he dropped his hand and crossed his arms over his chest. "I've taken steps to see that you're protected while I'm gone."

"Protected?"

"While the cat is away, the mice will play, as the saying goes, and His Majesty is the worst mouse of all. But I've arranged for you to stay with an old friend of mine. His Majesty will stay clear of you as long as you are at her lodgings."

Her. Another woman. How many women did Colin call friend? Were any of them more than that to him? "Who is this friend?"

"Her name's Aphra Behn. She's a widow who did some spying for the king in Antwerp at the same time I was there." A wry smile twisted his lips. "Unfortunately, the king had no monies to pay her. He was bad about paying any of us, but then, I didn't need the money. In any case, she had to borrow money to return to England. Since then she's been petitioning the king for the payment he owes her, but Charles, of course, won't spare her a pound."

He laughed bitterly. "It has made for a very uncomfortable situation between them. The king won't go near you as long as you appear to be Aphra's intimate friend and houseguest. He'll fear that if he beds you, you'll pressure him to pay Aphra. So you'll be quite safe with her."

She wanted to ask him so many more questions, but any of them would make her sound jealous, and her pride wouldn't allow her to let him see her jealousy.

"I—I don't know, Colin. I think I'd rather stay here. Isn't there another way to make His Majesty lose interest in me?"

His gaze on her was dark, penetrating, and terribly unnerving. "Not unless you leave the theater entirely and go into hiding. I didn't think you'd want to do that. Of course, if you'd rather, I could send you to one of my estates—"

"No, no," she put in quickly. His words made her heart plummet. *I could send you to one of my estates.* But he would not take her with him to Kent.

Well, he was right, she told herself, gathering her dignity about her like a cloak. She couldn't go with him and leave the theater. She mustn't lose her place in the duke's company, not with her vengeance still unaccomplished and her future uncertain.

His tone softened. "You'll like Aphra, I assure you. She's a witty, intelligent woman with a mind of her own . . . like you. She's young and carefree . . . she'll take your mind off your troubles."

Young . . . witty . . . the sort of woman Colin was attracted to. Was Annabelle to spend the next few days or weeks with a former mistress of Colin's, one he'd now relegated to the status of "friend"?

Stop this, she told herself angrily. *You're behaving like a jealous wife already. You don't know anything about this woman.*

Besides, no matter what the woman had been to Colin, Annabelle had willingly entered his world of rakes and free living. Now she must accustom herself to its rules, distasteful though they might be.

Yet she didn't have to like it. In clipped tones, she said, "I suppose this means I must delay my search for my father."

A strange anger flared briefly in his eyes, then faded. "For a short time. Don't worry, Annabelle. You'll find your father. I promise you that."

He sounded so sure. She stared at him a long moment, wondering what devious plans he was concocting in his head.

Then she sighed and dropped her gaze from his. "When do I meet this Aphra Behn?"

She hadn't realized he was so tense until her words made him relax visibly. He uncrossed his arms and held out his hand to her. "After you've eaten and you're dressed and ready. Charity should be here any moment, for I sent word to Sir John's. I must go make arrangements for my trip, but I'll return to accompany you to Aphra's."

Taking his hand, she stood. She winced as her headache attacked once more, forcing her to sway unsteadily as she pressed her hand to her head.

"Are you all right?" he asked, placing a hand under her elbow to steady her. His arm went around her shoulder, and he held her with solicitous concern.

No, I'm not all right, she wanted to scream. *You've turned all my plans topsy-turvy and I don't know how to right them.*

Since she couldn't say that, she nodded instead. "I have a headache, but it will pass, I'm sure. That medicine you gave me last night has apparently had its own aftereffects."

Guilt shone in his face for a second, but it went as quickly as it came, making her wonder if she'd seen it at all. "Are you well enough to go to Aphra's today? I suppose I could delay my trip one more day if—"

"I'm fine," she said firmly. She needed him to leave, to give her the chance to think. When he was around, she couldn't make a single logical decision without being influenced by him.

"You don't look fine," he said gently, then paused. A hardness entered his voice as he dropped it a fraction. "Sometimes I think you're not being completely honest with me."

Her gaze locked with his. Clearly he meant more than simply her honesty about the state of her health. His gaze peeled back the layers of her many roles to penetrate beneath the costumes and the pretense into her very soul. She wondered if he'd guessed that she hadn't told him everything. For a split second, she wanted to spill out the entire sordid tale, to tell him of her mother's hanging and of her quest for revenge.

Then she reminded herself that he hadn't told her everything either. There were secrets he kept from her still—she felt certain of it. What's more, at the moment, he had the upper hand. He knew the Maynards of London. She did not. If she told him everything, then she might as well give up her vengeance. And she simply wasn't ready to do that.

"I'm as honest with you as you are with me," she said in a trembling whisper, her chin tilted up in challenge.

His eyes widened. Then he lifted one eyebrow as a cynical smile curved his lips. "That you are, Annabelle. That you certainly are."

He dropped his hand from her shoulder and turned from her with an abruptness that sent worry stealing up around her heart like vines choking a tree. She should never have hinted that she'd been less than honest with him. Then again, she hadn't expected him to be so remote and brusque at a time like this, not after last night's kisses and caresses. His behavior had made it difficult for her not to want to rouse some emotion in him, even if it was anger.

His spare, indifferent words continued to dash her expectations. "I'll leave you to pack your belongings. Try not to take more than you need. Aphra's lodgings aren't large." With that, he strode toward the door.

"Colin?" she called out, wanting something more from him, some soft word or act that would show her how he felt after last night. She couldn't let him leave her like this.

He half turned to face her. "Yes, Annabelle?"

There was no softness in the chiseled planes of his face. It had fled since last night. He didn't seem at all the same man who'd made love to her with sweet tenderness and a passionate hunger bordering on obsession, who'd made her promise there'd be no other gallants in her life.

"N-nothing," she said, managing a feeble smile. "I'll be ready when you return."

He hesitated, his eyes searching her face. Then he nodded curtly and walked out, leaving her wondering how she'd ever soothe her bruised heart.

Colin's carriage inched along crowded, stinking Grub Street, but despite the din outside, there was a palpable silence within the walls of the carriage. Annabelle and Colin hadn't spoken the entire way. He sat on his side, staring out at the jostling crowds, and she sat on hers, watching him with a bleak expression. She wished Charity were there to break the tension, but they'd agreed that Charity should remain at Annabelle's lodgings while Annabelle was temporarily ensconced at Aphra Behn's house.

Then the carriage jerked to a stop before a ramshackle lodging house. Annabelle glanced out, but couldn't believe her eyes. Was this where his friend lodged, in the literally grubby environs of Grub Street? She'd assumed the woman was some nobleman's widow who spent her time hopping from one wit's bed to another now that her husband's money had made her independent. But no nobleman would leave his wife to live in such a disreputable place.

Annabelle cast a quizzical glance at Colin, but he was already climbing out of the carriage and shouting commands to the coachman. Still directing the coachman on where to put her bags, he handed Annabelle out of the carriage, then accompanied her inside and up the stairs.

When Aphra herself met them at the door to her lodgings, she met Annabelle's expectations in one respect. She was in her late twenties and quite pretty. Though she was olive-skinned and had a rather longish face, masses of dark reddish curls fell over her shoulders and she had a pouting heart-shaped mouth that would tempt most men. Nonetheless, the effect was somewhat ruined by the dust smeared across one cheek, over her pert nose, and along her wide fore-head.

"Come in, come in," she said in a hurried manner, swiping her hair back with one dirty hand and in the process putting a fresh smear across the other cheek. Then she sneezed a couple of times. "I'm sorry, Hampden. There's dust everywhere. I've been putting the place to rights since you came by this morning, but I'm not much of a housekeeper."

She flashed Annabelle an apologetic glance. "Can't afford a servant, you see, so I do it all myself, and I truly, truly detest cleaning."

Annabelle didn't know quite how to respond. After all, she still wasn't certain if she wanted to be here. Yet breeding and a natural tendency toward courtesy made her say, "You shouldn't have gone to any trouble—"

"Nonsense, nonsense." Aphra waved her hand dismissively as she ushered them into what was apparently her drawing room and motioned to the coachman to start bringing in Annabelle's luggage. "If you're letting a room from me, it ought to be clean, don't you think?"

Annabelle's startled gaze flew to Colin, but he was already reaching into his vest and withdrawing a small purse. "This should cover Annabelle's expenses while I'm gone," he murmured, pressing the purse into Aphra's hand. "You know where to reach me should you need more."

"Colin, I'm perfectly capable of paying for—" Annabelle began.

"No," he said quickly. " 'Twas my idea to move you from your own lodgings, and the cost is merely a trifle. Don't worry yourself over it."

An amused expression on her face, Aphra tucked the purse into a pocket of her apron, then winked at Annabelle. "It might be merely a trifle to you, Hampden, but for women of the world like your friend and me it's bread and wine for some time to come."

Annabelle wasn't certain what this peculiar woman

meant by "women of the world like your friend and me." Surely Colin hadn't brought her to the house of a . . . a vizard-mask, had he?

For the first time since Annabelle had arrived, she surveyed her surroundings. What she saw reassured her. Not that she knew what the drawing room of a vizard-mask would look like. Yet surely it would be more flamboyant and extravagant than this woefully cramped room filled with worn furniture and fraying rugs. Surely a vizard-mask wouldn't have piles of paper and pots of ink scattered about her drawing room.

Noting Annabelle's curious stare, Colin said, "In addition to being a spy and an adventuress, Aphra fancies herself something of a writer. She thinks to write for the stage."

"Yes," Aphra put in bitterly, "if I can ever give off writing petitions to His Majesty and letters to all of my friends and acquaintances from here to the Continent requesting their help in getting my due from him. I swear, I've one foot in the debtor's prison, thanks to the king and his tight purse, and no one gives a damn."

Colin raised one eyebrow.

Aphra laughed. "Except for you, of course, Hampden. You're a dear for thinking of me when searching for a place for your friend." Her smile faded. "I know this is your roundabout way of giving me charity, since I wouldn't take your money outright."

"Not at all," he insisted. "You'll provide the perfect haven for Annabelle."

Aphra brightened. "I do hope so. Aside from the help with the rent, I can use the advice of an actress." Aphra smiled at Annabelle. "You don't mind helping me with my plays, do you?"

"Not at all," Annabelle murmured, still not quite comfortable with this odd woman. At least the mystery of why the widow had such poor quarters was solved. Still, Annabelle burned with curiosity to know the woman's relationship with Colin.

Colin's gaze rested on Aphra with friendly warmth,

which didn't reassure Annabelle much. "As long as you keep His Majesty from Annabelle, I'm sure she'll be quite happy to give you advice." He turned to Annabelle. "Aye, dearling?"

It was the first time since last night that he'd used the endearment, and Annabelle noted that Aphra seemed intrigued rather than angered by it. Perhaps the woman wasn't a former paramour of Colin's, then, Annabelle told herself. It wasn't much, but it cheered her. "Aye," she said softly. "I'll be glad to tell you what I can, such as it is."

"Good, good," Aphra stated, "but don't worry. I'll not make you work for your keep. Besides, you'll be safe as a clam in a shell here. His Majesty avoids me like the plague these days." Her confident expression faltered as she added, "Unfortunately."

A moment of silence ensued, during which the three of them stood rather awkwardly waiting for the others to speak.

At last Colin cleared his throat and said, "Well, then. It sounds as if Annabelle will be fine here, so I'd best be on my way."

Aphra glanced from him to Annabelle, her shrewd eyes narrowing. Then she nodded. "I believe I'll tidy up the kitchen. I'm certain you two don't want an audience as you say your good-byes."

In a flurry of skirts, she bustled out. They could hear her sneezing as she entered the next room.

Colin laughed. "I somehow knew Aphra would be terrible at a mundane task like cleaning. She's much too absorbed with lofty ideas and schemes to bother. I hope you don't mind."

"No, it's fine."

At the quiet evenness of her tone, he turned to stare at her. "I know you don't like being thrust on a stranger like this, but I couldn't think of anything else. Believe me, I would have preferred that the king had never noticed you." His jaw tightened. "Unfortunately, no man with eyes in his head could have managed that, and certainly not Old Rowley."

The resentment behind his words, when coupled with his strange remote behavior toward her throughout the day, made something snap within her. "Yes, and we know how I led him on by trodding the boards before God and everyone. I ought to have realized that a woman has no right to put herself forward in public, even if she *is* simply trying to earn a living for herself. How foolish of me to expect to be treated with dignity instead of like . . . like . . . any common whore."

He cursed under his breath, then clasped her elbow and turned her to face him. "Surely you knew when you chose to be so conspicuously scandalous what would be expected of you. Yes, our society is unfair to women. It always has been, as you can well attest. Did you think the rules would change simply because you wanted them to? What did you expect?"

She dropped her eyes from his, then blurted out, "I didn't expect you to treat me like a whore too." Clapping her hand over her mouth, she instantly wished she could unsay the words that showed how much his behavior toward her bothered her.

"For the love of God, Annabelle, what are you talking about?" He gripped her chin in one hand, lifting her face to his.

She tried to pull away, but his other hand snaked around her waist, holding her tightly against him.

"I was told to expect this of men," she said shakily, fighting for control, ashamed of herself for being so emotional when he'd probably think her even more of a bother for it. "Once they bed you, they want nothing more to do with you. They toss you aside, they trot off to attend to their business affairs, and they abandon you. I've seen it happen before with countless actresses, but I thought—"

"Forget the other actresses," he ground out. "Forget every damnable lie you've ever been told about men. This is me, Annabelle, and I'm not abandoning you. If you think that one night of bliss with you could purge you from my blood, then you're a bigger fool than I gave you credit for."

She said nothing, but merely continued to stare at the buttons of his coat, her heart hammering in her chest painfully.

"Look at me," he whispered.

She shook her head.

"Hell and furies, look at me," he repeated in so urgent a voice she finally did as he asked.

"You want the truth, Annabelle?" His eyes glimmered with unreleased torment; his face was all harsh angles and mysterious shadows. "The thought of leaving you here with such little protection terrifies me. I feel I hold you only by the most tenuous thread, which will snap the second I leave this room."

"Do you trust me so little?" she asked shakily.

His gaze lingered over her face with dark intensity. "Promise me one thing, Annabelle."

"What?"

"Promise to wear my ring until I return. As a sign of your . . . your affection for me. The other gallants won't bother you if they know you wear my ring. Promise me."

How could she deny him, when he stared at her with such uncertainty, such pain in his eyes? "I promise."

He released a great breath. " 'Sdeath, I wish I didn't have to go, but I do. It's more important than you could possibly imagine."

How odd that he spoke with such earnestness of attending to his estates. He'd never spoken so fervently of them to her before. Perhaps more was amiss than he was letting on.

"I'm only sorry you feel abandoned," he continued.

"I'm merely being silly. Don't mind me," she said in a whisper, fearing that her emotional outburst would drive him away rather than entice him to stay.

That elicited another curse. "How can I not mind you? Even when you're not near, the pain behind your eyes haunts my dreams until I can't think without thinking of you. . . . The orange scent of you fills my nostrils until I can't breathe without breathing you."

Her pulse beat madly from his thrilling words. He pressed a kiss to her forehead. Then his lips trailed soft kisses along her temple to her ear, and he drew her against him so closely she could feel his arousal.

"Since last night," he murmured huskily, "when I discovered how soft you are, how wild and sweet under my caresses, I'm even more obsessed." He spoke the words as if they were forced from him. "So how can I not care what you feel? It's all I think about. The trouble is, you won't tell me what *you're* feeling. I know you keep secrets from me, but I don't know why. It kills me . . . not knowing why."

His lips against her hair were firing her blood as they had the night before. "I—I keep no secrets from you," she forced herself to say, although baring her soul to him sounded tempting at the moment.

Abruptly he went still. He held her against him, not moving, not speaking.

Then he released her and stepped back with a bleak, tight-lipped expression on his face. "No secrets, eh, Annabelle? Come, now, I know you too well for that. I can tell by the way you shy from me still that you hold a great many dark secrets behind your bright smiles."

She couldn't deny it again. She simply couldn't. So she said nothing, watching him with her heart slamming in her chest.

He stood there a moment, his flashing eyes boring into her, probing for the truths he seemed to know she hid. Then he muttered a low curse. "My mysterious swan, always hiding, always speaking one thing but meaning another. I pray that your secrets are worth lying for. Because I may not be able to control my fury if I discover they are not."

With that dire pronouncement, he whirled on his heels and left.

Chapter Fifteen

"O heaven, were man
But constant, he would be perfect."
—William Shakespeare, *The Two Gentlemen
of Verona*, Act 5, Scene 4

Three days after Annabelle had moved into Aphra
Behn's lodgings, Charity came over to help Annabelle
prepare her lines. That evening the duke's players were
to perform at Whitehall for the king, and Annabelle
was very nervous about it. This would be her first opportunity to test how well her alliance with Aphra
would keep the king from her.

Charity gestured broadly with her hand as she read
a line, and in the process knocked over a stack of
heavy tomes on the table beside her chair. "Odsfish,
don't this woman have a cartload of books!" she exclaimed in dismay.

"Aphra does seem to enjoy reading," Annabelle
murmured as she studied her part. Aphra had gone out
an hour before to deliver another petition to the palace
and should be returning any moment.

Charity eyed her curiously. "So what's she like?"

"She's very intelligent," Annabelle said without
glancing up. "She's probably read more books than
I'd ever dreamed of reading. She's bold, adventurous,
and willing to unravel any conundrum. I like her."

"John says she's a wild sort, likes to swagger and
talk of love like a rake."

With a smile, Annabelle thought of Aphra poring
over her journal in the evening by the dim light of a

candle. "She hasn't swaggered around me. She talks rather freely about love, 'tis true, although I wouldn't call her a wild sort. Actually, she's a lot like you. She's been married and widowed, and as a result has become rather cynical about the whole business of courtship. She says she'd rather take a lover of her own choice than marry some old bastard simply because he has money."

Charity's eyes flashed briefly. "She sounds like a wild sort to me."

"You took a lover of your own choice rather than marry," Annabelle said with a grin, amused by Charity's apparent resentment of Aphra.

"Aye, and I'm beginnin' to see the folly of that," Charity said in a far-off voice, dismissing the subject of Aphra abruptly.

Annabelle put down the script she'd been studying. "What's wrong? Is Riverton mistreating you?"

Charity shook her head. "He's been talkin' about settin' me up in a cottage in the country." Her voice hardened. "You know, where others won't know about me. When I threaten to leave him before I'd let him closet me out away from all my friends, he talks about wantin' me to have his children."

Choosing her words carefully, Annabelle said, "It sounds as if he's becoming quite serious about you."

Her normally amiable servant gave a resentful laugh. "Nay, not exactly." Her eyes narrowed as if she were trying to decide whether to reveal something to Annabelle. At last she sighed. "John has a fiancée. So he can't get too serious, can he, when he's got a viscount's daughter preparin' herself to marry him in the fall? Her family wants his money, and he wants their connections. 'Tis the same old story."

Although Charity tried to put on the airs of a worldly woman who understood about such things, Annabelle could see she was hurting inside. Annabelle could hardly blame her. "Oh, I'm sorry, Charity. I didn't know."

Charity waved her hand with nonchalance, but her

expression grew wistful. ''Nor did I. When I found out, I couldn't very well get angry with him, could I? I was the one told him I didn't want an attachment. I tell you, this Aphra Behn may talk about takin' a lover of one's free will, but 'tis not as grand as it would seem. Bein' free to take a lover means you leave him free too. With a man, a little freedom can go a long way.''

Annabelle thought of Colin. A little freedom could indeed go a long way. She touched the ring he'd made her promise to wear. Could Colin too have some fiancée hidden away? He'd already made it clear Annabelle wasn't to be part of his public life, the one that involved his estates. In how many other respects was she to be kept apart, so she wouldn't embarrass him? Or would he be one of those rakes who enjoyed flaunting their mistresses and public opinion be damned?

Neither possibility appealed to her, she realized, her insides twisting into knots. Dear heaven, how she wished Colin were here to kiss away her doubts. If she could feel more sure of him, it wouldn't pain her so much to think of a future as his mistress.

There were aspects, however, of being his mistress that seemed almost appealing. To have him to talk to over supper after a play . . . then to make love to until they both were spent. A blush stained her cheeks. Ah, yes, there could be some advantages to waking up every day in the arms of the man she loved. . . .

She stopped short at that thought. Dear heaven, the man she loved. No, no, she couldn't love Colin. She mustn't. He didn't love her, so she must protect herself from loving him.

But how could she protect herself when he'd already slipped beneath her defenses with his kindness and his fervent words and . . .

Admit it, she told herself sadly. *You do love him. You've loved him almost since the day he caught you alone in the tiring-room.*

Determinedly, she thrust that pleasant memory from her mind. She mustn't let him get to her this way, she thought despairingly. She couldn't let him change her into a pining, heartsick woman like those wives of philandering husbands she'd seen in the theater, trying to make their husbands jealous and carrying out petty vengeances on their husbands' mistresses.

Then the sound of footsteps on the stairs, bold, quick steps, interrupted her thoughts and made both her and Charity look up. For a fleeting instant, Annabelle thought it might be Colin. When the door opened and Aphra came in, she had to hide the quick expression of disappointment that flitted over her face.

"Good day," Aphra said to Annabelle, though she wouldn't meet her eyes for some reason. Instead, she stared at Charity curiously.

Annabelle introduced the two of them. Aphra seemed very agitated, but Annabelle couldn't imagine why.

" 'Tis a good thing you're here with Annabelle," Aphra muttered to Charity. "Yes, yes, a good thing indeed. She likes company."

Annabelle wondered at that peculiar statement. "How were things at Whitehall? Did you deliver your petition without any trouble?"

Picking up the books Charity had knocked over, Aphra began to restack them absentmindedly. "Oh, yes. It went well, though I hate dealing with the Master of Requests. He's a scurrilous man, he is. Nonetheless, he assured me His Majesty would attend to the petition soon. Which means, of course, that I'll be fortunate if the king even reads it in the next month."

From what Aphra had told her, this wasn't any different from before. So why was she so perturbed? When Aphra continued to stride about the room, straightening rugs, kicking crumbs under the table, clearing away the dishes she'd left out that morning, Annabelle wondered what was wrong.

"Did you hear any interesting gossip at Whitehall?" Annabelle persisted.

Aphra looked up startled. "Gossip? Er, no, not a word."

Aphra was definitely behaving strangely, Annabelle thought. Thanks to her and Aphra's many discussions over the past three days, Annabelle had come to know the woman amazingly well. They'd instantly discovered that they agreed on a number of issues, particularly the need for women to have better opportunities for education and independence. From their talks, Annabelle had quickly determined that the older woman was forthright and outspoken, not at all the type to be evasive.

"What is it?" Annabelle asked with concern. "Have you heard something about me at Whitehall? Has His Majesty somehow found out about the ruse Lord Hampden and I used the other night to trick him?" Annabelle had told Aphra about their deception, but had left Mina's name out of it, not wanting to hurt the woman's reputation. "You can tell me, you know. We can deal with it somehow. We can send word to Lord Hampden at Kent and—"

"Hampden's not in Kent," Aphra blurted out. Then she squeezed her eyes shut and grimaced. "Oh, pish, I shouldn't have told you. But you'd have been damned angry at me if you'd learned the truth and I hadn't said a word. Besides, you deserve to know."

The blood slowly drained from Annabelle's face. "What do you mean? Of course he's in Kent. He told me—"

"He lied." Aphra gave her a look of such pity that Annabelle knew in an instant Aphra was telling the truth.

"Why?" Annabelle whispered, her hands trembling. She tucked them under her arms, not wanting Aphra to see how much the news disturbed her. "Why would he lie?"

"I don't know." Aphra sighed. "I found out quite by accident. Rochester and Sedley were discussing Hampden. Sedley had apparently been heading out of town to attend to his own properties on the same day Hampden left. They happened to stop at the same inn, so they shared lunch before continuing on for some time together. They parted and Hampden went north. North, Annabelle, not south to Kent.''

"Perhaps he meant to . . . to . . .'' To do what?

"When Rochester asked if Sedley knew where Hampden had been heading, Sedley said Hampden wouldn't discuss it.'' The lines of pity on Aphra's face deepened. "Sedley did say, however, that Hampden asked him not to mention their meeting to you.''

Annabelle flushed with anger. Sweet Mary, and she'd been thinking how badly she loved him. This was what she got for falling into such a trap.

Dear heaven, how it hurt! Colin had lied to her. He had indeed cast her away to go off and pursue some secret business after having bedded her. Devil take the deceitful man! "I should have known he wasn't telling me the truth . . . he was so closemouthed about his trip,'' she murmured in a pained voice.

Charity jumped up from her chair and planted her hands on her hips as she faced Annabelle. "You stop this, now, dear heart, you hear me? Lord Hampden's a good man. He wouldn't lie to you. I know he wouldn't.''

Her eyes filling with malice, she turned to Aphra. "Why should my mistress believe your tales, I want to know? And why do you tell her such nonsense? Are you smitten by Lord Hampden? Is that it? My mistress has Lord Hampden's affections, and in your jealousy, you think to destroy what they share between them?''

Aphra's startled gaze swung to Annabelle. "Is this what you think, Annabelle? Because I assure you Hampden and I have never been more than friends, forced to rely on each other's wits when we were spies together in Holland. I didn't guess that you might assume—''

"I didn't,'' Annabelle snapped, casting Charity a quelling look. "Charity, I'm afraid, sees Lord Hampden as the solution to all my problems, and she fears my losing him for any reason.'' Annabelle's voice sharpened. "She's also been swayed by his money, I'm afraid.''

Not to mention that Charity was resentful of Aphra, Annabelle thought, since the older woman had become something of a confidante to Annabelle. Charity had never seen her mistress take another woman's advice and obviously disapproved of the whole idea.

Confirming Annabelle's suspicions, Charity sat back down in her chair with a sniff. "I see my opinions aren't wanted here by such fine ladies as yerselves. My ideas are too coarse, I suppose, and not at all fittin'."

Annabelle ventured a glance at Aphra, who cast her a sympathetic look in return, showing that she understood Charity's feelings.

Yet only Annabelle could soothe those feelings. "Come, now, Charity, you know I value your opinions. But I also know Aphra speaks the truth. Lord Hampden lied to me about where he was going. It's as simple as that, which means something is amiss." She added meaningfully, "You *know* what I'm talking about."

Charity glanced up as Annabelle had hoped she would. There was one thing Annabelle had not told Aphra, and that was her purpose in coming to London. Only Charity knew that, and it wouldn't do for the maid to reveal any of it. Charity's eyes narrowed; then her expression brightened, showing that she understood. The two of them had one bond that Aphra couldn't share, and it seemed to mollify Charity to remember it.

"Why do you think Lord Hampden wants to hide his destination from me?" Annabelle asked Aphra.

Aphra shrugged. "I hoped you could tell me that."

Annabelle pursed her lips. If she only knew. She thought a moment about everything Aphra had said, about Colin heading north. Why north? To the north lay . . . Northamptonshire. And Norwood.

A raw fear coursed through her, leaving an acid taste in her mouth. Could it be? Could Colin be going to Norwood to find out her secrets? For a moment, panic overtook her so completely she could hardly stop the shaking in her body. Sweet Mary, if he were on his way to Norwood . . .

She'd never told him she was from Norwood, she reminded herself. She'd merely told him her county. He couldn't exactly traverse the entire county searching for someone who knew her when he didn't even know her real surname. No one would respond to the name Maynard, and the name "Annabelle" was common enough to keep him from determining who she was.

Why, then, had he lied? Why? In light of Charity's revelation, all Annabelle could think was that he too had a fiancée or some other mistress in the country. Or perhaps even a wife, she thought with despair.

"Lord Hampden's not married, is he?" she asked as that thought gave her more torment than she might have imagined.

"Pish, of course not," Aphra retorted. Then, realizing how that sounded, she said, "I mean . . . well, not that he can't or anything . . . but he's always said . . ."

"It's all right," Annabelle whispered in a sad voice. "He's a rake, and they avoid marriage as best they can."

"Not all of them," Charity added bitterly. "Riverton's only too happy to leap into the marriage bed. Someone else's, that is."

"Riverton?" Aphra asked.

Ignoring Charity's warning stare, Annabelle bit out, "Aye, Sir John Riverton, Charity's lover. You know him. He goes to the theater quite a bit. Charity has found out that he's got a fiancée."

"Of course that don't mean he don't want me," Charity said defensively. "He wants to keep me."

"Aye," Annabelle snapped, "he wants to keep you in the country, so you and his fiancée won't bother each other."

Aphra shook her head dolefully. "Aren't we a happy threesome? I'm in love with a man who's courting a woman younger than I while at the same time claiming to love me to distraction." She sighed. "These treacherous, strutting cocks haven't an inkling of the precious fragility of love. They bid us be wantons with them alone, yet see no reason to stay faithful themselves.''

Annabelle thought of Colin making her promise that there would be no other gallants. He hadn't made a reciprocal promise, had he?

Colin wouldn't be unfaithful to me, she told herself sternly.

Then why had he lied and told Sedley to keep his destination a secret? To her torment, she could find no answer to that question except that he had some other woman hidden away whom he didn't want her to know about.

''It's time to declare war on our two-faced gallants,'' Aphra announced with her typical impetuousness. Finding a stool, she climbed up on it and posed like someone presenting an argument in Parliament. ''I ask you, ladies, why should we sit at home, waiting for men to take freedoms they won't allow to us? We of the soft, unhappy sex must fight this unequal division of love, this . . . this dishonest inconstancy!''

Charity cast her mistress a quizzical expression, but Annabelle merely shrugged. Aphra was prone to grand pronouncements, undoubtedly because of her aspirations to be a playwright.

''How do you propose we fight this battle?'' Annabelle quipped bitterly. ''We have no rights, no money, no weapons. All of the advantages are on their side.''

''Not all,'' Aphra insisted. Flinging her hair back over her shoulder, she struck a seductive pose. ''We have our beauty, our wit, and our own capacity for deviousness. And they have their weaknesses—their egos and their desires.'' She leveled a knowing glance on the two women seated at her feet.

Satisfied that she had their full attention, she continued more boldly. ''You know what possessive creatures these men are. If we contain our own passions, if we withstand their flattery and sly blandishments, then we might prevail upon them by flaunting our assets before all their friends.''

''I know what you mean,'' Charity said with a cynical twist to her lips. ''Try to make them jealous, aye? We refuse them our favors while flirtin' with the other gallants? We do that, and I promise they'll find other women who won't be so rebellious.''

''Perhaps,'' Aphra admitted. ''If they do, however, then what do we want with them? If our lovers treasure us only for our bodies and our docile natures, then they're fools, and we should find other, better lovers. No, we must make them crave our wit, our kindness, our singleness of attention. We must remind them that we too can find our pleasures elsewhere. They count on our sense of modesty and honor to keep us from being as wild as they, so we must set aside the shackles of modesty and honor!''

''And pretend to wildness to keep our men?'' Annabelle asked bitterly. ''Must we feign promiscuous desires to keep them company in theirs? Nay, I will not!''

She rose from her chair to pace the room. Already once she'd pretended to be a wanton for the purposes of her vengeance, and she'd not enjoyed it. She didn't relish doing it again simply to taunt Colin. Must she lower herself to mirror his falseness by breaking her promises to him?

Yet he'd made no promises to her, she reminded herself. He'd made no promises at all.

''Our men feign constancy,'' Aphra said softly. ''Perhaps if we feign inconstancy, then we can show them how wounding it can be.''

Annabelle shook her head, tears starting from her eyes. Aphra thought men could be educated to be more considerate of women's wants and needs, but that was merely wishful thinking. Men like Ogden Taylor and Annabelle's father would always believe that women were chattel to be used and cast aside, no matter what women did to educate them otherwise.

Still, she'd thought Colin was different. Her breath

caught in her throat as she thought how she'd believed him to be better than the other rakes. For heaven's sake, she'd even thought she could marry him!

"You know," Aphra intruded into her thoughts, "if Hampden came back to find you merrily flirting with the gallants and behaving as if you hadn't noticed he'd even gone, he'd not be so quick to deceive you next time. His pride would be pricked."

Eh, his pride would be pricked, she thought, and she wanted sorely to prick his pride after the way he'd left her so easily. Still, what if she were wrong about him? What if he had some perfectly innocuous reason for lying to her? Or what if Aphra had misunderstood Sedley's comments?

"I, for one, think it's a sound notion," Charity piped up. "Riverton thinks he can hold me by the strength of his passions without puttin' forth a whit of effort to keep me. Money, but not effort. I say, fie on that! If I'd wanted a married lover, I'd have sought one." She stamped her foot, her face growing as determined as Aphra's. "From now on, I'll run that fickle rake a merry chase. If he wants me, well, then, he must relinquish his fiancée." Her voice lowered. "Or I swear I'll find another man to keep me warm. I swear it."

The two women turned to Annabelle, a question in both their faces. "You have pride, don't you?" Aphra chided. "I'll admit I'd never thought Colin would show a woman such contempt for her feelings. But it seems he has. So what will you do? Will you let him return to find you pining away, while he has been blithely attending to some secret purpose?"

Annabelle turned her back on their eager faces, wanting to resist the ploys they proposed. Unwillingly, however, she thought of Sedley, of what he'd said. She thought of the smug smile he and Rochester would wear when she came to the theater. Aphra had said nothing of it, but Sedley and Rochester probably assumed Colin went to meet another lover. They'd smile at her like ministers carrying the king's secrets, mocking her for her faithfulness to a man who wasn't faithful to her.

That decided her. She wouldn't let Colin make a fool of her simply because her heart was breaking. She'd hide her pain; she'd tear out the love he'd planted in her breast.

Her vengeance required that she play the role of wanton, and she'd play it to the hilt. Let him wonder that she still flirted with all the gallants. Let him wonder about her broken promises. When he made the same promises to her, then she'd honor her own, and not before.

Slowly, she removed Colin's ring, tucking it into the pocket of her apron. She'd not wear it again. Not until he proved that it represented more than the fee paid to a strumpet.

"All right, then, ladies, let's be merry," she said stoutly, facing Aphra and Charity with a brittle smile. "Let's show our fickle lovers what blazingly brilliant women they've tossed aside."

Chapter Sixteen

"Trust not your daughters' minds
By what you see them act."
—William Shakespeare, *Othello*, Act 1, Scene 1

Edward Maynard sat in the box watching the play. It had been nearly five years since he'd been to the theater. Soon after the king had been restored to the throne, Edward had grown disgusted with the immorality of the London stages.

When one of the actresses came onstage wearing a painted face and a gaudy gown, he was reminded of why. He could scarcely believe there were women willing to make such fools of themselves in public. What an unfeminine occupation this acting was. Society would have been better off if it had kept to those days when men were the only ones trodding the boards.

The licentious behavior now common in the theaters was a direct result of actresses corrupting the morals of young men. Edward was sure of that.

He concentrated his attention on the painted woman now dancing about and wondered if she were Annabelle Maynard. No, according to the playbill, Annabelle Maynard would not appear until the next scene.

Edward shifted in his uncomfortable seat and peered at the stage. From where he sat far back in the box with one of the curtains down, he couldn't see as well as he'd have liked. Yet he dared not have sat farther forward or in the pit or some other conspicuous spot where he might be seen.

He ought not to be here at all, exposing himself, but

that damned Hampden had left him no choice. Edward's valet had questioned Hampden's servants when Hampden had remained silent for some days. The rogue had apparently left town to attend to his estates. In fact, he'd been gone nearly two weeks.

Edward clenched his fist about the head of his walking stick. How dare Hampden leave at the most crucial point of this whole matter! The marquis had promised to put his full attention to solving the mystery of Annabelle Maynard and then had trotted off to the country.

Edward fairly seethed to think of it. Oh, he'd have a few choice words for Hampden when the marquis returned. In the meantime, Edward's curiosity had gotten the better of him. Before, when he'd thought the girl might be a spy or enemy's lackey who'd uncovered the truth about what had happened at Norwood, he'd been less curious about who she was than what she was up to.

But ever since Hampden had told Edward the woman might be his daughter, he'd been plagued by a desire to see her in the flesh. The painted woman exited with an actor, and Edward tensed. The next scene was Annabelle's.

Then an actor walked onstage. No, it wasn't an actor, he realized after a moment. It was an actress dressed as a boy. How scandalous! Bad enough that there were women on the stage at all, but to put them in tight breeches and thin shirts . . . For God's sake, what was the theater coming to?

The woman wore no paint, not that any of the gallants in the pit cared, for they set up a cry the moment she appeared. Despite her apparel or perhaps because of her apparel, there was no denying she was a beauty with the kind of body made more alluring by breeches. The calls of "Silver Swan" from the pit taunted Edward. It was her. This wanton chit in boy's clothes was his daughter.

He would have recognized her in any case. Even in boy's clothes, she was the very image of her mother—

hair black as midnight . . . slender, tall form . . . long, graceful neck. Even her gestures reminded him of Phoebe.

Within moments of her entrance, he was transported back twenty-three years to those fearful hours when he and Phoebe had exchanged kisses in his room while he'd been recovering from the wounds he'd received at the Battle of Naseby. Phoebe had helped her mother attend him, and somehow she'd managed to steal a few moments alone with him here and there.

In time, they'd stolen much more . . . much, much more, in the middle of the night when everyone else slept. For a fleeting instant, he let his mind wander through those bittersweet memories. Phoebe had been soft and pliant as wax during their first night together. During the days, she'd walked about in a graceful dance, her cheeks perpetually flushed with her joy of him.

She'd been in love. And he'd desired her with a passion that had made him reckless to the point of insanity. He'd bedded her under the very nose of her Roundhead father, and not thought of the consequences that might come of it.

In truth, it had been more than desire. For him, she'd been part of the excitement of secretly thwarting the Roundheads. He'd been intoxicated with the thrill of spying, and Phoebe had been part of that intoxication. Then the wine had turned to vinegar when he'd learned that three Royalist spies who'd fled the Battle of Naseby were rumored to be hidden in the city, three men he knew well.

Suddenly it wasn't exciting or thrilling anymore. It was deadly dangerous work. He'd worried about what to do, then had raced to compose his coded poem and have Phoebe deliver it to the right person. He should never have trusted a woman with such an important task, and certainly not a woman of such ambiguous loyalties. Of course, she hadn't been the least interested in politics. She'd done what he'd asked because she was in love with him.

Or had she? Had she instead delivered it to the wrong person? He'd never known what happened, but he'd lived in terror of what she might do with that poem. All he'd learned was that the three had been arrested and the king's papers found on them. Then he'd fled, before he too could be caught.

That had proved to be the turning point in the war. In the hands of the Roundheads, the king's papers had been a weapon, revealing that Charles I was plotting with the Irish, Danes, French, and God knew who else, to help him regain power in his kingdom. That had given the Parliamentary forces popular support as nothing else had. From there, matters had steadily worsened until the king had finally been executed. And all of it due to his one act.

"Coward!" he hissed under his breath.

He thought about those wretched days, when he'd had to cover up what he'd done, to claim he'd never known there were Royalists in Norwood in the heart of the Roundhead camp. By heaven, if his peers, especially Buckingham and those young pups who now advised Charles II, had ever learned what he'd really done . . .

Shame washed over him again, as it always did when he remembered Norwood. He'd lived the next few years hiding his error, attempting to live down his failure, and trying to assuage his guilt. During those years, he'd worried that Phoebe would betray him to his fellows, or that she'd use the note to reveal his identity and betray him to Cromwell's men, since the message and her testimony together could link him to his code name. But after he'd heard nothing else from Norwood, he'd concluded that his secret had been safe with her. Probably, he'd reasoned, his message in a poem had been lost for all time.

Now he wondered if it had been. Had Phoebe passed on the poem to her daughter? Was that how this Annabelle knew his code name? It was possible. What's more, if she knew about the message, then she might know of his cowardice. After all these years of hiding his culpability, he didn't relish the thought of having it surface to ruin him politically and financially.

He gritted his teeth and stared at the stage. The debacle in Norwood should have been buried in the past. If it weren't for this insolent baggage named Annabelle, it would have been. She might resemble her mother, but she had nothing of her mother's meek bearing or pliant will. More was the pity.

"Pickworth!" he barked to his footman, who stood outside the curtained box. Pickworth stuck his head through the curtains.

Edward pointed at the stage. "You see that woman there, the one the fools in the pit are calling the Silver Swan? I want you to bring her to me as soon as the play is over."

"And if she will not come?"

"Don't be absurd. Make her come. You know how to strong-arm a wench, I should think."

Pickworth nodded and left.

The rest of the play Edward spent in fearful anticipation. He dared not let the woman know who he was, but he fully intended to find out how much she knew. Obviously, he could no longer depend on Hampden to attend to the matter, so by heaven, he'd do his own investigating.

Perhaps it was better this way. Edward didn't want Hampden to discover the real source of his concern about this Annabelle Maynard's use of the name Silver Swan. Unfortunately, the marquis's curiosity seemed to have been roused.

The play ended and the players took their bows. Edward noted grimly that Annabelle Maynard smiled coyly at every gallant in the pit. When one of them threw her a rose, she picked it up, sniffed it, then broke off the stem and tucked the bloom in the deep vee of her thin shirt to the delighted cheers of the men in the pit.

Edward grew sick at the sight. He could hardly believe he'd spawned this scandalous chit. He wished he could march down, whisk her from the theater, and give her the good drubbing she deserved. Then Hampden's words about the squire's beatings sprang into his mind. Many a man beat his daughters, Edward told himself testily, but if the squire had actually marred the girl's skin so that Hampden could see the marks . . .

For a moment, something akin to hate for the squire flooded him. Then he forced the feeling down. He was being absurd. Hampden had undoubtedly exaggerated, enamored as he apparently was of this Annabelle. If the squire had beaten her, it had undoubtedly been no more than she'd deserved, although it apparently hadn't done her any good.

In moments, the stage grew quiet, and the theater rapidly emptied. Edward waited, his fingers drumming on his knee with increasing impatience. Suddenly he heard voices outside his box.

"Listen, you cur," a feminine voice protested, "if you don't unhand me or tell me what this is all about, I'll have you thrown out of—"

Her words were cut off when she was rudely shoved in the box. She still wore her boy's clothes, and it lent her an oddly brave appearance. She stood there in the box a moment, disoriented, then turned around. Since Edward sat in the shadows, he knew she couldn't see much of him. Still, her eyes found him with unerring accuracy.

Her eyes shone blue in the light from the theater's candles, the same blue as his own. It jolted him, as did the sweet scent of oranges that clung to her.

But she broke the spell when she opened her mouth. "Who are you? I swear, you men think you can manhandle a woman without a whit of concern for her dignity or—"

"Dignity?" He gave a short, cruel laugh. "Yes, so dignified you are there onstage as you contort your body into lewd positions to tease those fools in the pit."

Her eyes flashed with a flagrant defiance he'd never seen on her gentle-tempered mother's face. She peered into the darkness, obviously trying to make out more of him. "Who *are* you?"

" 'Tis none of your concern, girl. Let's just say I'm a friend, concerned about your behavior."

Her eyes narrowed. "If you're a friend, then why do you hide in the shadows? What do you fear from me?"

"I fear nothing from you!" he barked out, half rising from his chair. Then he forced himself to regain control. He sat back down, steepling his fingers as he rested his elbows on his knees. "But you should fear me."

The nonchalant pose she then struck didn't quite belie the flash of alarm in her face. "Why is that?"

"You meddle in matters you don't understand. The Silver Swan isn't a name to use lightly."

That got her attention. For a second, he saw that his barb had struck home before she masked it with an expression of insolent bravado. " 'Tis a nickname, that's all. I can't help what the gallants call me."

He lifted his cane to tap her brooch. "Nor can you help wearing that silver swan brooch or showing a preference for silver, can you?"

She flinched away from his cane, abject fear shining briefly in her eyes. Once again, he thought of Hampden's tale of the squire's beatings. He dropped the cane abruptly, a mixture of emotions coursing through him.

"What do you care if I am called the Silver Swan?" she whispered.

"That's none of your business, girl."

At those words, she apparently decided to drop the pretense of not understanding what he was talking about. "Was it your nickname, then? What did you do to make it such a dangerous name?"

The chit was taking a stab in the dark, hoping to find out who he was, but her stab came uncomfortably close to impaling him. "*My* name? Because I come when I hear it? Nay, 'tis not my name. But as you say, 'tis a dangerous name, one that shouldn't be used by wanton girls without a thought in their heads."

"You know so much about my character," she said with heavy sarcasm. "Have you been spying on me, sir?"

The word *spying* jolted him. "Why do you have them call you the Silver Swan? Tell me that, and I'll spy on you no more."

She stiffened. "That's for me to discuss with the other bearer of the name. If you are not he, then I have nothing further to say to you." She started to leave.

"If I were to tell you that he sent me on his behalf?"

She hesitated, her face flushing. "I would say he should come himself if he wants the truth."

Damn the chit! What game did she play? She obviously didn't know the whole story or she'd have confronted him with it before now. Yet she had some piece of the story, that was certain, or she wouldn't be using his code name. How much did she know? That was the crucial question.

He had half a mind to lock her up in his house until she told him everything, but now that he'd involved Hampden, he dared not. Hampden would want to know why she'd gone missing, and when he got no satisfying answers to his questions, he'd find his own answers.

Edward couldn't take that chance. Furious at the futility of his questions in the face of her stubbornness, he growled, "You're a brazen, selfish bitch with not a virtue to commend you, do you know that?"

She paled slightly at his words, but stood her ground. "And you, sir, are a bastard. Now that we've both called each other sufficiently nasty names, may I go?"

"Aye," he exclaimed sharply, "you may go. I'll be watching you, girl, remember that. If you decide to explain yourself, leave a message for the Silver Swan at the Green Goat Tavern. I'll see that the Silver Swan gets it." He paused, lowering his voice to a menacing whisper. "But if you continue this foolish charade, you'll find that having me for an enemy is a torment indeed, perhaps even a hazard to your well-being, if you take my meaning.''

Fear flashed in her eyes for the briefest instant. Then she tilted her chin up and whispered with equal menace, ''You can go straight to hell!''

With that she whirled and left the box.

He stared after her a moment, aghast that a woman would use such language to him, especially the woman whom he was now certain was his daughter.

Then he recovered. ''Aye,'' he whispered as her steps echoed down the narrow hall, ''but if I go, I'll take you with me, girl. I'll damn well take you with me.''

Clutching her waist, Annabelle found a deserted box and slid inside. She was going to be sick. She fought her heaving stomach, grateful that she'd been able to find a place where no one would see her.

That bastard, that wretched bastard, she thought, shutting her eyes to squeeze back the tears threatening to spill forth. She wouldn't let him make her cry. She wouldn't.

But oh, dear heaven, was that horrible man her father? Could he possibly be?

He could be indeed, she told herself bitterly. After all, he'd abandoned her mother to a life of hell, and surely a man like that would be a monster.

Yet to treat her with such callous, hurting unconcern! Unbidden, the memory of that sneering voice coming out of the darkness intruded itself into her thoughts. Sweet Mary, she hoped that wasn't her father.

How foolhardy she'd been to embark on this . . . this insane search. Somehow she'd thought she could cause her absent father pain while remaining immune from it herself. She'd planned to shame and humiliate him while he stood quietly by, enduring his punishment until he admitted that he'd done wrong by her mother.

Then she would have graciously forgiven him. She

couldn't have done more, but she would have magnanimously accepted his protestations of regret and bestowed on him the mercy he craved.

"What a naive, stupid little fool you are," she hissed under her breath. She'd held some sentimental notion that he would regret his actions. But if he were the man she'd met tonight, he wasn't a man to regret anything. He was an unfeeling beast.

Still, the man in the box might not have been her father. Perhaps her father had indeed found someone to spy on her. After all, she'd thought at one time that Colin might be spying for her father. But now that the despicable man in the box had confronted her while Colin was gone, she couldn't believe Colin was also working for her father. Why would her father have two men to represent him?

Despite the anger that yet smoldered within her at Colin's deception, it gave her hope to think that Colin was not in league with her father or the despicable man she'd met tonight. She clung to that hope as she pondered what to do.

Obviously her nickname had upset the man she'd met tonight. But why? She'd thought it was simply a nickname, one chosen by her father and known by both her mother and the person to whom her mother had delivered the poem so many years ago. Yet the strange man threatening her had implied that her nickname had a deeper, more sinister significance.

What could it be? She thought once more of the peculiar poem that made little sense on the surface. What message had been hidden in those odd words? And why hadn't her father signed it with his own name?

Unless . . . unless he'd not wanted anyone to know what he was about. Annabelle thought of the soldiers who, according to her mother, had come to Norwood shortly after her mother had delivered the poem. What if her father had been involved with them? During the civil war, both the Parliamentary and the Royalist armies had fought back and forth all around the country.

Everyone had taken a side. No doubt her father had too.

Could he have been a spy? she wondered. It would explain the peculiar nickname. Undoubtedly it was some sort of code name. That could also explain why the despicable creature she'd met tonight had warned her about using it.

Yet if he'd been a spy back then, who would care now about his code name? The war in England ended years ago. Why was he so adamant about her not using the name?

Her eyes narrowed. Something had alarmed him, that was certain. Her father was clearly worried about being exposed. Why?

A thought struck her with powerful force. Her father was more worried about this nickname than about her behavior on the stage, that was certain. It was true that the man in the shadows had commented snidely about her wantonness, but the focus of his concern had been her use of the nickname.

Perhaps this could be turned to her good. Her vengeance had focused on humiliating him with her scandalous behavior, but what if she could do more? He'd clearly been up to no good all those years ago or he wouldn't be trying to hide it now. And he'd dragged her mother into it, which was the worst of it.

Briefly she remembered his threats, the sinister quality of that gravelly voice. What if he were sincere? What if this horrible man truly intended her harm?

It didn't matter, she thought sadly. He could hardly harm her more than she'd been harmed since she'd come to London. She'd long prepared her emotions for the fact that her father wouldn't want her. After all, he wouldn't have abandoned her and her mother if he'd wanted either of them. Her reputation was in tatters, thanks to her plans, so he couldn't ruin her in that manner. And Colin had wounded her heart more thoroughly than her father or his accomplice ever could, so her heart could hardly receive a more terrible battering. What, then, was left for him to do to her?

He could kill her.

Her blood chilled at the thought. Could her father actually wish her dead? She clutched her arms tightly about herself. Sweet Mary, surely even he could not be such a miserable worm. Then again, she thought despairingly, he didn't know she was his daughter, not yet. She knew nothing of his character either. For heaven's sake, she had yet to be certain of his full name.

Would he kill her? She thought a moment, her skin feeling almost too tight for her body. Surely he wouldn't kill her yet, not until he knew what she was up to. Well, he'd wait a long time for that. She wouldn't tell all simply because a stranger who hid in the shadows made idle threats. Still, now it was more important than ever that she discover her father's identity.

Unfortunately, it was clear she'd not be able to depend on Colin to help her in the search. The scoundrel hadn't so much as sent word of his whereabouts. He'd told her he'd not be gone long, yet it had been nearly two weeks since last she'd seen him.

Suddenly an alarmed voice calling her name outside the boxes intruded into her thoughts. It was Charity.

"I'm back here!" Annabelle called out. What in heaven would she tell Charity about her frightening encounter with the man in the box?

In moments, Charity had stuck her head between the curtains of the box. "Odsfish, madam, you had me worried, you did! One of the orange girls said some brute had taken you off forcibly! She didn't know what to do, and she couldn't find a man to help. What happened?"

Annabelle stood then, trying to regain her composure. "A man wanted to speak with me. He claimed to come from my father, or rather, from the man calling himself the Silver Swan, so I assume it was my father."

Stepping through the curtains into the box, Charity surveyed her from head to toe. "He didn't hurt you, did he?"

"Nay." She ducked her head down so Charity wouldn't notice her consternation. "He wanted to know why I used the name, and when I wouldn't tell him, he left."

Charity eyed her a moment longer, obviously curious, but at last she shrugged. "Do you still plan on goin' with the others to the supper?"

Annabelle groaned. She'd forgotten all about Aphra's supper at the Blue Bell, the ordinary where the players normally supped after the play. In keeping with Aphra's and Charity's new determination to behave outrageously and thus enrage their lovers, Aphra had planned a ribald diversion. With Annabelle's approval, Aphra was funding it out of Colin's generous purse, the one he'd left to pay for Annabelle's keeping. Annabelle could think of no better purpose for his money than to spend it on a wild supper, since she'd already decided to pay Aphra for her keep out of her own meager funds.

And the supper was to be wild indeed. Aphra had persuaded all the actresses, both those who'd dressed in boys' clothes for the play and those who hadn't, to come in male attire. The gallants who were invited were not to know about it until they arrived. Aphra knew well how much the men enjoyed seeing women in breeches. She wanted her supper to be a scandal-provoking affair, one that would prove a sufficient taunt to the men in the lives of her and her friends.

It was to be a merry supper with fiddlers and dancers and music till dawn. Despite Annabelle's recent growing disenchantment with the games that represented London life in the theater, Annabelle had been looking forward to Aphra's party . . . until now.

"Are you goin'?" Charity repeated. "The others have already left and Aphra will be waitin' for us."

Now that Charity and Aphra had joined forces against their men, Charity had lost all her resentment of the older woman. If anything, Aphra and Charity had become closer than Aphra and Annabelle, who couldn't share their wicked delight in flirting outrageously with all the wits.

Still, tonight Annabelle wanted more than anything to lose herself in such revelry. She wanted to forget that Colin had taken her virtue, then abandoned her. She wanted to forget that her father was a cruel man capable of wishing harm to her. Most of all, she wanted to blot out of her heart the love growing like a weed, choking out her very lifeblood.

"Yes, I'm coming," she retorted. "Let's go on, then."

By the time she stopped outside to empty her pockets for the urchins and she and Charity had found a coach, nearly an hour had passed. Thus the ordinary was already filled with guests by the time they arrived. Aphra bustled about, giving orders to the serving girls and urging the musicians to play. The din was nearly as loud as in the theater before a performance, but no one seemed to mind.

The second Annabelle walked in, she was surrounded by gallants complimenting her on her performance. Forcing a smile to her face, she parried the verbal sallies of one and tapped another with her fan.

When the third snatched her hand up to kiss it, then lingered over her fingers, his wet lips leaving a damp trail along her knuckles, it took all her control not to yank her hand away from him and slap him with it.

Colin had been right about one thing. As long as she'd kept his ring on her finger and allowed Charity to let it be known that Colin was her protector, she'd been safe from the groping hands of the wits and rakes. They'd treated her with respect, and she'd found she'd liked it. For the first time, she'd been able to perform her roles without having her concentration broken by rude remarks. Offstage, she'd been left blessedly alone, and she'd reveled in the chance to put all her energies into performing instead of being forced to deal with the advances of the wits.

But once she'd removed Colin's ring, the men at the theater had rushed to flock around her again, to sniff at her heels like staghounds in heat. What's more, this time everything seemed different. Somehow her biting humor and ability to play a role was no longer enough to fend them off. They no longer seemed pricked by her barbs, nor fooled by her role of haughty lady.

It hadn't taken her long to figure out why. Sedley's tale of Colin's secretive journey had spread among the men. When they had also noted that she no longer wore Colin's ring, they'd assumed she was no longer under his protection. Rumors buzzed among them about why she couldn't keep a man faithful to her, since she'd given her affections to two noblemen in rapid succession and both had apparently discarded her. It lent a faint contempt to the way they treated her now.

Though it brought anger smoldering within her to realize how unfair were their rules, she held her head high and always faced them with dignity. Still, she found herself being trapped first behind a curtain, then behind a scenery flat, and even one day on the stairs to Aphra's lodgings by men wanting a lusty kiss and much more. So far she'd kept her virtue intact, but she couldn't hold out much longer.

The theater world that had at first been her haven had become a treacherous bog where only by deft maneuvering and clever acting could she protect herself. She wished she could give up her many pretenses, yet she felt trapped.

As she stood amid her tormentors now, she wished she hadn't come after all. She'd been mad to think they could give her relief from her tortuous thoughts. The rakes only intensified her suffering over Colin's betrayal.

She had a headache, and she wanted nothing more than to go home. Yet she'd promised Aphra to perform her dance again for the gallants as part of the supper's festivities. She did owe Aphra a great deal for coming to her aid. She mustn't leave until she'd delivered the promised dance.

So she stood there, playing yet another role, the one

of outrageous actress, while despairing thoughts tormented her. She'd painted herself into a corner, it seemed. Dear heaven, where would all of this end? Was she ever to see the fruition of her plans? Would she ever feel as if she'd sufficiently avenged her mother's death?

And would her heart ever, ever stop aching over Colin?

Chapter Seventeen

"Why, I hold fate
Clasped in my fist, and could command the course
Of time's eternal motion, hadst thou been
One thought more steady than an ebbing sea."
—John Ford, *'Tis Pity She's a Whore*, Act 5, Scene 4

When Colin entered London, he'd been traveling hard by post horse since noon the previous day. Yet night had fallen, so it was well past time for the play at the Duke's House to be over. It would do him no good to search for Annabelle there.

To find Annabelle was his first aim. He spared only a few minutes at an inn to send a boy ahead to his house to let his servants know he'd arrived. Then he continued at his same frenzied pace, for if he didn't see Annabelle soon and confront her with all he'd learned, he'd surely go mad.

Little had he dreamed how much she'd kept hidden from him. He'd still not entirely recovered from his shock at hearing that Annabelle Maynard, whose real name was Annabelle Taylor, was the daughter of a woman who'd been hanged for killing her husband, or that Annabelle herself had been suspected of aiding in the murder.

The latter rumor he'd put little faith in, and his skepticism had turned completely to disbelief after speaking with one of the servants who'd witnessed the murder and could testify to the actual events. The servant had insisted that Annabelle hadn't participated in the murder, which had taken place with such speed and in such anger it could hardly have been planned. What's more, the servant's account of the murder had confirmed that some of those marks on Annabelle's back had indeed been made within the year. Apparently the squire had been beating Annabelle unmercifully when her mother had plunged a knife in his chest.

Despite his anger with her, sympathy for Annabelle welled deep within him. Oh, yes, Annabelle had truly suffered. No wonder pain glimmered constantly in her eyes. From what the servant had said about wails in the night and balms prepared to ease Annabelle's suffering, her account of her torment had been less embroidered than it could have been.

Oh, yes, much of what she'd told him was the truth, as he'd found out after speaking with Charity's father, Richard Woodfield. Colin had presented himself to Mr. Woodfield as Annabelle's distant cousin who wished to provide for her, and the kindhearted man had accepted his story. Colin had questioned the man at length, which had proved profitable. Apparently Charity had told her father of Annabelle's parentage before she and Annabelle had left for London, which confirmed Annabelle's claim to be a bastard. Annabelle's claim that she hadn't known about her bastardy until recently had also proven to be true.

Unfortunately, Mr. Woodfield had also told Colin something Annabelle had certainly never mentioned to him. Before she'd gone to London, Mr. Woodfield had said, she'd vowed vengeance against her real father. Mr. Woodfield hadn't known what form the vengeance would take, but he'd felt certain she'd carry out her purpose. "The girl is strong-willed," he'd told Colin. "She had to be so to endure that wretched squire's mistreatment."

Strong-willed wasn't the word for it, Colin thought as he turned his horse into Grub Street. She was a proud, defiant tigress with a capacity for deception he'd never dreamed of. To think that all this time when she'd pretended to have told him everything, she'd been plotting some vengeance that she'd kept carefully secret within her. She'd even used him to get to her father. Had she known of his relationship to Walcester? It was hard to say—she'd kept so much of the truth from him.

It half destroyed him even now to think that she'd not trusted him enough to reveal her true purpose for coming to London. In fact, he still didn't really know what her plans for vengeance might be. Unless . . .

Unless she planned to expose Walcester's past. And Walcester definitely had a past. Colin had discovered in Norwood exactly how tangled and tortured Walcester's past was.

'Sdeath, if ever there were father and daughter with common traits, it was those two. Walcester had claimed from the start to be afraid that an enemy might be out to trap him somehow, when he'd really feared being found out.

Not that Colin knew the entire story, but he knew enough. Unable to speak with Phoebe Taylor's parents, who were dead, he'd at last tracked down an old woman living ten miles away who'd been her parents' housekeeper. Thanks to her statements, Colin had unraveled a tale that had left him terrified for Annabelle and made him hasten back to London.

Walcester had been hiding a great deal from Colin to ensure his compliance. Not that Colin found it surprising. If Colin's suspicions were correct, then Walcester, highly placed officer of the king, had been a traitor during the war—and not just a traitor, but the man indirectly responsible for Charles I's execution. It was a horrific thought. Apparently Walcester regretted his treachery now and wished to hide it. Then again, perhaps Walcester, having hidden his true loyalties all this time, had moved up into his lofty position precisely so he could effect some change in the government. Whatever the case, Colin would find out the truth. It was his duty to uncover whatever treachery Walcester might intend.

But first Colin had to speak to Annabelle. Hell and furies, it had become obvious during his investigations that Annabelle must know something about her father's activities. After all, she had that coded poem in her possession, and she was using her father's code name on purpose.

She knew more than she was saying, and he feared she intended to use it against her father as part of her damnable scheme for vengeance.

Yet even as he wanted to hate her for being so deceitful and not trusting him with the truth, he couldn't. How could he, when he'd seen the marks on her back and heard the tale of the servant? 'Sdeath, only the coldest man alive would condemn her for wanting her vengeance.

Unfortunately, he wasn't the coldest man alive, not where she was concerned. No, she made him too damnably warm by far. Too warm, too weak, too absolutely smitten.

With a grunt of anger, he spurred the horse on. Two weeks away from her, two weeks of lonely nights and restless dreams, had only made his thirst for her grow more acute, his hunger more piercing. It so fevered his brain that he found himself wanting to forgive her for deceiving him.

In truth, he admitted, he'd deceived her as well, although not with such a nefarious purpose in mind. If he'd been honest with her from the beginning, he might have brought about some truce between Annabelle and her father.

Then again, thinking of the webs both daughter and father had woven filled him with a dull sickness that poisoned all his thoughts and cast him into a welter of indecision. He no longer knew what to feel for either his friend or his mistress, but most of all, for his mistress. A part of him truly suffered to think she'd been so calculating all the time they'd been together.

Why? Why did she have this effect on him? Why did it make him feel drawn and quartered whenever he thought of how much she'd kept from him? Women had held secrets from him before, and he'd never experienced this mind-numbing pain.

Nay, only Annabelle had the power to draw blood.

His pulse raced as he approached Aphra's lodgings. He couldn't believe it—his body already anticipated the moment when he'd see her again. What kind of spell had she wrought over him? Would he ever be free of it?

He tied his horse up at the post, then leapt from the saddle, but he'd scarcely made it inside when he met Riverton descending the stairs. Riverton paused a moment, his eyes widening at the sight of Colin with his clothing bespattered by mud from the roads and his hair a tangled, knotted mess.

Then a grim smile crossed Riverton's face. "If you're looking for Annabelle, she's not here. Aphra's neighbor tells me she and Aphra have gone to the Blue Bell to supper."

Colin stared at his friend blankly. Colin had been so single-minded in his determination to reach Aphra's lodgings that it took him a moment to realize he must now go to another place for his quarry.

"Why are *you* looking for her?" Colin asked when he'd recovered himself.

"I'm not. I'm looking for Charity," Riverton bit out. "I returned from the country a week ago to discover that Charity would no longer see or even speak to me. Mind you, I was in the country in the first place to find a cottage for her. To return and find her cold and distant . . . well, I'm afraid I was too angry to do more than refuse to speak to her in turn."

He passed Colin, who fell into step beside him as they headed for the door.

"I guess that was childish," Riverton murmured. "It didn't achieve the desired effect either. Instead of making her regret her coolness, it apparently made her consider herself well rid of me. For the last week, she's been blithely flirting with every man who pays her attentions."

Colin shook his head in disbelief as they left the house together. "I can hardly believe it. I would have sworn the woman was in love with you."

Riverton stiffened. "I think she was, until she

learned of my recent engagement to a viscount's daughter. Despite Charity's apparent free-thinking ideas, at heart she's a country girl.'' His voice softened. ''I suppose she expected me to— Oh, damn, I don't know what she expected.''

''Ah,'' Colin remarked.

''In any case, I've decided to convince her that this can work. By God, I miss the wench more sorely than I'd ever thought possible. She's a sweet-tempered lass, is our Charity. I can't stand by and let her go.''

Oddly enough, it wasn't Riverton that Colin sympathized with, but Charity. One thing about being a bastard—it had made him much more sensitive to the ramifications of a man's having both a mistress and a wife. Men like Riverton had never been the child of a mistress, so they couldn't possibly imagine what it was like to have a succession of ''uncles,'' to have their mothers' married lovers treat them like bothersome gnats. Nor could they know what it was like for the woman, who always had to share a man's affections. Colin knew, however. He'd watched his mother's way of life turn her into a cruel, brittle woman.

Colin had later been exposed to it from the other end, having been forced to face the disapproval of his father's dead wife's relatives once he'd come to England. They'd regarded him as an affront to the memory of his father's wife. He couldn't exactly blame them either.

As a result of all that, Colin had always been careful with his mistresses. He'd done his best not to sire children on them, nor to promise what he couldn't offer. Nor had he ever split his loyalties by taking a wife while he kept a mistress. He had sworn not to wed until he could find a woman who'd be a suitable wife for a marquis as well as someone to whom he could remain faithful. He'd never found that woman. Until now.

Hell and furies, where had that come from? he asked himself. He couldn't be thinking about Annabelle, whose capacity for deception would surely destroy any man's hope of a peaceful life. Yet it was indeed Annabelle he imagined as his hostess, sharing his days, warming his bed at night, bearing his children. . . .

'Sdeath, you truly are bewitched, he told himself as he and Riverton mounted their horses and began to ride toward the Blue Bell. *The woman has unhinged you.*

They reached the ordinary in a short time. Music and laughter spilled out of the building into the otherwise silent evening. Colin wondered if Annabelle and Aphra were part of that.

It took him only a moment to find out, for the moment they walked in the door it was apparent that the ordinary now held only one group of people, a group that had apparently long ago finished supping and now filled the room with loud conversation, wild music, and gay colors.

At first he was disoriented, for the front room appeared to be filled with men, though he could have sworn he'd heard feminine voices. Then he realized why. Although everyone in the room wore male clothing, nearly half of them were women.

He glanced around the room. Except for the scandalous male attire, the supper was no different than a hundred he'd attended himself. In one corner he saw a rake deep in conversation with a pretty blond woman whose hand rested on his thigh with familiarity. Another very buxom lady was flanked by two gallants who were making a game of trying to remove her mask as she tittered and slapped their hands away.

Oh, yes, this was a typical gathering among the wits and beauties and actresses. Yet it left him with a sour taste in his mouth to think that somewhere in the rooms Annabelle was playing these teasing, erotic games.

But not in this room, apparently. Hearing music floating in from an adjoining room, he followed the sound. As he passed the table, Riverton at his side, he spotted Charity sitting beside Henry Harris, the actor in the duke's company who was known for his wild, romantic exploits. Harris had his arm about her shoulders and she was laughing as she fed him a sweetmeat. Apparently Riverton saw her at the same moment as Colin, for he muttered a low curse and left Colin's side.

Colin didn't stay to see what happened. But when he entered the next room, he didn't at once see Annabelle. He did see Aphra with her back to him, dressed like the rest of the women, her hand propped on one hip as she argued with Sir William D'Avenant.

Then he noticed a cluster of people at one end of the room. He pushed forward through the crowd, but stopped short of the front when he caught sight of his quarry in the middle of the knot of revelers.

Annabelle was dancing, and not with the measured steps so common to English dances. She was whirling . . . and kicking her heels high . . . and tossing her hair with lively grace.

He could scarcely believe his eyes. What he saw was completely at odds with the foolish vision of his arrival that he'd nursed in his mind through the entire ride back to London. He'd thought to find Annabelle meekly awaiting him at Aphra's chambers, desperately miserable at his absence and ready to tell him anything simply to have him promise to stay with her. Yet here she was, performing for a crowd of gallants who cheered her every step. He continued to stand there for a moment, astonished into silence as he watched her.

Her face was flushed, lending her skin a rosy, seductive glow, and she laughed with every quick turn. What was more, she wore the costume she'd worn when he saw her dance in the play—snug-fitting breeches that molded her hips more closely than any skirt could ever do and the sheerest hose he'd ever seen. She'd apparently abandoned her coat, if she'd ever worn one, and she'd unbuttoned the shepherd's smock beneath that, so all she wore over her breasts was a man's thin holland shirt, which clung to her like a second skin.

A terrible anger began eating away at him like a

caustic poultice as he glanced to her hand to see if she wore his ring.

She didn't. The sight stunned him. He felt as if someone had driven a knife deep in his gut.

Suddenly the music ended, and before Colin could even react, the Earl of Rochester, who'd been watching the dance and who appeared to be quite drunk, pulled a protesting Annabelle into the adjoining room. Sick with a cold, jealous anger, Colin followed them, ignoring the murmurs around him as the crowd realized who he was and parted to let him pass.

Rage so overwhelmed him he didn't even acknowledge Aphra's presence when she pushed through the crowd toward him, words of greeting on her lips that died when she saw the fury in his expression. He had only one aim: to get to Annabelle and remind her of all her promises, her damnable broken promises.

He passed into the next room in time to see Rochester thrust Annabelle against a wall and force his knee between her legs as he covered her mouth with his and slid his hand over her breast. She struggled beneath him, but his mouth muffled her protest.

Colin grasped the hilt of his sword. He was so blinded by rage he could scarcely think, but as he stepped forward, Rochester let out a hoarse cry and jumped back from Annabelle.

"You bith my tongue!" Rochester cried in outrage, wiping away the blood trickling from his mouth. "Damn wenth! You bith me!"

"Aye, and drunk or no, I'll bite your fingers off if you ever touch me like that again, Rochester!" she retorted, fierce and furious.

Rochester's thick lips curled in ugly menace, and he stepped back toward her. That's when Colin drew his sword. The loud hiss of metal made Rochester whirl around. His bleary eyes showed first astonishment, then anger.

"You lay a hand on her," Colin said in a menacing tone, "and I'll do more than bite you, Rochester. I'll spit you like a joint of mutton and roast you over yon fire.''

He heard Annabelle suck in her breath, but he dared not take his eyes off the slender young man. When Rochester was drunk, he was wild and dangerous. Rochester's hand went to his own sword, and Colin tensed.

Then Rochester seemed to catch himself. Slowly, he dropped his hand from his sword hilt, although he didn't move from his position between Colin and Annabelle. The flow of blood from his mouth had slowed. He licked his lips with his tongue as if to test whether his tongue still worked.

Although he swayed a bit, he had enough presence of mind to sneer, ''So the marquis has returned at last from his secret trip.'' Apparently his tongue was functioning normally again.

Before Colin could even wonder how Rochester knew about his trip, the young man continued, ''Come to claim your woman, have you?''

Colin's gaze flicked to Annabelle. She stared at him wide-eyed, her hand at her throat.

''You could say that,'' Colin ground out, returning his gaze to Rochester. ''Now step aside, Rochester.''

''She doesn't want you anymore, you know,'' Rochester said, slurring his words. ''She's got other men to keep her company while you're out running about.''

Colin didn't even bother to answer that. ''Annabelle, come here.''

His gaze locked with hers. He couldn't tell from her expression whether she was pleased or not to see him, and for a fleeting second, he wondered if she'd actually wanted Rochester's attentions. Then she slid from behind Rochester and came to his side. Only then did Colin lower his sword, although he didn't sheathe it.

Rochester slumped against the wall, a half smile crossing his face. Then he shrugged. ''She's a damn fine dancer, you know.'' His smile broadened to an insolent grin as he spread his legs wide and thrust with his hips in a provocative movement that couldn't be misinterpreted. "I'll wager she's even better in bed."

Rochester was deliberately provoking him for daring to interrupt his pleasure. Nonetheless, Colin tensed at the mocking words, rage flooding him.

Then Annabelle's hand gripped his arm. "He's a drunken fool," she whispered, a hint of desperation in her tone. "You know that, so let him be. Please, Colin, let's just leave."

It was the "please" that affected him more than anything. Her fingers clutched at his arm as if it were a lifeline, and one glance at her pale face told him she wanted to be out of there as quickly as possible.

Grudgingly, he admitted he wanted to oblige her, but not before he did one thing. Jerking his sword up again, he thrust forward between Rochester's spread thighs, catching Rochester's full breeches and pinning them to the wall.

Rochester went white as he stared down at the sword, which had come far too close to his privates for his comfort. "Gadsbud, you almost unmanned me! Are you mad?"

"Nay," Colin hissed. "If I'd been mad, there'd have been no 'almost.' And if I ever see you with your hands on Annabelle again, you lecherous sot, there will be no 'almost' about it. Next time I won't miss. Is that understood?"

Nothing could sober a man up faster than the possibility of having his privates skewered, Colin thought as he watched Rochester straighten against the wall and his eyes grow amazingly alert.

"I understand," Rochester murmured. "I understand."

"Good." Colin withdrew his sword and sheathed it. "Because I won't mind repeating the lesson if you ever forget it."

Rochester began muttering curses under his breath as he checked himself to make sure Colin hadn't done any damage, but Colin didn't stay around to watch.

"Time to fly, my pretty bird," he said as he clasped

Annabelle's arm and thrust her toward the door. "You and I have a great deal to talk about."

Annabelle walked beside Colin in a daze. Although his gait was stiff, as if he were sore from riding for a long while, he strode quickly through the back room of the Blue Bell, forcing her to try to match his furious pace. His fingers were laced through hers, giving the appearance that they were in easy accord with one another, but she knew if she tried to break his grip, she'd not succeed.

Neither of them spoke as they walked together, not that they would have wanted to say much when surrounded by staring women and grinning rakes. She held her head high and proud, determined at least to maintain her dignity. Murmurs and whispers followed in their wake as the other people parted to let them pass, but she hardly noticed. She was still too busy recovering from Rochester's disgusting advances.

She stole a glance at Colin. Dear heaven, he was angry. His eyes held a feral gleam she'd never seen before, and his mouth had a hard edge to it that terrified her.

She couldn't believe the way he'd reacted to Rochester. He'd acted as jealous as any Othello, which just went to prove that men were two-faced rogues. He'd gone off and left her, possibly been unfaithful to her, and yet he stormed in after his trip and claimed her as if she were some horse he'd left at a stable to be picked up on his return. Sweet Mary, what right had he to be so furious?

Then again, she ought to be grateful he'd chosen that moment to return. Granted, she might have been able to handle Rochester, but Colin certainly had a way of driving his point home, so to speak, that made his solutions more permanent.

She thought of the expression on his face when she'd first seen him standing there, looking like the angel of vengeance come to force justice on the unyielding. Though his brow had drawn tight with fury, she'd seen only the accusation blazing from his eyes when he'd stared at her—accusation and hurt.

Devil take the man! As if he had the right to feel hurt! In any case, he deserved to suffer the same agony she'd suffered the last two weeks.

Unfortunately, it wasn't his agony that had her worried, but his anger. The strength coursing through his fingers now as he steered her into the front room reminded her he wasn't a man to be taken lightly. Still, she'd dealt with his anger before. She could do it again.

Yet when they approached the entrance doors, she balked, her terror of him making her halt in the entrance. She lifted her face up to his. "Where are we going?"

He looked like Adonis gone mad as he faced her, eyes glittering and chin set. "To my house, where I can be sure there will be no interruptions."

His house. Dear heaven, what did he intend to do with her there? "I don't want to go anywhere with you when you're this angry," she said in a trembling voice. "You frighten me."

He dropped his hand to the small of her back and forced her forward through the door. "Would you rather return to Rochester and his roving hands?"

"Nay. I—I could go back to Aphra's, however, and you could come see me there when you're less upset."

"Not a chance," he growled. Suddenly he stopped dead in his tracks and turned to glare at her. "You know, none of that mess with Rochester would have happened if you'd kept your promise to me and not removed my ring."

The nerve of the man! Her fear suddenly shifted to fury. "That ring proved to be only as good as the word of the man who gave it to me," she snapped. "Since I found him to be a liar and a deceiving, unfaithful rake, I didn't see much point in wearing it."

Her statement seemed to draw him up short. "What in the devil are you talking about?"

"Don't pretend you don't know. I'm quite aware you

didn't go to Kent. I also know you asked Sedley to keep it secret that you weren't in Kent.''

For a moment he looked startled by her statement. Then his eyes narrowed. "I see Sedley has trouble keeping his mouth shut,'' he muttered unrepentantly.

Any private hope she'd harbored that Sedley might have misunderstood Colin vanished with those words. "You . . . you wretched, lying . . . lying . . .''

"Bastard?'' he said with one eyebrow raised.

"Aye! Bastard! Your dear friend Sedley didn't say a word to me, but he told every other wit at court, and that's all it took for it to get back to me. Of course everyone realized at once that you . . . that you . . .''

He gazed down at her suspiciously. "That I what?''

"That you hid your destination from me because you were going to meet another woman.''

Now he truly looked astonished. "What in the name of— Hell and furies, you thought I was with another woman?''

The incredulous note in his voice and the expression on his face seemed awfully convincing, but she'd risk the fires of hell before she believed him again, she told herself. "Of course I did! Such infidelity is common among noblemen. You made me promise not to be unfaithful, but you gave me no similar promise, if you'll recall. Nor have you given me a reason to think you're any different.''

"Haven't I?'' he bit out. The fine string of curses that tumbled from his lips were more colorful than she'd ever heard him use before. He thrust her away from him, his brow knit in a forbidding frown. "Even when I protected you from the king and told you of matters no other man would ever have discussed with a woman?'' He shook his head. " 'Sdeath, I'd have thought our night together would have told you something about the way I feel.''

This time she couldn't keep the hurt from her voice as she stared off into the street that was barely lit by an early risen moon. "Not nearly as much as your abrupt departure the next morning and your attempt to cover up where you'd gone."

He winced as if she'd struck him.

Attempting to sound sophisticated, she went on, "After you left, I learned the painful lesson I should have learned long ago. Men and women look at such things differently. Riverton, for example. He expects Charity to share him with his fiancée. I would have thought he was different, too, but I learned I was wrong. Men want to have their pleasures sated, and they tire of one woman easily."

"Not all men," Colin protested. "I tell you, not all men!"

"Admit it, you lied to me about where you were going, because you wanted me to stay faithful while you did as you pleased, like Riverton and the others!"

"I'll not admit such a thing, because it's absurd."

"Then why did you lie to me, Colin?"

The wind ruffled his hair as he struck an arrogant stance. "I could ask the same thing. Why did you break your promises?"

"Oh, come now, I've already told you. Because you lied to me. I wouldn't have done it otherwise."

He continued as if he hadn't heard her. "You took off my ring . . . you obviously went on teasing every fop and whey-faced wit who caught your fancy until they began following you around like insolent pups. . . ."

The unfairness of his accusation tore at her. "Oh, it didn't take much effort on my part. When they learned you'd abandoned me, they were all too eager to leap into the breach."

A wildness lit his eyes at the bitterness in her voice. "For the love of God, none of them . . . they didn't . . ."

Her gaze shot to his as his meaning became apparent. "No, no! I can take care of myself when I have to. I don't need your help, Colin, in fighting my battles." It was a lie, but it gave her immense satisfaction to say it.

"Should I have left you to Rochester, then?" He crossed his arms over his chest, quietly watching her.

"I didn't lie when I told him I'd bite his fingers off," she whispered. "I would have too."

The ghost of a smile flitted over his face. "Yes, I almost think you would have." Then the smile faded. "So help me, dearling, I wanted to kill him for touching you. And before that, when I saw you dancing so blithely, without my ring on your finger, I nearly wanted to kill you too."

He could make her feel so guilty with just a few words. But he was the one who should feel guilty. He was the one who'd lied, who was still attempting to pull the wool over her eyes. "Where were you these past two weeks," she asked point-blank, "if not with another woman?"

He opened his mouth to speak, then snapped it shut. He glanced around at the people coming in and out of the ordinary, slowing as they passed Colin and Annabelle and cocking their heads to hear any interesting gossip.

Then he stepped toward her and took her arm, urging her forward once again. "I'll tell you as soon as we get away from all these ears. 'Tis not the place to discuss this."

"Yes, of course, more of your man's secrets." She spitefully resisted his attempts to make her move.

A look of sheer exasperation crossed his face. "Believe me, I wasn't with another woman. 'Sdeath, I can't even handle one woman at a time, much less two."

"Whatever you say, Colin."

At the biting tone of her statement, he lifted his hand to stroke her cheek, and she flinched away from his touch.

"You don't much trust me, do you?" he said softly, dropping his hand.

Unshed tears stung her eyes when she heard the hurt in his voice, but she was hurting too. "Sweet Mary, can you blame me? You—you leave town after tossing me a story that I learn is a lie . . . and then . . . then you waltz in here as if you hadn't been gone for nearly two weeks without a word.''

Realizing she was treading dangerously close to revealing the full extent of her feelings, she sucked in her breath and tried to force the bitterness from her voice. ''In any case, it doesn't matter. None of it matters in the least.''

The slip of a moon illuminated his face as he stared at her. Dear heaven, but that steady, heart-stopping gaze could still make her tremble to her toes.

''Oh, it matters, dearling, it matters very much, as you'll realize after we talk. But *not here.* Come on.''

Encircling her waist again, he pivoted on his heel and pulled her along with him to a huge, mud-spattered bay tethered near the entrance. He lifted her into the saddle with an easy grace, then untethered the horse before swinging up into the saddle behind her.

The click of his tongue sent the horse plodding wearily down the thoroughfare, which still bustled with people since it was still not yet eight o'clock. His arm slid around her waist to settle her more securely in the saddle, and her thighs rested on his corded, muscular ones. She could feel every sinew of those thighs beneath her legs through the thin breeches she wore.

And his arm, oh, dear heaven, his arm was fixed just under her breasts. Without the lacing and boning of a gown, the two soft weights rested on his arm, gently jounced by the gait of the horse.

Every touch, every sweet intimacy they'd ever shared sprang instantly into her mind, heating her blood and sending anticipation prickling over her skin. Sweet Mary, how could she have forgotten what it was like to be held by Colin?

Even as her anger smoldered, a lovely, erotic longing threatened to sweep away all her determination to resist his smooth words this time. It didn't help that the horse's pace had slowed or that Colin had begun stroking her thigh idly with his other hand.

Closing her eyes, she reminded herself that they'd soon reach his house and the spell would be broken.

He'd tell her where he'd been, and that would shatter everything, because he wouldn't have lied about it in the first place if it had been something innocuous. No, he knew she wouldn't like what he had to say or he'd have said it in front of the Blue Bell.

Her curiosity jabbered like a jester inside her, yet a part of her feared knowing where he'd been. She sensed that whatever he had to say to her would change everything.

It took them only a short while to reach his house in the Strand, one of the most fashionable districts in London, but it wasn't short enough to keep her apprehension and her doubts from growing. Nor did it help when they drew up before the imposing marble columns of a three-story brick edifice with a dazzling array of mullioned windows.

Sick at heart, she stared at the blatant symbol of the differences between their stations. No wonder he'd lied to her. Men who lived in mansions didn't deign to worry about what a lowly actress might think of them. What a fool she'd been even to dream of being Colin's wife. Colin would never stoop to marry a woman like her.

Seemingly unaware of the consternation eating away at her self-confidence, Colin dismounted, then helped her dismount as a footman came running out to take the post horse and return it.

Other servants greeted him the moment they entered—a gruff steward of indeterminate age, a cheery, matronly housekeeper, and a groom of the chambers who took Colin's coat and hat. Colin answered their many questions, resting his hand all the while in the small of her back.

When the steward cast her a furtive glance of sheer astonishment, Annabelle realized she was still dressed in her male garb. Embarrassment swept through her as she avoided the gaze of the servants. What on earth was she doing here? This awe-inspiring house, with its marble floor and its walls covered with the stern portraits of a long line of titled ancestors, was not the place for a scandalously dressed actress.

She reminded herself that Colin was a bastard like her, that he'd inherited all of this only because his father had sired no other heirs, but it did no good. The reality of his magnificent holdings had caught her up in a net of torment.

Why was she so stunned at this evidence of Colin's wealth? She'd known Colin had riches. She'd known he had power and a title. So why was she standing here, gawking in amazement like the street urchins to whom she fed oranges?

Perhaps because he'd never behaved like the other wealthy men who'd frequented the theater. He'd always treated her with respect . . . well, until recently . . . even when he'd been furious at her. He'd never emphasized the difference between their stations. She'd known so many pompous, ostentatious men who wore their wealth and power on their sleeves and spoke with contempt to the actresses that she'd half expected Colin's lodgings to be modest and small to match the casual disregard he seemed to have for his position.

Of course not, she thought sadly. She should have realized Colin would have a mansion and no less. Perhaps this was why he'd brought her here, to remind her of his power and standing, which surpassed hers as sunlight surpasses moonlight in brightness. Well, if that was his intent, he'd certainly succeeded. She'd been a fool to believe him when he'd said she held his affections. Who could hold the affections of a man who could buy anyone's affections whenever he wanted?

The housekeeper left and Colin turned to the steward. Annabelle tried not to feel conspicuous and out of place as Colin spoke with the steward, but she had little success.

Their conversation droned on a few minutes, during which Colin asked several questions about financial matters. Suddenly the steward said, ''I do hope you had no trouble finding Norwood, my lord. It has been some time since I traveled that way, and I'm not sure my directions were adequate.''

Norwood? Her head snapped around, and she fixed Colin with a gaze of pure fear as her heart began to hammer in her chest. His eyes met hers, inscrutable as the mysterious green ocean. Yet she could tell by the harsh expression on his face that she hadn't misheard the steward Norwood. Sweet Mary in heaven, Colin had been to Norwood.

Without taking his eyes from her, Colin told the steward, ''No, no, Jonson. No trouble at all. The trip only took me a day and a half. Thank you.''

Annabelle was trembling now, and she knew he could see it. *Colin has been to Norwood,* the chant began in her mind. As the ramifications of that hit her, her anger and jealousy over his apparent unfaithfulness instantly dissipated, to be replaced by an iron ball of terror dropping with a thud into her belly.

He'd been to Norwood. That meant he knew it all now, didn't it? Oh, yes, he must have found out about her mother, the squire, the murder . . . everything. There was no way on God's green earth that Colin could have gone to Norwood and not discovered every dirty secret from her past. The only thing he didn't know was her purpose for coming to London, but she had no doubt he'd try to get that out of her too.

Devil take him, who could possibly have told him she was from Norwood? She could have sworn she'd only told him the name of the county. Could Charity have said something to him? No, if Charity had told him, she'd have said something when she'd heard that Colin had left town and lied about where he was going.

Annabelle's mouth felt dry. Somehow Colin had found out where she was from. But why had he even bothered to search it out or to go to Norwood once he knew?

''If you'd like a bit of supper, my lord—'' the steward began.

"No, I've already eaten. Just bring some wine into my study."

"And for . . . for the young lady?"

Annabelle could tell the steward was choking on the phrase, but she no longer cared about the steward or the housekeeper or any of Colin's undoubtedly numerous servants.

"Annabelle? Would you like something?" Colin asked calmly, as if he hadn't pulled the rug out from under her.

"No," she whispered, "nothing." What she wanted was to disappear, and she doubted the steward could manage that for her.

"Very good," the steward murmured, and then left.

Since the housekeeper and groom had already gone off to follow other instructions, Annabelle and Colin were left standing alone in the hall.

"As I told you," he said softly, almost menacingly, "I have not been with a woman for the past two weeks. And you and I do have a great deal to talk about."

His words and his tone of voice hardened the resolve in her breast as he led her up the stairs to the first floor. Yes, they did have a great deal to talk about.

Nonetheless, whether he realized it or not, he had as much explaining to do as she did. And she'd make him explain himself if it took her all night to do it.

Chapter Eighteen

"Excellent wretch! Perdition catch my soul
But I do love thee! and when I love thee not,
Chaos is come again."
—William Shakespeare, *Othello*, Act 3, Scene 3

Her head was awhirl as they reached the top of the stairs. Now that he knew everything, what would he do? And for heaven's sake, how had he found out?

She had her answer to the first question soon enough. As soon as they'd moved down a hall and entered a large room lined with bookshelves, he faced her, his expression dangerously dark. "Why didn't you tell me?"

The time for truth had come, yet she couldn't get a word past the thickness in her throat.

"Why didn't you tell me your mother had been hung for killing your stepfather?" he demanded.

"It's not the sort of thing anyone would want widely known," she attempted to say offhandedly, meeting the feverish intensity of his eyes with a proudly tilted chin.

That only seemed to infuriate him. "Some in Norwood claim you had a part in the murder."

All her defiance dwindled into nothing. "I did not! Dear heaven, Colin, surely you couldn't believe that I—"

"Nay." His expression softened the merest fraction. "Nay, I didn't believe it. Fortunately, I found someone who'd seen everything and proved me right not to. Of course, it would have all been more clear if you'd told me yourself."

A knock sounded at the door, and Colin barked a curt command. A footman entered bearing a tray with a flagon of wine. Colin moved away from her to stand by the newly laid fire roaring in the grate.

Annabelle watched the footman, her emotions in turmoil. She scarcely paid attention to the odd glances she garnered from the servant for her apparel. She was too busy trying to make sense of what Colin had told her so far. He hadn't gone to meet another woman. Well, that hardly mattered anymore. She almost wished he had—it certainly would have made her life easier.

Instead, he'd gone to Norwood and learned about her mother's hanging. Why? And how had he learned that Norwood was her home?

Only with great restraint did she force herself to wait for the servant to leave so she could broach her questions. As the footman moved toward the door, Colin called out, "See to it that we aren't disturbed by anyone."

"Aye, my lord," the footman murmured, and left.

Annabelle watched the door shut behind him with growing trepidation. Drawing up the fractured bits of her courage, she managed to ask the question that was plaguing her. "Why did you go to Norwood, Colin?"

He didn't answer at first. Still staring into the fire, he rested his hand on the mantelpiece. The flames limned his golden hair with fiery lights that made him look like a tigerish devil, ready to tear into her with his claws. The fire stripped away the patina of civilization he normally wore and reminded her Colin could be almost savage when his ire was roused.

"Why did you go to Norwood?" she repeated with impatience. "How did you know to go there?"

He looked up at her, although a shutter went down over his face. "I went to Norwood because I wanted to find out all your secrets, even the ones you wouldn't tell me."

"But how—"

"I was a spy, Annabelle, remember? We have ways of finding out such things."

"Yes, but—"

"How I found out is neither here nor there," he exploded as he left the fire. He went to the flagon and filled a pewter goblet with wine, then downed it quickly before leveling a wild-eyed gaze on her. "The fact is, I did find out, and now I want some answers."

Her spine stiffened. She didn't flinch from his gaze, though the dark determination in it alarmed her. "Why should I give you any answers? You have no right to them. Except for protecting me from the king, for which I paid you amply," she said with biting irony, "you haven't given me many answers yourself."

He raked his hands through his golden mane agitatedly. "What answers do you want from me?"

"I want to know what prompted you to go to Norwood, and I want to know who my father is."

His eyes widened in surprise. "You think I can tell you who your father is." It was a statement, not a question, and he spoke it with an odd evasion.

She wasn't sure if he could tell her, but she had her suspicions, and she wanted them addressed. "You're the one who pointed out your abilities as a spy. All right, then. If you're such an accomplished spy, so powerful in London, so knowledgeable about the peerage, then why didn't you recognize that coat of arms? Why did you rush off to Norwood to root out all *my* secrets when you knew how much I wanted to know his identity?"

He seemed to debate that statement a moment. Then he wiped his face clean of all expression and said in an even voice, "Your father is Edward Maynard, the Earl of Walcester. His coat of arms matches the one on your signet ring."

Stunned to have him state it so bluntly, she searched his face for signs that he was lying. "When . . . how long . . ."

He tossed the goblet down, and it clanked on the tray. "As you say, I'm knowledgeable about the peerage. I recognized Walcester's coat of arms the night you showed me the ring."

Going limp as a piece of unstarched linen, she dropped into a nearby armchair. So the Earl of Walcester was her father. At last she knew the truth. She'd thought she'd feel more relief or anger or something to know it, but the words had little meaning for her. It was simply another name of a noble with a title. It meant nothing when she didn't know the man.

Then again, she wasn't certain that she didn't know the man. If it had been him at the theater tonight, then she knew him far too well. She wanted to ask more of Colin, to determine if that man and her father were the same person, but first she needed to know one thing. "Why didn't you tell me his identity that night?"

Colin's eyes narrowed. "Because I wasn't sure what you intended to do with the information. In truth, I'm still not sure."

She certainly wasn't going to tell him. He would construe it in the worst way.

Colin approached the armchair, leaned down, and rested his hands on the arms, trapping her in the chair. His face was scant inches from hers. "Now, Annabelle," he growled, "it's your turn. And don't think you can lie to me. I've told you what you wanted. I want my own questions answered now."

"You already seem to know all the important answers," she whispered. Her hands had grown very clammy, and she wiped them on her shepherd's smock with nervous movements.

"Yes, I know about the murder itself. Your mother killed your stepfather to protect you from him and was hanged for it. That needs no explanation."

The almost manic intensity in his gaze struck her with terror, despite his reassuring words. "S-so what is it you wish to know?"

"They told me in Norwood that you were a proper girl, even religious. They said that to all outward appearances, you were modest and respectable."

"It was either be modest and respectable in public or risk my stepfather's temper. Believe me, modest and respectable was not what I was inside."

His tone tightened. "They also told me that you were cut from your stepfather's will—"

"Because of my bastardy!"

"Yes, I realize that. But it means you had no money and, from what I hear, no man to protect you."

She nodded, bewildered by this trail of reasoning. If he understood all of this, then what was he so intent on learning? What was he so angry about? Simply that she hadn't told him any of it?

"So you found out you had no means of support, but you had a father in London. You and Charity set out for London. That much is perfectly understandable."

He paused a moment, his eyes playing over her face with a strange sort of hunger. Not certain what he wanted of her now that he knew so much, she held her tongue.

"What I don't understand," he said softly, "is why you chose to go on the stage. Why not find some employment more suitable to your upbringing—a position as a governess, perhaps?"

"I told you before—Charity had a friend in the theater."

Abruptly he straightened. Crossing his arms over his chest, he smiled, though it didn't bring any warmth to his eyes. "Ah, yes. Charity to the rescue. Still, that doesn't explain why you didn't use your real name once you arrived. Or why you didn't take more active steps to find your father. It took me a week to convince you to tell me you were looking for him. You could have shown that ring to a number of people who'd have brought you to your father. Yet you didn't. Why?"

She couldn't meet his eyes. "I wanted to be discreet."

"Rubbish. Try another tale, my lying swan. While you're at it, explain why a 'modest girl' would turn into a wanton in the city. And don't tell me any of that nonsense about its being the only way to protect yourself. Other actresses manage to live respectably and not be troubled by forward gallants."

"I could see no way to fend them off—"

"Stop it!" he thundered, leaning down again to trap her in the chair. "Stop lying to me! You came to this city and set yourself up as a wanton amongst the actresses with a purpose in mind. I want to know what that purpose is."

He was so unwavering, almost desperate, that it frightened her. "Why? Why do you care so much?"

Torment gleamed in his eyes for a moment, then faded. "Because I'm afraid I know what your purpose is, and it smacks of a deeper treachery than I'd thought you capable of."

Could he have guessed what she'd planned? Surely if he had, he could understand why. Unfortunately, the stark accusation in his glance told her he didn't. Suddenly she couldn't bear it anymore, his presuming to pass judgment on her.

She shoved him back, then leapt to her feet, feeling as if he were smothering her, closing her in a tight box of condemnation without even seeing her for what she was. She was tired of her role, tired of pretending to be someone else, especially with him.

As she paced the room, unable to meet his eyes, the words spilled out of her like corruption from a lanced canker sore. "Is it treachery to want to punish the one who abandoned my mother and me to a daily torment? Is it treachery to want vengeance for being discarded without a thought? Is it?"

He remained silent.

"You want to know my purpose? All right, then. I came to London to punish my father. I came to humiliate him before all the world and make him ashamed to lift his head in public." She whirled to face him, and added in a voice bitter and low, "I came to make him suffer for his crimes by being the bastard daughter of his nightmares. *That's* my darker purpose, my treachery."

Colin's expression altered subtly, the faintest hint of surprise in his furrowed brow. "You wanted to humiliate your real father? You sought to shame him?"

"Aye," she choked out, turning her back to him once more. "I thought to be the kind of daughter no man would want to own. Then I planned to reveal my identity publicly once I could determine who he was."

"I don't understand."

"No, of course you don't. Your father claimed you—a little late perhaps, but he claimed you. Mine didn't. As far as I can determine, he didn't care one whit that he'd fathered a child."

"Perhaps your mother never told him."

"That's not the point!" she hissed. "Mother was a virgin until my father came along. Because he couldn't keep his—his blessed 'sword' in its sheath, to use your phrasing, Mother was consigned to a life of hell. Hell, I tell you! You say you understand about the murder. Do you really? You weren't there. You don't know what it's like to see your mother, normally mild as a nun, take a knife and plunge it over . . . and over . . . and—"

She broke off with a sob, reliving the day as her heart pounded painfully in her chest. She scarcely noticed that he'd gathered her up in his arms, that he was trying to force her head against his shoulder.

She simply stared wild-eyed across the room at the mantel with its crossed swords. "There was so much blood," she whispered. "It . . . it splattered Mother . . . it splattered me. Mother was screaming like a madwoman. I tried to stop her, but she had this sudden incredible strength. She just kept stabbing and stabbing—"

"Hush," he murmured, cradling her head. "Oh, please, dearling, hush."

But she couldn't halt her babbling. "The squire was long dead before Mother stopped. One of the reasons that . . . the judge had no mercy for her was that she was so brutal. Of course, he didn't know or care why. He—he simply sentenced her to hang."

Only when Colin rubbed the tears from her eyes did she realize she'd been crying.

"I was there at the execution," she whispered, tears flowing down her cheeks. "I watched her hang."

He went white, his eyes staring in disbelief. "For the love of God, why?"

"I—I thought I'd save her . . . you know . . . cut her down and bring her to a surgeon who'd revive her." Her voice hardened. "But they wouldn't let me near the body. Charity took me away once Mother was h-hoisted . . . but—" her voice broke, "I—I heard she didn't die for some time. Oh, sweet Mary, Colin, I should have saved her! I should have stopped her from killing him! I should have—"

"Sh, sh," he murmured, holding her close. "It sounds as if you did everything you could, dearling, short of calling down a miracle from God."

"I did that too," she admitted solemnly. "He didn't oblige me by giving me one."

That seemed to send Colin right over the edge. With a choked cry, he lifted her and went to sit by the fire, cradling her in his arms, whispering soothing words, stroking her hair. The kindness was too much. She gave herself up to the tears clogging her throat, to the unbearable sadness that had lain in her for what seemed like years.

He let her cry. He didn't try to hush her or even kiss her. Instead, he cushioned her with his body and comforted her with his arms, giving no demands and asking no questions. It felt so good to have him hold her that she remained curled against his chest long after her tears had subsided, her hand clutching the now damp cloth of his vest. Shifting her in his arms, he reached for the flagon and poured her some wine. She sipped it gratefully, letting the sourness cleanse her dry, hot mouth.

She was afraid to speak, to break the spell and risk facing his anger and condemnation again, but at last she could avoid it no more. Staring up into his eyes, she searched for signs of his early anger, but all she saw was a kind of quiet waiting, a tender acceptance.

"Colin? You d-do understand why I had to punish my father somehow. I—I had to make him suffer the way Mother suffered. He took her innocence and abandoned her. He had to pay for that."

Colin sighed. He wrapped a lock of her hair about his finger, then lifted it to his lips and kissed it. "I can see why you'd want revenge, but I still don't understand how you'd intended to get it."

Sniffling, she set the goblet of wine aside and laid her head on his chest again. "I thought if I appeared to live scandalously, my father would be shamed before his peers. No man wants a daughter who's an actress on the stage."

"Most nobility consider trodding the boards to be one step above whoring," he agreed matter-of-factly.

She winced. "I—I had this dream, you see, of destroying his reputation by flaunting myself and eventually revealing my parentage."

"But you had to find him first."

"Yes. I took his surname . . . and . . . and . . ."

She paused, wondering if she should tell him about the poem. Why not? If Colin had been in the king's service, he might know something about such things. What's more, Colin *had* finally told her who her father was, and if Colin were in league with her father, he wouldn't have done that, would he?

"I—I took a nickname," she whispered. "I didn't tell you this before, but my father left my mother a poem signed with the name 'The Silver Swan.' That's why I wore that brooch and Charity and I did what we could to coax the gallants into using the nickname. All I knew was my father's surname and that nickname, so I used it on the stage, hoping to draw him out."

Did she imagine it or did he suddenly relax beneath her?

"This poem," he said quietly. "Why did it have such a strange signature?"

She shook her head. "I don't know. I thought it was some sort of . . . I don't know . . . lovers' code or something." Thinking of her encounter at the theater, she sighed. "Until today."

"What do you mean?" he asked sharply.

She thought of the man in the box at the theater. If Colin knew her father, then he could tell her if the man at the theater was him. Dear heaven, but it would be a relief to completely unburden herself to Colin, to have him at her side in this. The man in the box had truly frightened her, making her realize she might be in over her head. Colin would know what to do, she told herself. Colin would know.

Once her mind was made up, she told him everything—about the man's threats, his refusal to let her see his face, his statements about her use of the nickname.

Colin shifted her on his lap, staring into her face with a strained expression. "What did the man look like?"

"I told you. I don't know. But he had a gravelly voice and carried a cane."

Paling, Colin closed his eyes.

"Was it my father?" she asked in a whisper.

He hesitated a moment, then said, "I think so."

"I—I don't understand why my father fears my using his . . . his nickname. Unless . . . I mean, I have to wonder if it had anything to do with the poem and the task he asked of my mother."

Colin stiffened. "What task?"

She swallowed. "Mother told me that my father gave her that poem to pass on to his friend in the village. She did, but after his friend read the poem, he thrust it back at her. She waited, but when she saw soldiers coming, she fled."

"For the love of God," Colin muttered under his breath.

"It sounds as if my father was involved in some intrigue. What could he have done that makes him so fearful now?"

Clutching her against his chest, Colin groaned. "Annabelle, it doesn't matter what he did. You must promise to abandon this foolish quest of yours for revenge. Your father could be dangerous."

"I know," she whispered.

His eyes shot open, and he tipped her chin up until she was staring into his eyes. "Listen to me, dearling. I'm not saying Walcester doesn't deserve to suffer for what he did to your mother. He does. But if you endanger your life to punish him, then he has won, don't you see? He has destroyed both you and your mother and proven he can do as he pleases without answering to anyone."

Her mouth trembled. "I know."

As if he couldn't quite believe she was agreeing with him, he murmured, "This isn't about him or your mother or your stepfather. This is about you and your pain. Your pain won't be assuaged by hurting him, I assure you." He sucked in his breath. "The scars on your back won't heal because he's been punished. Nor will the scars on your soul. You must set about healing them by putting the past behind you and finding some new future."

Not only did his words make sense, they gave her an odd relief. Lately, she'd felt as if she were spiraling down into madness. The more she nursed her plans, the more she felt twisted on the rack. Only when she lost herself in the theater did she find release from her torment. And when she was in Colin's arms.

Telling him about her mother's death had somehow purged her. She still hated her real father, this earl, for abandoning her mother, but she'd lost the burning thirst to destroy him. Maybe Colin was right. Maybe it was time to put the past behind her.

He must have seen her agreement in her face, for his eyes suddenly glowed with some internal light. "I have no right to ask it of you, but you will promise, won't you, to abandon this plan of yours, before Walcester gets some wild idea about what you know of his past and decides to hurt you?"

She stared at him, at the longing in his face. This was the man she loved, the man who'd listened to all her plans for destroying her father and hadn't condemned her. He didn't care that she'd been deceiving him or that her mother had been a criminal. All he cared about was her safety.

He sat now, patiently waiting for her to promise she'd abandon her plans—not because he wanted to protect a nobleman, but because he wanted to protect her. What other answer could she give him?

"Yes, I'll give up my vengeance if you wish it," she said.

For a moment he looked stunned, as if he hadn't expected her to respond so quickly. Then sheer relief passed over his face. "Thank heaven. Walcester is a foe to be feared."

"You don't truly think he'd try to kill me, do you? I—I mean, I know he doesn't know I'm his daughter, but—but he's not the kind of man who would murder someone, is he?"

Colin's arms tightened around her. He seemed preoccupied by his thoughts for a moment. Then he said, "I don't know, dearling. I truly don't." He gave her a searching look. "I discovered some things in Norwood about your father that give me pause."

"What?"

"It's all very confusing, but apparently your father was at Norwood shortly after the Battle of Naseby, which, as you know, took place not far from there. After your father sent your mother to Norwood to deliver that message, three Royalists who'd escaped capture until then were caught and the papers of Charles I were confiscated by the Roundheads. The man who arrested them said they were betrayed by a traitor in their midst."

"You think my father was the traitor?" she whispered, her pulse quickening.

" 'Tis possible, I'm afraid, although I don't know for certain. I intend to find out, however." He cupped her face in his hands. "I tell you this only because I

want you to know what a risky game you've been playing with this vengeance of yours. I hope you mean it
when you say you'll abandon it.''

She'd be a fool not to, she thought. "I do.''

"I swear it would destroy me if something happened
to you, Annabelle. It would completely destroy me.''

The intensity of emotion behind his words struck
her dumb. All she could do was stare at him in amazement, love for him welling within her. Slowly, a
change came over him. The worry in his expression
faded to desire. Before she knew it, he'd pressed his
mouth hard to hers, making her forget about her father
and the Silver Swan and the terrible things that had
happened at Norwood. All she cared about was him,
his lips forcing hers apart, his hands cupping her head
to hold it still as he kissed her more and more deeply.

After he'd made her quite faint from pleasure, he
drew back, cupping her cheek in his hand. His eyes
flamed with the same hunger that was also building
inside her. "Hell and furies, it's been the longest two
weeks of my life.''

"Of mine too," she admitted with a shy smile.

For an instant, pain flashed over his face. "I suppose I understand why you . . . took my ring off and
sought to hurt me while I was gone. You were right. I
should have told you what I was doing. Still, I don't
think I could bear it again to see you mauled by a
lecher like Rochester.''

"Don't worry. It won't happen again. As soon as I
return to Aphra's, I'll put your ring back on and never
take it off.''

He smiled. "This time you'll keep your promise to
be mine and mine alone?''

"Aye, this time I will, my lord.'' Then she added
archly, "But only if you promise the same.''

To her delight, he said, "Easily.'' He clasped her
hands and held them to his chest. "I swear, Annabelle, by all that's holy, to be yours and yours alone,
to have no other woman in my bed, in my thoughts,
in my heart.''

In his heart? Was it possible that . . . Nay, it was only the gallant in him talking. Still, his words warmed her, as did his willingness to make the same promise to her that he wanted her to make to him.

She smiled through a mist of tears. "Then I swear, my lord, there will never be another man in my bed, in my thoughts, in my heart." She meant every word. It was the closest she could come to marrying him.

He sealed their promises by bending her back over the arm of the chair and kissing her with a devouring hunger more provocative than tender. When at last he tired of ravaging her mouth, he drew back and stared at her, his eyes glittering and his expression enigmatic.

Slowly, he rubbed his thumb over her kiss-bruised lips, then trailed it down over her chin to her neck. "Annabelle," he whispered, his jaw taut with unfulfilled desire. "I think our promises are not enough."

She swallowed, her breath stilling. "Wh-what do you mean?"

"I would have a more concrete assurance, a more lasting promise."

What could she possibly give him that would be more lasting? she wondered.

"I would have you in marriage," he whispered, his eyes earnest.

She stared at him, her mouth agape, though her pulse quickened. Surely he hadn't said what she'd thought he'd said. "M-marriage? But . . . but . . ."

"Does that mean you don't wish to marry me?" he asked solemnly. He clasped her hand and lifted it to his lips, grazing the knuckles with a feathery caress.

It almost broke her heart to watch him. "Please, don't toy with me like this. We aren't of the same station and—"

"The same station?" A fierce light entered his eyes. "You're the daughter of an earl and the granddaughter of a knight, are you not?"

"Yes, but—"

"I love you, dearling." He spoke the words fervently, but his eyes reflected that he was almost shocked to hear himself say them. He paused, then nodded as if to himself. "Aye, Annabelle, I mean it. I love you. And I want you more than I've ever wanted another woman. I want you in my life, in my future, in my soul. I couldn't stand to lose you. It would drive me quite mad. So to save my sanity, you must marry me. You must."

She wanted to cling to his beautiful words, to vow that she too loved him, but she knew better. He might mean it now, but he'd surely change his mind later when he realized what he'd done. She tried to wriggle from his lap. He wouldn't let her.

"You can't marry me, Colin," she whispered in desperation. "I'm an actress with a scandalous reputation, and a bastard—"

"So am I, remember? You and I are meant for each other. Who else could I find who would understand my sorrow and my peculiar sense of humor, who wouldn't secretly be embarrassed to be wed to me, who cares not a farthing for my money and position? Who else?"

"Surely you could find a wife who isn't—"

"Intelligent? Talented? Beautiful? Kind? Aye, I could. I don't want that sort of wife."

She ducked her head down, not wanting him to see the hope shining in her eyes. He couldn't do this. She couldn't let him. There were so many reasons it would be unwise.

Yet all she could think of was her dream of growing old with him, of sharing her future with him.

"Is it that you don't love me?" he whispered. "I could make you love me, Annabelle. I believe I could."

Dear heaven, if he actually worked at making her love him, it would kill her. "Of course I love you," she blurted out. "How could I not?"

He tipped her head up, his eyes gleaming with satisfaction. "Then marry me."

"You'd be the laughingstock of London. You'd never be able to hold your head high here again."

"Then we won't live in London." He clasped her hands in his and drew them to his lips, kissing them both. "There are other places to live, the colonies, for example. In the colonies, no one will know or care about your past. You know I've been considering going there, to find some purpose beyond my life other than whiling it away at court. The only reason I hesitated was because I couldn't bear the thought of going alone."

Her gaze flew to his. "You can't . . . you can't mean this," she said in a tone of incredulity.

"Yes, I can." His eyes glittered . . . with determination . . . with desire . . . yes, and even with love. When she stared into those eyes, she could almost believe he meant every word.

"How shall I prove I mean it?" he asked. "Shall I circulate a poem among the court that extols your virtues and announces my intentions? Shower you with jewels? Cry my love from the rooftops?"

Her eyes widened. These were the words a gallant would say, yet somehow she knew he meant them.

"Or perhaps you'd prefer something else." He trailed his finger down into the neck of her shirt. "Kisses, caresses, sweet words. They're all yours, my love, if you want them."

Abruptly he set her to one side and stood, leaving her curled up in the chair, watching him. With his hands at his sides, he stared at her. "Tell me what you wish, Annabelle. What trials will you require of your swain to prove his love?"

He knelt in front of her. "Shall I beg?"

His hand snaked out and clasped her foot. He withdrew the embroidered slipper, then reached up beneath the hem of her breeches to untie her garter and pull down her stocking.

Without taking his gaze from her, he caressed her instep. "Shall I kiss your feet?" he asked, then pressed his lips against the top of her small foot, sending shivers of delight radiating up her leg.

Suddenly desire struck her with such intensity, she thought she'd collapse under the power of it. He was offering himself to her, but she had no wish to see him write poetry or give her jewels. She wanted him. She wanted him to seal his promises with more than a kiss.

"Tell me what you want," he whispered in a low, seductive voice. "What trial shall you have me fulfill?"

Her pulse beat madly. Oh, yes, she wanted him. What's more, he was sending wicked thoughts scampering through her mind. Suddenly she felt daring and adventurous. So he wanted a trial, did he? Then she'd give him a trial that would take care of her desires as well.

"Take off your boots," she said, her tone at first shaky.

His eyes shot to hers, inquisitive, stormy. Then a half smile played over his face as he sat back on the floor and tugged off his heavy, mud-splattered jackboots. He tossed them aside, then turned his gaze to her, lifting one eyebrow in question.

"Stand up," she commanded, more firmly this time.

Without hesitating, he stood. She surveyed him thoroughly for the first time that evening. He must have ridden hard from Norwood, for the parts of his clothing that hadn't been covered by his coat were rumpled and dirty. He was dressed in unusually sober clothes, undoubtedly because he'd dressed for traveling in the cold weather.

Yet even though he wore rough fabrics and his breeches were spattered with mud, she found him more dangerously attractive than ever before, particularly when his face flamed with blatant desire.

Emboldened by that, she said, "Take off your vest."

His smile widening to a grin, he undid his sash, then unbuttoned his vest. In seconds, the plain, black velvet lay in a pile on the floor. Without his vest, it was easy to see his aroused member standing boldly beneath his breeches.

She knelt in the chair, wondering how far he would let her go. She was rapidly finding this game intriguing. "Now the shirt and cravat," she whispered, and he immediately complied. His shirt and cravat joined his vest on the floor.

Sweet Mary, but the sight of his bared chest nearly undid her. The blond hair sprinkled over it folded into a line in the center of his chest, which darkened the closer it moved to his groin.

Now Colin's eyes were gleaming, his smile broad as he watched her. Not a hint of embarrassment crossed his face. If anything, the arrogant man was cockier than usual.

Well, she knew how to destroy that arrogance. Slowly she too stood. It took her only seconds to shrug off her coat and vest, then seconds more to unbutton her shirt and toss it aside.

He was concentrating hard on not lowering his eyes from her face to her bared breasts, for she could see the strain in his still present smile. He reached for her, but she whispered "Not yet" and brushed his hands away. Then she moved behind him and hugged him close so her breasts flattened against him.

He sucked in his breath, and she smiled. She ran her hands over the muscles of his chest and teased the flat nipples. A groan escaped his lips.

She was certainly enjoying this, she decided. For once, Colin was at her mercy, and not the other way around. Pressing kisses over his iron-hard back, she trailed her hands down his chest until she reached the band of his breeches. She undid the button and his breeches slid to the floor.

Now he wore only his kerseymere long drawers and his stockings held up with leather garters. But when she reached for the ties of his drawers, he caught her hand. "That's enough, my demanding temptress," he murmured, lifting her hand to his lips. "You'll drive me insane if you don't let me touch you too."

"I thought you said I could ask any trial of you," she whispered coyly. "Well, your trial is to let me touch you until I've had my fill."

He moaned. "Hell and furies, you've chosen a good one."

"I know." She fought to keep the laughter out of her voice as she slipped her hand from his and undid the ties of his drawers. She slid the kerseymere down over his firm hips and muscled thighs, stopping to kiss one bared buttock.

He swore, but she merely laughed as she knelt to unbuckle his garters, then remove his stockings and the long drawers. He kicked them aside. For a long moment, she savored the sight of him from behind—broad back and shoulders, lean but muscular hips, and two well-formed legs. Slowly, she ran her hands down over that wonderful expanse of male muscle, watching fascinated as the skin grew iron-taut beneath her fingers. Then she circled around to stand before him.

The arrogant smile had gone completely. In its place was a look of such blazing hunger it fed the heat building in her belly. She swallowed, then lifted both hands tentatively to touch his chest.

That was all it took to break Colin's control. Before she could even think or wonder or halt him—not that she would have—he'd clasped her so tightly in his arms she could hardly move, much less resist.

He started to kiss her, then stopped an inch short of her mouth. His eyes locked with hers. Never had she seen them look so forbidding and mysterious . . . and very, very determined.

"Have I passed my trial?" he growled. "Have I let you touch me until you had your fill?"

She was tempted to say no, yet it felt so good to be clutched against him. "I suppose it could be considered—"

That was all it took to set him off. There was nothing slow or leisurely about the way he plundered her mouth or ground his hips against her to make her aware of every inch of his hardness. He was less than gentle when he lowered his head to tug greedily at her breasts with his mouth, laving them with his tongue until they felt tight and tender as ripe berries awaiting the picking.

He dropped to one knee to dart his tongue into her navel as he worked loose her breeches. He slid them over her hips with a grin and murmured, "I never thought I'd be undoing breeches for someone I wished to make love to. It feels odd."

As he bared her to his gaze, he went very still. Then, with a low groan, he kissed the soft thatch of hair between her legs. "Doing this, however, feels not the least bit odd." He tasted her there, then drew back. "No, it feels quite right indeed."

Then a wicked expression lit his face. He reached for her half-full goblet and trickled the wine between her legs. She shivered at the cold sensation, but in seconds his warm tongue was roughly lapping her . . . first her thighs, then her covering of hair, then deeper to tease and taunt the inflamed petals of skin. She gasped as he began to caress her with his mouth in earnest, his hands clasping her hips to hold her still as he buried his face in her most private place. Her breath quickened, and she clutched his head to draw him tighter and tighter still.

Then a sudden sweet burst of pleasure made her arch up to stand on tiptoe, and she lost her balance in the process. Yet it didn't matter, for Colin caught her, cushioning her fall with his body so they ended up on the floor with her sprawled atop him.

He shifted her until she straddled him. Staring up into her face, he brushed the hair back from her flushed cheek and cupped her chin in his hand. "You know, dearling, if we're to continue this very interesting test of my love, we should go to my room where I keep my sheaths."

She groaned at the unwelcome intrusion into her sensual haze. Trust Colin to have remembered the sheaths. She forced herself to concentrate on what he was saying. Then a startling realization hit her.

She no longer needed to protect herself from having a child.

"I thought you were going to marry me," she whispered.

"I am."

"Then it hardly matters if I . . . if I find myself with child, does it?"

A smile tipped up the edges of his mouth. "No, dearling, I don't believe it does."

Then he pulled her head down to his, kissing her with wild abandonment as he cupped her buttocks with his hands. His hardness pressed up behind her. It hadn't occurred to her until that very moment that there might be other positions in lovemaking than the one they'd used the first time.

Strange thoughts were running through her head, intriguing her. Slowly she drew back from him and sat up, then moved so his member was in front of her and not in back. She touched it experimentally, delighted when it leapt to her touch.

His smile grew forced. She stroked it as he watched, not stopping her. This could be very interesting, she thought. She raised her hips. His eyes grew stormy with desire, but there was no surprise in them. He knew exactly what she intended. Had he made love like this with other women before?

"You're a natural wanton," he murmured.

She glanced at him, startled.

" 'Tis a compliment, dearling. There are few inexperienced women who need so little teaching to make love the way you do."

She ran her tongue over her dry lips, not quite sure what to make of his statement, but she didn't think about it long. Both her curiosity and her passion roused, she hovered there on her knees a moment, uncertain what to do. Colin's hands tightened on her hips, and next thing she knew, he'd lifted her and was sliding up inside her, hot, hard, and heavy.

It was nothing like the first time. She felt no pain, and only a little pinching tightness, but it gave her a delightful sense of power to be over him like this. When she moved experimentally and he gasped, she decided she definitely liked this position.

"Annabelle, love," he whispered, "don't stop."

Ah, she thought, so his pleasure was now dependent on her whim. She stared at him a moment, at his brow shiny with sweat, at the clenched muscles of his face, and realized that he'd relinquished control on purpose, to please her.

Dear heaven, how she loved him, she thought as she began to move. She had only one thought, one purpose—to please him as much as he sought to please her.

Yet somewhere in the undulating motion, in the joining of their two bodies, she discovered that their two pleasures were as intertwined as the strands of a thread. When she ground down against him, they both sighed with satisfaction. When he caressed her breast, she felt propelled to a greater height, yet it was he who whispered how much ecstasy she gave him.

Annabelle leaned forward, bracing her hands against his chest as they rocked together, faster and faster and faster. She didn't set the pace alone—he thrust upward in time to her movements—so it was a joint endeavor to reach that hope of joy dangling in front of them.

Their bodies rode together, pounding, thundering, lifting and teasing. Their gait quickened as one; their rhythm became blended with the roar of the blood in their ears and the sweet wanton cries that escaped their lips until at last he gave one mighty thrust and she arched back in sheer delight to receive it as they reached the peak of bliss together.

It took several moments for her to regain awareness of their surroundings, to realize she was clutching his arms, leaving tiny half-moon marks in them with her fingernails.

His eyes were closed, his mouth parted, and sheer ecstasy shone in his face. Slowly he drew her down to his chest, cradling her against him apparently without the least bit of care for her weight atop him.

They lay there entwined for a while as he stroked her back and she relished the feel of his hard body beneath her.

Suddenly he pressed a fierce kiss against her hair. "I swear, Annabelle," he whispered fervently, "if you ever leave me, I'll die."

And she had to admit the feeling was utterly reciprocated.

Chapter Nineteen

"Those have most power to hurt us that we love."
—Francis Beaumont and John Fletcher, *The Maid's Tragedy*, Act 5

The woven rug covering the floor of Colin's study hardly helped to soften the hardness against his back. Yet he didn't move or ask Annabelle to move from her contented sprawl atop him. The hardness served as a kind of penance, even if it barely assuaged his guilt.

He should have told Annabelle everything—about his connection to Walcester and his reasons for first pursuing her. After all, she'd told him everything. He was certain of that. In return, he'd kept back something she would want to know.

So why couldn't he tell her? Because he was afraid. Afraid that she'd be so hurt, she'd lose her trust in him or that she'd suspect all his motives. 'Sdeath, he had to tell her sometime. He couldn't risk her finding out some other way.

Yet wouldn't it be better to marry her first, to prove his intentions were honorable? Yes, of course. They'd marry as soon as possible, and then he'd tell her. She'd be angry for a while, undoubtedly, but she'd not be able to doubt his love for her.

Hell and furies, how he did love her. He hadn't realized it until he'd said the words aloud, but then it was as if scales had fallen from his eyes and he'd seen the stark truth before him. How could he not love her?

He'd never known a woman in his situation—one who was a bastard reared gently, who'd suffered all the pains of rejection, but had only become stronger for it. She was amazing, as outspoken and daring as a man, but as incredibly soft and loving as a woman. He could think of no one else who could follow him to the colonies, who could face head-on the trials they were sure to find there, yet who'd not resent him for tearing her away from London's glittering society.

Suddenly a terrible thought occurred to him. She hadn't said whether she'd be willing to accompany him to the colonies. Perhaps she wouldn't want to leave the theater; perhaps she truly enjoyed the wild life of London. . . .

Then he remembered her eagerness to escape the party, her bitterness when she spoke of the gallants at the theater. It was possible she'd grown as disillusioned as he. His arms tightened around her. Somehow he'd convince her to go with him. Somehow they'd come to a decision about their future, and they'd do it together. He wouldn't allow himself to think she'd refuse him.

He smiled. Besides, she might be with child. Then he'd have her for sure, because she'd never bear a bastard. For the first time in his life, he blessed the fact that lovemaking could result in children. It was his trump card, and he'd use it if he had to.

After all, there could be no one else for him. No one. Annabelle had been right when she'd said there were other women he could have married, women of higher station, greater fortune, and impeccable reputation. Ah, but he'd never been like his peers, searching for ways to enhance his position in London society. He was far more concerned with finding a woman he could live with, and at last he'd found her.

Later he'd think about what to do with Walcester, for he must do something, if only to make certain the earl never tried to hurt Annabelle. It had all happened so long ago. Perhaps it would be best if Colin simply kept his knowledge to himself, or better yet, used it as a lever to get Walcester to agree to some terms on Annabelle's behalf. Could Walcester truly be involved in some conspiracy to overthrow the king? It seemed unlikely, the more Colin thought about it.

"Colin?" she whispered, interrupting his thoughts.

"Aye, my love?"

"Am I hurting you?"

He smiled. "Nay, but the floor is doing a fine job of stiffening my back."

Immediately she slid off him to kneel at his side. "You should have said something! Oh, dear, I'm sorry I—"

"I'm teasing you," he said with a laugh as he propped himself up on one elbow. "You'll have to get used to my teasing, love, if we're to be married the long years I intend." He sat up. "Although I'll admit I think it's time we moved our . . . er . . . discussion to a more comfortable room." His gaze darkened. "Like my bedchamber."

To his surprise, she blushed, eliciting a hearty laugh from him. "Hell and furies, Annabelle, no wonder you're such a fine actress. You're as unpredictable in reality as you are in the roles you play."

She managed a trembling smile. "And you, Lord Hampden, are a smooth-tongued rogue."

"Aye. 'Tis what makes you love me."

At her wisp of a smile, he stood and offered her his hand. "It's down the hall, but we ought to put some clothing on before we go sneaking about the house, don't you think?"

Laughing, she donned her clothes and slippers, but he noticed she didn't bother with the stockings. Instead, she stood, her adorable calves bared and her hands on her hips, waiting for him to dress.

He pulled on his breeches, but didn't worry about the rest. Then he took her hand. "Come, my love, let's see if we can get to my room without being spotted."

Like two mischievous children, they peeked out into the hall. Colin pointed out the door to his rooms.

Then, seeing no one around, Colin slapped her rump and whispered, "Quickly, now, dearling," and watched her run laughing ahead of him as he followed at a more sedate pace.

But as she reached the door to his rooms, Colin heard shouting in the foyer below. She paused with her hand on the door. He motioned her to go in the room, but she stared at him wide-eyed, for she'd apparently recognized the voice of the man shouting.

So had he. It was Walcester.

"I know he has returned," the gravelly voice echoed up the stairs. "I have ways of knowing these things. He's here, and I will see him!"

"His lordship is not to be disturbed!" the footman shouted.

"He'll see me, I tell you," Walcester growled, and they could hear his steps coming up the stairs, punctuated by the clicks of his walking stick. "He'd damn well better see me."

Colin heard the footman trotting up the stairs behind the earl, protesting all the way, but he didn't wait to see if his footman would be successful in ousting the earl.

Quickly, he turned to Annabelle and motioned her to enter his bedroom. When she stood frozen, her eyes wide and fearful, Colin strode to her side and opened the door, intending to thrust her through it. Then Walcester rounded the top of the stairs and spotted them.

For a moment, the three of them stared at each other, Walcester full of rage, Colin equally angry, and Annabelle completely stunned.

Walcester was the first to speak. "Well, well, this certainly explains a lot. Damn you, Hampden, how long have you been back in London, cavorting with her while you pretended to be helping me?"

Colin heard Annabelle's sharp intake of breath, and he clasped her arm. "Something wrong with your hearing? I distinctly heard my servant tell you I didn't wish to be disturbed."

Walcester's face was mottled with rage. "You deceitful bastard! I've waited nearly two weeks for your return. You had no right to leave in the first place—you promised you'd find out what I asked. But no, you trot off to the country without a word. Then, instead of coming immediately to my house upon your return from God knows where, you avoid me and come back here to serve your own ends and bed this . . . this chit!"

Colin stiffened. "Walcester, get out!"

But the earl was beyond reason. "Don't try to tell me you did it to find out her secrets for me. You're like all those other randy bucks, who can't keep their cocks in their pants and their minds on their obligations!"

"What obligations is he talking about?" Annabelle said in a low voice beside him. Her face showed her confusion. "This horrible man can't be Walcester." Then her tone sharpened. "Oh, but of course he is, which means he's . . . he's . . ."

"I'll explain it all later, love," Colin said, his throat tight with pain. 'Sdeath, he was losing her. He had to get Walcester out of here.

"Love?" Walcester growled. "I see you've pulled the wool over her eyes well, haven't you?"

Annabelle stared at the earl, pain etched in every line of her face. "You're my father, aren't you, the Earl of Walcester?"

For the first time since he'd arrived, Walcester turned his gaze on Annabelle. Bitterness twisted his mouth as he looked her over with ruthless unconcern. "You're a wanton, girl. No matter what your blood says, you're no daughter of mine."

Annabelle flinched as if she'd been struck. For a second, she stood there ashen, obviously not as pleased with the outcome of her vengeance as she'd expected. Nonetheless, she managed to pull herself together. Her hurt expression faded, replaced by one of harsh defiance.

In a low, caustic voice, she hissed, "What did you

expect, *Father*? When you forced a gentlewoman to share your bed and then set her loose among the wolves, you should have known you'd breed a wanton. I'm only taking after my dear old father."

The earl's head bobbed with the effort of controlling his sheer outrage, making the plume of his hat sketch wild patterns in the air. With a shake of his walking stick, he took a step toward her. "I was never a whore!"

Colin's eyes narrowed. Walcester wasn't exactly an old man. He was perfectly capable of injuring Annabelle if he wished. Quickly, Colin strode forward to place himself between Walcester and Annabelle. "If you ever call her such names again, I'll slit your body from throat to toe."

"Well, she's certainly got you fooled, hasn't she?" Walcester went on relentlessly, not the least bit worried. "Tell me, doesn't it bother you that she's played the wanton with every man in your acquaintance? Do you enjoy having a mistress bring you another man's leavings?"

Colin clenched his fists. "Let me tell you something about your daughter—"

"No!" Annabelle burst out. She stepped forward to clutch Colin's arm.

Turning to look at her, his heart sank at the expression of wounded anger on her face. "I'm going to tell him the truth," Colin said. "I won't let him continue with these base opinions."

Her fingers dug into his arm. "H-haven't you done enough already? Sp-spying on me? Lying to me about . . . about what you felt?"

The look of anguish on her face seared him through. He turned to the earl. "Walcester, give us a moment alone and I'll tell you everything you wish to know. Everything."

After a slight pause, Walcester nodded, though his hands clenched the top of his walking stick as if it were a club.

Colin took Annabelle aside and said in a whisper,

"I'm not going to let him think you're a whore. Don't you see? It serves no purpose to let him believe it."

"Oh? It doesn't prick his pride? Look at him. He's furious. And ashamed, yes, ashamed, as he should be."

At the desperate purpose written in her eyes, something twisted inside him. "You promised you'd give up this insane vengeance. You promised, Annabelle."

"Of course I did. You knew I would when you . . . when you seduced me and spoke sweet words to me . . . and, devil take you, told me you loved me!"

"That was not a lie!"

She shook her head, her mouth trembling. He could see the tears starting in her eyes. "Please, Colin, don't torment me anymore. You—you've fulfilled whatever cursed obligation you had to him. . . . Just leave me alone!"

He clenched her shoulders, wanting to shake her, yet understanding how betrayed she must feel. He should have told her when he'd had the chance. "Give me the chance to make it up to you, love. Please give me the chance. I know I deceived you about my association with Walcester, but I meant everything I said tonight. Everything!"

"What are you two whispering about?" Walcester bellowed.

Annabelle wrenched away from Colin's arms. Despite the pleading in his eyes, she gave him one last tormented glance, then stiffened her spine and turned to the earl.

"Father," she said in the most sarcastic voice Colin had ever heard her use. "You want to know everything about me? Well, then, I'll tell you. My mother was Phoebe Harlow Taylor, whom you bedded, then abandoned while she was with child."

"I didn't know she was—"

"She had no choice but to marry a squire, who dedicated his every waking hour to making her miserable. Yes, thanks to you, Mother had a painful life and a more painful death. She was abused and tormented by the man who hated her for bearing a bastard.''

When Walcester seemed at a loss for words, she went on relentlessly. ''So the next time you see me on the stage or hear of my scandalous exploits, you remember what you did to my mother. Because from now on, everyone will know I'm the Earl of Walcester's daughter. Everyone!''

''Annabelle, don't do this!'' Colin urged, but she left his side to stand two feet from the earl.

Planting her hands on her hips, she faced the earl with quiet rage, not the least bit embarrassed by her outrageous attire or her disheveled hair and bare calves, although Colin could see the unshed tears glittering in her eyes.

''And you know what?'' she hissed, leaning forward to look her father in the eye. ''The Silver Swan will rue the day he abandoned my mother to the torments of a cruel man. Because *I* am going to be a most unforgettable daughter. *Most* unforgettable.''

Walcester paled. ''What do you know about the Silver Swan, you damned impertinent wench? You'll tell me what you know or I swear I'll shake it out of you!''

Walcester reached out to grab her and Colin stepped forward, but she slipped easily from them both and fled down the stairs.

''Come back!'' the earl shouted as he strode to the top of the stairs. ''I say, you come back here, girl, or I swear you'll regret it! When I get through with you—''

''Leave her be!'' Colin ordered as he started to muscle his way past the earl and run after Annabelle. Then he heard the front door slam downstairs and paused. He must talk to her and set her straight. . . . He sighed. Unfortunately, he had to deal with the earl first. Whether she knew it or not, Annabelle had stirred up a giant hornet's nest with her last taunt about the Silver Swan, and Colin had to make sure the earl didn't try to make her suffer for it. Her safety came first.

Still he wavered at the top of the stairs, torn by his

desire to go after her. Walcester made his mind up for him when he whirled and snapped, "What did she mean? How much does she know about the Silver Swan?"

Colin's stomach roiled in disgust. "You've just wounded your daughter beyond all repair and all you can think about is your damnable code name? Hell and furies, man, don't you have an ounce of feeling in those iron veins?"

For the first time since Walcester had arrived, Colin saw ambivalence flash over the stern face, but it was quickly masked.

Walcester leaned forward on his walking stick. "When your past is as full of treachery as mine, when all you've worked for is in jeopardy of being ruined because some girl has taken it into her head to destroy you, you can't coddle yourself. Feelings are dangerous. You should have learned that by now, Hampden."

Unfortunately, Colin had learned it long ago. It was why he'd left the king's service. He'd wanted to feel again without worrying about repercussions. He'd wanted to be able to simply live, without trying to guess the meaning behind every smile.

Now here he was, embroiled in it all once more. This time, however, he had a purpose for his spying. "I can see why you regard your past as treacherous. But it's caught up with you at last, hasn't it?"

Walcester looked wary. "What do you mean by that?"

"I've been in Norwood for the past two weeks." He paused to let that sink in and was rewarded by the sight of Walcester stumbling back a pace.

Walcester recovered himself quickly. "Why did you go to Norwood?"

"To find out what Annabelle was hiding, and what you were so alarmed about."

"What did you discover?" Walcester's voice had grown very quiet, and he watched Colin with wary intensity.

"About Annabelle or about you?"

"Annabelle first."

"Everything she said just now is true and then some. As for her mother's death, I found out that Annabelle's mother went mad one day while her husband was taking a crop to Annabelle's bare back over some minor infraction, and she plunged a butcher knife into his heart."

Walcester clutched at his cane, a strange mixture of emotions passing over his face.

Pitiless, Colin continued. "Annabelle neglected to tell you that her mother wasn't the only one abused by that beast. She was also punished often, because her stepfather knew she was a bastard, had known it from the beginning of the marriage. That's also why he disinherited them both. And why, after Annabelle witnessed *her own mother's* hanging, she came penniless to London, hoping to find you and have her vengeance."

At last Walcester showed some hint of feeling. The veins of his neck bulged as he tried to clamp down on any emotion, but it was useless. He began shaking his head in disbelief, slowly at first, then more rapidly.

He fixed Colin with the kind of astonished expression people wear when they first realize a loved one has been taken from them. But Colin could dredge up little sympathy for the man.

"Phoebe was hanged?" Walcester asked in a still voice.

"Aye. Apparently her death was slow and painful."

Taking off his hat, Walcester rubbed his bald pate as if trying to rub away the thoughts going through his mind. "Phoebe, poor Phoebe. I—I'm afraid I never loved her the way she loved me, but she was a sweet slip of a thing, given to tender words, and very timid."

"Except, I take it, for when you bedded her." Colin's voice hardened. "Unless you raped her."

"Good God, no!" Walcester protested. " 'Twas not a rape. We cared for one another. I wouldn't have left her behind if I hadn't been forced to."

"You mean, when your Royalist companions were all taken prisoner and the king's papers confiscated?"

Walcester suddenly looked quite old and weary. He leaned heavily on his walking stick. "I suppose you should tell me what else you found out in Norwood."

Colin pursed his lips, wondering if he should even give Walcester the chance to explain. Then again, though he suspected the earl might be a traitor, he had no proof, and he couldn't in good conscience condemn the man without proof. No, it would be best to hear the earl's story. After all, Colin was quite adept at sorting lies from truth.

"I spoke with the Harlows' housekeeper. She told me you'd spent three weeks in the Harlow home recovering from injuries, though she didn't know, of course, what you'd been doing with Phoebe Harlow."

"We were very circumspect," Walcester said in a whisper.

"Apparently you were . . . that is, until you'd left, of course, and the family discovered that Phoebe was with child."

"Yes, yes, and married her off to the squire. You knew about that. What else did she say?"

"She said you fled after three Royalist spies had been arrested in Norwood and the king's papers taken from them. There was talk that they'd been betrayed."

"Aye, they had been." Walcester turned from Colin and walked to the stairwell, leaning heavily on the banister.

Colin stared at him incredulously, hardly able to believe that Walcester would admit his treachery so freely. "You sent a message by Phoebe to someone in the town."

Walcester whirled to stare at him, a startled expression on his face. "How did you know that?"

"Annabelle told me. Phoebe gave Annabelle the poem your message was hidden in and told her it was written by her father. Annabelle, of course, didn't realize it was a secret message, but I found it among her things and realized its significance at once. I just didn't understand why you gave it to Phoebe. Until I went to Norwood.''

Rubbing his bald pate distractedly, Walcester went rigid. ''The poem. Where is it? Where does my . . . my daughter keep it?''

''Why?''

''Don't you see? It proves everything.''

''I figured as much.''

Walcester couldn't mistake the suspicion and accusation in Colin's voice. ''No, no, you don't understand. It proves that I warned them off, that I warned them about the traitor in their midst!''

For the first time that day, Walcester took him by surprise. ''You mean you weren't the traitor?''

Walcester looked appalled. ''Good God, no! But there *was* one, and in the end he was successful in getting them captured. 'Tis obvious Phoebe never delivered the message. She kept it, and as a consequence, the Royalists were arrested!''

Colin regarded Walcester warily, but he didn't think the man was lying. Yet something wasn't quite right. ''Annabelle insists that her mother delivered the poem. Your friend read it and then soldiers came and her mother fled.''

A desperate look entered Walcester's eyes. ''Nay. The girl must be lying.'' At the fierce expression crossing Colin's face, he amended, ''Or mistaken. Yes, yes, either the girl misunderstood or her mother's memory failed her. Then again, perhaps Phoebe delivered the poem to the wrong person. Whatever the case, the men *were* arrested. If she'd delivered the poem, they wouldn't have been.''

''If you'd tried to save them, if you'd behaved as was your duty, then why have you been trying to hide all this from me?''

Walcester sighed. ''As I said, the Royalists *were* arrested.'' His expression turned grim. ''They were drawn and quartered. The king's papers were confiscated, and as you know, that turned the tide in the war. The king was executed. There was some question about why I hadn't done more to affect the outcome when I was so close by.

"Until now, I've always claimed I didn't know the men were there. But if my peers knew I sent a woman instead of going myself, they might think me a coward or, worse yet, suspect me of bungling it on purpose, of being a traitor." Walcester shook his head. "All manner of things might go wrong, and my political career would be over."

"You couldn't tell me all of this before?"

Walcester looked startled. "Nay. You might not have agreed to help me. You would have been contemptuous of my actions if you'd known the truth, and you would have been in your rights to be so. I shouldn't have sent a woman to do my work."

Silently Colin agreed. Poor innocent Phoebe Harlow should never have been forced to aid Walcester in such a dangerous task. "Then why did you?"

A bitter smile crossed Walcester's face. "Because I was a coward. The soldiers were everywhere, and I knew if they caught me I'd die a spy's death, drawn and quartered like the rest. 'Tis the only reason. But 'tis reason enough, isn't it? 'Tis reason enough for my enemies."

Colin couldn't quite believe him, yet Walcester's story rang true. If a man like him were exposed as a coward possibly responsible for setting in motion the events leading to Charles I's execution, it would indeed ruin his political career, if not open him to charges of treason.

"If you don't believe me," Walcester put in, "then look at the words of my poem. They prove my innocence."

Colin tried to remember the poem he'd memorized. Something about Portia and Beatrice treading nowhere near the martyr's plain. Then there was the line about keeping quiet or being forced "by crown-less hands/ To sing the hangman's lullaby." Obviously that was a warning about being caught by the Roundheads, the "crown-less hands."

"Who were Portia and Beatrice?" Colin asked.

"I see you've memorized the poem."

"Aye. Who were Portia and Beatrice?"

"Don't you know Shakespeare, Hampden?"

Colin thought about the poem. "Ah, yes, 'the bard.' "

"Indeed. Portia was the heroine in *The Merchant of Venice* and Beatrice in *Much Ado about Nothing*. Portia saved Antonio's life in the first play and Beatrice fell in love with Benedict in the second. Two of the captured Royalists were traveling in disguise under the names Anthony and Benedict. They were fleeing the Battle of Naseby and carrying the king's papers. One of them had been wounded and they were forced to take shelter in Norwood, posing as wealthy merchants. The message was for them."

Colin rubbed his chin as he pondered the possible truth of what Walcester was telling him.

"As for the rest of the poem," Walcester rushed on, " 'the martyr's plain' referred to St. Stephen's Street where they were staying in an inn. I was telling them to leave their present house before the soldiers could find them."

"How did the soldiers know about the men in the first place?"

Walcester's expression grew fierce. "There was a traitor among them—Paxton Hart. He'd sent word to the soldiers about where the Royalists were and what names they were using. Luckily, the message was sent to Phoebe's parents' house, where the Roundhead captain was supposed to be dining with some of his foot soldiers. Only he wasn't there, and you know how soldiers are. They couldn't decide anything without first finding their captain. Besides, they thought they had plenty of time. But they didn't reckon on me, of course. Since I was staying there, I heard everything. That's when I sent the message."

Colin thought a moment. " 'Her heart she must keep close and mute' . . . I see. You wanted to warn them to keep Hart quiet while they escaped the inn at St. Stephen's Street.''

Walcester nodded sadly. "I didn't dare write the message out the way I wanted, in case it fell into enemy hands, but I knew Benedict would understand the poem. So I sent Phoebe to him with it, because I feared to go myself and risk capture.''

"Instead you risked Phoebe's life, for they would have been no kinder to her if she'd been caught.''

Walcester blanched. "I'd hoped the coded message would protect her, but you are right. I should have done my duty and gone myself. Everything might have been different then. I've always assumed she never delivered the message.''

"Maybe the foot soldiers moved more quickly than you bargained for.''

"Probably,'' Walcester said sadly. "Or Phoebe moved too slowly.''

Colin shook his head. What a tangled story. Yet Walcester couldn't blame himself entirely for what had happened. The traitor Hart was as much to blame as any.

"What happened to Hart?'' Colin asked.

"They killed him with the others. They weren't foolish enough to keep a man alive who'd betrayed his own companions.'' Walcester paused a moment. "You know, the worst of it wasn't that I trusted Phoebe to do my work, but that Phoebe wouldn't have been regarded as trustworthy by anyone else. Her father was a Roundhead. Yet it . . . it didn't worry me. She said she loved me, and I thought she didn't care about political matters—''

"You were probably right.'' Colin managed a reassuring smile. "A woman in love can be fiercely loyal.'' He thought of Annabelle. A woman in love could also be vindictive. He'd tarried here long enough. He must go after her and convince her that he'd not betrayed her, not in the way she imagined anyway.

First he had to ensure one thing. "Walcester, you understand that Annabelle knew none of this."

Lost in his thoughts, Walcester didn't respond at first. Then he shifted his gaze to Colin. "What? Yes, yes, you've explained that. I suppose if she had known, she'd have found some way to punish me with the poem, since as you say . . ." He paused, a look of chagrin passing over his face. "Since, as you say, she has some cause to hate me."

"Some?"

"Perhaps more than some. If you've not lied about what became of Phoebe, then I suppose she has excellent cause to hate me." Each word seemed wrenched from him. Then he scowled and shook his head. "But for God's sake, man, you don't understand how it galls to see one's daughter playing the wanton on the stage! I have no children at all. At last I discover that I do have someone of my blood, and in the same day I learn she's become a wild trollop—"

"I can set your mind at rest about that. Annabelle's wantonness was a part she played and no more. The only man Annabelle has ever bedded is me, and that only because I seduced her, as you seduced her mother."

Walcester's eyes widened in disbelief and the faintest flicker of outrage as his gaze swung to Colin.

Colin faced him squarely. "Aye. Annabelle is no wanton. I can testify to the truth of that. She merely wished to humiliate you, and it seems she succeeded."

"And intends to continue at it," Walcester said with wry bitterness.

Colin's insides knotted up. "Listen, Walcester. Those threats Annabelle made . . . you'll not do anything about them, you hear me? You'll leave this to me."

For the first time that day, Walcester smiled, though it looked a bit forced. "Don't worry. Any fool can see that you have more influence with her than I." He surveyed Colin with grim satisfaction. "You care for my daughter, don't you?"

Colin met his gaze without a hint of remorse. "I love your daughter, Walcester."

Walcester's mocking laugh grated against him. "For God's sake, why?"

"She was courageous enough to survive her childhood and daring enough to take on all of London society, which is more than you would do. What's more, until you showed up today and tore her heart to ribbons, she was willing to bestow mercy upon a man who neither asked for it nor deserved it."

Walcester colored at that, but Colin paid him no heed. Instead he strode toward his study, where he'd left his clothes. "Now, if you'll excuse me, I intend to find your daughter and beg her—on my knees, if necessary—to forgive me for conspiring with you. Then I intend to marry her, if she'll still have me."

"Marry her?" Walcester said in astonishment as he followed Colin, the walking stick tapping along the floor.

"Aye. Marry her."

Walcester watched Colin don his clothes. "You and Lord Falkham with your common women."

Colin shot him a murderous glance. "She's no more common than you are, for your blood runs through her veins."

Walcester shrugged. "True. I suppose I can hardly complain if you choose to wed my daughter and make her respectable. I can't believe the girl would refuse. She'd be a fool not to marry you."

Bending to pick up his boots, Colin said, "Fear of being thought a fool doesn't always stop Annabelle from doing what she wishes."

Walcester snorted. "You have my permission to tell her I approve of the match."

The beginnings of a sarcastic retort sprung to Colin's lips as he turned. It died when he saw the hint of wistfulness in the hoary earl's features.

Somehow Colin managed to keep the coldness out

of his voice. "My association with you hasn't exactly endeared your daughter to me, so telling her you've given me your blessing would probably prompt her to refuse my proposal at once." He paused, noting how the earl suddenly looked quite weary. Softening his tone, he said, "But if you wish, I'll pass some other message on to her from you. I'll do that much."

Like a man who has lost his bearings, Walcester stared about him in distraction. Clearly, all of this was too much for him to contemplate. Walcester was of an older age, when men with titles would never have dreamed of marrying a girl of small wealth and bad reputation.

Suddenly Walcester surprised Colin by nodding. "Aye, pass a message to her from me. Tell her . . . tell my daughter that I'll claim her if she wishes." He hesitated; then his voice grew firmer. "Aye, you tell her I'll claim her. She'll be a bastard no more."

With a shake of his head, Colin sat down and began putting on his stockings and boots. He wanted to retort that society would never let Annabelle forget she was a bastard if Walcester claimed her. She'd almost be better off as Annabelle Taylor, the squire's daughter whose mother murdered him, than as Lady Annabelle Maynard, the earl's bastard. Colin also wanted to point out that Annabelle would benefit most from the words "I'm sorry."

But he held his tongue. After all, it undoubtedly took a great deal of effort on Walcester's part to give such a promise, and though she might not accept the earl's offer, it might soothe her pain to know he'd made it.

He stared at the earl, who leaned on his cane, his brow knit with worry about his political future and his hands clutching the walking stick. Suddenly Colin pitied the lonely, stern old man, whose dreams of power were his only sustenance. Colin stood, then stepped forward to place his hand on the earl's shoulder.

"I'll tell her," he murmured.

But first he must find her.

Chapter Twenty

"Heaven has no rage like love to hatred turned,
Nor hell a fury like a woman scorned."
—William Congreve, *The Mourning Bride*, Act 3, Scene 8

Annabelle warmed herself at the fire she'd made in the grate of the tiring-room. No one would look for her here at the closed theater so late in the evening. Not even Colin.

Colin. She couldn't bear to see him right now. She needed time to sort out her thoughts and decide what to do. And how to cope with the pain threatening to erupt from her throat in a mad scream. Dear heaven, how could she look at him again, knowing that he'd been in league with her father all along? Had his every word been suspect? Could he have been lying to her all those times he said he cared?

No, she couldn't believe that, or she'd have to believe that her every instinct was unreliable. He had indeed cared, and he seemed to have believed he loved her. Love. What did he know of love when he couldn't tell her the truth, when he could make an alliance with her enemy, then hide it from her? It appeared that even after he'd come to care, he'd continued to spy for that . . . that horrible man who apparently was her father!

Like a creeping poison, Colin's assurances to Walcester, when he'd promised to tell Walcester everything after speaking to her, seeped into her mind. Devil take him and his promises! she thought, a sob choking her throat. He knew what she'd been through and had seen what a blackguard her father was, and

still he intended to . . . to fulfill some obligation he
felt to the man! Had he no thought for her feelings at
all?

The thought of Colin and her father together sent
pain slicing through her. Had Colin given the earl daily
reports? Had Colin told her father about the drugged
tea and her naïveté and her pathetic tears when she'd
asked him to stay in London? She ground her knuckles
against her mouth to keep back the sobs. For heaven's
sake, how closely had Colin reported to her father, to
that wretched, uncaring man?

Sitting down on the cold, hard floor, she hugged
herself and rocked back and forth, trying to blot out
of her mind the sweet thoughts of making love to
Colin. But she simply couldn't. It was too recent, too
precious. She kept seeing Colin's anguished expression when her father had made his appearance.

Her anger dug in its heels. Yes, Colin had obviously
been distressed by her father's appearance, and maybe
he'd even felt ashamed that he'd not told her. But that
didn't take away the fact that he *hadn't* told her, that
he'd misled and lied to her.

Had he intended to keep it a secret from her forever?
Had he planned to marry her and never tell her that
he'd been spying for her father?

Marry. The word brought forth such a mixture of
emotions that her head shot up and her body went soft.
Colin wanted to marry her.

Her hand balled into a fist in her lap. How dare he
offer marriage to her while he was carrying on such a
deceit? Thinking of it made rage surge through her
once more.

It also made her hate her father all the more, for
using her and Colin to further his own hidden aims.
He deserved everything she could do to bring him
down. What a spiteful, horrible man!

Yet she had to admit her vengeance had brought her
a shallow victory. Although she'd bravely told him that
she would shame him publicly until he begged for
mercy, she didn't have the heart to do it anymore. Her

pride had made her speak the words, yet now that she'd witnessed his contempt for her, she didn't know if she could bear to witness it again.

Yes, perhaps he found her reputation a torment, but it no doubt made him all the more pleased that he'd abandoned the woman who'd borne him such an outrageous daughter. That was not at all what she'd wished to accomplish. She'd wanted to make him feel some shred of remorse.

But one look in his cold eyes had told her he didn't know the meaning of remorse. There wasn't a gentle bone in her father's body. Her dreams of retribution were just that—silly dreams. Walcester wasn't the kind of man to beg forgiveness or dissolve into bitter, regretful tears when she told him all her mother had suffered. No, all he'd cared about was her knowledge of his wretched nickname.

Exhausted from the emotional turmoil of the last few hours, she rested her head in her hands. Unfortunately, her mind seemed incapable of resting. She couldn't forget her father's cruel words, his lack of concern for her mother's suffering. All he'd cared about was her use of his code name.

She stiffened at the memory. Dear heaven, had Colin told her the truth when he'd hinted that her father might be a traitor? Why would he have said such a thing about his own friend unless it was true?

Her father had been awfully intent on questioning her about what she knew of the Silver Swan. The name *was* clearly an alias. Her father must have been some kind of spy. If he'd been a spy for the Royalists, why was he so afraid of anyone finding out now? What's more, how had her mother fit into all of it?

Colin had said that the poem her father had given her mother may have been a message of some sort, a traitorous message. Dear heaven, how could he have entrusted her mother with such a thing? Her poor mother had been betrayed not once, but twice by her lover—first, by being forced to bear his villainous message; second, by being forced to bear his child.

She pondered the poem, wondering what secret it held. She'd already figured out that the bard referred to Shakespeare. The poem had mentioned Portia and Beatrice. She remembered what Colin had said. Three men had been arrested. Her blood began to pump madly. What if the poem had contained the names of the men her father had betrayed? The names would be hidden in the poem, but obviously Portia and Beatrice referred to two of them.

A chill struck her. If her father was a traitor, then it was no wonder he'd cautioned her against using his alias. She remembered what Colin had said . . . that her father was a dangerous man. She had to admit that thus far, her father had given her no reason to believe he had any tender feelings for her.

Her father, a traitor. She wondered if Colin had known all along. No, perhaps not. He seemed to have found out most of his information in Norwood.

So her father was a traitor and Colin, being his friend, could not do anything about it. For some strange reason, Colin felt he owed her father something. She had no idea what, but whatever it was, it had put him in the position of spying for her father.

She, however, owed her father nothing. Her father had involved her mother in this treachery, then seduced her. Now her mother was dead. No, she didn't owe her father a thing. But she still owed her mother.

She'd promised Colin to abandon her vengeance, true. But that was before she'd known that he was indebted to her father, that the wily earl had a hold over Colin that would prevent Colin from betraying him. That was before she'd known the full extent of her father's treachery.

Colin had warned her that her father was dangerous. That was probably true, too, but how better to protect herself from such a dangerous man than to make sure he received justice?

The door opened behind her, startling her so much she nearly screamed aloud. She whirled on the intruder as she cast about her for a weapon, but it was only Charity standing in the door.

"I thought I might find you here. Y've got everyone worried, you have. Aphra's in a state and his lordship is beside himself wanting to find you."

Colin. He must not find her before she had a chance to avenge her mother and make things right once more. He would never approve. But she couldn't allow him to harbor a traitor, no matter what obligation he felt.

"Where's Colin now?" Annabelle asked, forcing herself to remain calm. "He's not here, is he?"

Charity regarded her oddly. "Nay, he went to Aphra's to see if you might have gone there, since you weren't at our lodgings."

Riverton stepped into the room behind Charity, and Annabelle groaned. So much for staying hidden. Nodding her head toward Riverton, Annabelle asked, "What's he doing here?"

"I didn't think Charity should be roaming the streets in the middle of the night alone," he snapped. "Nor should you, for that matter."

In Annabelle's anxious state, she had little patience with Riverton. "I'm surprised you have time to be so concerned about your mistress, Sir John. Your fiancée must keep you quite busy."

Riverton's face registered shock at her boldness, then anger. Placing his arm around Charity, he drew her close as if to defend her from Annabelle's words. "Aye, my fiancée is keeping me quite busy," he retorted.

Charity gave a shy smile as Annabelle stared at her in confusion.

"John's asked me to marry him, he has," Charity said softly. "He intends to go tomorrow to withdraw his offer for the viscount's daughter."

Annabelle continued to stare in disbelief. "Really?"

Riverton's face hardened at her obvious skepticism. "Listen here, Annabelle. I won't let you poison Charity with your hardhearted views about men. I admit

I've neglected her feelings in the past, but that's all
changed. Charity has helped me realize that our love
is more important than any social position.''

The loving expression he leveled on Charity tore at
Annabelle's already wounded heart.

''My father was a mere merchant,'' he continued,
''and my mother a chambermaid when he fell in love
and took her to wife. So you see, I have a rather humble lineage. I gained a knighthood only because of
service to the king.''

Charity gave him a blinding smile, which he returned. ''For a time, I forgot that my parents had been
happier in their love than any of the nobility I know
with all their titles and wealth. I nearly threw away my
only chance for happiness.''

''I set you straight, didn't I, love?'' Charity whispered.

Riverton nodded. ''Aye, when it came right down
to it, I found I couldn't stomach the thought of losing
you.''

To see them billing and cooing like two doves was
nearly more than Annabelle could bear, but she forced
herself not to say anything to dim their happiness.
Charity deserved this second opportunity for love. Annabelle could only hope Riverton's fidelity didn't prove
false in time.

''At any rate,'' Riverton said, turning back to Annabelle with a softer expression on his face, ''I hope
you'll wish us happiness.''

''I do,'' she said, and found she meant it, despite
her pain at seeing them together. She managed a smile.
''I truly do.''

''Now y've got to go after Lord Hampden,'' Charity
said fervently. '' 'Tis time for you to find yer own
happiness.''

Annabelle's smile faded. ''I'm afraid you'll have to
let me handle Lord Hampden in my own way.''

''But—'' Charity began.

Riverton cut her off. ''Nay, love, she's right, you

know. You must let them work out their own problems.''

Annabelle yearned to tell Charity of all that had happened, but Charity's loyalties were with Riverton now, and Riverton would immediately tell Colin what she was up to. Dear heaven, she was surrounded by spies. No doubt Riverton had known all along what Colin was doing for Walcester. Or had he?

''Sir John,'' Annabelle blurted out.

''Aye?''

''Do you know the Earl of Walcester?''

''Of course. He's a powerful man.''

Annabelle fought to keep her chagrin from showing. ''Is he also a friend of Lord Hampden's?''

Charity was regarding her suspiciously, but Annabelle ignored her.

Riverton shrugged. ''I suppose you could say that. I know Hampden regards him highly because the earl once saved his life. The earl also got Colin his position in the king's service. But I don't know that the earl makes many real friends.''

Her heart sank. *The earl once saved his life. The earl also got Colin his position in the king's service.* No wonder Colin felt indebted to her father. Owing so much to the earl, Colin would never help her bring her father to justice. After all, for all his secrets, Colin was an honorable man.

But her father didn't deserve such consideration.

''Why do you ask?'' Riverton said.

''N-no reason.'' She cast Charity a warning glance, hoping the maid wouldn't say anything to Riverton, for Charity knew that Annabelle suspected the earl of being her father.

Charity stiffened. ''John, love, could you give Annabelle and me a moment alone?''

He nodded, then stepped out into the hall, closing the door behind him.

Charity stepped closer. ''What the devil is going on?''

Annabelle twisted her hands. "The earl is indeed my father. And Colin has been spying on me for him."

"Are you sure?"

Annabelle nodded. "I don't think Colin intended for me to find out. He must have known how it would hurt me to know. But I have found out, and he's upset. The thing is, I've also found out . . . well . . . something else. About my father. And I can't keep silent about it. But I know Colin would want me to."

Planting her hands on her hips, Charity stared at Annabelle as if trying to decide whether to press her for more information. "So what are you planning to do?"

With a sigh, Annabelle asked, "Would you do one favor for me?"

"Anything."

"Would you fetch my special box from our lodgings and bring it to me here? The key is in the binding of the book of poems on the bureau."

Charity regarded her quizzically. "Aye, but why?"

"Please don't ask. Do this one thing for me, and I'll be forever in your debt."

Shrugging, Charity turned toward the door. "Whatever you wish."

"And Charity? Don't tell Colin about it, and whatever you do, don't tell him where I am."

Charity pivoted to stare at her with suspicion. "What are you up to, madam?"

"You'll know soon enough," Annabelle said. "Now go."

To her relief, Charity nodded and left. Then Annabelle began to search for a costume. She had to look her best tonight.

For she was going to meet a king.

At midnight, Annabelle stood in the small room off the Privy Stairs of Whitehall Palace, waiting for William Chiffinch to return from sending her message in to the king. As she stared about her nervously, she clutched her box against her chest.

Dear heaven, what would His Majesty think when he saw her here so late, dressed in the elaborate gown she'd found among the costumes at the theater? It didn't much matter. After she spoke with him, he'd be set straight, if her note hadn't already quelled all interest he might have in her body.

A moment's guilt assailed her. What she was about to do was unforgivable. Even if her father ever could find it in his heart to accept her, he'd not do so after this. She reminded herself of what Colin had said, that her father was almost certainly a traitor. So she was doing this for her country and her king, for all those men who'd died in the Royalist cause.

No, she thought, forcing herself to be honest. She was doing this as much to punish her father as anything—for not caring, for being so callous about his abandonment of her mother. And for making Colin spy on her.

She stiffened. She wouldn't think about Colin, not now. Opening her box, she looked for her father's ring, wanting to look at it one more time to remind herself of his treachery. Instead, she caught sight of the ring Colin had given her.

Emotions flooded her—pain, resentment, longing . . . and yes, love. She loved Colin so much. And he'd undoubtedly be furious when he heard what she'd done.

Yet she had to do this. She had to.

She took out his ring, then tucked it into her apron pocket. The king mustn't know about her association with Colin. Oh, he'd probably heard some rumors, but he mustn't know the truth. She didn't dare risk that Colin might be tarred with the same brush as her father. She couldn't bear to think of Colin being arrested, simply because he'd fulfilled some ancient obligation to the treacherous Earl of Walcester.

Forcing thoughts of Colin from her mind, she snapped the box closed. It was her father and his punishment alone that must concern her. She was about to ruin him, but then he deserved to be ruined if her suspicions were correct. Besides, how else could she keep him from hurting her? As long as he knew of her knowledge of his past, he'd hound her. No, the earl was a hard man, and the only message he would understand was a hard one.

Chiffinch appeared in the doorway. "His Majesty says he will see you, madam, but he can only give you a few moments. He has guests."

Guests? she thought. Of course. The king rarely went to bed until the wee hours of the morning, or so she'd heard.

Annabelle followed Chiffinch up the Privy Stairs and into the king's chambers with increasing trepidation. His Majesty was presiding over a small supper. She recognized an actress from the king's company and Barbara Palmer, the king's current mistress, who flashed her a glance of scathing contempt as she entered. Buckingham, one of the king's advisers and Barbara Palmer's cousin, was there as well. Unfortunately, so was Rochester. To her grim satisfaction, he was wearing different breeches than before.

The king himself met her with a sober expression on his face. She swallowed as she stared up at the man she'd heard so much about. He was tall, much taller than she'd expected, and handsome, with thick brown hair that fell past his shoulders, a sensuous mouth, and heavy-lidded eyes. No wonder the women all wanted him.

Still, he could not compare to Colin.

He watched impatiently as she belatedly remembered to fall into a deep curtsy.

Offering her his hand, he murmured, "Good evening, Madam Maynard. I do hope you've fully recovered from your illness."

She was so nervous at being in his presence, she nearly forgot what he was talking about, but she caught herself in time. "Yes, Your Majesty. I'm feeling much better these days."

"That was a very interesting message you sent just now," he said. She'd always heard he was an amiable man, but he wasn't smiling at the moment. "I'll admit it roused my curiosity. I hope it wasn't intended as a ruse to do just that."

"Nay, Your Majesty!" She glanced around the room, then swallowed. "But if it please you, I would prefer to discuss the matter in private."

The king regarded her oddly for a moment, then nodded. Taking her hand, he murmured "This way" and led her into an adjoining drawing room.

He shut the door, then turned to look at her. "You said you had information about a traitor to the Crown. You do realize what a serious charge that is?"

She sucked in her breath. "Aye."

"Would you mind explaining what you mean?"

It was time for her to present the truth, or most of it, for she wouldn't tell him of Colin's involvement or her mother's hanging. But the rest . . .

"First I must tell you that my suspicions aren't based on hearsay or speculation."

"Yes, yes, go on," the king said with an impatient wave of his hand.

She drew herself up. "I don't speak merely as an actress either. I speak as the daughter of the Earl of Walcester."

Now she had his full attention. "What in the devil are you talking about?"

"I'm the earl's illegitimate daughter, conceived shortly after the Battle of Naseby in a town called Norwood."

The king's eyes narrowed. Obviously he knew about both Naseby and Norwood. Perhaps he even knew of her father's presence there.

"You have proof of your parentage?"

"Aye." She opened her box, then took out the signet ring and handed it to the king. "This is the ring he gave my mother. It bears his coat of arms, as you can see."

The king's eyes narrowed. He turned the ring over in his fingers, frowning as he did so.

Then she handed him the poem written by the Silver Swan. "He also gave this to my mother."

He scanned it quickly, then paled. "You'd best tell me everything."

She related an abbreviated version of how her mother and father had met and how her mother had come by the coded poem. Then she told him why her mother had married the squire. She told him her mother and stepfather were now dead, but didn't say how the deaths had occurred. Finally she explained how she'd come to London penniless to seek out her father, though she made no mention of her plans for vengeance.

When she finished, the king looked astonished. He read the poem again, then dropped his hand to his side, though he still gripped the piece of paper.

"This is most disturbing, most disturbing indeed," he muttered. "You say your mother delivered this message before the three men were taken and my father's papers confiscated?"

She nodded.

"Buckingham!" the king shouted, making Annabelle jump.

The door into the other room opened, and Buckingham entered with Rochester. Annabelle's stomach sank. Had the king not believed her? Why did he call for the others?

"Buckingham," the king stated, turning to the portly, middle-aged lord. "You were well acquainted with what happened at Norwood after the Battle of Naseby, weren't you?"

"You mean when those men were captured and your father's papers confiscated?"

"Aye. It proved a severe blow to our cause at the time. Wasn't the Earl of Walcester questioned in connection with the incident?"

"Aye, Your Majesty. I was one of the men who questioned him."

"Didn't Walcester claim he knew nothing of the three Royalists who carried the papers until after the men were arrested?"

Buckingham's eyes narrowed as he rubbed his full

chin. "As I recall, that is true, sire." His shrewd gaze flitted to Annabelle, then back to the king.

"You know Madam Maynard, don't you?" the king said, waving his hand toward her.

Buckingham nodded, the hint of a smile playing about his lips.

Rochester was less conspicuous as he listened to the conversation. "Aye, Your Majesty," he interjected slyly. "We *all* know Madam Maynard."

Charles flashed Rochester an impatient glance. "If you must listen to all this, Rochester, keep your tongue to yourself. This business happened while you were still a pup, so I'm sure you have little to add to the discussion."

Annabelle relaxed. After what had occurred earlier in the evening, Rochester no doubt was itching to strike back at her. At least the king wouldn't tolerate his behavior.

His Majesty returned his attention to Buckingham. "Madam Maynard claims to be Walcester's illegitimate daughter."

After a brief moment of surprise, Buckingham regarded her with new interest, but Rochester merely smirked behind him.

"I am inclined to believe she is telling the truth," the king continued. "In any case, she has some information about the fiasco at Norwood. Do you remember Walcester's code name during the war?"

Buckingham thought a moment. "Silver Bird . . . Silver Swan." He fixed Annabelle with a curious gaze. "Yes, Silver Swan. That was it."

Rochester's eyes widened as he glanced at Annabelle. She avoided his gaze, but could feel it on her, probing, menacing.

Charles handed Buckingham the rolled-up paper. "Look at this. 'Tis a message that Madam Maynard claims was sent by Walcester to someone in Norwood shortly before the men were arrested. Do you remember the names the men were going under at the time?"

"Anthony Gibbs, Benedict Cooper, and Paxton

Hart.'' Buckingham read the poem several times over as Annabelle waited, resisting the urge to twist the overskirt of her gown. She mustn't appear anxious, or they'd never believe her.

When he reached the bottom of the poem, he murmured, ''Ah, the Silver Swan.''

''So you think he probably did write the poem,'' the king said.

''Probably.''

Charles frowned as he turned to Annabelle. ''To whom did you say your mother was charged to give this?''

''I don't know. She never said. All she told me was that my father sent her into town with a description of the man to whom she was to deliver the message.''

A calculating expression crossed Buckingham's face, lingering there long enough for Annabelle to see it, but not long enough for it to be noticed by the king.

''I'm curious, Madam Maynard,'' Buckingham said. ''Why have you chosen to bring this to our attention?''

She faced him boldly. ''I wish to see justice done. All I have seen of my father tells me that he is dangerous. I felt it my duty to expose his treachery to those who could end it, before he has the chance to do any more damage.'' She added truthfully, ''And before he can hurt me for what I know.''

''I see.'' Buckingham bent his head to read the poem again. ''It seems to me, Your Majesty,'' he said in a considering voice, ''that this is a message in code, governed by the reference to the bard. It contains the three names of the men who were taken.''

He showed the king the paper, gesturing to a line. ''Here 'Portia' is meant to be read as Anthony, 'Beatrice' as Benedict, and down here, 'heart' is meant to be Hart. The 'martyr's plain' no doubt refers to St. Stephen's Street, where the men were staying. 'Tis clear that Walcester wanted to identify the men and where they were staying, so he embedded their names and location in a poem, which he sent to the soldiers, who promptly arrested the men at the inn in St. Stephen's Street.''

This was the first time Annabelle had heard where the men had been captured. The line of the poem that Buckingham claimed referred to St. Stephen's flitted through her mind—''Far away from the martyr's plain.'' If her father had wanted to betray his companions, then why would he have sent a message to the soldiers bidding them tread far from that street, when that was where their quarry was staying?

The king nodded, his brow furrowed. ''What a nasty business. Yet it does seem as if you are right. What of the rest of the message?''

Buckingham folded the paper carefully and tucked it into his pocket. ''Mere words to throw the reader off the track. You know how these communications work: a lot of frivolous material to cover up the meat.''

Annabelle was no longer paying attention to Buckingham. Quickly, her mind ran through the poem as she tried to remember all the key phrases. *Your heart you must keep close and mute.* If that was a reference to the man Hart, then why would her father have admonished the soldiers to keep him silent, but not the others?

Then there were the lines ''Lest ye be forced by crown-less hands/ To sing the hangman's lullaby.'' Crown-less hands. The Roundheads?

A cold chill assailed her. Could she have been wrong about the poem? Was it possible it wasn't a message of betrayal at all but a warning?

That made no sense. Her father would have had no reason to hide the fact that he'd tried to warn the Royalists. But if he'd been involved in some treachery, then of course he would have wanted her to keep silent.

Still . . .

''Your Majesty?'' she said. ''It seems to me that one line of the poem might have meaning.''

Buckingham shot her a wary glance, but the king regarded her seriously.

"Oh?"

Rochester was watching her with malignant interest and Buckingham's eyes were riveted on her. She licked her lips. "I mean, the line about the 'crown-less hands'—"

"Means nothing," Buckingham finished for her. "Unless it refers to the Roundheads' desire to take the crown from the king."

"No, I meant—"

"I think you'd best leave this sort of thing to the men," Buckingham broke in again, fixing her with eyes of deadly coldness. "You're quite talented on the stage, Madam Maynard, but as a woman, sorting out messages in a logical orderly fashion is not within your purview."

She bristled at the typically male comment, but sensed that there was more to Buckingham's determination to keep her silent than a simple disdain for women.

"Perhaps you're right, Your Grace," she murmured, fighting the urge to give him an angry retort, "but after all, I know more about the situation than any of you, since my mother was there."

"We should speak to the mother, you know," Charles interjected.

Annabelle's heart began to pound. "I told you, sire. My mother is dead."

He sighed. "Yes, yes, you did tell me that."

The door to the room opened, and Barbara Palmer put her head in. With scathing thoroughness, she surveyed Annabelle from head to toe, but it was the king she spoke to. "I swear, what are you three taking so long about? I thought we were going to play a game of whist. Peg and I are near to tears with boredom out here waiting for you." She shot Annabelle another contemptuous glance.

Charles turned to flash his mistress an ingratiating smile. "Yes, yes, a moment more, darling. State business does sometimes intrude, you know."

"State business. Ah, yes," Barbara replied with

arched eyebrows and another glare at Annabelle, but at Buckingham's wave of the hand, she pouted and shut the door.

"In any case," Charles remarked dismissively as he turned back to Annabelle, "Buckingham is absolutely correct. You were right to come to us with this, but you must leave it to us to address the problem now, my dear. Buckingham is quite well versed in the ways of spies. I have complete faith in his ability to sort out the truth of this matter." Clearly, the king no longer wanted to be bothered with it.

Buckingham looked quite pleased with himself, and Annabelle despaired. After all, she might be wrong. Now that she thought on it, the poem could be interpreted in more than one way.

"Your Majesty, I think perhaps I've been hasty in my accusations—"

This time it was Rochester who interrupted her. "So like a woman to be fickle. Have you suddenly figured out that your Lord Hampden won't take kindly to your exposing his ally as a traitor?"

Annabelle paled. Where on earth had Rochester drawn that from? Then again, he'd been spoiling to have his revenge on her ever since she'd arrived.

"Lord Hampden has nothing to do with any of this," she asserted, trying to sound nonchalant. "I can't imagine why you'd think he would."

"Can't you? He's your lover, yet you're exposing his ally—your father—as a traitor? Have the two of you had a falling out?"

Buckingham seemed perturbed by this turn in the conversation. "I don't see what Lord Hampden has to do with this."

"Come on, Buckingham," Rochester retorted as he sidled closer to the three of them, his lip curling with disdain. "The girl has been prancing about the stage under the name the Silver Swan, her father's own code name."

The king waved his hand dismissively. "She explained all that to me before the two of you came in. She did so to find her father.''

''But that proves my point. She shows up using Walcester's code name, and suddenly Hampden, Walcester's only close ally in London, displays profound interest in her. A bit too pat, don't you think? It smacks to me of a conspiracy.''

''Nay!'' she cried with alarm. ''What conspiracy?''

Rochester shrugged. ''You could say that better than I, but it sounds as if Walcester's been deliberately misleading his peers all these years about what happened at Norwood. And to what purpose? Does he have secret ties to the king's enemies? Are he and Lord Hampden up to some treachery?''

''Lord Hampden had nothing to do with any of this,'' she repeated through gritted teeth. ''You're merely angry because he shamed you at the Blue Bell tonight.''

Rochester colored and cast her a look of disbelief that she would dare to mention his humiliation before the king.

''What's this?'' the king asked.

''Lord Hampden put his sword through his lordship's breeches,'' Annabelle said with scorn. ''Lord Rochester was behaving like a drunken lecher . . . as usual.''

The king managed to hide his laugh behind a discreet cough, but that only infuriated Rochester.

''One thing has nothing to do with the other,'' he said haughtily as he faced Buckingham and the king. ''The fact remains that Hampden and Walcester have been intriguing together in this matter. Hampden obviously knew about the whole thing and sought her out for that reason. Then perhaps the two of them drew Madam Maynard into it for a while until at last she came to her senses and decided to do her duty by her country.''

''Your Majesty,'' Annabelle pleaded, ''all of this about Lord Hampden is sheer nonsense! Rochester's just being spiteful because—''

"Enough!" the king said wearily. "Listen to me, Madam Maynard. You have presented us with important evidence, and for that we are grateful. Now you shall have to trust me and my advisers to sort out the truth." He gave her a condescending smile. "These are weighty matters. I promise you we are more qualified to deal with them than you. You have done your part. Now you must let us do ours."

"But—"

"Are you questioning the integrity of His Majesty or his advisers?" Buckingham asked sternly. His eyes sparkled with something that looked suspiciously like triumph. Why did he seem to be so pleased with all of this?

"I repeat," Buckingham said, "are you questioning His Majesty's integrity?"

"Nay." She fought the trembling in her belly. Dear heaven, she could say no more without giving the king insult. But how could she let Rochester sway them with his insane lies?

"That is settled, then," the king announced with a smile. He turned to the door, obviously ready to get back to his mistress. "Buckingham, we must discuss this at length in the morning. Something must be done about Walcester, of course." He cast Rochester a considering glance. "Hampden, too, if indeed he is involved."

Annabelle stood there helpless, wanting to do something, anything, to stop this madness. But she'd started it, and she could hardly stop it now. They'd taken it out of her hands.

Sweet Mary, what had she done?

"Rochester, will you accompany Madam Maynard downstairs?" His Majesty said as an afterthought.

Rochester practically licked his lips over the prospect. "Of course, sire."

"I—I can see myself out, Your Majesty," she ventured to say. "His lordship need not trouble himself."

"I shall see you out," the Duke of Buckingham inexplicably interrupted.

''Very good,'' said His Majesty, and opened the door to the other room. ''Come along, Rochester. We have friends to entertain.''

Buckingham led her out behind them, then took her arm and prodded her toward the door leading to the Privy Stairs.

As soon as they were on the stairs and the door shut behind them, he murmured, ''I have a suggestion for you, Madam Maynard.''

''Aye, Your Grace?'' She was still reeling from the rapidity with which they'd gone from scarcely believing her story to condemning both her father and Colin.

''I wouldn't speak to anyone of what happened here tonight, if I were you.''

She stopped short on the stair and fixed him with a suspicious gaze. ''Why not?''

His lazy smile didn't mask the cruelty about his eyes. ''You may not realize this, but I have more influence with the king than you could ever dream of. One word, and I can make it seem as if you too were part of this absurd conspiracy Rochester wants to propose.''

Only with great effort did she keep from letting him cow her. It was time to play another role. ''His Majesty is not so lacking in discernment, I hope, as to think that a frivolous actress like me would be interested in such boring affairs.''

Buckingham's eyes rested on her bosom with rapacious enjoyment. ''Perhaps. But then, as you saw just now, His Majesty would rather dally with his mistresses than concern himself with matters of state. He will listen to me when I suggest that he keep your name out of the entire affair—for propriety's sake, of course.''

''Of course. And what do you wish of me in return?''

''Simply that you do not mention that poem to anyone, especially not to Lord Hampden.''

Her control slipped a fraction. ''Lord Hampden has nothing to do with this, as I said before.''

He smiled. "Yes, well, we shall see. But in truth, I have no doubt that he's innocent, and I'm sure the king realizes it as well. Rochester can spout absurdities when he's angry, but that doesn't mean anyone will credit it."

The tension in her chest eased a little.

"Nonetheless, 'tis true that your lover is a close ally of Lord Walcester. If justice is to be done and your father to be punished, we mustn't have Lord Hampden stepping in to confuse the interpretation of the poem, if you know what I mean. Better that he not know about the poem at all."

Her pulse quickened as the truth hit her. Buckingham didn't care what the poem really said. He apparently hated her father and was taking this chance to rid himself of an enemy. She ought to delight in that, but all she felt was an overwhelming guilt at her part in the madness.

It was one thing to betray her father if he were a traitor deserving of punishment, and quite another to see him pay for a crime she wasn't certain he'd committed.

She didn't know why he'd hidden the truth about Norwood all these years, but part of her wondered if he might have had just cause. What if she were setting in motion the condemnation of an innocent man? He might not have been innocent of abandoning her mother, but if she were truly fair, she must admit that his punishment for that shouldn't be as severe as the punishment for being a traitor.

Dear heaven, was she sending her own father to certain death or imprisonment? What kind of woman was she to do such a thing? Nay, she couldn't do it, for it would make her as low as he. More important, she couldn't let them take Colin.

"You do want to see your father arrested, don't you?" Buckingham said with an oily smirk. "Didn't you say you wanted to see justice done?"

She had to find some way to solve this dilemma. She had to save Colin and find out the truth about her father. But Buckingham would be no help to her, that was certain. Gathering her courage about her, she forced a smile to her face. "Of course. I do want to see justice done."

And she would see it done, she thought as he nodded his approval, then took her arm once more and continued on down the stairs. She'd see justice done somehow for both Colin and her father. For in the end, it was her soul that lay in the balance, and she suddenly found that she wanted to keep her soul.

Chapter Twenty-one

"The quality of mercy is not strained,
It droppeth as the gentle rain from heaven
Upon the place beneath: it is twice blessed;
It blesseth him that gives and him that
takes."
—William Shakespeare, *The Merchant of Venice*,
Act 4, Scene 1

Hell and furies, where is Annabelle? Colin thought once more as he pulled his horse up before his town house in the early morning hours. He'd sought her at the Blue Bell, at her lodgings, at Aphra's lodgings, even at Riverton's house, but she hadn't been at any of them. Riverton and Charity had at last admitted that they'd seen her at the theater, but when he'd arrived there, she was gone.

Finally he'd returned to Aphra's and spent several hours there, hoping Annabelle would appear, but she hadn't. He'd dozed on Aphra's settee, and when he'd awakened, he'd faced the fact that she wasn't returning. Still, he'd gone again to all the places she might be. But he'd not found her.

The long day and night had taken its toll on him. First his grueling ride, then his discussion with Annabelle and their lovemaking. . . . A bitter smile crossed his face. He could hardly complain about their lovemaking last night. For one sweet moment, he'd had her entirely within his grasp, before Walcester had arrived and shattered everything.

He dismounted and tied up his horse, his jaw set grimly. 'Sdeath, but he'd have her again. He'd find her if he had to comb all of England, and somehow he'd make her understand and forgive him for deceiving her.

He was so caught up in his thoughts as he walked wearily into his town house that he didn't at first pay attention to what his footman was saying as the man took his cloak.

Then he caught the words "she would not leave."

"What did you say?"

"The woman who accompanied you home last evening is in the drawing room awaiting you, my lord. I was not certain whether I should allow her to stay, but she simply would not leave."

"You did the right thing," Colin said, relief coursing through him.

Quickly, he strode into the drawing room, then stopped short at the sight of the slender form asleep in an armchair before the fire. "Annabelle."

Her head came up as she rubbed her eyes in momentary confusion.

"Where have you been?" he cried, going to her side.

At the sound of his voice, she widened her eyes and stared at him. Her momentary expression of sleepy confusion faded to one of wariness as she regarded him with the same suspicious expression she'd worn the first day they'd met in the tiring-room. He wondered how long she'd been there. She'd changed her clothes, but he didn't think the lavish silk gown she wore was hers. Where had she gotten it and why was she wearing it now?

It was all he could do to keep from gathering her up in his arms, but judging from her expression, he dared not.

She settled herself demurely in the chair, trying to smooth her rumpled skirts, her eyes dropping from his. "Colin, I need to speak with you, if you'll spare me a moment."

"Spare you a moment?" he said incredulously, wounded by her formal tone of voice. "I'll spare you a few years if that's what it takes. You and I must have a long discussion. I have to explain—''

Her head snapped up, her eyes filling with tears. "There's no time for that. Please. Let me say what I've come to say, and then I'll leave you alone."

Oh, no, you won't, he thought, but he restrained himself from saying it aloud. He must handle this carefully if he was to get her back. "All right, then. Speak your mind."

He noticed for the first time since he'd entered that clutched in her arms was the box he'd seen on her bureau before. Why had she brought it?

Rising to her feet, she faced him, eyes wide with sorrow and lips trembling. "I've done a terrible thing, Colin."

He reached for her, but she shied away from him. The blood pounded in his ears as he asked in a barely modulated voice, "And what is that, dearling?"

The endearment did gain him a quick surprised glance from her, but then something oddly like guilt flooded her face and she moved even farther away to stand by the sideboard with her back to him. She placed her box on the board, then rested her hands on either side of it, staring down at it as if it held the key to a mystery.

Even from behind, she looked heart-wrenchingly beautiful in the gorgeous gown, part of her hair swept up in back and tied with a ribbon while the mass of it cascaded down her back. It made his blood race to see her thus. Once again, he wondered why she was dressed so formally.

After a moment, she sighed and turned to face him. "You know that poem I told you about? The one my father gave Mother?"

His gaze flew to the box, then back to her before he caught himself. He reminded himself that she didn't know he'd seen the poem, that he'd drugged her to get a glimpse of it. One more secret for him to make penance for. "Yes. I remember the poem."

"After I left here," she went on, "I—I was so angry, so furious with you. And with my father. I could tell that you were indebted to him, and it hurt to think you'd helped him.''

"I helped him in the beginning, Annabelle," he interjected. "I'll admit that, but as you say, I owed him a lot. He saved my life once, so I didn't feel I could refuse him when he asked me to find out what you were up to."

"Yes, I see," she said, almost distractedly.

He wasn't sure she saw at all. He plunged on, blindly afraid of that strange distraction in her eyes. "I took the trip to Norwood on my own, because I'd already fallen half in love with you and had to know what I was getting into. I swear to you, that's the truth."

She stared at him, a gut-twisting sadness in her expression. "It doesn't matter anymore what you did or what you meant to do. I've done something far worse, I'm afraid. Far worse."

"What do you mean?" Dread built slowly in him at the words, heavy as stones, that dropped from her lips.

She couldn't seem to keep her gaze on his face, but kept glancing away, as if looking at him would kill her. "As I said before, after I left here, I was furious with both you and my father and all your spying. It seemed to me that my father had given me nothing but grief, and now to see how he'd used you against me . . . I—I simply went a little mad." She paused. "You'd already told me that you thought my father was a traitor."

At that statement, his eyes narrowed.

"I read the poem again," she continued, "but I could make no sense of it. It did seem to me, however, that I ought to do something. If my father truly was a traitor, he deserved . . . deserved to be punished." Her voice grew more distant with every word. "I knew you would not stand against your friend, and I knew of no one else who had the power to see that justice was done." She drew in a sharp breath. "Except perhaps one man."

A cold chill struck him. "Who?" he asked in a barely modulated voice.

She licked her lips nervously and turned away from him. "His Majesty."

He felt as if someone had just knocked the wind out of him. Lost for words, he stared blindly at her, a million thoughts going through his head. She'd gone to the king after all the pains they'd taken to keep her safe from the man? Was that why she was dressed as she was? He thought of the king speaking with Annabelle in the dead of night, and his blood rose. Surely that wasn't the "terrible thing" she spoke of, that had her feeling so guilty. Surely she wouldn't have let His Majesty lay a hand on her.

Yes, but would she have had a choice? He managed to choke out the words, "You went to the king?"

"Aye," she said, facing him once more. She nervously twisted a hank of her gown overskirt. Then her words came out in a rush as she lifted pleading eyes to him. "Aye. He was with Buckingham and some others. I showed him the poem, I explained everything to him, but it all got turned around, and before I knew it Rochester was accusing you of treason and Buckingham was calling for my father's arrest and—"

She broke off with a sob. "Dear heaven, Colin, I didn't want to hurt you. You may not believe this, but I love you. That's why I had to warn you about what they intend to do."

He didn't know whether to feel relieved that the king hadn't touched her or horrified that she'd told the king stories about him and Walcester. Hell and furies, had she been that angry?

"Perhaps you should start at the beginning," he said through a throat thick with pain. "Tell me everything."

It took him several minutes to get the entire story out of her coherently as she paced the room and blurted out bits and pieces of her encounter with the king, but when at last he understood what had happened, he realized she'd not tried to implicate him in treason at all. What she'd done was certainly serious and would no doubt have dire repercussions for Walcester, but Colin himself was not in any real danger. And it was his safety she seemed most concerned about.

On that he could reassure her easily. "Annabelle, don't worry about me. If indeed His Majesty believes Rochester, he'll simply have me questioned and then dismiss the matter. Rochester isn't out for blood, but he wants to humiliate me for shaming him in public. I can handle whatever he throws at me."

"Don't you see? It's bigger than that now," she whispered. "If they prove that my father was a traitor, then you'll be seen as one too!"

"Your father wasn't a traitor," he stated. "I can assure them of that. In fact, he was something of a hero if they can be made to realize it."

She stopped her pacing and faced him, a fearful expression on her face. "What do you mean?"

He didn't want to increase her guilt, but she would learn the truth eventually. Once he presented it, it would be all over London. Quickly he related all her father had told him. The longer he talked, the paler she grew until she stumbled back against the sideboard, shaking her head.

"Dear heaven, oh, dear heaven, what have I done?" she began whispering over and over.

"When they question Walcester, he'll explain everything, and when I add my testimony—"

"You don't understand," she broke in. "Buckingham will do anything to destroy my father. The duke will never let them hear the correct version."

She seemed so sure that it worried him. He forced a lightness into his tone. "Nonsense. Buckingham's a fair man. I'll admit I've been away from the court for some time and am not as familiar with the political alliances among the nobles as I used to be, but Buckingham was always Walcester's ally. Surely he'll champion your father."

She shook her head. "There's something I haven't told you yet. Buckingham accompanied me out of

Whitehall. He . . . he warned me against showing you the poem. Of course, he didn't know that you already knew of it, and I certainly didn't tell him.''

"What *did* you tell him?''

After she recounted the conversation in a few terse words, a terrible sadness stole over him. It sounded as if she was right about Buckingham. What's more, the duke was powerful enough to ensure her father was punished, even though his crime had been committed so long ago. Certainly her father would never finish out his years in England. Most likely he'd be exiled as Clarendon had been. And of course, his dreams of political power would be over.

She stared off behind him at the fire. "So you see,'' she whispered, "my father will be destroyed no matter what you or I say. Perhaps you're right and Buckingham doesn't care about ruining you, but he most certainly will ruin my father.''

He couldn't resist saying, "That should make you happy.''

Shame flooded her face. Shutting her eyes, she hugged herself tightly. "Nay, I would not have wished to see him so thoroughly destroyed. I—I suppose I had some dream of making him feel regret for what he did to my mother, but I never wanted to see him exiled or imprisoned or . . .''

She trailed off, but he knew what she didn't dare to say. She'd already seen one parent hanged. She didn't wish to see another suffer the same fate, even if he deserved it.

Her expression was so woeful it roused every protective instinct within him. "Listen to me, dearling—'' he began.

"Don't call me that!'' she burst out, half in tears. "Haven't you been listening, Colin? For heaven's sake, I've ruined your life and betrayed my own father, who may be innocent, to a pack of hounds eager for his blood. Don't pretend you can feel anything but contempt for me now!''

He strode up to her and clasped her shoulders, forcing her to look at him. "Annabelle, I feel a great many emotions at the moment, but contempt isn't one of them. I'll admit I'm stunned by all you've told me. Your father is a callous man, but I don't think he deserves exile for it. Still, I know you felt it was your duty."

Tears began to stream down her cheeks. He wiped them away with the back of his hand, wishing he could somehow take her pain into his body and suffer for her.

"You should hate me for what I've done," she whispered.

He rubbed her arms. "I can't hate you. I'm a little hurt that you didn't feel you could trust me with the problem. I'm angry at myself for ever deceiving you in the first place and starting this entire mess."

Her eyes met his now, the yearning in them so palpable he felt his heart twist in response.

"Most of all," he whispered, "I'm sick with fear that you won't believe me when I say I love you. But I do love you, no matter what you've done, no matter what happens."

Annabelle could hardly believe what Colin was saying. She wanted to believe him. She loved him to desperation, but her shame still made her fearful. "I've ruined your life. And the life of your friend, my father."

"Your father can take care of himself, dearling. As for me, you haven't ruined anything, except that you've made it impossible for me to live without you," he said so fervently it overwhelmed her. "If the choice is you and ruin, or no you, I'll take the ruin."

He smiled. "I don't feel, however, as if my life has been ruined. From the moment I saw you onstage that first time, I knew I had to have you for myself, regardless of what Walcester wanted me to do with you. And I do have you, don't I?" His smile faded. "You're going to forgive me, aren't you, for misleading you, for not telling you about my relationship with your father?"

Annabelle's anger at him had dimmed in the face of her fear that he might be arrested, but his words reminded her that he'd told her father her secrets even while he pretended to be helping her. She remained silent, torn by the urge to chastise him, which she hadn't yet had the chance to do, and to assure him that it didn't matter, not if he loved her.

"It wasn't as bad as it looked," he said in a rush. "Even as I arranged that first meeting, I didn't solely have Walcester's request in mind. He asked me to spy on you and find out why you'd come to London, and I agreed because I found you so intriguing. But after I began to pursue you, I only went to him once and that was to discover what he was hiding."

Once. But what did he say on that one occasion? she wondered, her heart aching. How much of their intimate relations had Colin told her father? "Did you tell him about . . . about . . . what we did?"

It seemed to take him a second to figure out what she was talking about. Then he clutched her to him. "Hell and furies, of course not! What kind of man do you take me for? I told him about the ring, and I asked him if you were his daughter. That's all. And that's when I found out you were from Norwood, for he remembered your mother well."

She stood in his arms a little stiffly, her head bent. "When was this?" she asked in a hoarse whisper.

He remained silent a long time. Then at last he sighed. "After we made love the first time, while you were asleep."

Sorting through her memories, she came up with one that made her breathing grow heavy once more under the weight of betrayal. "That physic you gave me was a sleeping draught, wasn't it?"

He sighed. "Aye. While you slept, I searched your room and found the key to your box. I read the poem and then I went to Walcester. I didn't tell him about the poem, because by then I didn't know whom to believe or trust."

She fixed him with a hurt stare. "That's when you decided to go to Norwood."

He nodded, a strange expression of despair on his face. Did he really care so much? she wondered. Then another realization hit her.

"That's why you were so cold to me that morning. That's why you acted so strangely when you left me at Aphra's."

A hint of chagrin touched his unsmiling lips. "Aye. I knew you were lying to me about the Silver Swan, and I feared you had some dire purpose in mind."

Shutting her eyes, she tried to back away from him, but he held her tight. Sweet Mary, but it still hurt to think of him having so little faith in her, but then she had never completely trusted him either. Yet he still claimed to love her. She certainly knew she loved him.

"I've told you everything now," he murmured, nuzzling her hair with his stubbled chin, "every way I've deceived you or kept the truth from you. I believe you've told me everything as well. There are no secrets between us anymore. So tell me. Do you feel contempt for me for what I did? Am I to lose you because I couldn't trust? Because I guessed you were lying to me and sought to find out the truth at your expense?"

She shook her head helplessly, lifting her hands to rub her temples.

"I love you," he repeated. "You've said you love me. Can't we go on from there? Make a new beginning?"

"So many untruths, so many roles," she choked out. She opened her eyes to look at him with soulful longing. "Can we really say we love each other when our love is built on a foundation of misunderstandings and lies?"

For a moment, he stared at her stunned, as if he could hardly believe she'd fight him like this. Then his jaw stiffened in fierce determination. "There were some truths between us from the very beginning, dearling. I never lied about wanting you. The moment I saw you standing so regally on the stage, I wanted you with a thirst I'd never experienced before. I may not have told you about my association with Walcester, but in every other way, I was myself when I was with you—a shade too quick-tongued perhaps about everything, but truthful.''

She swallowed, watching him silently.

He stroked a tendril of hair back from her face. "Nor were you as duplicitous with me as you seem to think. You never lied to me about your pain. Even when you disguised it, I could sense and understand it, because I've suffered some of that kind of pain myself. And you never lied about your innocence. Whether you knew it or not, it showed in your every word and smile.''

More tears stained her cheeks as she dropped her face, filled once again with the overwhelming shame of what she'd done. "Innocence . . .'' she murmured bitterly. "There's little enough left of that now.''

He caught her head in his hands and wiped a tear from her cheek with his thumb. "Aye. You're not an innocent any longer. You've learned that the world can be crueler even than your stepfather was. And perhaps for the first time, you've committed an act that's left you feeling genuine guilt. But it's also helped you determine what you really want for yourself. It's helped you find the core that is Annabelle, the woman beneath the roles.''

"I don't know who Annabelle is. How can you?''

He smiled. "Oh, but I do. So do you, if you'll see yourself through my eyes. Annabelle is too softhearted to see her father go to prison, despite the things he's done to her. Annabelle is determined, the kind of woman who'll take on a king before she'll relinquish her dignity. She's strong enough to withstand a beating, though I hope to God she never has to do so again, and kind enough to feed oranges to the street urchins. Yet a soft, wild part of her wants to shed her protective roles and simply live.''

Dear heaven, how could she let a man like this slip away? She'd known many a gallant and none of them had ever seen into her soul the way Colin had. "You make me sound much better than my father did."

Colin's eyes went hard. "Your father's a bastard, dearling, no matter what his lineage may say. When he calls you names, it's truly a case of the pot calling the kettle black."

She was touched by the way he leapt to defend her. "You don't seem fond of him."

"I'm not. Believe me, loyalty and fondness are not the same thing," he said, arching one brow. Then his gaze grew intense. "But I'm very fond of his daughter. Now tell me. Is his daughter very fond of me?"

The earnest expression on his face made her breath quicken. "I'm fond of the Colin who gave Aphra enough rent money to last her a lifetime—"

"Which she used for a wild supper," he interjected wryly.

So he'd noticed, had he? Annabelle thought with a smile. "Aye. And I'm fond of the Colin who told me about sheaths and protected me from the king." Her voice dropped to a whisper. "I'm very fond of the Colin who said he loved me and promised to marry me and take me to the colonies."

His slow smile made her heart catch in her throat.

"Then you're fond of me, dearling," he said in a husky whisper, "for there was and is no other Colin."

His words brought her almost more happiness than she could bear. "Then I suppose I'm quite inordinately fond of you," she whispered sweetly.

With a groan, he buried his face in her neck. "Thank God, Annabelle." He nuzzled her neck. "Hell and furies, how I love you."

He began kissing her then, and she gave herself up to the kiss with complete delight. For the moment, her fears were eclipsed by the fire in his touch, by the heat his impassioned avowals had roused within her.

Then her joy was shattered by a loud knock at the front door.

It didn't seem to concern him. "The servants will get

it," he murmured, and kept kissing her, but she drew back and listened intently as the footman opened the door.

Surely they couldn't have come for Colin already, she thought, unable to quench the fear growing within her.

Then they both heard a loud voice announce, "I'm Captain Lockley of His Majesty's Guard. Is your master at home?"

Her blood raced. She clutched at Colin's coat. "They've come for you. Oh, sweet Mary! You've got to slip out of the house and escape! You can't let them take you!"

He seemed more irritated than afraid, and she wondered how he could be so calm.

"You mustn't worry," he said as he thrust her gently from him and turned toward the door. "Everything will be all right. Just stay here, and I'll speak with them."

"Colin!" she protested in a distraught voice, unable to believe he was actually going to meet the soldiers.

But he was already striding into the foyer, closing the door of the drawing room behind him. The man was insane if he thought she'd hide in here while the soldiers took him off.

She opened the door and walked boldly into the foyer to stand beside him, her heart leaping into her throat when she saw the captain standing there, looking uncomfortably about him as he slapped the dust from his riding breeches with two burly hands.

Colin motioned to her to go back in the drawing room, but she glared at him. Didn't he realize she was not the one in danger?

"Good day, my lord," the captain said with a bow, forcing Colin to shift his attention from her.

"Good day, Captain. Can I be of service to you?"

The captain's discomfort grew. "His Majesty has given me orders to accompany you to the Tower. My men await us outside."

Her worst fears had been realized. They really were going to arrest Colin, weren't they, despite what Buckingham had said. If she ever caught sight of that wretched Rochester, she'd do more than bite off his fingers—she'd plant a knife in the spot Colin had deliberately missed.

"His Lordship has done nothing wrong," she couldn't keep from protesting. "Why on earth is he being taken to the Tower?"

"Annabelle, let me handle this," Colin said through gritted teeth. "Go upstairs and stay there until we leave."

For the first time, the captain seemed to notice her standing there. He took one look at her extravagant gown and apparently decided she was Colin's wife.

"My lady," he murmured, bowing again.

Dear heaven, the man was arresting Colin, and he still behaved like a gallant at the theater. Well, she wasn't a wife yet, so she fully intended to make certain she got the chance to become one.

"What is my . . . what is his lordship charged with?" she asked.

Colin's face went stony. "Captain. May I have a moment alone with my lady?"

The captain shifted from one foot to the other, his face reddening, but he nodded.

Colin pulled her back into the drawing room. "Listen, dearling. You mustn't concern yourself with this. This is a tricky business, and if I'm to survive it, I must comply with whatever is asked of me. Otherwise, they'll assume I truly am guilty and I'll be dead for sure."

She paled. "But you've done nothing!"

"Aye, and the king will realize that the moment I present my case. Don't worry." He flashed her a wry smile. "The king has a certain fondness for me. He'll throw me in the Tower for a few days to satisfy his honor. 'Tis his way of disciplining his nobles. Last year, Buckingham himself had a stint in the Tower, as did Rochester for eloping with an heiress."

She knew about Buckingham and Rochester, but she still couldn't quite believe Colin's words. The strain in his features belied his assurances. This was, after all, a far more serious offense than either of those two lords had ever committed.

"Can't you simply tell them you knew nothing about my father and had nothing to do with his spying on me?"

He forced a smile. "I could. But as much as I dislike your father for what he's done to you, I can't betray him like that. It would truly make me a man of no morals. I couldn't live with myself if I let them eat him alive without saying what I know."

She fought back tears of desperate futility. "Don't you see? Thanks to me, he's lost for good. You mustn't let them take you down with him!"

"It will be all right," he merely repeated, making her heart twist painfully.

This was all her fault. Dear heaven, she had to find a way to stop this madness! "Perhaps if I go to the Privy Council and explain the poem—"

"You know they'll not believe what you say—not now, after you've come forward with a different story. They'll simply say the same callous things they said before—that you're a woman and too emotional to be trusted. 'Tis better for you to simply stay out of it and hope for the best."

But she couldn't stay out of it. She couldn't!

His expression grew fierce. "Promise me you'll do nothing to jeopardize your own safety," he bit out, gripping her shoulders with his hands. "I'll go mad in the Tower if I think you're risking your life or . . . or your dignity for me. Promise me you won't go to the king or Buckingham or Rochester!"

She sucked in her breath. He was right. None of them would help her anymore. But perhaps she could find another way.

"I promise," she whispered.

But she didn't promise not to try to save him. She'd find a way to stop the madness. Somehow she'd find a way.

He searched her face a moment. "Do you have my ring?"

She stared at him distracted, then bobbed her head and drew the band from her pocket. He slid it onto her finger, then closed her hand in his.

"Wait for me, dearling," he murmured. "Someday,

we'll have the chance to be together without all this. I promise.''

Then he released her and strode out to the captain. She watched him go, her blood pounding in her ears and her hand throbbing where he'd squeezed it. She wished she could believe it. But despair reared up in her heart as Colin turned to his footman, spoke to the man in a low voice, then left with the captain.

She flew to the window and looked out, the despair growing as she saw the guardsmen who moved to flank Colin, their expressions serious. She couldn't let this happen. She couldn't!

But how to stop them? Colin was right—it would do her little good to speak with the king again. He'd obviously made up his mind as had Buckingham.

Why were men such fools? They were more concerned with political connections and power than with the truth. They never recognized the truth—all they saw was what they wanted to see.

Her entire career had been a perfect example of that. Colin had seen through her roles, but no one else had. The other men had merely seen a scheming actress. Dear heaven, they'd believed her more easily when she was playing a role than now when she was telling the truth.

That's when it hit her. Her blood began to race as thoughts tumbled through her head one after another. A plan formed in her mind, a plan of outrageous, ridiculous proportions. Yet it might work.

She didn't pause to ponder it anymore. There was no time. It was time to act.

The footman was still standing with his mouth open in the foyer. When he saw her leave the drawing room, he told her with a faintly disapproving air that his lordship had said to make her comfortable in the house until his lordship's return.

She'd have none of that. ''I need a coach,'' she said in the most imperious voice she could muster. ''I must be taken to a friend's house at once.''

''But his lordship said—''

''I'll be returning, I assure you, but I have to speak

with my friend. If you want to see your master free, then please do as I ask.''

His eyes widened, but he nodded quickly and went off to call for a coach. She waited impatiently, wondering if Aphra would cooperate. Oh, of course she would. She was Colin's friend, after all.

A short ride later, Annabelle climbed the stairs to Aphra's rooms and opened the door, relieved to find the woman poring over a book.

"Annabelle!" she exclaimed. "Colin's been looking for you everywhere! What has happened? He wouldn't tell me anything, but he seemed pretty upset.''

"Colin's been taken to the Tower.'' She told her everything, relieved when Aphra didn't condemn her for what she'd done.

"That explains one thing, in any case,'' Aphra remarked.

"Oh?''

"A messenger came from Buckingham this morning with a purse for you. He said to tell you that His Grace considers it a small payment in exchange for your cooperation.''

Annabelle groaned. "Dear heaven, he truly hates my father.''

"What are you going to do?'' Aphra asked.

Annabelle clasped her friend's hands, her mind racing. The money from Buckingham could work into her plan quite nicely. But she had to have Aphra's help.

"Aphra, you want to be a playwright, do you not?''

"Yes, but I don't see—''

"I need you to write a scene. It's got to be the best thing you've ever written and very convincing.''

"What on earth are you talking about?'' Aphra asked, regarding Annabelle as if she'd gone mad.

"I'm talking about a scene that will free my father and Colin. I'm talking about a scene to be performed before your most discriminating audience yet.''

Aphra's eyes narrowed. "Who?''

"His Majesty.''

Chapter Twenty-two

"Still in the paths of honour persevere,
And not from past or present ills despair:
For blessings ever wait on virtuous deeds;
And though a late a sure reward succeeds."
—William Congreve, *The Morning Bride,* Act 5, Scene 3

Soft violin music wafted from the musician's box to where Annabelle sat in one of the special boxes, the one next to the king's. It felt odd to sit across from the stage instead of behind it. It felt odder still to wear a mask, although she knew no one else would remark on it.

Yet except for the mask and her seat in the box, tonight was no different from any other night she'd spent in the theater. Her hands were clammy with both nervousness and the rush of excitement that came before a performance. She still wore a costume, even if it was just an expensive gown she'd purchased with Buckingham's money in a very ostentatious manner.

If everything went according to plan, however, her audience would be far more limited . . . and far more discerning than usual. It had taken her three days to pull everything together and this certainly would be the role of a lifetime. It had to be absolutely convincing or His Majesty would never believe it.

Thank heaven Sir William D'Avenant had agreed to help her and Aphra by pushing up the production of George Etherege's new play, *She Would If She Could.* Etherege was popular with the wits and gallants, so she and Aphra had reasoned that a new play of his would draw everyone.

And it had. Everyone of any import was here. The

seats had been filled by two o'clock even though the performance wasn't scheduled until three-thirty. Still, she'd not been able to rest until the king and Buckingham had arrived. Once she'd heard noises in the box next to her and had recognized the king's bored tone and Buckingham's lazy voice, she'd relaxed. Everyone was in place now.

She only hoped her plan would work. She hoped she could say Aphra's skilled lines with some degree of sincerity and that Aphra's first attempt at acting would turn out well. As for Charity, Annabelle knew her maid could do her part with ease.

Yes, it was up to the three of them now. They had to succeed. They had to make sure they could effect the release of her father, so that Colin would also be freed.

The curtains opened, and the first part of her plan fell into place as Sir William himself announced that Annabelle Maynard wouldn't be playing the part of Lady Cockwood as scheduled. Mrs. Shadwell would play the part instead, he stated, to some isolated boos from the wits.

As soon as he left the stage, the whispering started in the pit. Annabelle could see one gallant after another beckoning to Charity, who moved about and muttered first in one ear, then in another. Fortunately, no one noticed her sitting alone above the pit. Not that they would have recognized her with her mask on.

Everything was in motion, yet Annabelle couldn't quite relax. So many things could go wrong. She only hoped they didn't. It was a good thing D'Avenant hadn't asked them too many questions about their plans. He would throttle all three of them when he realized how they intended to disrupt his big night.

As she waited for the agreed-upon scene, she fidgeted in her seat, unable to dull the edge of fearful anticipation in her blood. Her anxiety was only slightly alleviated when she heard Sedley enter next door and repeat to His Majesty the rumors Charity had circulated below. When His Majesty laughed, she relaxed a fraction. That hadn't been in the plan, but it was perfect. His Majesty had taken the first nibble at the hook, thanks to Sedley's gossiping tongue.

Time passed far too slowly after that. She felt as if she were watching it all from underwater, unable to hear or see with any accuracy. But at last Henry Harris made his entrance on stage and spoke the lines she'd been waiting for. It was time.

Right on cue, Aphra swung open the door to Annabelle's box. "Annabelle Maynard! I should have known you'd be skulking about in here, hiding behind a mask! You ought to be ashamed of yourself!"

"Keep your voice down, Aphra, if you please!" Annabelle retorted in a stage whisper that would carry quite easily to the box next to her. "I don't want Sir William to know I'm here. He thinks I'm ill."

"So he does." Aphra dropped into the chair next to Annabelle and surreptitiously squeezed her hand before continuing in a scathing tone, "But we both know why you don't wish to trod the boards tonight."

The voices in the next box had grown quiet, as well as those in two of the other boxes. Annabelle bit back a smile. She made her tone haughty. "I don't know what you mean."

"I heard what Charity's telling everyone in the pit. All that rot about you not taking the stage because you're distraught over your newly found father's arrest. You ought to be ashamed for letting them believe such lies."

"I *am* distraught over my poor dear father's arrest," she said in the sarcastic tone she'd perfected when sparring with gallants. "Here I am, having just discovered that the man is my father, and now he's been whisked away from me."

"Such fustian, and you know it! If you hadn't lied about that poem, then he'd not have been arrested at all."

Annabelle gave a dramatic sigh. "I didn't lie. My father *did* give that poem to my mother to deliver to someone in Norwood."

"Aye, but to one of the Royalists, as you well know. You didn't bother to tell them, did you, that the poem was sent to that Benedict fellow, or that the line about Hart was meant to warn his friends that their companion was a traitor. Nor did you happen to mention that the reference to 'crown-less hands' referred to the Roundheads. It clearly stated that if his companions didn't leave St. Stephens they'd be captured by the Roundheads. Of course, you kept that all quite secret.''

Now a gallant was looking up from the pit at them. He nudged his companion and they focused their eyes on the two women conversing above them. She and Aphra had pitched their voices to stand out slightly over the hum of audience noise that always accompanied the plays, so she knew that anyone who paid attention to their conversation would hear it.

"I didn't see the need to tell His Majesty *everything*," Annabelle said smugly, but she wondered if the men in the next box could truly be so dense that they wouldn't realize all of this was staged. Then again, they'd been pretty dense in other matters.

Besides, it didn't matter if they figured it out. She'd still have made the situation public in a way that the king dared not ignore.

"Aye, you told them exactly what you wanted them to know," Aphra hissed. "I take it you didn't tell them that you hold your father responsible for abandoning your mother."

"That was none of their affair," Annabelle said with a sniff.

Aphra gave a mocking laugh. "Nor did it suit your plans. I hope you're happy now. An innocent man is in prison because of your lies. Thanks to you, your father is being treated as a traitor instead of the hero that he was.''

"Why do you care about my father anyway?" Annabelle said in her stage whisper. "You know it was monstrous of him to abandon my mother and me. What does it matter to you if I wish to avenge that?''

"I don't care a whit for your father. But thanks to your insane desire to see vengeance done, my friend Lord Hampden is in the Tower. That's what you should be ashamed of. After all, he *was* your lover."

"Was. Until he ran off somewhere to meet another woman, leaving me here without so much as a shilling to see me through his absence."

Aphra sighed loudly. "Yes, well, he is a wastrel, but I could have told you that. In any case, you landed well enough on your feet."

"What do you mean by that?"

"I mean I know about that tidy sum Lord Buckingham sent to you this morning in payment for your lies about your father."

They both heard the gasp in the next box, but Annabelle continued the conversation as if she'd not noticed at all.

"I suppose you'll want some of it now to help you pay off your debt," Annabelle said hotly.

"Well, I have been lodging you at my house, after all. I don't think you should begrudge me a little of Buckingham's money."

Now the people in the fourth box over were straining forward to hear the conversation that had risen in loudness since they'd begun. Annabelle shot Aphra a questioning glance through the slits of her mask. How long should they continue this before they'd said enough? The first act was ending, and once the interlude came, they'd not be able to be heard by anyone, even His Majesty.

Annabelle sighed and gave an exaggerated shrug. "All right, then. I'll give you some of it. Trouble is, the gold's not going very far. This gown cost me nearly all of it, but it was worth it to be able to buy a decent gown for a change. I swear, Lord Hampden was terribly lax about such things."

"That's not provocation enough to have him put in the Tower, for God's sake," Aphra retorted slyly.

"I didn't have him put in the Tower. That was all Rochester's doing. He was angry, you know—"

A tap at the door to the box made her break off. *It took them long enough,* she thought.

Now the more difficult part of her performance would begin.

"Enter," she said, making her voice sound more normal.

Rochester opened the door, his face blanched in rage. "Madam Maynard? It is you under that mask, isn't it?"

Annabelle nodded her head regally. "I wish to be alone just now, Rochester—"

"I beg your pardon, madam," he said, his voice heavily sarcastic, "but His Majesty has sent me to request that you accompany me to his box."

She stared at him, her mouth dropping open in feigned surprise. "Oh, dear heaven, is His Majesty here tonight?"

"Yes." His eyes shot daggers at her. He, at least, was not fooled by her little scene, but then he wasn't the man she needed to fool.

Rising to her feet and flashing Aphra an exaggerated look of horror, she followed Rochester into the passageway and then into the next box. His Majesty had apparently sent away his other companions, except for Buckingham. They'd also pulled the curtains so that the box was now a self-enclosed room, cut off from the noise of the theater, although she knew every eye was probably upon those closed curtains.

She only hoped enough people had overheard her and Aphra's conversation to ensure that the king couldn't take her statements lightly.

"Madam Maynard," the king remarked, his eyes cold on her as she gave him a curtsy. "If you would be so kind as to remove the mask—"

"Of course," she murmured, and did as he asked.

It made it easier to see his face, which looked quite flushed even in the dim light of the sconces.

" 'Tis very rude of us, we know," the king announced formally, "but we couldn't help overhearing your conversation with Madam Behn."

You certainly couldn't. We made sure of that, she thought, but gave him a stricken expression. "Oh, dear heaven, I had no idea that—"

"We must say your conversation has us very disturbed, very disturbed indeed."

It was all she could do to keep from looking at Buckingham to see how he was taking this, but she imagined he wasn't taking it well.

"I don't know what to say," she murmured.

"You have said enough already," the king retorted in a tart voice. "Egad, what kind of woman would deliberately set out to ruin her father's reputation?"

She drew on all her acting abilities to look devastated and afraid. "Oh, Your Majesty, 'tis not at all the way it sounded. Aphra is peeved at me, so she has made up these insane accusations—"

"Enough of your lies. Lord Hampden as well has pointed out the alternate interpretations of the poem. We did not believe him, of course, because Walcester is his friend and we assumed he was misled by the man, but now we see that he told the truth after all."

"But Your Majesty—" she protested.

"Silence!"

The king turned to Buckingham and only then did she dare venture a look at the duke. He kept his features carefully indifferent, but she could see the anger seething behind his eyes. Something told her he definitely understood what she'd just done. Now she'd certainly made an enemy of him, but that couldn't have been helped in any case.

"Buckingham," the king remarked, a sternness in his voice that made her quake for the duke, "how do you suggest we handle this terrible situation?"

Buckingham regarded her a moment longer with glittering eyes. Then he blinked and turned to the king, an ingratiating smile on his face. "I would humbly propose that Lord Walcester be released, Your Majesty. It appears that a gross error has been made, thanks to this woman's lies."

The king nodded wearily, for the first time not looking quite so in command as he had heretofore.

She wondered if His Majesty had really believed her little scene, or if he'd been forced to accept her presentation of the matter because he knew if he didn't, his subjects, many of whom had also heard the entire exchange, would rise up in outrage to demand the earl's release. After all, it wouldn't do for him to appear to mistreat a hero at the word of a woman whom all regarded as scandalous anyway. He had enough trouble dealing with his subjects' dislike of his many mistresses and their pensions.

In any case, her father was apparently going to be released, so His Majesty's reasons for doing so hardly mattered. But no mention had been made of Colin. Was he to be released as well? She could hardly ask the question, when she'd been pretending she was indifferent to his plight. Still, how could they keep him imprisoned now?

"Your Majesty, what are we to do with Madam Maynard?" Buckingham asked, bringing her abruptly out of her thoughts.

Dear heaven, she'd tried to ignore the possibility that they might punish her for falsely maligning a noble, but deep down she'd known it was a possibility. What was more, they had every right to do so. And of course they would. That was the way these things were handled. For a moment, horrible memories filled her mind . . . her mother's cell, her mother's last ride to the gallows, her mother with the noose about her neck. . . .

"What do you think?" His Majesty asked, turning a shrewd gaze on Buckingham.

Annabelle's heart pounded in her chest, but she reassured herself that Buckingham's hatred for her could work to her advantage. Unfortunately for him, everyone knew he'd given her money to keep silent. They would assume, if he ordered some cruel punishment, that he was retaliating, and that wouldn't look good either.

Buckingham stared at her for a moment, obviously itching to torment her. Then he seemed to restrain himself. In a bored tone, he remarked, "She's a woman, Your Majesty, and women are weak in matters like these. They think only of their petty emotions and strike in fury without giving the matter the more considered thought that a man would give it."

Annabelle tensed. She certainly didn't have to pretend to hate Buckingham at this moment. It was so like a man to consider a woman's maneuvering to be motivated by petty emotion, while his own was motivated only by sound logic. Buckingham had schemed more than she had, that was certain. And for his scheming, he would get a few words of disapproval from the king. While she was to be given . . . what?

"The only thing for it, I think," Buckingham continued, "is to order that she be dismissed from the duke's players. That way you'll prevent her from continuing her scheming among the nobility. I think that's a suitable punishment."

A suitable punishment, Annabelle thought bitterly. Aye, he would think so. An actress dismissed from her company generally had one of two choices—find a protector or sink into the darkness of the whorehouses. And since she'd offended every nobleman's sensibilities and betrayed her father, Buckingham no doubt thought she'd have only the latter choice.

But she knew better than that. She'd always find a way to survive. The theater had taught her that. If Colin wouldn't have her after this . . .

She thrust that thought aside. She must take things one at a time. At the moment, she must escape this place without finding herself sentenced to the Tower.

The king appeared to consider Buckingham's suggestion. Then he nodded curtly. "All right, then. That sounds most appropriate." He leveled a stern gaze on her. "Madam Maynard, we hope that away from the theater, you will reflect upon the error of your ways."

She knew she'd best make a token protest. "But Your

Majesty, how will I live? I have nothing but the theater."

Charles II waved his hand dismissively. "You should have thought about that before you embarked on this terrible scheme. Now begone. We are fast tiring of your deceitful countenance."

After falling into a deep curtsy, she stormed dramatically from the king's box. Outwardly, she pretended to be furious about the entire matter, but inwardly, she worried that she'd not been successful in freeing Colin. Still, she hadn't dared ask the king, not if she'd wanted to maintain her necessary fiction.

As soon as she'd moved into the passageway, Aphra met her, but Rochester was standing there watching them both, so she couldn't say a word to her friend. She passed Aphra in silence, knowing that later Aphra would find her at her lodgings and want to know everything. But right now, she had to maintain her role.

With hurried steps, she left the second tier, conscious that the interlude had begun and people would soon be milling about. She had to get out before that. Not that anyone would bother her, but the story of what she'd done would be spreading through the theater, and she didn't feel like enduring the murmurs and contemptuous remarks.

How ironic, she thought to herself. *Now that I no longer care about it, I've succeeded in making myself truly scandalous.*

It was probably a fitting punishment for a woman who'd betrayed her own father. Well, at least she and her father were even on that score. He was once more the revered member of the nobility, and she was, as always, the despised bastard.

Oddly enough, it no longer bothered her. After tonight, she knew she could do anything she put her mind to. By heaven, if Colin weren't released in a few days, she'd manufacture some other scheme for his release.

Feeling a little better, she walked through the foyer, doing her best to maintain her role of affronted actress. Just as she passed Sir William's tiny office near the front doors, however, two hands reached out and dragged her forcibly into the office, shutting the door behind her.

Thinking some forward gallant had waylaid her, she whirled, a hot retort on her lips that died when she saw who'd grabbed her.

"Colin!" she exclaimed in a whisper. "But . . . but how? I thought . . ."

He wore a frown, but the sparkle in his eyes belied his attempt to look severe. "Now, now, dearling. I could hardly stay in the Tower with Buckingham buying you gowns and Aphra calling me a 'wastrel,' could I? Besides, having left you without so much as a shilling, I had to at least correct that injustice."

She colored. "You heard . . ."

"Aye." He grinned from ear to ear, all pretense of anger gone. "Leave it to you to find a way to make the king eat his words, and before an audience, no less. I assume he *did* eat his words when he took you aside in private."

She nodded quickly, unable to keep back her exuberant smile. "My father's been freed, although Buckingham's mad as a hornet about it."

"Not surprising. He's just found himself outwitted by a woman, and not quite certain if it was intentional or simply bad fortune on his part." His grin faded. "Annabelle, dearling, you are amazing."

Her breath caught in her throat at the searing look he gave her. With a low cry, she threw herself into his arms and he clasped her so close, she thought he'd crack her ribs. But she didn't care. He was safe and free, and he wasn't angry at her. That was all that mattered.

"We have but a moment," he murmured in her ear. "As soon as the interlude is over and the next act begins, we have to leave, before someone figures out that you're not at all peeved to see me. I've got a coach waiting to take you to an inn on the outskirts of London. I'll meet you there in my own coach and then we'll set out for my estate at Kent together. But we mustn't be seen together until then. I wouldn't have all your machinations go for naught.''

She pulled back. ''I'm sorry I had to make you sound so pathetic, but I didn't want them to realize I was trying to save you. Speaking of which, how on earth did you manage to get here?''

He opened the door a crack and peeked out to see if the interlude was over yet. It was just ending. ''They released me this afternoon, so of course I went looking for you and finally ended up here. Charity saw me enter and told me I'd best hide in one of the boxes or I'd ruin everything. Of course, she didn't explain what I'd be ruining, or I'd have put a stop to it at once. You shouldn't have risked yourself like that, dearling.''

''Yes, yes,'' she muttered impatiently, ''but how did you get released?''

He smiled. ''As I told you, His Majesty could hardly condemn me on such little evidence. He did make one suggestion, however, to squelch any talk that might arise.''

''What?'' she whispered.

Colin's eyes twinkled. ''He suggested I leave England for a while, at least a few years. He pointed out that the colonies would be a likely place for my talents.''

''You know His Majesty won't expect that of you now. You can stay if you like.''

His expression grew sober. ''I don't want to stay. Do you wish to stay in England, my love? Does the theater mean that much to you?''

She managed a shaky laugh. ''You may have been given a suggestion, but I was given more than that. The king has ordered that I be dismissed from the company, so I don't have much choice, do I?''

''Whose idea was that?'' he asked, glowering.

''Buckingham's. Who else?''

Colin regarded her with narrowed eyes. ''Did Buckingham really give you money to keep silent or were you making that up?''

"Oh, no. He really sent me a bag of gold." She grinned. "And I really bought this gown with it too."

"Wonderful." He chuckled. "That part had everyone in the theater silently cheering, I'm sure. Most of them hate Buckingham."

"True, but now most of them hate me more." She dropped her eyes from him. "I'll be considered the worst harlot imaginable, ruthless and scheming to have my hallowed father imprisoned. I suppose that's mostly true anyway, even if I thought I had good reason for it."

Colin tipped her chin up, staring into her eyes. "You're no harlot. You and I know the truth, dearling. That's all that matters. You and I know you just did a very, very brave thing. You gave up everything to right a wrong when what you wanted was to leave your father to the wolves. It took incredible courage and a goodly measure of wit to abandon your quest to see him punished. I know it, and so do your friends— Riverton, Charity, and Aphra. None of the rest of them matter."

She swallowed. " 'Twas not so noble a thing. I didn't do it solely for my father. I thought I was doing it for you too."

"I know." He pressed a kiss to her forehead. "That makes it no less noble to me. You were willing to give up your vengeance for me. That means more to me than you can ever imagine."

"Yes, but now you've been made to look like a fool for being my lover and—"

"Who cares? I don't. All I care about is having the woman I love beside me when I set off for my new home." His jaw tightened. "Can I count on that?"

She stared up at him in disbelief. He still wanted her. Despite all that had happened, he still wanted her. Sweet Mary, what had she done to deserve such a man?

At her hesitation, he said, "I know I've been a rogue in the past, but—"

"Hush," she murmured, putting one finger to his lips. "Surely you know I love you. But you must be mad to want a woman of such scandalous reputation as I.''

"Where we're going no one will care, dearling," he murmured. Then he paused. "Let me set you straight on this. I love you. If I wanted to live in England, I would, and I'd marry you all the same. I'd say to hell with all the naysayers, as I have ever since my father first brought me here. We'd simply be the most scandalous couple in London.''

His voice deepened. "But I want to marry you and go to a place where you and I can begin again, where no one knows or cares that we're bastards, where there are no memories of hangings to torment you and no court manipulations to disturb me. I want to own my soul again. Will you go with me?''

How could she resist him when he offered her something she'd wanted all her life? A place where she could be herself, where the one person she cared about knew all her tormented past and didn't care. A place where she could love and be loved.

A beatific smile spread over her face. It was Annabelle, only Annabelle, who gave the answer.

"I'll follow you to the ends of the earth, Colin Jeffreys.'' Her love for him swelled with sweet delight within her. "Yes, my love, I'll go.''

Chapter Twenty-three

"A brave world, Sir, full of religion,
knavery, and change: we shall shortly
see better days."
—Aphra Behn, *The Roundheads*, Act 1, Scene 1

Annabelle and Colin stood on the deck of one of Riverton's ships, waiting for it to set sail. Riverton and Charity had found the idea of starting afresh in the colonies an intriguing one, so they too had decided to make the trip. They'd married only a week ago, not long after Colin and Annabelle's quiet private wedding at his estate. Riverton and Charity were already below, settling into their quarters.

But Annabelle had wanted to watch the ship leave, to say good-bye to England, as it were. No, her memories weren't all fond, but they were her memories after all. They were what had made her what she was, and she wouldn't go without making some sort of peace with them.

"Shall you miss the theater very much?" Colin asked softly, pulling her close against him.

She grew pensive, thinking of the months she'd spent trodding the boards. "I don't know. I did enjoy the time I actually spent on the stage, the experience of holding people in thrall." She sighed. "But once I left the stage, I was never allowed to be myself. I always had to fend off advances and think up sharp retorts for the wits."

"It can be a hard place, I suppose," he said.

She nodded. "For a woman, it can." She paused. "I think . . . I think perhaps the theater isn't ready for

women yet. I don't think a woman with any character
or depth of feeling will truly enjoy trodding the boards
until she's allowed the same freedom to work that the
actors have.''

''And the same respect?''

She nodded, and clutched him tight. Colin was completely different from any man she'd ever known. He
took it for granted that women should have some priv-
ileges. He seemed to guess her thoughts before she
spoke them. It was a constant amazement to her.

Staring up into the sky, she thanked God for this
man whom she loved with every breath in her body.
Then her eyes narrowed as she realized that she'd just
said a prayer, her first since God had abandoned her
mother to the gallows. She watched the seagulls dip-
ping toward the ship and felt the comfort in Colin's
close embrace. Yes, God had chosen not to save her
mother. Yet he'd given her this other wonderful gift,
this caring, loving man. A tear slipped from her eye.
Maybe it was time to put her anger toward God aside
as well.

Her throat tightened as she lay her head on Colin's
chest. Aye, God had been watching out for her all this
time. He'd given her Colin. How could she hate him
after that?

Feeling peace steal over her, she stood in Colin's
embrace awhile longer, awaiting the ship's departure.
Suddenly she felt him tense.

''What is it?'' she asked.

''Your father.''

Startled, she searched the docks, her heart beginning to pound when she caught sight of the balding
figure walking briskly toward the ship, his cane tapping the wood as he came.

''What does he want?'' she asked.

Colin shook his head, then left her side to greet him.
She followed after, too curious to stay back. She hadn't
seen her father since that terrible night in Colin's
house. She'd heard he'd been freed, but at Colin's estate there'd been too much to do for her to spend much

time thinking about a man she barely knew. Colin hadn't seen him either, although he'd told her in detail about their last encounter and her father's statement that he'd claim her if she wished. No doubt he had changed his mind about *that* after she'd gone to the king.

Her father took Colin's proffered hand and came on board, standing there awkwardly looking about. Colin stood between him and Annabelle, but her father saw her anyway and stiffened a little.

"I hear you're taking my daughter off to the colonies," he muttered to Colin, though his watery eyes stayed fixed on her face. In the bright light of day he looked older than he had before. Strangely enough, she suddenly pitied him. Colin had told her about him—that he had no family, no heirs. Only his political aspirations to keep him company. Such a lonely life he must lead.

She met his inquisitive stare without flinching.

"I'm taking my *wife* to the colonies," Colin retorted. "And I'd thank you not to do anything to upset her."

"It's all right," Annabelle said. "Truly it's all right, Colin. I . . . I wish to speak with him a moment, if I may."

Colin turned a speculative glance her way, but at her pleading expression, he gave a reluctant nod and stepped aside. Her father came close, his eyes narrowing as he surveyed her from head to toe. He seemed pleased by what he saw, by the demure gown she wore.

"Sir," she said, her throat tight. She couldn't bear to call him "Father." "I would like to know something if I may. Before she died, my mother said she loved you, that you were the only man she'd ever loved. Did . . . did you perchance love her? Even a little?"

She didn't know why she needed to know, but she did. Perhaps it was because her mother had found so little love in her life. Or perhaps she really wanted to believe she'd been conceived in love. Somehow that would make everything else bearable.

He looked completely taken aback by her question. For a moment, his eyes misted over, and his broad hand gripped the top of his cane fiercely.

"I don't know if I've ever loved anyone," he murmured hoarsely. "But the closest I ever came was with your mother. She was a sweet, giving woman, and I truly hated leaving her behind."

Annabelle swallowed, unable to say anything.

"Annabelle," he continued, astonishing her by using her name for the first time, "if I'd known about you, I believe I would have gone back." He began to nod. "Aye, I do believe I would have gone back."

Tears welled in her eyes, tears of grief, of pain for lost chances, and yes, even of happiness. "I'm sorry I went to the king about the poem," she whispered, and suddenly she knew this was what she'd been waiting for, the chance to find some sort of absolution from him.

He gave her a trembling smile then, the wrinkles in his brow tightening. "I'm not. For many years, I've lived in fear of having it be known what a coward I was. When at last it was all made public, I knew only relief. Now I can finally have some peace."

He stared at her a moment, then gave a raucous laugh. "Besides, even though I shirked my duties, they've not been as harsh toward me as I thought they might be. They pity me for my treacherous daughter and gloss over my past sins. You must have painted quite a picture in your little scene at the theater. I hear you gave Buckingham fits. It was worth a few days in the Tower to hear how my sharp-tongued daughter made a fool of that duplicitous snake before His Majesty and everyone."

He looked as if he might say more, then fell silent.

An awkwardness descended upon them both. The other times they'd spoken, it had been with bitter words. With all the bitterness evaporated between them, there seemed little to say. The silence was broken by the call of "All aboard!"

He glanced about him anxiously, then fixed her with

a yearning gaze. "You'll tell me if I have grandchildren, won't you?"

She glanced at Colin, who smiled. Then she nodded. When her father flashed her a grateful look, she added impulsively, "And you may visit them anytime, if you wish, although I admit it will be a long journey."

"I may surprise you and accept that invitation someday." He stepped forward, and before she realized what he was doing, he leaned over and pressed a kiss to her forehead. "May God keep you well, daughter," he murmured softly.

As he turned to go, she clasped his arm, then kissed his dry cheek. "And you," she managed to whisper through the tightness in her throat.

He nodded, his eyes misting again, then walked less confidently back to the edge of the boat, where he was helped off by a crewman.

Colin came to her side. "Are you all right?"

She nodded wordlessly, wiping away a tear with the back of her hand. He drew her into his arms, and she lay her head against his chest, her love for him so intense she could feel it throb in every part of her.

"You know, it's odd," she whispered, "but all this time I thought that all I wanted was to hear him say he was sorry for what he'd done, that he regretted it. He didn't really say that even today, did he?"

Colin remained silent, somehow knowing she expected no answer.

"Yet I didn't care. Because he said enough. He finally said enough."

"Do you wish you were staying now, so you could get to know him better?"

She lifted her head to gaze at him. "Nay. The only person I want to know better is you."

A slow, secret smile crossed his face as the wind whipped his golden hair about him like a halo. Crewmen scurried around them, casting off and hoisting the sails. Then the ship slipped away from the dock, and Colin steadied her in his arms as the boat rocked.